The Guardian
and the FarCaller

The Guardian and the FarCaller

A SPOONWORLD Novel

Chuck Marsters

Copyright © 2007 by Chuck Marsters.

Library of Congress Control Number:		2007904286
ISBN:	Hardcover	978-1-4257-4852-4
	Softcover	978-1-4257-4842-5

All rights reserved. No part of this book may be reproduced or transmitted in any form or by any means, electronic or mechanical, including photocopying, recording, or by any information storage and retrieval system, without permission in writing from the copyright owner.

This is a work of fiction. Names, characters, places and incidents either are the product of the author's imagination or are used fictitiously, and any resemblance to any actual persons, living or dead, events, or locales is entirely coincidental.

This book was printed in the United States of America.

To order additional copies of this book, contact:
Xlibris Corporation
1-888-795-4274
www.Xlibris.com
Orders@Xlibris.com
36979

Contents

Prologue 9

Part I: The Legacy 21

Part II: Find That Spoon! 33

Part III: The FarCaller 57

Part IV: Collision 93

Part V: Collisions 185

Part VI: Picking Up Pieces 249

Part VII: Retribution 313

Part VIII: Housewarming 333

Part IX: The Mystery 339

Acknowledgments

My writing "career" started early one morning in 1993 in Riyadh, Saudi Arabia, when I woke up and couldn't not write. (If you work at it, you'll decode that sentence.) I sat down at my Mac and began typing away and, with months here and there when writing was impossible, I've been at it ever since. My first effort was a science fiction novel that I hope to publish soon.

This book carries only my name but couldn't have been written without help from too many people to list. However, not telling you about at least some of these friends would make me appear remiss, conceited and thankless. They are the friends and relatives for whom I have the greatest thanks.

This book, *The Guardian and the FarCaller,* was inspired in about 1998, and has gone through no less than 20 revisions. For the inspiration to write this book, as well as its sequels and other books already written or in work, I thank God. It may sound trite to some, but I am absolutely sincere. For support during the beginning of writing this book, I thank my late wife, Naomi. Her assistance was invaluable. At nearly the same level of appreciation is my present wife, Jeanie, who read through at least 10 versions of this book, giving her suggestions (some of which were giggles) about how better to say what I meant, or delete what I said and didn't mean. Next comes a good friend, Craig Holland, whose editing was amazingly fast, to the point, and which helped me keep in mind the purpose for this book and the need to give up some of my deathless prose so the book would be better.

For additional support I thank other members of my family: my son David, my daughters Nancy and Sandi, my grandkids Darla, Brandon and Devin, my sister Colleen, and my brother Dave and his wife, Tommie. Every one of these people gave their time and thoughts to making this book better. (Believe me when I say that early versions REALLY needed help.) Also high on my list is James Gunn. Yes, THE James Gunn, the famous science fiction author, historian, and Grand Master of Science Fiction. He first gave me the courage and confidence to attend his Science Fiction Writers Workshops at the University of Kansas. His comments, as well as those of the other wannabe writers, deftly pared away any inflated ideas I had about my skills and replaced them with specific suggestions on how to make the ideas, plot and descriptions more vivid and compelling. Also meriting thanks is THE Kij Johnson (she's another of those who would best be addressed in that manner). Kij is an amazingly talented writer and teacher who goes out of her way to help those of us struggling to get our thoughts out to the public.

The cover art was designed by Phil Morales, my son-in-law. His wife, my daughter Nancy, acted as the book's self-appointed censor whenever my prose became too earthy. (I must admit Jeanie also acted in that capacity.)

There are certainly many others who helped. They know who they are and I thank them very much.

So here it is: the culmination of much work and cooperation. SPOONWORLD: THE GUARDIAN AND THE FARCALLER, is the first of at least five books about both of these men and their worlds. I hope it'll make you look carefully at every silver spoon you see for the rest of your life.

Chuck Marsters
Oakdale, Minnesota
June 2007

Prologue

Excerpt from the FarCaller Annals, Volume 1
(Edited by Daniel Kaaler)

Earth date: June 1589 (reconstructed)
Place: FarCaller's World

Hondras the Promised was quietly but desperately searching for the one person needed to enable her to fulfill her destiny. A beautiful redhead with a strong but lithe frame, gentle voice, and graceful carriage, she enjoyed traveling across her magnificent homeland, through its thick forests of giant, nut-bearing hardwoods, through rippling streams glittering and dancing over moss-draped rocks, and along rich fields, undulating with windblown kernel crops. The woods sheltered thousands of animals, birds, and insects, as well as roots, herbs, and multicolored berries, all of which provided Hondras her nightly feasts. Sometimes she'd catch a fish or snare a rabbit or grouse to complement the other foods. When that happened, she'd masterfully use the herbs, berry juices, and honey to turn the lean and gamey meat into something suitable for the gods—whom she daily thanked for their largesse.

Enjoyable as it was, the trip had a serious purpose. The varied styles of clothing and the magical masks and wigs she brought with her, along with the shape-shifting spells pounded into her memory by her father before he died, enabled her to travel without leaving a trail. This was important for many reasons, not the least being that there were felons about, men who'd attack a lone rider to steal anything of value. In the case of a woman traveling solo, they'd subject her to ordeals so dreaded that she'd prefer death. However, Hondras could defend herself, sometimes by skillful use of the small daggers she kept in secret places in her clothes and sometimes by magic. One of her defenses was a spell that hid her flashing blue eyes and made her face so ugly it discouraged all but the most wretched attackers. She always used it when traveling on the rutted and dusty roads that connected villages—but never in the villages or hamlets themselves.

During the midday meal at each village along her meandering route, she'd inquire about its history and people, seeking clues to help her find the master craftsman for whom she searched. She always received the expected questions about why a woman of her gentle voice and graceful carriage would be traveling alone. Her answer was ready, although untrue: "To my father's home returning am I," she'd say. "Frightfully ill has he been, and before he dies see him I must, to again tell him how much him I love." And always, before leaving, she'd pass on "rumors" she'd concocted about FenWraith the Evil during her travels. "A witch she is," Hondras would whisper to anyone who'd listen, "who would your soul steal and curse!" The people seldom asked how she knew this, partly because they loved to hear new stories about evil persons and partly because Hondras would always weave a spell that made them believe her words and suspend their normal skepticism about anything told them by a stranger.

"Short is she," Hondras would say, holding her hand barely shoulder high to most women, "and ugly! Black her hair is, where insects and maggots abound. Her swollen black eyes from her dark red face bulging are, and a large red nose has she, with purple veins and green warts." Hondras would then tell the listeners—now surrounding her—gobbling every word as if priceless, "The only sound when moving makes she, the shuffling of her large boots is." As she said that, she'd shuffle her own small and delicate feet, the deerskin boots making scarcely any sound on the tavern's floor. "Little says she, but at the sound of her voice, snakes in their tracks stop."

Before people could ask more questions, she would smile, her blue eyes disarming them. "To my father's home continue I must," she'd say and then pick up her small hand-woven pouch of thistle-bush bark. Her purse was small, barely the size of a man's fist. It was clearly not a place for a traveler to carry valuables. The message: she was poor, like those to whom she spoke.

Mounting her large draft horse, its black tail, mane, and body contrasting with her ragged blue riding cloak, she'd then leave the village as she found it—except now the villagers feared that FenWraith the Evil would appear some dark, moonless night.

Several months into this sojourn, after countless nights in as many inns, after telling the story of FenWraith the Evil many, many times, she arrived at a village larger than any of the others she'd seen. Well-tended fields of grain, corn, and root vegetables surrounded it, with neatly trimmed farmhouses sprinkling the countryside. Some of the fields were already harvested of their bounty and were now being tilled by farmers driving teams of horses or oxen pulling large iron plows. Invariably the farmers would wave in response to her arm raised in greeting, and more often than not, they'd offer to share their modest lunches with her. She always accepted and, like the previous villages, introduced herself with a false name, usually Sunset or Promise or Morning Star. They were unusual names, beautiful in their simplicity and poetry, and much different from the names most often used by her new friends. Hondras suspected that a year or two after her visit, a newborn girl would be given one of her special aliases, and she took pleasure from that.

She spent nearly a week in one of the small inns in this village, quietly going about her business of looking for the special person needed to complete her search, but never telling anyone what she was doing. They liked the pretty and vivacious woman, enjoyed hearing about places she'd been, while "to my father's house traveling," and, at nights in the inn, gathered to hear about FenWraith the Evil.

This village, Fair Water, fascinated Hondras because its citizens openly boasted of the skills and artistic talents of one of its tradesmen, Ewan the Smith. He was a tall, rangy man with arms strong enough to bend steel bars but was gentle enough to wipe the noses of the many small children who gathered around his smithy to watch him turn hot iron into knives or horseshoes or pitchforks. And on rare occasions, the people told Hondras, he'd hammer sheets of copper or silver into beautiful pitchers and bowls and then sell them to the richest families in the area. Always they were perfectly made, with no visible hammer or file marks, their surfaces shining so brightly that everything around them was mirrored and bent into amazingly beautiful reflections.

As she joined the crowds quietly watching Ewan work, Hondras joyfully realized her search was over. Early one evening a few days later, after the usual crowd of onlookers had gone home to their evening dinners, Hondras acted. Using the noise of Ewan's work to hide her chants, she conjured a spell that put him under her control. She then covered his head with a loosely woven black hood and led him outside the smithy to her horse. Gently coaxing the huge horse to kneel, she told Ewan to sit just behind her saddle. When he was properly seated and steady, she put a rope around him and attached it to the saddle so he would not slip off. After confirming he was as comfortable as possible, they rode for three days over one hundred twenty kilometers through rough, heavily treed hills. Throughout this trip, Ewan remained under her control, eating when told, sleeping when told but unable to speak. They passed through forests rumored (according to the stories she spread in the villages she visited) to be the homes of vicious, man-hungry creatures. As with the tales she'd spread about FenWraith the Evil, the dangers in the forests were also figments of her imagination. Because she knew country people and how they lived and thought, Hondras was certain they'd never follow anyone—even her—into those "dangerous" forests, lest vicious beasts would capture and eat them. In these forests, she and Ewan would stop for meals and sleep in safety en route to her home.

On the far side of the forests, away from all the roads she'd traveled and villages she'd visited, Hondras rode into a rocky ravine to the base of a brooding cliff, then through a small vine-covered opening into a hidden cave. She carefully slid

Ewan, still blindfolded and under the spell, off the back of her horse and onto some soft straw to rest. Her spell had protected him from the pain of traveling so far and so long. Next she unsaddled, carefully and lovingly groomed her horse, and put out fresh water and apples for him—a reward for traveling so far. That accomplished, she led Ewan from the stable into her living area in the middle of the cave and released him from his spell. It had blocked out all his memories of their travel, so he recalled working in his shop until she cast her spell over him. When she removed the hood covering his dark eyes, the thoroughly shaken man was astonished at what he beheld.

Through his friends at the village, Ewan had heard of FenWraith the Evil and fully believed she had captured him. Thus, his mind was full of the stories of how the ugly witch lived in a cavern full of bats and spiders and venomous serpents, how she ate terrible and distasteful things cooked into a dreadful stew in a large iron pot, and how she imprisoned her captives in spells and forced them to slave for her until they died. Instead, the terrified man stood in a large room brightly lit with torches and tapers. Its walls were covered with gold-framed mirrors and hung with tapestries depicting bright sunlight, spring and summer flowers, deer, bear, eagles, and flocks of colorful songbirds. Ewan slowly turned around, feasting on the beautiful decorations and tasteful furniture.

Then he looked at his dirty and ugly captor in her dark fur outer garments and hood of woven reeds. As he stared at her monstrously unattractive face, Hondras removed her hood to reveal scraggly black hair and then shed her heavy bearskin robe. Beneath it, she wore a loose dress of soft red velvet draping her slender and very female body. When she stepped out of large wolfskin boots, he could see her feet and ankles were clean, small, and delicate. Lastly she reached over her head with both hands, grabbed her grimy, matted black wig, and pulled it straight up, set it aside, and recited the words that canceled her facial disguise spell. What emerged from below the filthy mop was a head of striking red hair framing a beautiful face.

Ewan's gasp broke the strained silence. "By the gods! Your beauty also a spell is?"

Her tinkling laugh only confused the smith. "For the kind words I thank you. People a witch think me, so when my purpose it suits, that form I assume. Often into villages and inns go I, and vegetables from the greengrocers purchase, but always my dirty clothes and mask without. Not only good food can I buy, but also what around that area is happening I learn. And eavesdrop can I on what about FenWraith the Evil they say." She flashed a brilliant and contagious smile at Ewan. "Some of it even me scares! But FenWraith and all the tales about her, from my imagination I conjured."

When the humor of the moment passed, Hondras walked up to stand close by Ewan, her expression serious. Looking up into his rugged and handsome face, she placed both hands on his shoulders and said, "That I had to use my powers to bring you here against your will I regret, but your help vital to me is because the finest smith in this entire area you are. No other certain way to get you to come with me knew I. Certainly, no offer from FenWraith the Evil would you accept, I knew." Her smile returned as she continued.

"So you I kidnapped, and through the Haunted Hills into the Devil's Woods, to a witches lair we rode." She gestured around the room proudly. "This place."

Realizing they were standing, a touch of discomfort still in the air, she motioned Ewan toward a wooden chair that he recognized as being made by a master furniture maker and good friend. "Several months ago, purchased this did I," she said. "My first guest you are."

As Ewan enjoyed the fit and feel of the chair, Hondras excused herself and left him alone. Shortly she returned carrying a black enameled tray on which she had placed a red stoneware teapot, a small plate, and two handmade cups matching the teapot. On the plate were four warm rolls bursting with aromas of honey, butter, and cinnamon. "In a cup of tea would you join me?" Hondras asked. Then, blushing slightly, she added, "The pastries some time ago I baked, but fresh with a spell kept them." Shyly she said, "Like them you will, I think."

* * *

Hondras knew she had been "guided" by her gods to find a man with the skills she needed to fulfill her destiny. When she first saw Ewan, she realized something else: she was strongly attracted to this handsome, quiet, and confident man. It made his kidnapping even more painful for her, because she knew she was taking a wonderful, gentle man from his home and friends and was causing him pain. Never before had she experienced such feelings, and hurting someone to whom she felt so strongly attracted hurt her. Nevertheless, she had to do it. Disregarding that, she gracefully lowered herself onto a small settee placed at the foot of Ewan's chair. Then she straightened her flowing dress and said, "And now, why I brought you here will I reveal."

Ewan nodded, uncertain about what to say.

"A very special legacy must I leave. The skills of the finest metalsmith need I for that legacy fulfilled to be.

Confusion colored Ewan's face. "I understand not."

Hondras screwed her face into a wry smile. "First, if I may, something must I confess."

"Please."

"The burden and role of mistress of powers not understood by anyone else, truly I carry." She said no more, obviously signaling Ewan to indicate any interest he had in her words.

"Again I understand not, beautiful lady," he said, responding as she hoped.

"As first you feared, Master Smith," she said, looking into his eyes, "possessing and manipulating magical powers can I. In truth, of your master's touch to protect those powers, your assistance I beg."

Ewan was suddenly consumed with interest. "Still your words my feeble mind understands not. You, then, a wizard are?"

"A sorceress am I. The skills to manipulate powers not of this world I wield, as do wizards."

"My doubts endure I cannot," Ewan said. "These powers the black arts are?"

"No, Master Smith, evil they are not," she answered. "But to those unknowing, often so they seem."

"How, then, can I assist?"

* * *

For his task, Hondras provided Ewan the purest gold, finest silver, and most surprisingly, copper and tin—the ingredients for bronze. Over the next several months, infused with a personal compulsion to design and craft the most perfect pieces ever, Ewan labored long and hard to produce three identical sets of plates and spoons, one of silver, one of gold, and one of bronze. If he needed any special tool or materials, the slightest word was enough to motivate his beautiful "employer." The object he needed would appear the next day. Yet, despite her keen interest in the progress of his work, Hondras never asked Ewan how his efforts were proceeding but listened eagerly whenever he discussed his progress. Neither did she visit his smithy, built for him in the back of her cave. It had a vent whose workings Ewan never understood; but it removed the extra heat, smoke, and fumes from his workplace without assistance from an apprentice.

Hondras obviously trusted Ewan, and however curious or impatient she might feel, she was willing to wait until he decided his task was complete. And throughout this period, they shared meals and talked of many things.

Ewan told Hondras of his betrothal to a beautiful young woman and her tragic death after a friend's horse threw her to the ground. Ewan learned of Hondras's father—a wizard—and her beautiful mother—a sorceress—and how both simply disappeared after her education in magic was completed. She told of her fear of the magic she practiced and how her parents had infused in her a strong sense of responsibility about using those powers.

Hondras cooked their meals and washed dishes and clothes while Ewan toiled in his forge. In the evenings, they occasionally walked in the forest that protected Hondras's home. He learned to identify mushrooms and wild roots and berries. She loved how he talked of his joy in crafting beautiful and useful objects from raw metal. As they shared, they grew fonder of each other, Ewan's kidnapping forever forgotten.

Five weeks after Ewan's arrival, when all six pieces were finally completed, he proudly carried them to the great room. She was preparing their dinner and was totally involved in what had become for her a labor of love. Surrounded by the aromas of onions, carrots, venison, and an amazing admixture of herbs and spices, all making his mouth's juices flow in anticipation, Ewan quietly placed his work on the dining table. Then he tiptoed up behind her, put his arms around her waist, and gently kissed the back of her neck.

At his first touch, she jumped slightly then recognized his male scent and touch. Her reaction was to slowly turn around within the circle of his arms and lovingly and enthusiastically return his kiss.

After dinner, two things happened for the first time in either of their lives. The first occurred in the great room, lit by torches whose flickering flames were multiplied thousands of times by the mirrors covering much of each wall. There Ewan watched Hondras weave spells on the three sets of implements. It was the first time he had ever seen her actually employ her magic, and it sobered his enthusiasm for his accomplishment.

She spoke unfamiliar words and used peculiar gestures over each pair of the devices, none understood by Ewan. For this occasion, Hondras wore robes of purple velvet whose only decoration was a piping of gold thread sewn along the edges of the long and spacious sleeves. Her expression was grave and her effort intense, her fair-skinned brow speckled with beads of perspiration colored gold by the open flames of the torches, adding an eerie quality to the frightening feeling already growing inside Ewan. After enabling the third set—the bronze—she covered it with a black velvet cloth and immediately turned away, leaving the others uncovered, gleaming in the torchlight.

The second wondrous event occurred that evening: they conceived a male child. Hondras said their son would be named FarCaller because he would have far-reaching power and the moral strength to use the silver plate.

"But," Ewan said, still basking in the glow of their love and holding his beloved close to him, "again, understand I not. With the silver plate and spoon, how does 'far-reaching' power relate?"

She smiled, returning his joy at this togetherness she had so long desired. "Because FarCaller the only person in our world will be who its powers can employ."

"How?"

She lifted her head and kissed him, slowly, tenderly, then intensely, pulling him close to her with surprising strength. "My beloved," she whispered, "let us our lives together relish. The time will come when all of these things clear to you can be made."

* * *

After celebrating the birth of their son eight years earlier, Hondras called her son and her husband to her. FarCaller was already a strong young lad, the handsome features of his father and the beauty of his mother blended into his countenance. However, instead of his father's brown hair or his mother's ravishing red hair, his was black as ebony. His eyes radiated a joy of living and love that gave both parents intense pleasure.

"My son," Hondras began, "for you to know more about your life and your heritage, now time it is." They sat in a circle in their great room, Ewan in what had quickly become his chair—the handcrafted one Hondras offered him the day she brought him in bondage to her home. Young FarCaller perched on his favorite low wooden, three-legged stool just to the right of his father. Hondras sat in a soft chair crafted for her by Ewan, with a frame of darkest iron polished to a glow, upholstered in the hide of a giant black bear that fell into a crevasse one winter and died of its injuries. "Many things there are about your life that tell you now I cannot," she continued, "but some of them you must now know for your destiny to prepare."

She reached beneath her chair and withdrew an object swathed in red velvet. As she slowly removed its soft and plush protection, Ewan recognized the silver plate he produced nearly nine years earlier and that he hadn't seen since.

"This," Hondras said to both her men, "a powerful instrument is, which you, FarCaller, for the next ten years will use. Today to you I am giving it so that familiar with its appearance, feel, and some of its powers you can become." Before he could say or ask anything, she withdrew a silver spoon from a pocket in her dress, holding it up for both men to see, then turned toward Ewan.

"This spoon its counterpart is. Much of the power of the plate it shares, my husband, which to use every day you must, until the next step in your role I reveal." So saying, she solemnly handed the plate to her son and the spoon to Ewan. Returning her attention to FarCaller, she said, "Your father both of these lovingly crafted. Now, on this day, to him and to you their purposes will I reveal.

"These instruments powers contain, that only for good can be used. With them, their users to communicate over long distances enabled are." So saying, she smiled at Ewan and looked at their son. She was now answering the questions Ewan had asked her the night of their son's conception. "You, my son," she said, looking directly the boy, "the plate will use; your father the spoon. To master—together—these instruments your tasks are."

She now leaned toward FarCaller, stressing the importance of what she was about to say. "A time there will come when you must these instruments use over distances greater than you can imagine, so diligently practice." Turning to Ewan, she said, "And you, beloved, must the power of this spoon master. The most important task in both of your lives this is." So saying, she returned her attention to the black-haired boy. "Now, my son, your father and me alone please leave. About something not yet of concern to you talk we must."

After FarCaller left, Hondras gazed intently into her mate's eyes, communicating to him that this was to be an important talk and he was to listen closely and learn. Ewan started to ask what Hondras was doing, but she silenced him by gently touching his lips with her finger. "Hush, my beloved. Listen."

He nodded and tried to relax, but even the comforting and familiar shape of his favorite chair didn't help.

"A time is coming when part we must," she said.

When Ewan's eyes constricted from fear and concern, Hondras touched his knee in what had become one of their most intimate gestures: he was not to worry.

"During this absence neither of us will suffer, but the needs of the future this separation necessary makes. When that happens, prepared and willing must you be. From this time onward, only with the powers of the silver spoon mastering must you yourself concern."

"But what about the other sets? They, to FarCaller, mention you did not."

Hondras nodded at the question. "Their own uses and their own time they have," she answered. "The golden set and the bronze and silver spoons on a journey take you will, but the bronze and silver plates must here remain. When the time comes, everything else you must know, you will I tell."

"But their powers are what?"

Hondras thought about his question, remaining silent for many seconds, her eyes glazing over in the manner he had learned to associate with deep thought. When her sense of attention returned, she said, "Only this can I say. For its users to communicate over long distances, the silver set makes possible. The golden set powers has which, if misused, could harm. Most I fear the bronze set, but exist it must. In contrast to the others, that set, and it alone, for evil could be used."

More questions came to Ewan's mind, but again Hondras sensed them and silenced him with a touch to his lips. "This tell you I can, beloved. FarCaller and his descendants for many lifetimes the silver plate will use and will its secrets to their firstborns pass. For this reason, our son the key to success of this matter is. You, my dearest, another role will have, one which to you at the proper time will I reveal."

* * *

On FarCaller's eighteenth birthday, he and Ewan proved to Hondras their skills in communicating using only the silver spoon and plate. Shortly thereafter, she fell ill, and no medication or treatment reversed her slow voyage toward the end of her life. Near death, Hondras summoned her men, her voice weak but filled with an intensity of love and dedication that amazed both of them.

"Soon to a place of peace go I," she began, hushing their denials with a slow wave of her hand. "It is time your destinies to reveal." Looking at Ewan, tears running down both his cheeks and his chin quivering in an attempt to keep from sobbing, she said, "You, my beloved, to another land will soon travel. It is one I have never seen, but the one to which the silver and bronze spoons, and the golden set, must be taken. You to that place are to go, knowing my love will with you always be. While there, another mate you will find, and—"

"No!" he shouted. "Another mate will I *never* have!"

Hondras smiled weakly but said, "Yes, my love, you will. And as you have loved me and I you, love you she will, and such joy you will have that already it pleases me." She coughed deeply, a racking cough whose sounds almost hurt her husband and son, but she shook off their offers of help and continued. "You, my love, must the title of 'Guardian' assume, but only to your mate and your firstborn this reveal. In addition, the silver spoon always must you protect, and with our son to communicate.

"Your firstborn a son will be, and on his eighteenth birthday, teach him the wonders of the silver spoon you must. He the next Guardian will become. The secrets of our two worlds, and of the silver set, you and all Guardians must protect."

Hondras turned to FarCaller, now unashamedly crying. "You, FarCaller, the same will do, but in this place. You also a mate will soon find. She loving and generous will be and will your children joyfully bear. To your firstborn—a daughter—the secrets and use of the silver plate must you teach until mastered them she has. She, then, these secrets to her firstborn must pass. And so must it ever be. To the firstborn, boy or girl, and to no other, these secrets taught must be. And each firstborn 'FarCaller' must be named."

"Ewan, my darling," she said, looking at the only man ever to share her life, "at the proper time—which know you will—the golden set to one of your descendants you must pass, but *not* a firstborn. That person instruct you must, to pass it to a member of his family, and tell them, as they are led, to pass it on. At the proper time, another of your descendants, a future Guardian, receive it will, and with it both his world and ours will protect. In a similar fashion, the bronze spoon you must pass on but to any of your descendants not. Its ultimate owner it will find, but I know not how long that will take."

She coughed, clearly losing strength, but she shook her head to prevent anyone from touching her and looked back at her son. "FarCaller, ever the silver plate keep safe you must, but the bronze plate also pass on. However, no instructions concerning it are you to give, for once passed, its proper recipient by its own powers will find. When this will happen I know not, but not for many generations will it be."

She then looked again at her husband. "Both you and our son, my beloved, ways to keep these secrets from prying eyes and minds must develop. A method to identify our family you need, before secrets to them you reveal. Up to you that leave I. The method flawlessly must work, every time needed it is. When the proper time arrives, the Guardian and his FarCaller to communicate instantly and flawlessly must be able. They, and only they, the powers needed to help each other overcome dangers to themselves, their unique heritage, their families, and possibly their countries, will have."

She closed her eyes, breathed deeply, and then weakly opened them. "All these things in your minds keep. In them you must your descendants test and instruct. Only then in peace will you rest." She exhaled—a deep, shuddering effort. Then, her voice barely a whisper, she said, "More than I can say, you both I love. By doing as I have said, honor me."

As her eyes closed for the final time and her life force rose from her body, Ewan disappeared from that world, transported by the power of the silver spoon to a different place, the world of his destiny. FarCaller suddenly found himself alone, standing beside his mother's body, holding a silver plate and not knowing what to do next, or when, if ever, he would again see his father's face or hear his father's voice.

Part I

The Legacy

Chapter 1

The Last Task

Bend, Oregon
May 2000

Ima Kaaler Mainor was more concerned than she could ever remember. In past years, she worried about her son's birth, about her husband's failing health and subsequent death, even about the birth of a grandchild. She'd never worried about money or personal possessions—her unusual heritage had removed those things as "worries" decades earlier. Now, however, she could sense her own approaching death. She was to have accomplished her most important task three years earlier, but through circumstances beyond her control, it remained uncompleted. Worse, it was barely started.

Ima was unremarkable in many ways. Shorter and more slender than most women, she was blessed with an amazing capacity to care for and about people. She had invested wisely, cautiously, and quietly, telling almost no one about her wealth. Her husband had been a master carpenter and cabinetmaker. Their family always had enough food and clothing, so there was enough money to take one family trip each year, usually to some place like San Francisco or Boise or the Grand Canyon. Even when her husband died, she kept her estate separate from his business so none of her family would know its unusual size. Then she announced her grandson Lee's high school graduation gift: a full scholarship to any school he wanted to attend—anywhere.

"But, Mom," her son protested, "you're talking about tens of thousands of dollars each year! That'll take much of what Dad left you. You could do something for yourself and let me take care of Lee's education. I mean, we really appreciate the gift, but—"

"Faar," she interrupted, her dark blue eyes gleaming and her still-pretty face firmly set, "you can't stop me from doing what I want with my own money." Then she flashed the smile he recognized as the "I won" signal. "Can you?"

So the little old lady with the cloud-white hair and lean body got her way—again. Lee chose the college he wanted: it was Willamette University, in Salem, a liberal arts college with a small campus and a big reputation, only a few hours' drive from their home.

Thus, it was that day in May of 2003 when Ima Mainor called her only grandchild and asked him to come back to Bend from college immediately to talk with her. Normally Lee did almost anything she asked, out of love for her and appreciation for all she'd done for him.

"Grandma," Lee said, his voice not betraying how much her call had destroyed his concentration for his comprehensive oral exams, "I can't come until next weekend. Next week is finals week. My orals are Friday morning, so I can see you that evening if I can get packed up soon enough."

"But, Lee," she began, her voice already in its "I'm going to convince you" mode.

"No, Grandma," he responded, uncharacteristically cutting her off in midsentence. "I'm a senior. If I don't pass my orals, I might have to go to summer school; and neither of us wants that, now do we?"

Before she could respond, he added, "No, of course not. So I'll see you a week from Friday, after dinner. Now goodbye, Grandma. I wish we could talk longer right now, but I really have to study."

The click on the line, followed by the dial tone, ended Ima's hopes for the talk she wanted to have with Lee that weekend.

Even though she felt weak and ill and suspected her death was near, her mind was still sharp. She immediately went to Plan B, although she wouldn't have called it that. She first scheduled a meeting with her attorney for the next afternoon. Then she began devising some unusual puzzles certain to capture Lee's imagination. She also wrote a series of letters to him, hoping against hope she'd have the time to write them and the skill to tell him what he needed to know. It consumed all of her time and energy.

She finished at noon of the following Friday, just as Lee finished his orals. She died that afternoon, never having had the opportunity to tell her grandson how much he meant to their family's future and how much he had to learn about it.

Chapter 2

Who Wants 'Em?

The Cascades Scenic Highway, Oregon
July 2004

As Lee Kaaler drove back toward his apartment in Bend, Oregon, he was absorbed in the beauty of the lush farms of the Willamette Valley and the green canopies of fir and pine covering the Santiam Pass highway over the Cascade Range. He smiled as he thought about his weekend frolicking in the bracing Pacific waters and flying kites on the beach with his friends. On short vacations, like this one, he most enjoyed camping and hiking in the Central Oregon desert or going to the Pacific coast.

This Sunday afternoon, however, once he crossed over the summit of the Cascades and headed toward the little town of Sisters, his thoughts kept alternating between the fun he had at the beach and memories of his grandma Mainor. Strangely, he hadn't thought about her in almost five months. It had been nearly four years since she passed away. Nevertheless, whenever he thought of her on this day, a weird feeling, a sense of approaching trouble, seemed to envelop him. It didn't frighten him, but the fact that it arose at all was odd.

His apartment was on the second floor of a modern cement and steel complex overlooking Mirror Pond in the center of Old Town. The three-story building had a Southwest theme; its eaves and arches reflected a Mexican influence and its grey-tan stucco finish complemented that impression.

After the four-and-one-half-hour drive, Lee parked his Volkswagen, grabbed his knapsack, and climbed the single flight of stairs to his apartment. He took one step inside and stopped. "What the h—?"

Every piece of living room furniture had been overturned, its stuffing removed, and every pillow had been cut open. His living room lamps were knocked over. All his books, DVDs, and CDs had been pulled from their towers and strewn across the slate blue Berber carpet. In the kitchen, the cabinet doors were agape, and much of his stoneware was in pieces on the kitchen floor, its traditional Mexican design complementing the bright Southwestern motif on the vinyl flooring. The utensil drawers were either pulled out as far as possible or turned upside down on the floor, their shiny contents adding to the visual cacophony of bright red, yellow, blue, and green shards.

In shock, Lee looked at the remains of the first place he could call his own and remembered how much effort and cash it had taken to furnish it. He recalled the joy he got from decorating it, piece by piece, as he saved enough money from his banker's salary to make this place his own. He loved the warm feeling he had every time he walked through the front door. Now his home, his space—his very self—had been violated.

One glance down the short hallway to the two bedrooms and the bathroom confirmed what he expected: they too were ravaged. He called 911.

Two police cars arrived in less than five minutes. First out was Sergeant Virgil Kinglit, one of Lee's old high school buddies.

After explaining what he found, Lee gestured toward the open door on the second-floor landing. "Do your thing, Virge."

Once the crime scene investigation team departed, Virge joined Lee at Lee's car.

"What'd you find?" Lee asked before his friend could say anything.

"You didn't touch anything when you opened the door?"

If Virge hadn't been a high school classmate, Lee would have been upset at the amount of time it took to get answers, but he accepted that Virge was just doing his job and didn't want to let friendship get in the way. Lee took a couple of deep breaths and pushed his mussed and sand-filled salt-and-pepper hair back from his forehead. "I walked in, saw the damage, called 911, and walked out. That's all."

"That's what we thought," Virge said. "There are lots of fingerprints, but our tech thinks they're from the same person, so they're probably yours. No tool marks, no shoe prints, no strange threads, no pieces of fabric—nothing. A professional job. Can't prove what I'm about to say, but since there've been no other break-ins like this in all of Central Oregon, I'd guess you were a specific target."

"Why? I don't have anything valuable. Just my entertainment stuff, plus an iMac and a printer, but they're pretty common. And they weren't taken."

"Well, whoever hit your place took his time, because that much searching takes a lot of effort. My guess is that the perps knew you were gone. Logic tells me they must have been watching you, maybe saw you pack up for your weekend at the coast. If they did that, they'd know you wouldn't be back for at least a day or two." He changed he subject. "When you were in your apartment, did you notice anything missing?"

"Didn't look around much, and haven't been inside since you and your people arrived."

Virge walked toward the steps leading to Lee's apartment, gesturing for Lee to follow. "We found one interesting thing."

He led Lee through the front room into the little kitchen, stepping around the mess on the living room and kitchen floors, then pointed to a drawer next to the small slide-in electric range. "What went in here?"

"My silverware, mostly."

"Why don't you pick it up and put it back? I'll even help."

Lee thought that was a ridiculous thing for a police sergeant to do but chalked it up to their friendship. Sifting through the rubble, he found forks, knives, kitchen knives, and peelers—doodads found in nearly every kitchen. All but . . .

"Where are my spoons?"

Virge nodded and smiled. "That's what we noticed: no spoons. Look around carefully and tell me if anything else is missing. It's all been checked for prints, so you can touch and move anything."

Twenty minutes later, Lee collapsed onto his oak rocker in the living room. "It's all here, Virge. Everything I own—except spoons. Eight teaspoons, eight soupspoons, a couple of serving ones, and a few I use for cooking. Why would anyone in their right mind do all this work and cause all this damage for about two-dozen spoons?"

Chapter 3

Same Song; Second Verse

Bend, Oregon

One week after Lee returned from the coast, his parents called to tell him their home had also been broken into. Only two days earlier, he had finally put his apartment back together from the chaos of his own robbery and clearly remembered how much the break-in had upset him. From that, he knew how his parents had to be feeling, so he sped to their home on the eastern edge of Bend.

Even before his mother could make her customary offer of a cup of tea, Lee started asking questions. "Are you both OK? Was anything taken? When do you think this happened? Have you called the police?"

His father, most often calm and collected, immediately began swearing and cursing; and with every such word, Lee's mother would say, "Now, Faar, don't talk that way! Lee understands how you feel without using profanity."

Not surprisingly, that made him swear even louder.

Lee's quick look around the house convinced him the break-in was by the same lowlifes who hit his apartment. Nothing was in its customary place, cushions and upholstery were ripped or sliced open and stuffing removed. His mother had already cleaned up her kitchen and seemed to be working her way out from there to put the rest of the house back into order.

They adjourned to the living room with their cups of tea. Lee sat in his favorite rocker by the fireplace; his dad and mom shared the love seat, as always. Shreds of furniture upholstery and petals from the silk flower arrangements his mother had made and so loved still hadn't been picked up.

After drinking their tea, during which Lee's mother forbade Lee's father from swearing, he calmed down enough that Lee felt he could raise the subject of robberies. "This looks just about like my place did," he began. "They went through it like a tornado."

"It's stupid!" his father said, his voice just short of a shout. "They left our antiques, our oil paintings, and even my first editions, tore the place apart upstairs and down, and took only spoons." The older man, a bit shorter and wider than Lee, his hair a bit thinner, could never have been missed as Lee's father if seen with his son, but their temperaments were completely different. Lee's favored his mother's. "Every blasted one of them!" his father bellowed. "It'll cost more to repair the mess those bastards made than to replace those spoons."

"Did the police say anything useful?" Lee asked.

"Only that it looked like the same guys hit here as hit your place. Big help that was."

Before Lee could say anything, his dad added, "This is more like what should have happened to your grandmother. She was always involved in kooky things: antiques, family heirlooms, family trees, puzzles. Once, when I was a teenager, she asked me if I'd like to learn about an heirloom spoon. I told her I didn't want anything to do with any of the crazy things she was involved in." He thought about his talks with his mother, then said, "She never brought them up to me again, either."

Lee gracefully excused himself as soon as he could and slowly drove back to his apartment, thinking about the heirloom spoon his dad mentioned. It was the only thing his grandmother bequeathed Lee. It was sterling silver, wrapped in a blue velvet cloth, and kept in a small wooden box. It had been in his safety-deposit box since her will was probated—nearly four years earlier. He hadn't seen or thought about it until his dad—not the robberies—reminded him of it.

One thought spiraled through his mind: *That has to be the only spoon left in either of our homes. Could that be what they wanted? If so, why?*

Chapter 4

The Fan

One of the things Lee liked about starting his banking career in a branch bank was that he usually wasn't terribly busy—except for this day. Getting the spoon out of his safety-deposit box was easy; finding time to inspect it wasn't. Almost every time he tried to get a few moments to open the small box and look at the spoon, he was interrupted—telephone calls, questions from tellers, the manager going to lunch and leaving Lee to cope with another hour of interruptions by himself. Each time he had a bit of peace, he'd take the spoon's box out of his pants pocket and start to open it. Then he'd have to respond to a telephone call or something else that demanded his attention; so he'd close the little box, replace the rubber band holding it shut, and put it back in his pants pocket. It was frustrating. Making matters worse, thoughts of the spoon kept popping into his mind to the point where he sometimes couldn't think of anything else.

In mid afternoon he finally gave up trying to look at the spoon. The bulge in his pocket looked awkward but felt safe. It was also the first time in his life that he wished he could comfortably wear a sport coat in the hot Central Oregon summer; the inside breast coat pockets made much better hiding places for bulky objects than pants pockets.

At five thirty, after laboriously toiling with the tellers to bring the daily balance sheet into order, Lee sped home. His apartment was only a few miles from the bank, and the rush hour traffic was waning, so he made it in ten minutes.

Once home, he locked the door and carefully inspected the spoon, not remembering anything about the object other than its deep silver luster.

He was disappointed. It resembled most of the silver spoons he'd seen all his life, especially when he accompanied his grandmother haunting her favorite antique shops. Its bowl had the normal shape but was larger than most tablespoons. The handle was slightly fluted, like most old spoons, but otherwise was perfectly plain except for an unrecognizable mark where he expected to see an initial.

Forgetting that for the moment, he held it at arm's length, tilting it back and forth to see if there was anything of particular note in the bowl. Finally he gave up and just sat, thinking, staring at the shiny spoon. He expected to see his face reflected in it, but instead there was the image of a ceiling fan slowly turning. It was unexpected, fascinating, and wrong.

Very wrong.

Slowly, apprehensively, unexplained fear rising in his chest, he shifted his attention from the image in the spoon to the ceiling of his living room, confirming what he knew. *My apartment doesn't have a ceiling fan!*

"What the . . ." He peered closely into the spoon, holding it exactly as he had first done, hoping he'd dreamed the fan. There, just as before, he saw a ceiling fan turning lazily in a room somewhere . . . else.

Part II

Find That Spoon!

Chapter 5

The Secret Revealed

Monterey, California
The Estate of Thomas Gerit

February 1940

The Monterey coastline was noted for its rugged beauty: jagged tan and black rocks jutting out from foaming surf, powerful waves pounding the shore. Clouds of seabirds swooped into the sea, emerging with silvery fish grasped in razor-sharp bills. Above the high tide mark, the edge of the beach was green with grasses.

Everyone living on that section of the California coast was accustomed to seeing the surf pound the rocks, but no one was comfortable when devilish, raging storms struck the area. Nobody liked seafoam blown high and far enough to cover the two-lane road known as California 1. This was partly because such storms were rare but so vicious that most people just stayed inside their expensive large homes and pulled themselves closer to the fireplaces. There they could let the comforting warmth help them forget nature's wrath. It was worse when the storms struck at night because they seemed to carry the aura of dark and nameless beings seeking to destroy anyone or anything trying to exist in the open. Those hapless souls were soaked, buffeted, and coated with sheets of foam and items of flotsam, as if Mother Nature was proving she was the most fearful entity in the entire world.

On one stretch of this coastal highway, a large private estate lay between the road and the cliffs. Its borders were delineated with tall green laurel hedges and red, yellow, and purple rhododendrons, punctuated by grossly misshapen pines, bent but unbroken in their efforts to withstand the continuous onslaught of ocean winds. This, the estate of Thomas Gerit, was known for several things among the locals. One was its size and manicured beauty, the other its owner—the most eccentric of all the local eccentrics. Thomas Gerit dressed in the style of Abraham Lincoln and spent much money traveling around the world to seek and capture unusual and exotic insects for his private collection.

He hadn't earned his fortune; he inherited it. His father, Philemon Gerit, founded a pharmaceutical empire that began by making and selling snake oil to the gold prospectors flooding California in the mid 1800s. Once Philemon made his first million, he expanded the company's product line into cosmetics, then athletic pain medicines, then women's hair products. By the time he retired, he had more money than he could have spent in two lifetimes. But that didn't stop his children from trying to get it for their own spending—all except his son Thomas. Thomas stayed home and helped his father, watching his younger brothers and sisters get married and move away. When Philemon died, bachelor Thomas inherited the bulk of everything. It didn't endear him to his siblings, but he didn't care.

The grandfather of winter storms hit the manor house just after dinner when sunlight was reduced to a cold and eerie glow. On nights like this, Thomas would often celebrate his contentment by standing at the huge bay window looking outward toward the ocean, trying to count the lightning strikes. On this particular night, the sky was almost constantly alight from dozens of lightning bolts hitting the ground and extending long, crooked fingers between clouds. Much to his servants' dismay, the tempest calmed Old Man Gerit, as he was privately called. It was during these storms that Thomas most wanted to have deep and philosophical discussions with his servants on why certain butterflies had blue or orange wings and whether that had some cosmic significance. These times were so important to their master that none of the help dared ask for time off in order to join their families huddling in fear from the storms, and none dared reveal any outward sign of his or her own fear.

During the height of this storm, while Thomas was deeply engrossed in examining one of his favorite dung beetle specimens, and discussing it with Sally, the entomologist he hired to catalog his collection, his estate manager entered the room and interrupted them. In most cases, this led to a severe tongue-lashing and threats of loss of employment; but the man's coat, pants, and shoes were sopping wet. His face was wind reddened and his hair plastered to his forehead. That he would dare enter the den in such a state stopped Thomas from his normal tirade: he knew something was very wrong. "What is it, Matthews?"

Before Matthews could respond, the room was plunged into darkness, broken only by blue flashes of lightning ripping through the skies around them.

"Master Gerit," he began, using the archaic term Thomas Gerit demanded, "the telephones are down, the roads are flooding and impassible, and now the electricity is off . . ."

Before Matthews could say anything more, Thomas Gerit stopped him. "So I see." Looking up at Sally, who was cataloging the beetles that so fascinated him, "Well, then, we'll have to continue this by lamplight, won't we?"

Sally walked across the room to the cabinets that held oil lamps kept just for such situations, but Matthews remained, holding his dripping hat in both hands, obviously not caring about any potential damage to the floors or carpets.

"Something more, Matthews?"

"Yes, sir. I was checking the approach road, and by the main gate I found a man lying in a ditch, nearly dead." He took two deep breaths before continuing. "I took the liberty of carrying him to the house, sir. Wouldn't want to die in a ditch myself, if you know what I mean."

"You brought him here? To my house?"

"He's not dead, sir. I felt you, as a good Christian, wouldn't want him to die alone in a muddy ditch but would at least want him to have some comfort in his last hours. Madeleine and George are cleaning him up as we speak. I thought some hot soup might help the poor soul."

Even though Thomas Gerit realized he was being manipulated by words about religion, he also believed Matthews might be correct. Thomas was eccentric but not stupid and wasn't about to let his salvation, if there was such a thing, be lost because he refused care to a dying man.

Sally was having difficulties in lighting the oil lamps, so Thomas motioned for Matthews to lead the way to the victim. As they reached the door to the den, George, the butler, appeared with two oil lamps.

The flickering golden light from the lamps added an eerie glow to the feeling of danger inherent in the rain and roaring wind battering the mansion. The infernal din of thunder was so close it sometimes shook the house. Saying nothing, Thomas Gerit took one of the lamps and nodded to Matthews to continue leading the way. Dutifully, Sally followed, the light from her lamp providing a respite from the oppressive darkness and causing her beautiful auburn hair to glow almost as if surrounded by a halo.

It didn't take long for Thomas to realize the man in the mud wasn't a hobo. His clothes were well made and he carried over a hundred dollars in cash—a significant sum. He had no identification, just a letter written to a "John" someone, possibly "Caller"—the last name was smeared—of Philadelphia, Pennsylvania, from a brother in Monterey. The writing was so smeared by the rain and mud thoroughly soaking his clothes that no other words were legible.

Once stripped of his sopping garments, then bathed and wrapped in warm blankets, the visitor began muttering.

"What did he say?" Thomas asked, moving next to the low bed so he could better hear the words.

Before anyone could answer, the ashen man whispered urgently, his eyes wide open, looking around furtively but apparently not seeing anyone. "Tell guardian. Earn musch more money." He obviously didn't know he was surrounded by strangers, because his words seemed to be meant for trusted friends or family. His voice was weak. Four people strained to hear more.

"Money?" Thomas asked. "Did he say 'money'?"

"I think so, Master Gerit," Matthews responded. "I think he said, 'much money,' but he slurs his words."

The patient, wheezing and coughing, weakly shook his head back and forth as if desperately trying to free himself of some invisible bonds. "Keep shecret!" His mumbling was interrupted with more wheezing, but he seemed determined to speak. "Protect shilver shpoon. Powerful magic. Keep! Get rich. Use challenge."

Thomas Gerit, his butler, and his estate manager all believed the ravings were gibberish. Matthews and George dismissed them as the those of a badly injured man, but they fascinated Thomas Gerit. The visitor was immediately given some warm soup and placed in the third best guest room in the manor, even though he was still not expected to live very long. Three days later, however, the guest had improved to the point where he could, at times, respond to some of the questions asked: his name was John, he was from somewhere near Philadelphia, and he was somehow associated with money. Thomas Gerit assumed John was an investor or antiques dealer because when asked about money, John would begin spouting the words "magic silver spoon" and rave about "seeing the future" and "making fortunes—hundreds of thousands of dollars." Once John gestured as if he wanted to draw something. Thomas responded by handing his guest a large pencil and a pad of paper.

John was no artist, and his hand shook, but he drew something resembling a man's face framed in what looked like the bowl of a spoon. While doing that, he said nothing intelligible except "challenge." When questioned about "challenge," he would always speak the same words in the same order. Thomas was so intrigued that he copied them down and checked them whenever John responded to a question about the challenge. John's speech remained slurred, however, so Thomas wasn't always certain he wrote exactly what John said. But unlike anything else John spoke, those words were always repeated exactly the same way and in the same order. Only one person in the room knew that what Thomas wrote down was incorrect, and she said nothing.

The morning of his fifth day in the Gerit mansion, John's fever suddenly spiked and that afternoon he died. Matthew and George promptly returned to their normal duties, no longer required to maintain a vigil over the stranger. Sally, however, remembered every word John had spoken.

As Thomas Gerit thought about the fortunes John spoke of, he became more and more enraptured with the mystery of what John had said. He began making detailed notes of everything spoken by John and poring over John's childlike sketches.

That evening, Sally drove down the winding coastal road to her father's four-bedroom, two-story Victorian home. A curved driveway teased visitors with scenes of the house peeking between stands of coastal pines, but Sally totally ignored the artistry involved in designing such an approach. She parked her car and rushed up the mahogany staircase to her father's office, not even taking the time to greet her mother and younger brother.

Philip Kaaler, the Guardian, was slender, fairly handsome, with hair that appeared to be turning from the medium brown of his youth to the gray of middle age. In reality, his hair had always been "salt and pepper," a characteristic of Kaaler firstborn males. Sally rushed in breathless from excitement and concern. "Daddy, Old Thomas Gerit knows about the silver spoon and the Challenge!"

Chapter 6

The Enemies

The Home of Philip Kaaler

If Sally had painstakingly conjured a method of obtaining her father's undivided attention, she couldn't have chosen a better one. Philip Kaaler, the Guardian, was writing a letter when she burst upon him; but when he saw her serious expression and heard her words, he immediately put down his pen. Gesturing for her to sit in one of the overstuffed chairs used by most visitors to this *sanctum sanctorum* of the Kaaler family, he took a deep breath and smiled just enough to tell his daughter that she should relax a bit. "Now, Sally," he quietly said, "whatever it is, start from the beginning."

She told him how her uncle John, her father's younger twin, was found and cared for and of his ravings about the silver spoon, the Challenge, the Guardian, riches, and secrecy. Lastly she told of John Kaaler's death. She also told her father that John, in his delirium, had repeated the Kaaler family Challenge many times. More importantly, she described how Thomas Gerit meticulously copied it but that the words Old Thomas wrote were not correct.

Tears filled her father's steel-gray eyes. He was silent as the shock of his twin's death sunk in. After a few seconds, he looked at her, his narrow face now taut, his expression intense, jaw muscles clenching. "John never was one to spend his money. Or anyone else's, for that matter," he began. "Lord knows he could have taken a taxi here for just a few dollars and kept himself out of the storm, but it wasn't in his makeup. Now he's gone, and we can't even grieve publicly or give him a burial with his real name, for it would compromise us." He took a deep breath. "Tell me exactly what John said when he was reciting the Challenge."

Sally recited what Thomas Gerit had written, after which it was her turn to smile slightly. "It was *almost* correct."

Her father nodded. "Actually, as it turns out, this is a kind of blessing." He shook his head quickly, as if erasing part of what he'd just said. "Not John's death, of course, but the fact that he couldn't speak the Challenge clearly. It means anyone contacting us with *that* version of our Challenge is somehow an enemy. And," he said, now smiling, "just by using that version of the Challenge, they'll identify themselves and its source to all of us."

He returned his attention to his desk, picked up a pencil, and scratched a few notes. "We'll have to warn everyone about ensuring that the Challenge is repeated *exactly* as taught by our ancestors. If they ever hear it spoken incorrectly they have to break off the contact and report all the circumstances of it through the family line to the Guardian, whomever it may be at that time." Looking up at his daughter, he smiled proudly and added, "You'll be the next Guardian, Sally. You've already done our family a great service, one that may well save Kaaler lives and the role we are destined to play, whatever it is and whenever it comes to pass."

Chapter 7

Useless Fortune

The Estate of Thomas Gerit

From the second John died, Thomas Gerit ignored his insect collection and dedicated his life to collecting and studying antique silver spoons, all kinds, shapes, and places of origin. His travels changed as well. Instead of visiting jungles and pristine areas looking for insects, he fought for and bribed to get accommodations on commercial and private steamers plying the sea-lanes of the world carrying war materials and occasional contraband. Wherever the ship docked, he haunted antique shops, jewelry shops, and museums. In each, he looked at every spoon available and then, for reasons he never discussed, was very selective in his purchases. Every spoon, whether plain or decorated, large or small, was solid silver. He never saw, spoke to, nor thought about Sally again.

Whenever his relatives visited, Thomas would show them his spoon collection and read to them from his increasing number of journals in spite of their obvious disinterest. But he never showed anyone, including his servants, where he hid those journals. It wasn't until after he died that they were found—stashed in a niche behind a walnut bookcase in his study. In the ten years between finding John and his own death, Thomas Gerit filled nearly thirty journals with sketches or photos of every spoon he purchased. He included anecdotes about spoons, about the people he heard talking about spoons of any type, and even what he believed were the best methods to polish and preserve silver spoons. The first journal contained the story of John "Caller," the guest who first revealed the existence of a silver spoon with supernatural powers that would make people wealthy and let them see into their futures.

* * *

Thomas Gerit died in 1983; and his grandnephew, Philemon Gerit III, inherited the spoon collection. Philemon first believed the hundreds of pounds of silver might be worth more if melted down and sold in ingot form. He was astonished to learn from an antiques appraiser that his great-uncle had accumulated nearly one hundred thousand dollars worth of seemingly ordinary, if aged, flatware. Of further importance, the appraiser recommended they be kept in a secure place and preserved as an investment. Up until that time Philemon thought his great-uncle was a lunatic. Given that financial appraisal, however, his opinion changed: his great-uncle was a bit "tetched" but smart enough to know how to invest his money. That made Philemon believe Thomas Gerit's journals also might be valuable. After reading the first one, however, he decided they were the ravings of a madman and promptly forgot about them.

Chapter 8

Jeff Gerit

Palo Alto, California
September 1997

Every few years, Jefferson Gerit, Old Thomas's great-great nephew, would dive into one of his large home's many storage areas and clean them up. This year's target was the attic above the first bay of his four-car garage. He vaguely remembered stashing a number of cartons there a few years after his uncle Philemon died but couldn't remember opening any of them. Today he planned to take care of the entire matter.

Jeff resembled most of the Gerit men: medium height, fair complexion, wiry rather than muscular. His usually gentle voice became a strident tenor when he was angered. His eyes were a soft blue, belying his inherent drive for getting what he wanted. Jeff would usually just plow through anything slowing progress toward his goal. His father, on the other hand, was much the same in normal matters, but very selective in what or whom he chose to eliminate.

The first three boxes of Philemon's possessions contained mostly old clothes and photo albums that were probably prepared by his great-grandmother: useless to Jeff but of possible interest to one of his aunts. The fourth contained a journal simply labeled "Volume 15." That by itself intrigued Jeff, because never before had he heard of anyone in his family keeping a journal, let alone one having fifteen volumes. Curiosity forced him to stop his examination of other cartons.

He sat on one and opened the volume, illuminated by a bare bulb, its light reflecting softly off his nearly bald head. As so often happened when he immersed himself in something, Jeff blocked out all distractions, so he didn't hear the traffic moving on the street in front of his estate, didn't hear the birds chirping, nor the squirrels as they scampered about on the roof above. He was vaguely aware of the lack of fresh air, but it didn't interfere with the task at hand.

The first page grabbed his attention because of the intriguing title: "Searching for the Spoon of Power."

Jeff stopped reading right there. He let the journal rest on his lap and stared at the rafters, so lost in thought that he actually perceived nothing. His initial curiosity immediately changed to intense interest. One thought kept repeating: *Why would someone write a journal of fifteen volumes, over many years? What could be so all important to my great-great-uncle that he would obsessively document everything he did to locate some "power spoon?"*

He put volume 15 on the floor and began searching through the remaining cartons, looking for volume 1. He found it in the ninth carton he opened. From the first page, Jeff was engrossed.

Chapter 9

Murder

January 14, 2004

From the San Francisco Chronicle:

Mysterious Attacks Continue

San Francisco—A series of burglaries, muggings, and anonymous threatening phone calls continues to terrorize many Bay Area families.

Police report finding only two common elements among the more than thirty such crimes. Every family attacked shared the same name, not yet released by police, and only silver spoons were stolen. However, according to our sources, several of the first break-ins earlier this year were at homes owned by people named Caller. When asked about this, the spokesperson for the police department had no comment.

Anyone having information regarding this strange series of crimes is asked to contact the San Francisco Police Department.

* * *

July 15, 2004
Daly City, California

Before approaching the ranch-style house on the outskirts of Daly City, the two thieves, a man and a woman, pulled on tight black gloves, covered their faces with black ski masks, and donned helmets containing infrared lamps and night-vision goggles. Both wore black pants, shirts, and canvas shoes.

Silently bypassing the puny back door lock in seconds, they moved straight to their assigned areas. Franco headed for the bedrooms and hall closets, Marnie for the kitchen and dining areas.

Confident in his stealth and ability to search every bit of storage space without waking the sleeping occupants, Franco slipped open the bottom drawer of the dresser, quickly touching and squeezing everything in it, covering every cubic inch of enclosed space. That completed, he left it open, checked the drawers in the dresser and the lamp tables, then moved to the closets.

Marnie's method was almost the opposite. Where Franco relied on a refined sense of touch and a sixth sense about where things might be hidden, she relied more on her night-vision optics, checking all surfaces, compartments, and display cases for every piece of silver flatware. She found a set in a black wooden box on the top shelf of a small closet in the dining room. She gently pulled it down and removed the solid silver spoons one by one, wrapping each in a soft cloth so they could make no sounds. That done, she put them into a pouch hanging from her utility belt and replaced the box.

Within an hour, both searches were complete. The burglars met in the kitchen, Franco silently shaking his head to indicate his hunt was unsuccessful; Marnie responding with a thumbs-up gesture. Still almost invisible in the darkness, they retraced their route to the back door, removed their night-vision goggles, and placed them in pouches attached to their utility belts. As they reached the door, they were blinded by an intense light suddenly flooding the room, accompanied by the soft click of a light switch and the hard click of a pistol being cocked.

"Stop," the male voice demanded, "or you're dead!"

Even before their eyes adjusted to the bright light, both intruders fell back and, in unison, from their utility belts they withdrew snub-nosed pistols with silencers and fired at the silhouette of the man they couldn't yet see in detail. They knew he'd be reluctant to shoot; they had no such compunctions.

The graying middle-aged homeowner grunted as blunt-nosed bullets slammed into him with more noise than the silenced shots themselves. Even as he began sliding to the floor, blood was pumping down the front of his pajamas. Ignoring the dying man, the burglars slipped out of the kitchen, turned off the light, and locked the door behind them.

Chapter 10

Ben Gerit

From the eighth page of the People section of the Chicago Tribune:

Homeowner Killed

Daly City—Richard Caller, well-known local entrepreneur, past president of the Chamber of Commerce and a former president of the local chapter of the American Cancer Society, was killed last night. Police believe he surprised burglars and was shot as they attempted to leave his house. His wife, Mona, said only a few items were missing.

The Callers are longtime residents and are well-known for their charity work and their private art collection. No artwork was reported missing; only silver spoons.

Local police reportedly have no leads to either the motive for the break-in or the motive for this murder.

Anyone having information on this crime is asked to contact the Daly City police department.

* * *

Chicago, Illinois

Ben Gerit was fuming! The only thing protecting his target from physical injury was distance: Ben was in Chicago, his son Jeff was in San Francisco. "I told you to quash that story!"

"No one, not even the President of the United States, Dad, can control every reporter on every paper or TV station around San Francisco."

The older man calmed down some—still angry but more in control. His spacious and beautifully decorated office helped him relax. Its lush decor, however, contrasted with his dour, balding countenance, slightly jaundiced skin, and conservative gray business suit with its ever-present maroon necktie. "Those kinds of stories can really hurt us. Your people have to be more careful."

"Already told them to lay off for a while. Besides, we still don't know who or where the Guardian is."

"You doing everything we planned?"

"Of course." Jeff's tone of voice revealed his resentment at the question. "I've got people checking personal ads in all the major papers from San Diego to Seattle looking for anything referring to Callers or Calling or anything like that. Same for the Mormon Church records. It's a lot of work, but we're at it."

As he talked, the older man picked up a yellow wooden pencil. "How 'bout training?"

"Monday nights we stage mock raids on houses, bypassing perimeter defenses and alarms, setting up countermeasures for any security systems in use, things like that. Plus we change practice locations every week. On the other weeknights, we hit real homes."

"By now your guys are probably so tired of all that training they've lost their edge."

Jeff chuckled. "Not likely. We're 'renting' them out—for a lot of money—to customers who need those skills but can't afford their own people. Everyone benefits. Except the targets, of course.

"Stopping our activities right now will hurt, but we have to protect the plan," he continued. "Maybe we should move on to other areas. A few jobs in Denver, perhaps Dallas/Fort Worth. Even Chicago, or Cincinnati. If we plan well enough, no one will ever find a pattern. Besides," he added, "it'll widen our search without needing more people."

"OK. But *keep low*! I don't want the Guardian to hear about us."

"Anything else?"

"Yes. How many of your people know the Challenge?"

"Only two right now. We're not telling break-in teams."

"Sounds OK. But *be careful.* I've invested a lot of money in this, and so far all I'm getting is bills." He ended the call by poking the "off" button on his speakerphone then sitting back in his black leather chair and thinking about how silly their goal might sound to outsiders—yet how very real it was. Thirty stories below his office, people, cars, elevated trains, and taxis moved about like ants, each in its own world, seemingly directionless. He smiled at that image, a cold and cruel smile devoid of humor. *Those idiots think they know what they're doing, but they have no idea what dedication to a cause really is. We've been working for generations to find the Guardian and finally have some techniques that'll probably work.* He thought about that press report. *If we don't step on ourselves first.*

Chapter 11

John Who?

San Francisco, California

His dad's call about the murder was expected, but Jeff still resented it. Their rivalry started when Jeff was a teenager and rebelled against his father's attempts to control his life. Adding to Jeff's animosity, the older Gerit never admitted fault. No matter what happened, even if Jeff had nothing to do with it, it was always Jeff's fault because it *couldn't* be his dad's.

Although they hadn't yet found the spoon, Jeff had done so much careful research on the discovery that he knew they were on the right track. Yet, in his heart, he knew he might have made a mistake; so several months after their first break-in he retrieved the key volume of the Thomas Gerit journal from the bottom drawer of his desk and opened it to the page where he found the first indication of his family's involvement with that thing. He had read the entry so many times, he almost had it memorized.

"Bad thunderstorm last night. Lost three trees to winds; rain washed most soil from rose garden.

"Grounds Manager found injured man in front yard this evening. Probably hit by car during storm. Brought man into house without permission. Started to chew grounds manager out, then saw man was badly injured. Treated him.

"No identification. Letter in his coat pocket addressed to John someone. Writing blurred. Last name possibly 'Caller.'

"Old man mumbled odd words. 'Tell guardian. Make a fortune,' and 'Keep shecret!' A bit later he said, 'Hide spoon. Tell future. Magic,' then, 'Use challenge.'

"When asked about 'magic' and 'spoon' he repeated certain phrases, again and again, exactly the same way: series of questions and answers he called the 'challenge.' Sounded like,

"First Statement: I'm looking for a different career path, and think I may have found a new calling.

"First Response: A new calling can be very hard to find. Did you have a preference?

"Second Statement: Something in long distance.

"Second Response: Worldwide, I presume."

Jeff usually stopped reading at that point in the journal, but now he thought about something that had eluded him for years. He'd been so absorbed in the story, and struggling so much with the poor quality writing, that he hadn't seen the obvious. In those first entries in the Gerit journal—his guide to finding the Guardian and taking the power he wanted so badly—he had never doubted "Caller's" last name was C-A-L-L-E-R. Because his people had been unable to find anything unusual in any of the spoons they had stolen, and because all of the victims told the police exactly what was taken, they didn't seem to be hiding anything. If their spoons really had special powers, Jeff believed the victims would have said nothing about their loss. Their total openness about the thefts now made him think he and his people were looking in the wrong places.

Do we have the wrong targets? After all this time and effort?

He slammed the journal shut and looked up, almost as if praying. "My idiot ancestor might have misspelled John's last name, so even if we know how to challenge someone, we can't find them. Maybe all we've been doing for years is wasting money. Worse, that's just what Dad said."

After more thought, he reopened the journal, found where he'd stopped reading, and, with slow and steady attention to every word, began looking for anything more on the subject of the Callers and the supposedly powerful, magic spoon. Every time he saw the word "spoon," Jeff shook his head in disgust. "I can't believe anyone as smart as Thomas Gerit really believed that John guy was talking about a spoon. But whatever it was, old Great-great-uncle Tom was serious, and my dad believes this is real or we wouldn't still be looking."

Three hours later, in an entry made almost ten weeks after John "Caller's" death, Jeff found something he'd paid no attention before. Accompanying the journal entry was a map of a suburb fifty miles south of San Francisco, with certain places marked in yellow circles. The largest circle enclosed a tract of land identified by the words "Gerit Estate." A mile north of it, the road in front of the Gerit estate crossed a set of railroad tracks. That intersection was marked with a circle surrounding the words "Market Station."

Shaking his head to clear his thoughts, he read the entry just below the map that had been so carefully pasted into the journal.

"Continued looking for information on Caller guy. Started by talking with everyone in the house when we found him.

"Madeleine Smythe, cook

"Sally Kaaler, entomologist

"George Foch, valet
"John Matthews, grounds manager."

Jeff turned back to the map and began searching the area around the Gerit estate. After skimming around for a while, he decided to become more systematic and started by putting his finger on the road in front of the estate. He traced it up the map to the railroad station then slowly moved it down the road, away from the Gerit place and the railroad station.

Scarcely three inches from the place where John was found by the road, Jeff found the outline of a much smaller home, its name only partially legible due to the poor quality of the map copy. Retrieving a magnifying glass from his desk drawer, he peered at the writing. Struggling with some of the letters, he used a sharp pencil to fill in places where he thought there might be gaps in the lines and serifs. Then, almost as if looming out of a mist, he saw the word "Kaaler."

Heart pounding in excitement, he looked again at the list of household help his great-great-uncle hired. There it was.

"Got you!" Jeff screamed at no one in particular, his finger stabbing Sally's name. "She probably told her whole family about what happened, and they've been laying low for nearly sixty years. My beloved ancestor was so involved in spelling that he didn't say the names out loud. The Guardian's name isn't Caller, it's *Kaaler*."

Jeff closed the journal and thought about all that happened since they began their search for the silver spoon and the Guardian. It had been fun, frantic, and, until the death of the guy in Daly City, invisible to the public. He understood his dad's anger at the newspaper article and even shared some of it, but he knew there was nothing they could do now except lie low and keep searching. His biggest surprise after finally getting the Guardian's name correct: there were only two Kaalers in Oregon's telephone listings, less than fifty in California—and no others in the entire western third of the United States. He'd even done an Internet search on the white pages and found fewer than a hundred other Kaalers in the twenty most populous states.

I don't believe Great-great-uncle Thomas could have imagined the spoon and its powers. If that John guy's last name was Kaaler, and that Kaaler woman was right there and heard all his ranting and raving, she probably told one of her relatives—that Guardian guy?—about it, and they went into hiding even more than they were before all of this happened. It all fits! We're losing a chance to gain control of a major industry because we can't look into our future like old John Kaaler babbled about. He touched the redial button on his telephone, barely able to control his excitement, but aware he was about to anger his dad. He'd be right, but he'd be blamed.

Chapter 12

He Was Right!

April 2004
Chicago, Illinois

"Dad, I think we missed something." Ebenezer Gerit, in his condominium in Chicago, didn't like being included in a group that made a mistake. "What's that mean? You said 'we' were doing everything on the list." Ben's grip on the handset tightened until his knuckles were white.

"We are," Jeff replied, not rising to the bait about who did what, "but I think we need to check something basic."

"Something else? What else *could* we check?" The elder Gerit fingered a gold nugget paperweight given him by his wife when he made his first million dollars. He was ready to throw it across the room to release his anger at this whole subject. Especially the hint that he had done something wrong.

"Calm down," Jeff insisted. "I've been doing some checking in the old family records, and I think we may be chasing the wrong family."

His statement met confused silence. Still, his father wouldn't say anything to accept responsibility for an error.

"Go on," Ben responded. He sounded calm. Frighteningly calm.

"We've had no luck chasing C-A-L-L-E-Rs. It feels to me like our search may be aimed wrong. So I need your help."

"Go on." *Now* Ben was interested: Jeff implied *he*, himself, had made the error.

"The Callers whose homes we've hit apparently have no clue as to why, and that doesn't ring true if they're the correct targets. I think we should be looking for people with family names sounding like 'Caller' but spelled differently. Like

K-A-A-L-E-R. I found a reference to a Kaaler in Old Uncle Thomas's journals. I really think that's where we should be looking."

For generations the Gerits had used the first spelling in the record as the name of the family possessing the spoon his ancestor wrote about and hadn't checked out any other possible spellings. Now, nearly a half century later, Jeff checked. Ben's real choking point: Jeff found the oversight, not Ben himself.

He let loose with a stream of obscenities, each worse than the other, and finally ran out of new curses to use. After that, to himself, he whispered, "He's right!" He threw the paperweight, hitting one of the five-by-eight glass windowpanes squarely in its center. Had the window not been made of bulletproof glass, it would have showered razor-sharp shards onto the street thirty stories below.

But he fumed anyway. *Our job's ten times bigger than we ever thought!* He lowered his shoulders in defeat, then spoke into the telephone. "Hit every name that sounds anything like 'Caller.'"

Chapter 13

The Real Jeff Gerit
April 2004

In spite of what his dad directed, Jeff Gerit was unwilling to start searching all newspapers, the Internet, the telephone listings, and the Mormon genealogical database for every family whose name sounded like "Caller." Not only would it have been an incredibly large and expensive job, it would do the very thing he most wanted to avoid: call attention to himself and his people. *Dad's wrong on the way to make this search. Since we're probably way behind where we thought we were anyway, it's more important to be accurate than to rush into a huge job and miss something important. Besides, we already know the Guardian's last name is probably Kaaler.*

He slowly walked to the window overlooking San Francisco Bay. From his small, new and expensive apartment he could see Alcatraz, Sausalito, and the north end of the Golden Gate Bridge. A beautiful and pricey view. Well worth the move from Palo Alto.

When he thought about that last conversation with his father, Jeff's cold, dark eyes flashed with anger. To calm himself, he took a long sip of bourbon. As soon as it hit his stomach, he tilted his head back and moved it from side to side, stretching the tight muscles and releasing the tensions that talking with his dad always brought.

It angered him that no one had thought to check the source material before but pleased him that he was the one who did. *No doubt Dad is having a fit about my finding the error and being right. But on this he screwed up, and we both know it.*

Another thought hit him, one he really liked. *If I do this correctly, I can delay passing the best stuff to Dad until I'm ready because he'll think that I'm making that great big search he wants. That might give me a head start at capturing the Guardian and getting control of that power spoon for myself.*

He smiled at his own brilliance.

Part III

The FarCaller

Chapter 14

The FarCaller
July 2004

Filled with a combination of curiosity and fear, Lee used his handkerchief to furiously polish the spoon until it was absolutely spotless, hoping to erase the image of the ceiling fan. Then he slowly looked into it again. The fan's image was gone, but his pleasure was short lived. The image of the ceiling fan had been replaced with that of a man's face. Lee wanted the image to be his own, reversed and upside down as it is when looking at concave surfaces, but it wasn't. The other man's image was in full color and right side up. He had black hair; Lee's was salt-and-pepper brown. Lee was clean shaven; the other had a wide black mustache. Lee's eyes were steel gray; the other's were almost black. Lee had thin arching brown eyebrows; the other man's were bushy and black. Before he could make further comparisons, Lee heard an unfamiliar voice say, "Guardian?"

Lee nervously looked around the room, trying to locate the speaker, but couldn't. Neither had he heard the doorbell nor any knocks. Slowly, hesitantly, he returned his attention to the spoon, again hoping he'd see only his own face. His hopes were dashed when the image of the same man remained, this time smiling joyously. "At long last, the Guardian!" the man blurted out. His eyes radiated pleasure and pride, as if he had just accomplished something so wonderful he couldn't hide his elation.

Feeling foolish and stupid, Lee slowly said—to a face in a spoon?—"My name is Lee Kaaler."

The other wasted no time on niceties. "Many years for you have I sought, Guardian," he said. "My grandfather last to speak with a Guardian was. His Guardian a woman was."

Lee's eyes widened in surprise. "A woman? An old woman?"

"Yes. Ima was she called."

Lee couldn't fathom what was happening. The image in the spoon was clear and undistorted. A spoon seemed a stupid device to use for any kind of contact—let alone audiovisual. But the man he was looking at mentioned Lee's grandmother. That couldn't be. Unless this man in the spoon said things that made some seemingly odd and unrelated events begin falling into a pattern.

"Ima was my grandmother," Lee said. "She died four years ago."

"Four?" The man speaking from the spoon was visibly shaken. "To believe, difficult that is. Over twenty years ago was it that my grandfather and Guardian Ima last talked."

Once more Lee looked around the room, hoping no one was watching him talking to a spoon, but he knew he was absolutely alone. "She willed me this spoon," he said. "I've never even looked at it before."

"Why we never met before now clear is. Much worried I." He stopped talking, the seriousness of his expression disappearing into a grin. "The grandson of the FarCaller who with Guardian Ima closely worked, I am. My grandfather FarCaller also is gone. My father, in our family's secret powers, no interest held, so Grandfather FarCaller of this responsibility told me. *Your* FarCaller am I."

Lee again looked around the room, trying to find any sign of a television camera or small speakers near his chair or the end table next to it or some kind of hidden candid camera whose pictures would be used to embarrass him. Yet he knew the full, realistic sound was somehow coming from the spoon. Or through it, because he both heard FarCaller's words and felt them in his mind.

FarCaller continued. "A long history between our families there is. But before that, about something important to you I Sense. Compelled am I to tell you."

Lee was having difficulty following FarCaller's style of speaking but mostly understood FarCaller's meaning. "What do you mean—'Sense'?"

FarCaller's dark eyes widened in surprise. "Ignorant of Sensing you are?"

"I told you, I know nothing about any of this. I'm not even certain I believe what's happening right now."

FarCaller hesitated a few seconds. "Grandfather FarCaller several truths about being the FarCaller taught me. One was that the Guardian and the FarCaller short distances into the future of the other can Sense."

"Do you really believe that?"

Two very slow nods, FarCaller's eyes never leaving Lee's. "Grandfather FarCaller said it was so, and now just such a Sensing have I. Quite clear my Sensing is: something in writing to you important is. Something to you near. Something about us, perhaps."

Lee stopped looking into the spoon and let his gaze roam mindlessly around the room while he tried to make sense of the man's words. His mind raced, trying to associate the strange image he saw when he looked into his grandmother's spoon with anything written. Then an idea surfaced. *Grandma's will! That's the only written thing that could possibly fit FarCaller's words. It said to contact her lawyer if I found something strange about my inheritance. She was writing about this spoon!*

Before Lee could think about what he needed to do next, FarCaller said, "Your grandmother's death sad makes me. Some important things about being Guardian she told you not, I believe."

"FarCaller, I've been told nothing, I've seen nothing at all in writing, and I know no one who knows anything about it. I don't know enough to talk to anyone about a Guardian, let alone anything about being one. I'm pretty certain not even my dad knows anything about the spoon or you or any of this." Lee then realized he had become comfortable talking to someone he could only see in the bowl of his spoon, but he flushed that thought and continued. "I don't know what a Guardian is, for pete's sake, let alone what a Guardian is supposed to be or do. If you have anything that can help, please tell me."

FarCaller's black eyes blinked in thought, and his grin disappeared. "Being Guardian for the Kaalers and for their world very important is, my grandfather taught me. Also, just *about* the Guardian knowing, a special secret for Kaalers was, he said."

"You mean I have relatives who know what I'm supposed to do as Guardian?"

"Not. That a Kaaler Guardian exists, and that they to help him are, the Kaaler relatives would know, Grandfather FarCaller told me. Who the Guardian is or what he does always would be secret kept. Only the Guardian could those secrets tell, and then only to another Kaaler."

"Talking to you makes me feel like I know nothing about my own family: I'm ignorant of things I should have been told long before this." No sooner had the words left his mouth than Lee recalled the telephone call he received from his grandmother just before finals week, four years earlier. *Was that why she called me? Was she trying tell me about this Guardian thing?* He closed his eyes and let his head drop. *That makes this whole ignorance thing my fault and no one else's.*

FarCaller ignored Lee's comment, his eyes still blinking in thought. "One of the things my grandfather about the Kaalers liked, their way of identifying themselves to each other is. Have you even of the Challenge not heard?"

Lee didn't understand FarCaller's question, but he clearly understood that he needed more information about being a Guardian. Since his father thought Lee's grandmother was eccentric or unbalanced on some matters, Lee knew that he had to see whatever was written for him by his grandmother—something his father almost certainly had never even looked at. "No, I haven't," he said. "Not yet." He glanced around his apartment, looking for something—anything—that might give him a thread to hang a memory on and make sense of what was happening. "I need to look for something, FarCaller. I'll be back in a while, but I don't know just when."

Before FarCaller could respond, Lee put the spoon into his shirt pocket and looked around his small apartment, seeing little, thinking much. *If FarCaller is right, how can I—*He shook his head in disbelief tempered with curiosity and reluctant acceptance, then returned to his initial thought. *If FarCaller is right, I have to look at Grandma's papers.*

Chapter 15

Finding Grandma

During a break from work the next morning, Lee called the office of Robert Kravin, his grandmother's lawyer. When the secretary didn't mention Kravin's name in her standard greeting, Lee immediately sensed trouble.

"May I speak to Mr. Kravin, please?" he asked.

After an awkward silence, the secretary said, "Sir, Mr. Kravin passed away over two years ago. His cases are being handled by Mr. Kravin's former partner, Mr. Maestre. Would you like to speak with him?"

Now what? I thought Kravin would be my contact with Grandma, and now it's turned out to be someone I don't know and who probably didn't know her. Well, not much else to do. "That would be fine, ma'am."

He heard a click followed by instrumental music. A few seconds later, a silky baritone voice said, "This is Clem Maestre. May Ah help you?"

After introducing himself, Lee explained his problem. "I think my grandma, Ima Mainor, may have left some papers for me with Mr. Kravin, and I'd like to look at them. Can you help me?"

"Mr. Kaaler, Ah know nothin' about that estate, but Ah'll be pleased to look into it for y'all. Ah'm busy right now, but Ah'll get back to y'all later today."

"Later" was four o'clock that afternoon, six slow hours after an impatient Lee made his telephone call. Clem didn't apologize for the delay since, Lee reluctantly believed, the lawyer probably had plenty of other clients—paying him $185 an hour.

After summarizing how case files are split up among partners if one of them leaves or dies, Clem simply said, "They're not here, Mr. Kaaler. As near as Ah can tell, they're in a secured storage area across town."

"Well, then, how soon can I see them? And please call me Lee."

"That depends on several things, Lee. Most importantly, y'all must first obtain the approval of the present executor of the estate: that's your father, not someone heah in this office. Y'all can see whatever he approves for y'all to see. Y'all's access is limited by law to what the executor approves."

"Meaning I have to get Dad's approval every time I want to see something?"

"That's how it works."

This is going to end up in some kind of fight with Dad, I just know it.

Chapter 16

Our Real Name's Not Kaaler

Lee loved both his parents very much but was much closer to his mother than his dad. Now he had to ask his father to let him see Grandma Mainor's papers, a subject Lee knew his father didn't like to discuss. He vividly remembered hearing his father talk about his eccentric mother and how the robbery would have made more sense if it had been against her house instead of his.

Regardless of these misgivings, Lee went to his parents' home after dinner that evening to get permission to look at his grandmother's papers. He received the exact reaction he had expected.

First, a series of questions from his father. "What has arisen four-plus years after she's gone that makes you so anxious to look at Mom's things? Why are you just bringing it up now?"

Lee hadn't put enough thought into his approach on the subject or he would have developed a good set of reasons and explanations. As it was, he could only respond with, "I'm just getting interested now, Dad. I looked at that thing she gave me and don't understand how to use it. I thought there might be some instructions in her papers."

His dad immediately asked, "That little box? What was in it, anyway?"

Lee ignored the question and returned the conversation to his desire to see if there was anything useful to him in his grandma's papers. The discussion lasted over two hours, at the end of which Lee's father said, "There's nothing in there that could do anyone any good, and I don't see any reason you or anyone else should go pawing through it."

Fortunately for Lee, his mother was able to accomplish miracles where her husband was concerned. She could see Lee's discomfort at asking his father for anything involving her mother-in-law and, just as Lee was about to leave, intervened. "Faar," she said in a smooth, innocent voice, "what harm can it do to let Lee just look? Besides," she added sweetly, "he might become more interested in our family tree than he has been until now. That would be a real blessing, don't you think?"

When she finished, Lee's dad made a helpless, what-else-can-I-do smile and shook his head to show resignation at the inevitable. Waving his hand as if sweeping something distasteful away, he said, "OK, Lee. Go ahead. It's in East Cascades Historial Repository, off Twenty-seventh Street. I'll tell the lawyer it's OK." As Lee rose to leave, his father opened a drawer in the end table next to his chair and pulled out a yellow key ring from which a single shiny steel key dangled. "It's unit number 636; the entry code is on the key ring." On the way out the door, Lee heard his father say, "I think all of this nutty stuff started when Mother paid us $5,000 to take her family's name of 'Kaaler' instead of my father's family name of 'Mainor.' For some reason I can't define, I think agreeing to do that was a mistake."

* * *

On the drive back to his apartment, Lee felt he'd been successful, but his thoughts were tempered with concerns that his grandmother did some weird things—like the unexpected revelation from his father about their name change. He had wondered about that some years ago but now was even more curious. Lee *now* remembered something about the facility where all the materials from her estate were stored. His bank used that same place for many of its nonsensitive historical documents because it had heated and air-conditioned rooms. The bad part was that the storage area kept the same weekday hours as the bank. Lee couldn't get into the files until Saturday. He had to wait another three days.

Chapter 17

She's a Puzzle Nut!

Lee barely slept the next two nights, his brain humming with thoughts about what might be in his grandmother's documents. When Friday night finally arrived and he knew that the next day he'd be able to see everything that had been removed from her house, he was certain he'd not be able to sleep at all. However, after only fitful sleep for the entire week, instead of again remaining awake, he awoke on Saturday morning almost groggy after nearly eight hours of intensely deep sleep. As soon as he could think, it hit him: *today's my day!*

After opening the storage unit so he could start his trek through his grandmother's papers, he realized they were in some order not resembling any kind of filing system he'd ever seen. Some times the papers were generally chronological, other times they weren't. That kind of disorderly filing was most uncharacteristic of her, but Lee had enough faith in what she did that he was certain it was done intentionally. One thing he knew: his father didn't care about them and had merely obeyed the instructions in her will about keeping them safe.

After leafing through over twenty separate plastic boxes of family financial data going back more than forty years, Lee saw nothing of particular interest. He next searched cartons marked Estate-related. Each box had the caveat Do Not Destroy printed in her neat hand. On the cover of one of the boxes were the words "For Lee: Puzzles." He almost tore off the cover. Lying flat on top of the folders was a spiral notepad labeled Important Puzzles. *Grandma, this was the best possible way to keep Dad from reading anything in this box.* On the first page of the notebook, in his grandmother's delicate script, were the words "The Challenge."

When he saw the word "Challenge"—a word he'd just heard FarCaller use, Lee felt as if he'd received a message from the grave. It was the eeriest feeling he'd ever experienced—next to talking to a spoon—causing him to breathe deeply and feel dizzy. He sat on the floor, leaned back against one of the stacks of boxes, and tried to relax. After taking several slow, deep breaths to help himself get over the shock, he pulled the box closer and began inspecting each item. He set aside those that seemed to deal with the spoon or the Challenge or anything else that might have seemed "eccentric" to his father.

The spiral notepad seemed to be the most important and was filled with incomplete sentences, unusual abbreviations, and apparently obscure references. After one of those references, he found a series of odd entries beneath the words "The Challenge." It was clearly a set of related items almost begging Lee to try to make sense of them. Just seeing them reminded Lee of his father's comments about how much time his grandmother wasted on crossword puzzles. But instead of the anger or frustration his father showed, Lee had always found them interesting. Now, seeing this notebook clearly left for him, he immediately began trying to decipher what she had concocted. He knew she'd never have gone to all of this work, certainly designed just for him, without a good reason. "This is a hit below the belt, Grandma," he said aloud. "You know I can't pass up the chance to solve a puzzle like this."

Very quickly he realized that task was going to be difficult. Rather than trying to solve the puzzle while sitting in the storage vault, he put everything back into the carton, took it to his car, and drove home. There he spread the contents over his small dining table. Opening one of the yellow notepads he kept in one of his end tables, he opened his grandmother's notebook to the page with the peculiar puzzle and started trying to solve it.

* * *

The Challenge

R1C1	to
C1E4	found
R1F2	?
C1B2	different
R2A1	world-
C1A1	I'm
R2D1	presume.
C2B1	in
C2D1	distances.
R1D1	you
R1F1	preferences

C1A3	for
C1E3	have
R1B3	very
R1A2	new
C1C2	path
R2C1	I
R1B1	may
C1A2	looking
R1E2	any
C2C1	long
C1C1	career
R1D2	you
R2B1	wide,
C1F2	new
R1B4	hard
R1C2	find.
C2A1	Something
C1D2	think
R1B2	be
C1E2	may
R1A1	A
C1B1	a
C1D1	and
C1E1	I
C1F3	calling.
C1F1	a
R1E1	have

Chapter 18

Reading the Unreadable

It took Lee all evening to solve the puzzle. His first assumption was that the second column contained definitions, much like normal crossword puzzles. The first column, however, was much more difficult to decipher. After many attempts, he eventually realized that each set of symbols described the first column of a two-column matrix. Since this puzzle was called "The Challenge," he assumed the letter C probably stood for "Challenge." That could mean the capital R stood for "Response" or something like that. He decided to procede from there, using C1 as the first Challenge element, R1 as the first Response element, and so on. The third symbol was the trick: it simply broke the sentences into sections, with no other apparent purpose. The last digit showed where, in the appropriate sentence, that word appeared. Very shortly Lee realized his grandmother had also included subtleties in the clues. When the "definitions" were capitalized, the capital letters had to be used in the puzzle's solution. Similarly, when the words were followed by punctuation marks, those marks had to be retained and used in exactly that order.

At 11:45 that night, he sat back in his chair, stretched his legs, and raised his arms as far back as he could, trying to relieve the discomfort caused from sitting in one place for such a long time. But he was smiling.

The Challenge

Challenge 1: I'm looking for a different career path, and think I may have found a new calling.
Response 1: A new calling may be very hard to find. Do you have any preferences?

Challenge 2: Something in long distances.
Response 2: Worldwide, I presume.

Lee looked at the pile of crumpled yellow sheets on the floor all around the table then at the neat notes in front of him. "I've worked all day on this thing, as Grandma probably expected, and finally solved it. Now all I have to do is figure out why she went to all of this trouble to make it almost impossible for Dad to want to solve and impossible for me to ignore.

Chapter 19

Grandma's Fairy Tale

Lee fell asleep almost as soon as his head touched his pillow, waking seven hours later to the insistent beeping of his alarm clock. Seldom a heavy sleeper, he usually woke before the alarm sounded; but this morning, especially after such an exhausting and rewarding evening, he was so tired he could scarcely pull himself out of bed. Once on his feet, he relied on habit: showering, shaving, and dressing in his banker's "uniform." Then he realized it was Sunday and he didn't have to go to work. After thinking about how much he wanted to get back to that puzzle he'd just solved and to look through his grandma's papers, he decided to go to the 8:30 church service instead of the 10:30 one he usually attended. He would spend the rest of the day just learning about things his grandma thought important enough to hide from his father. Besides, going to church would let him start the day refreshed and with the sense of peace he always got from attending a worship service.

He returned home immediately after church and went directly to the dining room table. Taking a deep breath to steel himself for a day possibly full of detailed research into his grandmother's work, he pulled the box of material from his grandma's estate next to him and began searching for something important enough for FarCaller to be "Sensing" it, something Lee still didn't believe was possible. Nothing looked particularly interesting until he got near the bottom of the box. When he saw it, he smiled then sobered as he realized FarCaller's "Sensing" about something written might well have been true.

A small packet of light blue envelopes neatly tied together with a narrow blue satin ribbon caught Lee's attention. Each was numbered, with Lee's full name—Faerleigh Faar Kaaler—written in his grandmother's neat, careful script.

Struggling against an urge to tear the envelopes open, Lee used a paring knife to carefully open envelope number 1 and began reading.

> My dear grandson,
> You are no doubt surprised to find this letter. But now that you are aware of some of the powers you have that are released by the Kaaler spoon, you need to know more about this talent we firstborn Kaalers are blessed with. Your father could have developed his talent, but he refused to let me explain what he thought were my "eccentricities." So I passed the spoon on to you. He knows nothing about it. Unfortunately for both of us, you were at college or working on your summer jobs when we should have discussed this. Now I have to write these letters and hope I've done an adequate job.
> You know much about FarCaller's world and the story of our unusual partnership, but you can't remember it. On your fifth birthday, I told your mom and dad I had a special present for you. That "present" was to take you upstairs to my bedroom and put you into a light trance so I could tell you about a world you had never seen. Like I was telling you a fairy tale.
> Before you next contact your FarCaller, hold the spoon in your hand and say the words "Grandma's Fairy Tale" aloud. You'll be surprised, I assure you.
> Open my second letter after hearing "Grandma's Fairy Tale."
>
> Love,
> Grandma Mainor (Ima *Faar Kaaler* Mainor)

Lee moved to his rocking chair, sat back, and thought about his grandmother. He remembered the many times he sat in her living room, surrounded by her mementos of decades of travel and excitement, engulfed in the ever-present fragrance of strawberry potpourri. He also remembered his fifth birthday, when she said she had something wonderful to give him and led him up to her bedroom. He could hardly contain his excitement. But instead of handing him a gift-wrapped package, she made him sit up straight in that uncomfortable old chair of hers, the one with the back that looked like a ladder.

She was smiling, as if wonderfully pleased. Then she retrieved a small box from her end table, opened it, and unwrapped something silver. It was the first and only time he'd seen the spoon until the lawyer gave it to him when her will was read. On that occasion, the spoon was wrapped in a small package with instructions that he was to open it only in private. No one in the room understood why, but he'd learned never to doubt his grandmother.

This isn't the time to reminisce. This is the time to follow her instructions, no matter how silly they sound.

He reread her letter then took a firm grip on the spoon and said, "Grandma's Fairy Tale."

Inside his head a hidden door in his mind popped open, releasing a torrent of new facts and images into his consciousness. He felt exactly as though he were back in his grandmother's bedroom, except he remembered that his eyes had been closed much of that first visit. This time he had an eye-opening experience, beginning with hearing his grandmother's voice sounding as if she were sitting right next to him.

"Dear Faerleigh," she said, "listen very closely to what I'm about to tell you. When you grow up, it will be very important. You must remember my words exactly and do precisely what I ask. Do you understand?"

"Yes, Grandmother. I understand."

"Good. Now listen:

> "The first Guardian, Ewan, our grandfather many generations ago, received a gift—a silver spoon—from his wife, Hondras. She told Ewan that the spoon, brought here from his home world, had special powers that could help all Guardians assist members of their family, and even to protect our country. Ewan had to swear to tell no one except his new wife and their firstborn child about the spoon and its powers. Each succeeding firstborn, Hondras told Ewan, would have the gift of using the spoon. The spoon always had to be passed on to the Guardian's firstborn, whether boy or girl. No later than his or her eighteenth birthday, that child had to be informed about it either in person by the Guardian or by some other reliable method the Guardian could use.
>
> "When Ewan arrived on this world, he took the family name of Kaaler and the middle name of Faar, to remind him of his obligation to be mindful of his son, the first FarCaller, on his home world. Hondras told Ewan that all of his descendants must be told about the Guardian, but few would ever see or know one. Each of those relatives should carry the family name 'Kaaler' either as a middle or a maiden name, and should become the source for wives and husbands of each future Guardian. Distant cousins would make ideal mates and would be strongly attracted to Ewan's descendants.
>
> "Should any Guardians' firstborns decide to marry outside the Kaaler family and thereby prevent themselves from becoming the next Guardian, they must be convinced to let their firstborn's grandparents tell the child a 'fairy tale' on his or her fifth birthday.

"Since your father refused to learn anything about his Kaaler heritage and becoming its Guardian, it is my duty, instead of his, to tell you about your heritage. And since I may not be able to do so before I pass on, I must let this trance give you that information. Listen carefully.

"The spoon is the most valuable thing you will ever possess, but remember it belongs to the Kaaler family, not you alone. It can help you in many ways, and just as surely help your FarCaller. Remember to use it only in secret and to tell no one about it except your wife—who *must* be a Kaaler—and your firstborn. That woman must be distant both in her Kaaler lineage and in where she lives. She will protect the secret and you with her every breath and will be a loving wife and wonderful mother to your children.

"I love you very much, dear Faerleigh, and know you will be a good Guardian. Remember your obligations and never shortchange a family member or use your talent illegally. *Always* protect the spoon, our family secrets, and your FarCaller.

"With all my love and hope for you as Guardian,
"Ima Faar Kaaler Mainor"

The scene disappeared, and Lee found himself back in his living room, alone, holding a silver spoon, and feeling both silly and amazed.

Chapter 20

The "Talk"

The Thomas Kaaler Willards family had just sat down for their Sunday meal: father, mother and two daughters. They had done this after Sunday church services for as long as their older daughter, Vera, could remember. Vera was called Verry because as a little girl she couldn't say "Vera." At twenty-five years old and five feet six inches tall, she was essentially a taller version of her mom.

Before the blessing could be asked, her mother said, "Verry, how old are you?"

Verry let her shoulders droop, took a deep breath, and closed her eyes to brace herself for another "When are you going to get married?" talk. "Golly, gee, Mom," she began, "I'm so old I've forgotten." *And,* Verry thought, *I'm not certain this meal is worth suffering through another one of these talks.*

"I'm just trying to look out for my older daughter," her mother continued. In one of her usual ploys to get her way with her family, her voice assumed a whiny, defensive, and apologetic tone. "You didn't find a husband in college, you hardly date anymore, and in your first job after graduation, you're stuck in the basement of the student union editing the alumni newspaper. Now you only meet younger men. Surely you don't plan on growing up with a stream of lovers instead of a husband and children."

"Mom!" Verry's sister, Drella, shouted. Like Verry, she was taller than her mother. She got her nickname from Verry: little Vera couldn't say "Dorella" any more than she could say "Vera." Drella's exclamation was nearly drowned out by her father's "Velma!"

Verry, ignoring all of them, her large dark eyes open wide in feigned innocence, said, "Should I say grace?"

Sunday meals were usually long on homegrown vegetables: steaming ears of corn, mountains of mashed potatoes streaked yellow with cascades of butter, and a huge bowl of freshly cooked peas or green beans with bacon and onions. The main course was either a large chicken, a ham basted with a honey mustard glaze, or a beef roast. And, of course, warm homemade bread. Today's dessert was peach cobbler drowned in homemade vanilla ice cream. The meal was incredibly delicious and brought with it all the feelings of home and family. It also required the women to diet for the next several days to keep from ballooning out of their clothes, but all of them knew the joy of the dinner outweighed the low-cal regimen it forced on them. Their dad, much to their dismay, seemed to be able to eat large quantities of almost anything fattening and never gain an ounce.

After the many laughs and the sharing that kept their family strong, Drella left to go to her job as an ICU ward nurse in the city's general hospital. Like Verry, she was attractive, intelligent, and capable.

Once the leftovers were in the refrigerator and the dishwasher was groaning under its usual Sunday load, Verry and her folks moved to the family room. Her dad, still wearing his dark Sunday suit pants and white shirt, wiggled down in his overstuffed rocking chair and tuned the TV to the Kansas City Chiefs game. His wife sat at the far end of their large brown sofa from where she could watch television and either knit or sew. Verry sat at the other end of the sofa so she could see both her parents.

After a few minutes of silence, her mother resumed her talk. "Verry, honey," she began in the same tone of voice she'd used earlier, "have you ever thought about marrying a Kaaler? Maybe a good-looking shirttail cousin—five or six times removed?"

Both Verry and her dad looked at her mother in surprise.

"I can't believe you said that, Mother," Verry responded, her eyes wide in astonishment. "First, I've no intention of trolling for a husband. Second, there hasn't been another Kaaler in this area, except for Dad and a few cousins, in who knows how many generations; and I'm not about to marry one of them. Third, I don't think getting married right away constitutes an emergency."

Before her mother could respond, Verry's dad spoke. "She's right, Velma. This isn't an emergency, and finding an outside Kaaler is a pretty serious thing."

"I know that, Tom, but I still think about my daughter's future. And I think she'd do best if she married a Kaaler."

"Mother, we haven't talked about the Kaaler family for probably five years. Why are you suddenly acting like it's *the* solution to a problem I don't even think exists?"

"Well, on the TV news a while back, I saw a thing about a series of break-ins in the San Francisco area. Thirty homes, no clues, never solved, but all the victims were named Caller—C-A-L-L-E-R. And in Daly City, there was a break-in and murder of a man named Caller." Before her family could interrupt, she continued unabated. "Then, just a few weeks ago, I read a short squib about similar robberies in Oregon. It wasn't against '*C*'-Callers but against two families named Kaaler. That's Kaaler with a *K*—just like our heritage name." Her husband and daughter exchanged puzzled glances but said nothing.

"That made me feel maybe all of us Kaalers are in danger," she continued, "and I don't want my daughter to be alone if something bad happens to any of us." She quietly began to cry. Verry, moved by her mother's obvious love for all of them, slid across the sofa and embraced her. Watching this exchange between two of the three people he loved most, Verry's father sniffed then grabbed a tissue from the reading table next to him and blew his nose.

Her mother's words cut deeply but still raised questions in Verry's mind. She hugged her mother, clearly touched. Then she looked at her father and asked, "Does mother always read newspapers so thoroughly?"

He nodded and smiled. "Every day, every section, every page. Even the personals."

The older lady sniffed a few times, dabbed her cheeks with a rose-scented handkerchief, and said, "Well, Tom, it worked for us, didn't it? We wouldn't have met if you hadn't placed a Challenge ad in the Des Moines paper. And you lived in Detroit at the time. Aren't we both Kaalers, and don't we have a pretty good marriage?" Her question didn't require an answer; but her husband rose from his chair and went to her, then knelt, pulled her head to his, and gave her a long kiss. "You betcha," he said. "Like it was made in heaven." He rose, gave her a quick peck on the lips, then returned to his chair.

Verry said nothing for a few seconds, then, "Mother, if Kaalers are in danger, why should I even consider marrying one?"

"Because a Kaaler husband would *understand*, Verry. And he'd know how to contact other Kaalers for help if the two of you needed it. If you didn't marry a Kaaler, you could never explain to your husband what was happening to any of us, and you'd be all alone with your fear." With that, the crying resumed.

While wiping tears from both her own and her mother's cheeks, Verry quietly but reluctantly conceded that her mother was correct. There was nothing she could say to counter a persuasive argument for worrying about her own safety. She didn't want to be alone the rest of her life, and she hadn't met any guy she considered as even a slight candidate for a husband. Another obvious element: her parents were distant Kaaler cousins, came from different parts of the country, and met through a method of contacting other Kaalers that would only be recognized by Kaalers.

Her parents had a wonderful marriage, and she wanted the same. So maybe looking for a Kaaler husband wasn't such a bad idea. And maybe she didn't have as much time to find a husband as she thought.

Chapter 21

Spoonworld

Lee stared at his grandmother's letter then glanced out his large picture window onto Mirror Pond. On most days, the magnificent sight infused him with a deep sense of peace. But not this day. In the last week, his world had turned upside down. He lived in one world but could now see and interact with someone who lived in another, a world he knew nothing about and the existence of which evoked question after question. *Where is this "Spoonworld?" Do all its people speak English in that strange way? What are they like? What does FarCaller use to talk to me, and who made it? How did my spoon get to Earth if it was made on Spoonworld? He's been looking for me for decades. Where did he get such dedication? And why?* And on and on. Most astonishing, denying all logic and laws of physics Lee knew about, his window into FarCaller's world was a silver spoon.

Crap! I forgot to tell FarCaller why I stopped talking to him last Sunday. He looked around for the spoon then remembered he'd put it in his fireproof document safe below his desk in his small second bedroom. Retrieving it, he returned to his rocker and looked into that silver window. He again wished he'd simply see his own image, reversed and distorted, but knew it wouldn't be so.

In the bowl of his spoon, he saw a room resembling the great room in a hunter's cabin. The only wall he could see was made of unpainted, roughhewn boards reaching from floor to ceiling. On the left hung a picture—a landscape, its bright colors contrasting with the browns and dark tans of the wallboards.

Lee slowly became aware he was squinting, as if trying to pull details out of a miniature painting. He hurried the few paces down the short hall to his office—his second bedroom—where he kept most of his college mementos and books. He retrieved his magnifying glass and returned to his rocking chair, focused the lens on the spoon, and saw—FarCaller's face.

"Guardian?" The man in the spoon was clearly confused by what he saw.

I would be too if I looked through a magnifying lens into someone's face. Probably look like an ogre, if they have them on Spoonworld. "Yes, FarCaller," Lee responded, lowering the lens. "I was trying to see more of your house." A thought jumped into his mind. "How do you keep your spoon high all the time? Judging from what I see, it's about eye level, probably on a wall."

FarCaller smiled back and shook his head. "No spoon have I, Lee. My portal into your world a silver plate is. Eight sides it has, and correct you are: to the wall of my great room attached it is."

"That's why you don't have to squint to see me."

"Through it a view that moves as you do, I enjoy," FarCaller responded.

"Like television?"

FarCaller's face wrenched into a frown. "No such word have I heard."

Criminy, Lee thought to himself, *he doesn't have anything like television.* He thought about the things he and FarCaller had discussed then recognized another item he didn't understand.

"Tell me about the ceiling fan I saw the first time we spoke. I haven't seen it since."

FarCaller smiled broadly and looked up at something out of Lee's view. "Here it remains, but after talking we began, the plate I lowered. Easier to see you it is. Hence, the fan no longer can you see. Very well it works. Like it, do you?"

"Yes," Lee said, nodding to emphasize his point, "but I don't understand how it operates. I'm beginning to believe you don't have the same power sources as we have, like electricity, so I can't visualize what makes it turn."

Again a confused expression appeared on FarCaller's face. "Wind have we always, so often its power we use. The fan by a loop of thin rope is powered, from my attic to a very large fan on a high post outside the house it leads. The wind both fans turn." Another big smile radiated from his face. "A good idea?"

"Very good, FarCaller," Lee said. *I'd better not discuss electricity. It would make his inventions look primitive and hurt his feelings.*

Before Lee could say anything more, FarCaller shifted the subject completely. "Away for forty days you have been. To where, can you tell me?"

"You mean six days."

"No, forty days has it been since last we spoke."

Lee said nothing, just looked at the little image, wondering why FarCaller would say such a thing. Then he remembered his grandmother's letter telling him he could always trust his FarCaller.

"You just taught me something important, FarCaller," he began. "Only six of my days passed since we last spoke. During that time I found some important things my grandmother wrote and read a little about you and your world. I also learned about the Challenge. And I've thought a lot about this amazing . . ." he searched for the right word " . . . *gift* we share." He leaned back, closed his eyes, and shook his head in the wonder of all that had already happened this day. "And please call me Lee," he continued. "My family name is Kaaler, and it sounds like yours. My friends call me Lee."

"FarCaller my name is."

Lee nodded, regained his train of thought, then continued. "It seems that one hour in my time is more than a day on your world—except when we speak to each other. That might explain why you thought my grandmother had been gone so long."

"Never did my grandfather this tell me," FarCaller said. "Contacting each other more difficult now is, because when our partner to hail never can we know."

If I'm supposed to use this spoon thing, there has to be a way to call each other.

Before he could vocalize that thought, FarCaller spoke. "When one of us to the other must speak, a method to alert one another must we have. My grandfather to Guardian Ima called by very hard about her thinking. That could we try?"

Doubt clouded Lee's face as he listened. *Telepathy?* "That means I have to keep the spoon close to me all the time."

"Not. My grandfather did not. Most all of the time the plate hidden kept he."

Lee let that pass. "One thing really bothers me. How did you know about the letter my grandmother wrote to me?"

"Your question I understand. The Guardian and the FarCaller another gift have, besides to each other speaking. Sometimes what to the other will soon occur, we Sense. About something to you written a strong feeling had I. This to you I passed.

"'Sensing' my grandfather named this," FarCaller continued, "and right now another have I. My grandfather often Guardian Ima helped money obtain. My Sensing is that money you could make, if in a company with the word "pyramid" in its name somehow involved you were." He faltered, obviously trying to find something else to tell Lee. "A device to make cloth also I sense. Such a company in your future is."

Market tips? From Spoonworld? Lee thought about his grandmother's large estate. *If this is how she got it and she felt it was OK, maybe I should give it a try.* "I'll see if I can use your advice, FarCaller," he said, "but I have no such talent."

"Both the FarCaller and the Guardian this gift possess, my grandfather told me. Perhaps something related to this Sensing soon to you will happen."

Chapter 22

Buy!

Following FarCaller's advice, Lee told his broker to locate a stock with the name Pyramid and something about weaving or looms. After searching her data base, she found a company called Pyramid Textiles, Inc.

"Buy a thousand shares, Jackie."

"But that thing's at a dollar and a quarter a share and going nowhere! For the same twelve hundred and fifty dollars, you can buy some stocks that will do a lot better." When she felt strongly about something, her voice always seemed to raise at least an octave in pitch. Right now it was almost there.

"Humor me, Jackie. Buy as soon as you can, and let me know what happens day by day."

"It's your money, Lee. Just remember this conversation in a week or so."

Lee sat back in his recliner, looked into the spoon, and began concentrating on FarCaller's face: dark complexion, black hair and mustache, dark eyes, ready smile. *Are you there, FarCaller? Does thinking about you really work?* When nothing happened after about five minutes, he put the spoon on his lap and contemplated what was happening. *I'm sitting in my living room, thinking about a man I've never really met, using a silver spoon as a two-way television connection, and I actually believe all of this is happening! No matter what Grandma said, anyone would have to be a little nuts to even consider doing it.*

His thoughts were interrupted by the same small voice as before. "Guardian? Hear me can you?"

Allowing himself a quick headshake to acknowledge the silliness of the whole thing, he looked into the spoon. There, as he hoped, was FarCaller. *It works!*

"Why this call make you?"

"No special reason, FarCaller. Grandmother's letter said I should try to learn all I can about this"—he searched again for the proper word, settled on—"gift, so I thought I'd try it again."

"On that company with the pyramid in its name, my meaning you understood?"

"Yes." Lee allowed himself a quick smile at the way his broker responded to the buy order. "My broker found the company, and I invested a small amount of money in it. With any luck, in a few months we'll know if your tip works out."

"Months?" The confusion on FarCaller's face infused his voice. "My grandfather said only a short distance into our futures Sense could we—days or hours."

"You mean you think something will happen right away?"

"Clearly. Otherwise, when in times of danger approaching, helping each other impossible would be."

"FarCaller, I want to think about something for a while. I'll point the spoon at something beautiful for you to see while I'm away."

Before his new friend could respond, Lee took the spoon into his kitchen and tilted it to point across Mirror Pond. Then he called Jackie at her home and directed her to buy five thousand more shares of Pyramid Textiles, much to her consternation and against all her advice. *That wipes out all my savings. If this Sensing thing doesn't work, I'll be flat broke.*

After the call, Lee retrieved the spoon from the window ledge and turned it so he could see FarCaller. "Did you like the view?"

"Wonderful it was!" FarCaller looked slightly confused. "Across the waters large buildings were, with beautiful gardens to the water's edge reaching. They were what?"

I shouldn't have done that. Now he knows we're more advanced here than his world, or at least his village. "Those are homes, FarCaller. Homes of people who have much money."

FarCaller slowly nodded. "So thought I. In my village no such homes have we. The sides of those homes smooth and colored are, more than one level they have, and many windows. Here windows we have, but not so many, nor so large." He stopped, then said, "A question ask may I?"

Here it comes! "Of course, FarCaller. Whatever you wish."

"Your home like one of those is, Lee? Rich are you?"

Lee couldn't suppress his smile. "No, FarCaller, I'm not rich and I don't live in a home like that. I live in an apartment—like a small house, but in a long building which has many such small places to live. I work in a bank and don't make much money."

"For your honesty I thank you, Lee." He took a deep breath then smiled lamely. "A beautiful scene was it."

It was finally Lee's turn to smile. "When the snow falls this winter, the view is at least as beautiful, but completely different. You'll really be surprised."

His new compatriot immediately changed the subject. "About 'winter' and 'snow' nothing know I. But believe you now that only by thinking to each other call we can?"

"It's hard to be skeptical when faced with proof. But I'm still not accustomed to any of this. I was brought up believing there was no such thing as real magic, and now I find myself sort of practicing it." He looked at the spoon and just shook his head.

Chapter 23

Warnings

After ending his talk with FarCaller, Lee walked back to his office and opened his safe, where he now kept all his grandmother's documents concerning the spoon and being Guardian. He picked up the package of blue envelopes and removed envelope number 2 then closed the safe and took the letter into the living room. Again sitting in his rocker, he opened the envelope and began reading.

>Dear Faerleigh,
>
>This is a *warning* about your talent. You *must* heed it! Later, when certain things happen and you read the other letters I've written, you will understand the need for this caution.
>
>1. Tell *no one* about the spoon or what you see or hear in it or through it. Not yet.
>2. Use the spoon only in private, and learn all you can by using it to talk to your FarCaller as often as you can.
>3. The FarCaller is someone you can trust, and he expects the same from you.
>4. If your FarCaller is as talented as mine was, he'll sense ways to help you earn money, perhaps a lot of money. Follow his advice, but tell no one of your successes. Don't change your lifestyle just because your estate has grown; live within the limits of your wages. One day, by rummaging through my papers, you'll learn some of the challenges I faced as Guardian and will realize that the fun of talking to someone on another world can be greatly outweighed by your responsibilities.

But be responsible. You can help many people by wise use of your gifts: giving to charities, helping someone in dire need by directing them to people you've hired (anonymously) to provide the assistance that person needs—things like that.

Open my next letter after a Sensing that you feel might change your life.

Your Guardian's gift is real and, as you'll learn later, powerful.

Now enjoy yourself with Spoonworld. (That's what I called it. Would be interesting to know your name for FarCaller's world.)

I love you very much and know you'll be a wonderful Guardian.

Grandma

Chapter 24

Matchmaker?

The next evening, Lee discussed with FarCaller his grandmother's second letter, especially the words about danger and being responsible in how he used his powers as Guardian. As Lee spoke, FarCaller's expression changed from its normal pleasant and sunny countenance to a much more serious one. Thoughtfully he said, "What Guardian Ima said about carefully acting understand do I, Lee, because here enemies also have I."

"Really? Are *you* rich?"

FarCaller smiled. "Not. Because my neighbors, harder than I, must work, it is. My grandfather much land to me left. People on it live, and many crops grow. A small share of the harvest as rent receive I, but that greatly disturbs those who as fortunate as I not are."

"I can understand that," Lee said. "But what do these people do that makes them your enemies?"

"Most commonly part of my share of the harvest steal they, sometimes before the carts can even to my barn arrive. Other times my barn they to blaze put, or my carts, and once my house even."

Lee's eyes and mouth opened wide in astonishment. "But that's illegal! Did you call the sheriff or police or whatever you have to enforce laws against theft and arson?"

"All your words understand I not, but from them I believe someone who protects you against such actions have you. To do such things for us no one have we: only a warder who small disputes settles have we, but on large problems work not will he. Often we our own problems must solve, but easy it is not."

"So what did you do to those who stole from you or damaged your property?"

FarCaller's grim expression softened a bit. "One time my renters I told, because my share of the harvest never arrived, another cart full of the harvest to send to me must they, and continue to do so until received it did I."

"Didn't they complain about that? Did they think you were being unfair?"

FarCaller chuckled. "Oh yes. All that. But, most important, the robberies stopped. Never again stolen my food was, but still the burning occurred."

"What do you do about that?"

"Ofttimes, to protect my barn, guards hire I. Sometimes in the forest around my homestead these guards hide, for enemies trying here to sneak at night to capture. When enemies caught are, flogged are they. The floggings any bones don't break, but the intruders sore for many days, sometimes weeks, are." He smiled weakly. "Many more times it makes them think before other attacks trying."

Lee quietly said, "I wish I could help."

FarCaller's response was not what Lee expected. "Believe you, do I," he began, "but how I know not. Perhaps, after some time about each other learning, such help to provide, develop can we.

Before Lee could comment further, FarCaller said, "These weeks of talks most enjoyable have been. Much about your world and yourself learned have I."

"I'm having fun too," Lee responded. "Certainly I didn't know there were people in Spoon—" He stopped. Rephrasing his thought, he said, "I didn't know there were people in your world who were against you. I assumed everyone there knew about what the two of us do and accepted it as normal."

"Our worlds very much alike seem."

"Except here I think the people who want the spoon could be better organized."

"And possibly more dangerous." FarCaller stopped talking and closed his eyes as if concentrating. Then he looked curiously at Lee.

Lee sensed the depth of their conversation had changed. "Is something wrong?"

"I know not." A surprised and confused expression clouded his face. "But a Sensing which affects you just had I."

Now peering closely into the spoon, Lee asked, "What is it?"

FarCaller's expression told Lee much. His friend was smiling. "Pleasant, think I."

"Tell me."

"In your world a place with many great fields of grain is there. A place where the land with fields, many times farther than I could see, is covered. In that place a person whom you should meet—a woman—lives."

A farm belt? The Plains States? "Anything else?"

FarCaller's eyes flitted back and forth, his brain obviously disconnected from what he was seeing, concentrating on what he Sensed about Lee's future. "A boon to you will she be." His eyes widened in sudden surprise. "Perhaps a wife."

Now Lee smiled: he needed something to break the stress. "I'm supposed to go somewhere in an area covering about a third of our country and find a wife?" He peered at his friend as if trying to make certain everything was all right on Spoonworld. "Is that a common prediction? Are you a matchmaker?"

FarCaller missed the humor. "The term 'matchmaker' no meaning to me has, but quite real this Sensing is—like that Pyramid company Sensed was. What that meant I also didn't understand, but good for you it was, yes?"

Lee nodded. Pyramid Textile's stock had made him almost half a million dollars in less than a week. That little company had developed a material that made space suits lighter, tighter, and less expensive than ever before. Jackie got her tiny broker's commission, of course, and even bought some of the stock herself after the stock's price soared; but her returns were minuscule compared to Lee's. She nearly had a heart attack when she saw its price climb with no warning. Now she was asking Lee for hot stock tips instead of giving them.

"If it's that kind of Sensing, FarCaller, I'll do something. But I'll have to think about it first. Goodbye for now." He put the spoon in his shirt pocket and sat still, thinking hard. *What am I supposed to do? Place an ad saying "Kaaler Guardian seeks mate?"*

Chapter 25

Grandma's Rules

Lee's first impulse after that talk with FarCaller was to tear open his grandmother's third letter, but out of sensitivity as to how she would feel if he did so, he carefully opened the envelope with his paring knife.

> My dear Faerleigh,
>
> So now you know! Our family history. The gift. And about the people of Spoonworld. It is absolutely vital that your gift be kept secret, because there are others in this world who want to use it for their own gain. They know a great deal about our family, including the Challenge. But they will give it incorrectly! *That* is the most important secret for you to know at this time. If a Challenger does not respond *exactly* as taught here, he or she cannot be trusted! No matter *what* you are told by them (man or woman). Even if they themselves believe what they are saying, they lie. You now know the Challenge. Memorize it then destroy the letter which contains it. You may keep the puzzle. Might be a fun way to teach the Challenge to your firstborn.
>
> Another important part of being the Guardian is your "team." Being a Guardian often involves tasks that are too big for one person. You need to select people whom you can trust—which means they'll probably be Kaalers. That may be more difficult than it seems, because Kaalers are no different than any other group of people; they have jealousies and arguments and reconciliations. I had a small team of close friends who often helped me, but none were Kaalers. When I started making money from my investments, some of them became jealous and tried to learn how I did it. That led to arguments and the

team's eventual dissolution. Those things are very painful, Lee, so keep them in mind when you need help. Be extraordinarily careful about what you tell your team members, even if they are Kaalers.

Your first Challenge may come from someone falsely identifying himself or herself as a Kaaler and might even be someone you know. Remember to do nothing to reveal you know they are enemies but get my next letter *as soon as possible.* Whenever you receive a correct Challenge, though, you can almost certainly trust that person. Still, don't talk about your gift or the spoon or any other Kaaler secrets until you know and trust those people implicitly. You have to be convinced they really *must* know those secrets in order to perform whatever tasks you've requested their help with. See what I've written below.

You've come a long way as Guardian already, or you wouldn't be reading this letter. Clearly, working with your FarCaller has sharpened your skills and refined your judgment.

There are other letters, as you know, but you'll have to use your own judgment as to when you read them. Don't hurry, however, just continue learning.

I love you, and deeply regret I couldn't teach you these things in person.

Sorry this isn't all sweetness and light, but life just isn't like that.

Love,
Grandma

Kaaler Identity Challenge Rules

If *any part* of the Challenge is not correct, cut off the contact and give a response that shows you have no more interest in the discussion.

The plurals are significant. Without them the responses are wrong. This lets someone being coerced into giving the actual Challenge and Responses to "cooperate" while giving clues signifying force is being used to compel him or her to reveal the Challenge. Kaalers must do everything possible to find and eliminate the source of the incorrect challenges and responses, because it almost certainly means a Kaaler is either in extreme danger or has been killed to obtain that information. In either case, *any person with an incorrect Challenge must be treated as an enemy.*

To find other Kaalers, you can place a Challenge ad in a newspaper. If you do, give only a hint about a "calling." A Kaaler—good or bad—should pick up the significance. Regardless, even if they understand the ad, *Challenge them!*

Part IV

Collision

Chapter 26

You Did What?

Ebenezer Gerit's Office in Chicago

Ben was a miser at heart. He also was obsessed with increasing his fortune and political power, and was willing to spend his money to do so. The power spoon was one of those ways. He smiled as he thought about it and how it would help enrich him. In the middle of those thoughts, his telephone rang.

Before he could say anything, his son blurted out, "We got it, Dad!" Excitement colored Jeff's baritone voice. "We went through the names that sound like 'Caller,' checked where the people lived, and compared their immigration histories with the information we have in Old Uncle Thomas's journal. There was a lot of 'em, but combining the information we have on them with all of the information in the journals, I'm convinced the Guardian's name has to be 'Kaaler,' spelled K-double A-L-E-R, and he has to live on the West Coast."

His father's response was what Jeff expected. "Never heard of 'em."

"That's the whole point. The Kaalers've laid low for over a century—essentially invisible. Nondescript. Except they *have* to have that power spoon!" He slowed his breathing, not wanting to sound so excited that he would lose whatever credibility he had with his father. "And we're about to start the Challenge calls."

Ben's voice suddenly turned strident. "Without telling me first?"

Jeff was very glad he'd just calmed himself; otherwise he had no chance to soothe his father's anger. "Dad," he began, his voice calm and even, "we've been practicing this for a long time, and you know that. Each member of the contact teams knows the Challenge by heart and has been trained in how to approach these people. Everything you've had us preparing for is about to happen. Why are you so surprised?"

"Because—" The older man stopped, apparently unwilling to give Jeff credit for anything well done. "Because I'm paying for this whole thing," he began again, "and you didn't tell me about contacting anyone before you started. You left me out of the loop on the most important step in our hunt!"

He's "tap dancing!" I caught him in something his own directions brought about, and he's trying to find some way to blame me. Jeff shook his head at his father's ego. *Right now I'll do whatever it takes to get him off his high horse and let us continue doing something useful to find that spoon. We're too close to wait.* "Sorry," he said. "Guess I didn't think far enough ahead. Want me to call off the contacts?" *He won't even consider it.*

"Just keep me informed."

Chapter 27

The Real Goal

Jeff Gerit smiled as he cut off the speakerphone and ended the talk with his dad. The plan to find the Guardian and control the power in the spoon was going Jeff's way, not his father's. He enjoyed the results of his teams' two break-ins at the Kaaler homes in Oregon several months earlier. They hadn't found that spoon in Oregon, which let them concentrate their burglaries in California. It also was a smart decision to stop chasing "Callers," even though his dad would have disagreed if Jeff had told him ahead of time. But his dad didn't have to do all the work, and sifting through Kaalers was much easier than searching through potentially hundreds of databases for anyone with a family name that sounded like "Caller."

Jeff had been directly involved in the hiring and training of all of his burglary teams. Weaknesses weren't tolerated, so when his teams reported not finding any unusual spoons in either of the Oregon homes, he was satisfied that neither of those homes held the powerful spoon his great-uncle Thomas had written about. Having eliminated the two Oregon Kaalers as possible Guardians of the spoon, his team was concentrating on the remaining Kaalers in California—all in the San Joaquin Valley, most around Fresno. He hadn't expected the murder of that Caller guy; but it, like the Oregon break-ins, convinced Jeff the spoon wasn't at that particular home. His conclusion: the murder was justified because he learned so much from its aftermath.

He sipped his bourbon on the rocks, concentrating entirely on how his Challenge teams would be contacting the Kaalers who lived in California. It took only a few seconds for him to decide to stop further burglaries until detailed surveillance of the targeted Kaaler families had been completed. He directed his agent there to have his people start watching all the Kaalers in the Fresno area, beginning with the richest and slowly working through the phone list.

If careful surveillance, Challenge telephone calls, and selected break-ins didn't locate the spoon in California, they'd head to the state with the next most Kaalers. Through the Internet telephone directories, he had already identified more than a thousand Kaaler families in the United States, and he knew there would be more because married Kaaler daughters would have different last names. But his people would find those women. And they would find the spoon. And they would report their success directly to Jeff. He fully expected to become powerful in his own right and no longer have to rely on his dad for money. That John Kaaler—the guy whose ravings first told Great-uncle Thomas about the power spoon and how it would help its user get rich—had given Jeff many good ideas and schemes. He let that thought bounce around his brain for a few seconds. *With the spoon's power, I might even send Dad to a nursing home and take over Gerit Pharmaceuticals.* That *would be fun. And* very *profitable.*

Chapter 28

Real Power

After the call from Jeff ended, Ben Gerit sat still, looking around the room but seeing nothing, thinking about the significance of what his son had just told him.

We've finally got a real chance to find that Guardian guy and get that spoon that makes him so powerful. A few more seconds of thought. *Once we have it, I'll put it to my own uses.* His face wrinkled into a cold, cruel, calculating, terrible grimace.

He reached for his telephone and pressed the button marked Atty. After two rings, it was answered; a familiar female voice said, "Yes, sir. What can I do for you?"

"Remember the conversation we had a few days ago, Belle?"

"Yes, sir," came her steady alto answer. "I did just as you asked."

"What did you learn?"

"There are several good candidates for takeovers, sir. It seems the only real problem is getting enough money together to purchase the stock—plus all the things we'd have to do with the Securities and Exchange Commission."

"I can take care of the money. What's the SEC need?"

"They'd be concerned about monopoly power, sir. Of course, you could buy several companies at first and not be any kind of monopoly threat because our market share wouldn't be very big." Before Ben could respond, she added, "At least not at first."

"OK, Belle. Start down the list."

After closing the phone circuit, he leaned back and thought. *In the near future, I'm going to be head of the largest pharmaceutical conglomerate in the United States. We'll set our own prices, have all that lobbying power working for us in Washington, and be able to call the shots in every aspect of the drug business. Prices, sources, international agreements, laws—you name it. Now, that's* power!

Chapter 29

Are You a Kaaler?

August 2004

Grandma's first letter instructed Lee to trust FarCaller. Now FarCaller had Sensed a woman Lee should meet, possibly his future wife. *Hunting for a woman goes against everything I ever felt about dating. Like not taking anyone's word about how wonderful some girl might be—because the one they're trying to set you up with might be an ugly cousin, or something like that.* He'd heard coeds talking about how many toads they had to kiss before they found their prince, and he didn't want to be one of those toads. But he couldn't go on in his life alone. He was to pass his Guardianship to his eldest child, and Grandma said his wife should be a Kaaler. *What kind of woman wants to date a man who may be more interested in her fertility than in loving her?* Then he thought back to one of his grandma's letters. *She said such a woman would love the Guardian and would lovingly bear his children. Does that mean she would love me even if we met through an ad in the personals?*

Regardless of his reservations, he decided to search for the woman Sensed by FarCaller. Even if he didn't find *the* woman, he might find some Kaalers who could help him learn about his family and its history and, possibly, help him find that special woman. The idea that this search might lead to someone who wouldn't love him disgusted Lee, but he knew he had to trust this whole weird Guardian/FarCaller thing he'd found himself in. He wanted to find the right wife. But hunting for one instead of just living his life and letting things happen? He didn't like that.

Following another of Grandma's suggestions and FarCaller's Sensing, he planned to place a series of Challenge ads in key newspapers throughout the Plains States. Via the Internet, he placed the first ad in the Oklahoma City *Oklahoman*.

He felt he had the best chance of making contact in Oklahoma because of the size of the population and its location in the middle of wheat country. If unsuccessful there, he'd place ads in newspapers in other key midwest cities.

Placing the ad was easy; waiting for responses was maddeningly slow. He placed the ad so it would appear over a three-day weekend and flew to Oklahoma City on Thursday. Adding to the pressures of this trip: he had to take some vacation time and had almost none. *If this Guardian thing takes much more time, I'll lose my job. I could live on the investments I made using FarCaller's leads, but that would reveal that I've suddenly come into money.* He shook his head in frustration and disgust. *There doesn't seem to be any easy way to do anything.*

He'd made his reservations without really thinking about the cost and was shocked at the rates when he checked in. It was one of the most beautiful hotels he'd ever seen: decorated in a Mexican theme—bright colors, photos and posters of Mexican deserts, beaches, Aztec ruins, and lovely cities. The uniforms of all the employees carried the same theme, and the daily cost of the room—as fine as Lee had ever seen—was half a week's salary. Before giving the hotel his credit card to guarantee his charges, his one thought was, *This had better be worth it!* Then he remembered that a credit card charge could be traced to him. He excused himself, withdrew from the ATM in the lobby more than enough cash to pay for his stay, and gave it to the clerk. The clerk didn't like it but ultimately agreed after Lee gave more than three times what his weekend could cost. *It's really bad when cash isn't good enough to let you stay in a hotel.* After completing his registration, he went directly to his room to prepare for what he hoped would be a useful weekend. Expecting he'd have many responses to his ad, he scrupulously carried his rented cell phone wherever he went.

There were nine Kaalers listed in the Oklahoma City area telephone books. His first thought was to call them directly, but he decided to follow his grandma's advice to use the Challenge ad, then after two days, he still had no responses. Sunday morning, in the hotel coffee shop, he looked at the ad again, trying to find something—anything—wrong with it, anything that might keep someone from calling.

Looking for different career path.
New calling. Contact 405-555-4515

No, it's all right. Someone should have contacted me. All the Kaalers can't be oblivious to the need to check for Challenge ads. Another thought struck him, the first ever of its kind. *Maybe, as Guardian, I should try to make Kaalers more conscientious about keeping abreast of the welfare of other Kaalers, to include regular checking for Challenge ads in their newspapers.*

No sooner had Lee finished that contemplation than his cell phone chirped. He jumped at the sudden brash interruption, took two deep breaths, and flipped open the cell phone cover. "Hello."

"You place the ad about a new callin'?" The caller's voice was deep and raspy. Excitement began to build in Lee's chest. *Is this it?* "Yes, sir, I did."

"Well, what kinda job you offerin'. I'm outta work and need somethin' bad. 'N I'm a good worker, man."

Offering? Then the reality of the call hit Lee. *He thinks I have job openings.* He shook his head quickly, his jaws tight in frustration. *Couldn't be more backward if I planned it.* He took a quick sip of his iced tea before speaking. "I'm sorry, sir, but the ad wasn't about job openings. I'm looking for a new career path, not offering one to others." Before the man could respond, Lee added, "I'm sorry for any misunderstanding this caused," then flipped the cell phone shut. He emptied his glass of iced tea and signaled the waitress for a refill.

A few minutes later, his phone chirped again. This speaker wasn't looking for a job but was offering Lee a grand and glorious opportunity to make more money than he thought would ever be possible: a career in direct sales. He could sell household goods, cleansers, party gifts, and on and on.

In the next hour, Lee received five responses from people either needing jobs or offering Lee "opportunities." With each, he became more frustrated and disappointed. Drinking the iced tea helped him relax but didn't solve his problem—no useful responses to his Challenge ad.

As he finished those thoughts, his cell phone chirped again. By now he was so disappointed in the lack of useful responses to his ad that he absentmindedly picked up the cell phone, unfolded it, and reluctantly put the instrument to his ear. "Yes?"

"Did you place an ad in the *Oklahoman?*" A man's voice: smooth, comforting. "One that mentioned a new calling?"

Suddenly things became serious. Lee's heart pounded in his ears, his hands became clammy, little beads of sweat sprang from his forehead. "Yes."

"Well," came the reply in the same smooth tones, "I'm looking for a new career path, and think I may have found a new calling."

The Challenge! Lee was almost too excited to speak but knew he had to follow the Challenge rules. Even though he'd practiced it hundreds of times, he had to think about what to say. Collecting his thoughts, he carefully recited the required response. "A new calling can be very hard to find. Did you have any preferences?"

"Something in long distance."

Contact! I've finally . . . His brain immediately overrode his emotions. Something was wrong: *"long distance" instead of "long distances?"* The enormity of that difference hit him hard: *I'm talking to one of the bad guys!*

"Sorry, sir," he said, "I'm on a cell phone and couldn't hear you very well. Would you repeat what you just said?"

"Of course," was the smooth response.

He doesn't sound nervous. Maybe it's just me.

"I said," the man continued, "'Something in long distance.'"

Fear replaced excitement. For the first time in his life, Lee felt he was in danger. Rising as he spoke, he strode out of the coffee shop, the cell phone against his ear. "Sir, I have no interests in that area. But have a nice day."

Snapping the cell phone closed, he walked quickly to the hotel desk, turned in the cell phone, settled his bill, then took the elevator up to his room and threw clothes and toiletries into his suitcase. Riding the elevator down to the parking garage and jumping into his rented car, he thanked God he'd not used his real name or address at the hotel. He drove out of the underground garage as fast as he could and headed directly for the rental car office at the airport. Lee didn't notice the man who went to his table just after Lee left it. Even before the busboy could clear the table, that man carefully picked up Lee's empty iced tea glass, touching only its base, and left the coffee shop with the glass wrapped in pages from Lee's newspaper.

On the road back to the rental car lot, Lee tried to think about what just happened and why he was so frightened. He reached a conclusion just as he turned into the rental car return area. *I used an alias and rented a cell phone from the hotel. Whoever that caller was, he shouldn't be able to trace anything back to me, so I shouldn't be frightened.*

But he was.

Chapter 30

The Fun Begins

"We found one, Dad!"

"One what? What're you talking about?"

Jeff's inherited short temper began to exert itself. He knew better than to blow up at his own father, but stupid questions like that were almost impossible to ignore. *I'll try just once more.*

"Dad, we've been tracing Kaalers continually since our last talk. I've had people in every major city checking newspapers and TV for anything that had the same words as the Challenge old Great-uncle Thomas wrote in his journal. Three days ago we found an ad in the Oklahoma City paper that used some of the words in the Challenge. Using the cell phone number in the ad, we traced it to a guy staying in a hotel there. Then we tried to check his hotel registry against the cell phone he rented so we could get some idea of what he looked like. The front desk wouldn't help us at all on that, so we bribed a bellboy to point the guy out for us. That worked, and we tailed him. He stayed around the hotel the entire time, even brought a copy of the daily newspaper with him to his meals and concentrated on doing crossword puzzles and on the personal ads page—the one with the ad that caught our attention. Did this for two days before I called him and gave the challenge." He waited for another idiotic interruption, but his dad was silent. *For once the old man is listening!*

"So this morning, while that guy was reading the Sunday paper in the coffee shop, I called the number in the ad. Just like we thought, he answered it, so I started the challenge. At first it went fine, but then he said something dumb, shut off the call, checked out of the hotel, and raced to the airport."

He could hear his dad breathing: fast, shallow, excited. "What did your man in the hotel do?"

"Traced him to the rental car return place then lost him."

"Didn't that idiot know what to do? Ben pounded his desk with his fist. "Jeff, this is the closest *we've ever come!*" He stopped ranting for a few seconds, long enough for Jeff to speak again.

"Dad," his son said slowly, evenly, soothingly, "we didn't learn what airplane he left on, but we got his photograph and lifted his fingerprints from his drinking glass. Best of all, for a small bribe at the car rental place, my guy got the man's name and address. He's Faerleigh F. Kaaler, and he lives in a place called Bend, in Oregon."

Chapter 31

It's Really Wrong

For the fifth time in an hour, Ben Gerit pored over the recording Jeff sent him of his Challenge call to that guy in the Oklahoma City hotel. As he had done each time, the older Gerit carefully checked every word of the Challenge against the document written by his ancestor.

"I'm looking for a new career path, and think I may have found a new calling," came Jeff's voice.

Exactly as written, Ben noted to himself.

"A new calling can be very hard to find. Did you have any preferences?"

The Kaaler guy. Just like we expected.

"Something in long distance."

Word for word.

"Sorry, sir, but I'm on a cell phone and couldn't hear you very well. Would you repeat what you just said?"

Possibly true, cell phones don't always operate perfectly. Or it could have been the way the Challenge was spoken.

"Of course. I said, 'Something in long distance.'"

Jeff said it correctly. Should have been no problem.

"Sir, I have no interests in that area. Have a good day."

"Then he hung up and ran!" Ben yelled, slamming his fist on his desk in frustration. The pens and photos bounced in response, his glass of scotch and water wobbled, splashing some of the amber liquid onto the polished wooden surface. "Damn it! What went wrong?"

He thought back the four months to when his son said the Gerit family journals might have an incorrect spelling of the Guardian's family name. *Jeff was correct that time. But could there be something wrong with our Challenge?* The enormity of that possibility was almost too much for the old man to contemplate. *If that's true, we aren't much closer to getting the Guardian's power than we were. It's as good as locked in a vault. What's wrong?* His musings were interrupted by the telephone. *That's what I need: a distraction.*

"Gerit here."

"This is Jeff.

My scheming son. "Why are you calling?" When Ebenezer Gerit was angry, he was a man of few words and a very short fuse.

"I wanted to give you an update on what we're doing."

A nice change. "Go ahead."

"We've isolated our search for the Kaaler in Oklahoma City to that first guy we ransacked in Oregon—Bend, Oregon."

"And?"

"He lives in an apartment in the center of town, and it's hard to find out what he's doing without being noticed. If he lived in a house, we could plant minicams and stuff when he was at work. That's nearly impossible in his apartment house."

"So what's the update? Sounds to me like you've identified him and aren't sure he's even the Guardian."

"That's not true, Dad, and you know it. Just finding the guy took a lot of work from a lot of people, including me. Now we've at least got a person we can watch instead of trying to chase down thousands of possibilities. That's real progress."

"But he didn't respond to the Challenge, did he?"

Jeff was silent: his father finally landed a telling blow. "No, he didn't, and we don't know why. Had any luck with your review of what was said?"

He's got me back in the blame loop! "With the little you gave me, there's almost nothing I *could* do."

"Didn't find anything significant, did you?" Jeff asked.

Reluctantly he replied, "No." Before Jeff could say anything else, his father added, "Your men better keep close tabs on that Kaaler guy. I want that spoon, and if he doesn't have it, I'll bet he knows where it is, so they'd better not screw this up!"

Chapter 32

Trolling

Early November 2004

Verry had a busy fall. Not only was there a lot of work editing the alumni newsletters and inputs to the college's recruiting brochures, but she'd been dating a lot. Her mom was right: once she got into the dating circuit, men seemed to pop out of the woodwork. Even good-looking ones.

For six weeks she'd dated Rick almost exclusively. He was a nice guy, fairly good looking, a super dancer, and treated her lovingly. Her folks and Drella liked him, even though he wasn't a Kaaler. Her mom was less than subtle when talking about their future together and how much she looked forward to having grandchildren. *If she only knew how awful that makes me feel. And how uncomfortable Rick gets. But Mom won't change.*

So maybe I have to. She tried to visualize a wedding with Rick as her groom, but all she could see was the decorations and activities. Nothing with the two of them together. *This isn't right! If I'm going to marry the guy, shouldn't he be in my thoughts all the time? If I love Rick, shouldn't I want to make love with him and have his children?*

But those thoughts didn't come. She liked him, and he probably loved her. But . . . She exhaled a loud sigh and then picked up the Sunday paper to check the personals. The idea didn't appeal to her at all, but she decided not to continue the relationship with Rick, and she didn't really like the guys she'd dated before him. Maybe there were some new opportunities there. If she could just get past the ads for guys wanting lovers—male or female.

She sat down at her small dining table and placed the paper on its blue Formica top, carefully pushing the crocheted place mat to the side. *Mustn't get newspaper ink on Grandma's doily.* Shaking her head, letting her auburn hair swing back and forth, she tried to relax. Humping her shoulders up and down didn't help much, but it helped some. One of her grandma's seemingly ancient prescriptions for nervousness floated into her mind: she made herself a cup of chamomile tea. If it didn't make her feel better, at least it would make her sleepy.

Pulling her fuzzy white robe around her, she thought about its pattern of tiny yellow daisies. *Looks a lot like Iowa in the spring. Maybe that's an omen that I'm doomed to stay in this place.*

As usual, the ads were awful. Just when she thought she'd found something interesting, at the end there would be a comment like "AC/DC" or "experience required." *Terrific! A "relationship" with someone with the morals of an alley cat. That's all I need.*

She stopped reading and sat back in her chair. *I'm going about this all wrong. Mom said the break-ins at Kaaler homes were in Oregon. Why am I looking at ads here in Des Moines, when I can place one in a newspaper in an area where I know Kaalers live?* More thought, her eyes randomly looking around her room as her brain churned. *Mom said she and Dad met through a newspaper ad. If it worked for them, it's probably pretty well written. Why should I try to invent one for myself when I can use their Challenge ad?*

She moved to her desk and turned on her computer. *First, find the newspapers in Oregon then pick a couple and start trolling.*

Chapter 33

Second Challenge

November 14, 2004

Earlier that week, Verry had placed Challenge ads in the Sunday editions of the two biggest Oregon newspapers, the Portland *Oregonian* and the *Eugene Register-Guard*. It was now late the following Sunday afternoon. She hoped there would be at least a few calls, because her mother had been thrilled when Verry asked to copy the ad her dad had used to help them find each other. The downside of that: her mother was certain to call that evening to see if any responses were received. If not, she would surely pester Verry to place ads in other newspapers. Bottom line: her mother wanted Verry to meet a potential Kaaler husband. Soon.

* * *

Over the preceding three months, Lee had placed Challenge ads in eight Plains States cities, using an 800 number he leased so he didn't have to leave home unless there was a successful contact. That also protected him from the trauma he experienced in Oklahoma City. He received responses to all of the ads in all of the cities, but none from Kaalers. One thing was obvious: many people were looking for work, and most of them sounded beaten down. He believed the lack of responses from any Kaalers at all went against the odds, but it didn't change the results. As he often did when faced with challenges or puzzles, he tried to find the clue that would solve them. In this matter, he came to three conclusions about his relatives. First: the Kaalers in the areas where he placed the ads either didn't read or wouldn't respond to personal ads no matter how enticing or real they looked. Second: if they read the ads, they were afraid they'd been placed by someone posing as a Kaaler and didn't want to let the false Kaalers know anything about the themselves. Third: he needed to keep running the ads until he got some useful responses. The problem with that was that he might find himself suddenly overwhelmed by responses from some of the cities. Eventually he'd have to spend more time and money traveling so he could meet the people who called him. That would cost him his job. In any case, the Challenge ads hadn't seemed to work so far. He'd decided to give up the search for a while, hoping for some better way to find the woman FarCaller Sensed.

It was Sunday afternoon, over three months since he'd placed the first Challenge ad in the Oklahoma City newspaper. He'd finished watching the Seahawks game and decided to take a short nap. But after less than fifteen minutes of restless sleep, his mind churning with thoughts about his search for other Kaalers, he woke with a start. *I'm just as bad as all the others! I'm not checking the personal ads any more than they seem to be.* He grimaced with dissatisfaction at his own lack of action then rose from his bed and went into the living room to check the Sunday issue of the *Oregonian*. It was the biggest paper in the state, and if someone really wanted to sell something or get in touch with someone, this was probably the best paper to use.

Once he found the classified ads section, he thumbed through the pages until he found the personals. He then read each one, methodically checking it off with a ballpoint pen as he did. After twenty minutes of fruitless efforts, he saw something that made his eyes open in surprise and his stomach contract.

> Looking for a different career path.
> New calling. Cell phone 515-555-4321.

Lee stared at the ad for several minutes, his thoughts flitting from unbelievability to wariness to delight, then back through the same path. Finally he said, "It's exactly like the one I used! How is that possible unless"—he blinked at his own conclusion—"a lot of Kaalers know it!" He then realized he'd been holding his breath, and he exhaled deeply. As he did, he felt relief from the strain of worrying about how to find other Kaalers flow out with the breath. "Didn't expect I'd do the calling." Smiling and shaking his head in amazement, he picked up his telephone.

* * *

Verry returned to her apartment right after dinner that Sunday evening so she could answer any responses to her ads in the Oregon papers. In the middle of wondering if anyone in Oregon even read the personals except those from people wanting to expand their sexual experiences, Verry heard the opening of the fourth movement of Mozart's Forty-first Symphony: it was her cell phone ring! The caller ID said Unknown Caller, temporarily dashing Verry's hopes for a legitimate call. *Probably a telemarketeer. Couldn't call at a worse time.* Swallowing hard and clearing her throat, she flipped the cell phone open. "Hello."

"Uh, did you place an ad in the Sunday *Oregonian* personals?" It was a man's voice.

"Yes." She sat erect now, paying careful attention to every word, trying to sense every nuance. *I really hope this isn't one of those AC/DC guys.*

After a short hesitation, the man said, "Well, I'm looking for a different career path, and think I may have found a new calling."

Oh! Excitement built inside her. *It's the Challenge!* Swallowing again, she said, "A new calling may be very hard to find. Do you have any preferences?" *Let it be right!* she prayed. *Let it be right!*

"Something in long distances."

It was correct! He was a real Kaaler. Verry completed the code with, "Worldwide, I presume." With that out of the way, she knew it was her turn to say something else. "I, uh, don't know exactly what to say."

"Well," said the caller, "since we have the same interests in new callings, perhaps we should meet."

"That's a good idea," she said. "But first I have a lot of questions. Like, who are you? Why did you answer the ad? Where do you live? Don't you think we should know a bit more about each other before meeting? After all," she said, "it's a long way from Oregon to where I live, and I wouldn't want you to spend a lot of money flying here for no real purpose."

The caller stopped speaking, so Lee spoke. "Actually, that makes sense. And since you at least know I live in Oregon, please tell me where your home is."

"Iowa."

She heard a sudden intake of breath, then, "He was right!"

Their conversation started with a question, "Why did you say that?"

"Say what?" he said, trying to sound innocent.

"You said, 'He was right.' What's that mean? Who's 'he?' It sounded like something was wrong."

That was so stupid! Lee thought. *I can't talk about FarCaller's Sensing, so I have to think up some kind of lie. Really stupid.* "Well," Lee began, speaking slowly so he could concoct a good response, "I've been having trouble contacting Kaalers. Placed a lot of ads in a lot of papers but got mostly either requests for work or offers to go into direct sales and make my fortune."

"I hate those calls too." Verry giggled a bit. "Go on."

I need more time to think! "I have a friend whose hunches are almost always right. He suggested that I would have success in contacting another Kaaler if I . . .

uh . . . looked for them in the Great Plains states. So, trusting his hunches, I placed Challenge ads. I started with ads in big city papers, beginning in Oklahoma City, then Kansas City, St. Louis, Omaha, Chicago, and Minneapolis. My next one was going to be Des Moines. I never got a useful response. Then, today—"

"You saw my ad," she said, finishing Lee's thought. "No wonder you were surprised. Are you going to stop your hunt now? I'm only one Kaaler, and there have to be lot more."

"I'll stop now, certainly. Even though you found me rather than the other way around, the important thing is that both of us were looking for Kaalers, and each of us found one. So before I resume my search, I'd like to know something about you. I live in Bend, Oregon, and am the assistant manager of a small bank. What do you do in Iowa?"

Their conversation continued for two hours. They discussed their ages, educations, marital status, vocations, and why they placed Challenge ads. Both gave ambiguous reasons on that subject; neither wanted the other to know they were looking for mates. When it ended, Lee was smiling and looking forward to future contacts with Verry and felt certain she felt the same.

They agreed to continue their talks, and they did. For many weeks. In that time they learned much about each other, began e-mailing back and forth, and exchanged photos. As they continued their contacts, they became good friends and confidantes; both knew they needed to see each other face-to-face. But Lee didn't want to put his job at risk by taking time off to fly to Des Moines, and Verry was tied up in her own job. They decided to meet in the spring, perhaps April.

Both could hardly wait.

Chapter 34

Surveillance

Mid November 2004

"What're you doin' about that Kaaler guy in Oregon?" Ben asked. He was sitting on the leather sofa in his private office, using the speakerphone. It let him have both hands free for his scotch and water. Besides, it was already early evening—happy hour in Chicago, even though it was late afternoon in San Francisco, where Jeff lived.

"Right now we're trying to keep track of the guy without being noticed," Jeff answered. "He lives in an apartment, like I told you, and there are residents messing around the place all day long. We haven't yet found a way to get to his phone lines or put in a video camera to watch him, 'cause someone would see it and ask questions."

Ben's jaw muscles began to twitch. "So you're doing nothing?"

Jeff could hear the anger and impatience coloring his dad's tone of voice. "I didn't say that, and its not true. I've got guys—good ones—checking the place out. As soon as they find a time when they can do their stuff without being noticed, they'll do it, and we'll have a good handle on what that Kaaler guy does and when and with whom. We know he was looking for other Kaalers, and we know someone named Kaaler was the Guardian when old Great-uncle Thomas first learned about the power spoon. Now we're using the only strong lead we have to zero in on who has it. I think that is definitely 'doing something,' but it takes time. Don't forget, Dad, we've come a long way in the past several months. I know you'd like it to go faster, but we've really gone a long way on our path to getting that power thing."

"Yeah," his dad responded, "but this is costing me a bunch of money, and I don't like paying people to sit on their butts and just look around. I want them to be doing something useful."

Jeff leaned back in his desk chair so he could look out his picture window at the Golden Gate Bridge. "They are, Dad. They are." He hung up before his dad could say something to counter Jeff's claim.

But he's right. We have to show some kind of useful results pretty soon. He mentally searched for useful tasks his people in Bend might be able to do to at least look like they were making headway, when a new thought popped into his mind. *We could set up a team to wash the windows of the entire unit—as an advertising ploy. That'd get us there, in plain sight but essentially invisible, and let my people put cameras and electronics near the Kaaler guy's apartment windows.* He thought some more. *His back windows look out on the water, so few if any of his neighbors could see us installing cameras.* He smiled at his own brilliance. *That may just do it.*

Chapter 35

Magic You Have?

Mid November 2004

It was a chilly, lazy Saturday morning, and Lee had no motivation to do anything. He had worked hard all week helping people with loans for Christmas and beginning the process of refinancing their home loans. It wasn't terribly difficult, but it demanded attention to detail. He hated working with details because he knew he wasn't good at it, but it had to be done. Knowing he often made errors by both action and inaction also didn't help. Adding to his frustration, he had been up past midnight talking with Verry, something that was becoming more and more important in his life. And, according to Verry, just as important in hers. Sitting quietly, thinking about Verry, reminded him of just how he first learned about her—indirectly, at least—from FarCaller's sensing.

"FarCaller," he said aloud, shaking his head in exasperation at his own negligence. "I've been so busy with my own world that I forgot about him completely." He rose and retrieved the spoon from his bedroom reading table, no longer keeping it in his safe. "It's time to—"

He was interrupted by a familiar voice. "Guardian? Can you hear me?"

Chuckling and smiling at the timing of FarCaller's call, Lee lifted the spoon chin high, saw his friend's face in it, and said, "Absolutely, FarCaller. I was just about to call you."

"Many days talked we have not," FarCaller began. "Things with you all right are?"

Lee nodded as he responded. "Very good, in fact. Do you remember your Sensing about a woman who lived in a place with large fields of grain?"

"Yes. To contact her wanted you. Successful were you?"

Lee's smile broadened. "Yes, indeed. In fact, we have talk to each other nearly every night."

FarCaller frowned. "But far away she lives. Talking to her possible is? How?"

"We have a small device, shorter than my silver spoon, that lets us talk to people long distances away. I used one of those to talk with her."

FarCaller concentrated intently on what Lee said, clearly having difficulty understanding it. "Magic have you? Grandfather FarCaller mentioned it not."

Here goes! "It is not magic, but it seems so. And I cannot explain how it works because I don't understand it. However, it works well, and she and I are getting to know each other better every time we talk."

FarCaller shook his head, looked down, then returned his attention to Lee. "But another Sensing have I," he said. "Perhaps more important than magical talking it is."

Lee's attitude immediately changed. If FarCaller called about a Sensing, Lee had to understand it. "Tell me."

"Someone watching you will be. From the window that onto the water looks. Dangerous to me it feels."

"You mean they could see us talking like we are now?"

"Yes," FarCaller said. "Soon watch you they will."

As he spoke, Lee looked up at the window FarCaller was talking about. Holding the spoon high enough so that FarCaller could see the window, he rose, walked over to it, and closed the blind. As he returned to his favorite chair, he thought about the significance of FarCaller's Sensing.

"FarCaller, I think that means the person or persons who called me with that incorrect Challenge have somehow found me." He leaned back and let his eyes relax. A few seconds of thought and he looked back at FarCaller's image, but now his mouth was tensed into a straight line and his eyes partially closed in anger. "If it's them, I have to be very careful."

"True," his friend offered. "While we talk, watch us they must not. The true purpose of the spoon revealed to them would be."

Lee thought some more then smiled. "You know what I'm going to do?"

"Not."

"First, I'll keep the blinds open when I'm not here, but close them whenever I'm home. That won't necessarily reveal I know I'm being watched, but it will keep them from seeing anything I want to keep private." He smiled some more. "Then, in a few days, perhaps a week, I'll have that window, or maybe all of my windows, covered with a film that reflects everything outside it but lets me see through it. That'll let me look at their sensors, or whatever they have, without letting them see me at all. And one of the good things about that approach is that it is logical around here: the sun is very hot in the summer, and the homes cool off a lot during the winter, so the insulation provided by that film will help solve both problems." He looked at his friend's image. "That's what I'll do, and I owe it to your Sensing. Thank you, FarCaller."

"No problem it is, Lee. But of what you just said, little I understand."

Chapter 36

Cameras and Mirrors

Late November 2004
Bend, Oregon

"Your were right, boss," Mackie said to Jeff, making no attempt to hide his chortling. "They went for the window-washin' thing like flies to cowpie. When I said we'd do the whole buildin' for free just to show how good we were, it was over. We start tomorra and should have the whole thing done in a couple of days." Before Jeff could ask anything, Mackie said, "I checked around the windows of the Kaaler guy's place. There's a tree on each side of the window, so the only people who might see us messin' around his place would be the people across the river. They're so rich I'll bet they don't even know the apartments 're there."

Jeff nodded at Mackie's report. "Sounds good. When'll we start getting useful information? Installing cameras and window mikes is one thing; getting good stuff is another. My dad's getting antsy, and I've gotta have something to show this is working."

"It'll prob'ly take a coupla more days. Gotta make sure everything works with the video recorders n' stuff like that."

"How 'bout phone taps?"

"That's a lot harder. I'll get back to you on that."

"Make it soon."

"Will do. Should have some kind a plan in a coupla days at most."

* * *

Ben Gerit was so furious he couldn't hold his telephone handset. Throwing it down, he pressed the speakerphone button on his telephone base and yelled. "That Kaaler guy did what?"

Again Jeff was glad he and his dad were separated by over a thousand miles, because that saved him from a longer tongue-lashing as well as a probable beating by one of his dad's meanest men. "He put that mirrorlike film over all his windows this afternoon. We can't see a thing inside his place except sometimes in the evenings, when he keeps his lights on. But much of the time he closes the blinds just after he returns from some trip, so all we see is an empty apartment until he gets back."

Ben took several deep breaths, trying to control his anger. "So," he finally said, "he's on to you and your idiots."

Jeff ignored the jibe. "Don't know why he put that film on the windows now, but it's not unusual around here. It's just that his timing is fishy."

Jeff's comment was met by a stream of invectives, then an ominous silence. "So what's your next step?" his dad demanded.

He's already divorcing himself from any blame on this, Jeff thought. *Just like he always does.*

"Phone taps, I guess."

"Do it, but do it RIGHT!"

Chapter 37

The Problem with Plans

November 23, 2004, 7:00 p.m. (PST)

Lee's life was busier than he could remember it ever being, with the possible exception of studying for his final exams in college. He was working full time, talking to Verry almost every night, and thinking about whomever was trying to watch him. He talked with FarCaller two or three times a week, but mostly in generalities, letting each of them learn more about the other's world. The talks with Verry, however, were becoming more and more important to both of them and seldom lasted less than two hours.

Their latest talk was about the weather in Iowa—at least on the surface. The real agenda, however, was if and when Lee would fly there so they could meet.

"Tell me about your December weather," he said. "We have snow and cold here in Central Oregon, but not like I've heard Iowa has."

"It's really not a big thing," she responded. "Our forecasts are pretty accurate, so we usually have several days' notice when bad storms are coming. Surely you're not afraid of snowstorms."

Lee could hear the smile in her voice as she chided him but decided to rise to the bait. "Not the results, but if I got caught in one that kept me from getting back here to work, I might lose my job. Don't want that to happen, but I do want to see you. I'm just trying to decide when would be a good time to—"

"Why don't you come early next month?" she said, cutting him off in midsentence. "The bad weather hasn't started; you could leave Friday afternoon or evening and be home Sunday night. You might be tired Monday morning, but at least you wouldn't miss work."

He was silent, thinking, then quietly said, "I like that. I'll get back with you on when I can leave."

Lee had too many things to settle before he could make flight reservations, not the least was dodging whoever was watching him and what he could do to get out of Bend without them knowing about it so they could follow him and learn about Verry. He couldn't leave in less than two weeks.

* * *

Immediately after his call with Verry ended, Lee's images of her were punctured by the now-familiar voice from—where? He still didn't know what to call FarCaller's home world, but since once thinking of the word "Spoonworld," the name had stuck. And his grandmother called it the same name.

Apologizing to Verry for cutting off their talk, he closed the telephone circuit and pulled the silver spoon out from his shirt pocket. "Yes, FarCaller. I'm here."

FarCaller's expression was serious, but after looking at Lee, his eyes narrowed and his eyebrows dropped into a frown of confusion. "Something good is?" he began. "Smiling broadly are you."

Lee's smile broadened even more, and he nodded. "Don't doubt it. I was talking to Verry when you called."

"Sorry am I for your talk interrupting." He leaned forward as if to study Lee's face in detail. "But happier now than for many weeks you look."

Lee's smile changed from one of personal joy to that of simple amusement. He and FarCaller talked three or four times a week, yet FarCaller talked as if they hadn't talked for many weeks. *It's that time compression and expansion thing between our worlds. Don't think I'll ever understand it.* "I am happier," he responded. "I will visit her soon. Then perhaps I will learn if your Sensing about a possible wife is accurate."

"Always before it was. Still doubt you?"

"Not exactly," he said. "But it isn't easy to become accustomed to." Before letting this conversation continue, he changed the subject. "Why did you call?"

FarCaller's expression changed from amusement to seriousness. "My Sensing about someone watching you remember do you?"

"Of course. Shortly after that I covered my windows with something that makes them look like mirrors from outside. We talked about it before. Is there something wrong with that? Should I change the film or something?"

FarCaller shook his head back and forth. "Not. My latest Sensing related may be, but the same thing isn't."

"Tell me, then," Lee said. "I don't like feeling I'm in danger all the time and was just beginning to relax, knowing they—whoever they are—couldn't see me anymore."

"My Sensing not about seeing is, friend Lee," was FarCaller's response. "What I see I understand not, but important it is."

"Tell me."

"Difficult to describe, but try I will." He looked down as if trying to clear his mind, then looked back at Lee. "Two things I Sense. Related they *must* be."

Lee nodded as if to say, "Go on. I'm listening."

"One part of the Sensing is you. In your home you are, holding something small to your head. Dark blue it is. Many small round things on the side near your face it has. One end against your ear is, the other your mouth near. On the top of the device, near your ear, a short, straight gray stick is. Talking and smiling you are." He looked at Lee, his expression again curious. Or puzzled. "Understand this can you?"

Lee nodded. "Yes. You're talking about my telephone." He reached over to the reading table near his chair and retrieved his cordless telephone, turning the spoon so it pointed at the device. "Is this it?"

FarCaller immediately smiled. "Exactly. This is the device use you to people far away to talk? Our spoon and plate like?"

"Sort of. But what about it?"

"Oh yes," FarCaller said, shaking his head in exasperation. "About the rest of my Sensing now I can talk." He took a deep breath. "As you speak, others listening to you seem to be. Two men. Each has a device, your blue telephone like, against their ears holding. Just after you stop talking the telephone put down, the same with the devices holding they do. Then something on a small black box in front of them they touch, and intently listening to it they begin."

As FarCaller described this part of his Sensing, Lee's stomach cramped and his heartbeat accelerated. "Let me understand this clearly," he began. "You Sense me talking to someone over the device I call a telephone, and while I am doing this, you Sense two other men apparently listening to what I was saying. Is that right?"

"Exactly. None of the Sensing do I understand, but you do. That you understand glad makes me. It's meaning to me explain can you?"

"Absolutely. And you say that this will happen in the near future if I don't do something to prevent it?"

"What I believe, that is," he said, his expression serious, his words cautiously pronounced. "What to change it you can, I know not, because none of it understand do I."

One quick nod. "Your Sensing tells me that someone will soon be listening to my telephone calls. Since I've broken no laws, I must assume those men must be listening illegally." He shook his head back and forth slowly, all the while looking at the floor. "I was hoping I'd be through worrying about someone trying to watch me and what I do, but I guess I was totally wrong: they're not only going to continue watching me, they're going to listen to my telephone calls.

"I thank you, FarCaller. This is bad news but a good warning. I have an idea what I can do to protect myself from their listening. When it's done I'll tell you about it." Without waiting for a response, he said, "Good night, friend," and returned the spoon to his pocket. Then, to no one in particular, he simply said, "Crap!"

Chapter 38

Dangerous Fun

Thanksgiving Eve 2004

Lee had just gotten home from shopping when his telephone rang. Since he received few calls on weekdays, it made him think perhaps something had happened to his folks. He dropped his package on the sofa and snapped up the handset, his heart beating loudly in his ears. "Hello," he said, his voice quavering.

"Hi," came a lovely, soft, sensuous woman's voice. "Thought I'd surprise you. What's up? Made your reservations yet? Glad to hear from me?"

A smile immediately replaced his serious expression as he sat down on the sofa. He let his shoulders slump, relaxing from relief. "You surprised me, Verry. I've not made the reservations yet, and yes, I'm glad to hear from you. I just didn't expect you to call so early." He glanced at his watch. "Oh, guess I shouldn't be surprised. It's nearly 8:30 in Iowa, isn't it?"

"Yep. I've had my Greek salad, had a sip of delicious white wine, and am ready to talk."

Nothing significant was said in the next hour, but both Lee and Verry thoroughly enjoyed their talk. Just as he was about to end the call, he remembered why he had purchased his cell phone in the first place: to keep from using telephones that could be tapped by the people FarCaller sensed. "Do you have a cell phone?"

"Doesn't almost everyone?" She sounded surprised and a bit confused at the question.

"Until today I didn't," he confessed. "How 'bout we use them for our calls?"

"If you want. But why?"

"For one thing, it'll let me make long-distance calls for free. How 'bout that?"

"OK with me," she said, "as long as we keep talking. I usually call by cell phone anyway, and I really enjoy these times, Lee."

Nodding as she spoke, he said simply, "Me too. A lot." Ending the conversation as soon as he gracefully could, Lee opened the box containing his new cell phone and began reading the operations manual.

Chapter 39

The Gushy Call

Late that afternoon, Jeff Gerit's concentration on finding Kaalers was interrupted by the chirp of his telephone. The raspy voice at the other end was its own introduction. "Mr. Jeff, we got the telephone bugs installed, 'n' I think they're workin'."

"What's that mean, Mackie? You 'think' they're working? I thought they either worked or they didn't." Jeff let his impatience with what he thought were stupid answers put an edge on his voice.

Mackie heard it; his attitude immediately changed. "Installed it early yestiddy mornin', Mr. Jeff. Got it workin' for a while yestiddy evenin'. Had a problem after 'bout 'n hour, so we missed the end of it. Got right on the problem, and it's fixed now, I'm thinkin'. Got nothin' from the tap since then, tho."

Jeff thought before responding. "You're telling me he was using his phone, and now he isn't?"

"Don't know that 'cuz we heard jus' that one call, sir." Before Jeff could respond, Mackie added, "But I larned somethin', sir."

"What?"

"Got the name of the gal what called him, Mr. Jeff. They din't say anathin' 'ticular useful, but I thought you'd want to know 'bout her."

Jeff nodded slowly, as if he were talking to a first grader. "You're right, Mackie. Tell me."

"Din't get the caller ID, Mr. Jeff, that was part of the problem with our gear, so all I got was her name 'n' somethin' 'bout Iowar. Her name's odd, sir—sounds like 'Very.' 'Very' from Iowar."

Jeff controlled his anger enough to ask, "And how'd they sound, Mackie?"

"Gushy, Mr. Jeff. Like they's gettin' ready ta do it, if you know what I mean. He's goin' ta Iower ta visit her, so I 'spect they'll be talkin' a lot more 'tween now 'n' then."

"So Kaaler has a girlfriend in Iowa but you don't know where?" The silence on the other end of the line gave Jeff his answer. "And her name sounds something like 'Very.' Did I get all of that right, Mackie?"

The response was barely a whisper. "Yes, sir."

"Send me a copy of the tape." Before Mackie could respond, Jeff's voice turned mean. "And keep listening! Next call, I want the name and phone number of the caller along with a complete tape of what they say. All of that! Got it?"

"Yes, sir, Mr. Jeff. I'll keep listenin'."

Chapter 40

Stupid Calls

Two days after his call about Lee and Verry's "gushy call," Mackie again phoned Jeff Gerit. "Somethin's changed, Mr. Jeff," he began.

"What's that mean? Is the phone tap working?"

He heard his man swallow loudly, as if preparing to say something that might anger Jeff, then take a deep breath. "Mr. Jeff, the taps workin', but we're gettin' nothin' but stupid calls from his fam'ly. Either he just doesn't make many phone calls or doesn't get very many or he's usin' a cell phone. Got no way of checkin' that out because we can't tap cell phone calls. But the way he 'n' that Iowar woman were talkin', he's gotta be talkin' to her a lot. 'N' we don't have a bug in his apartment, so we can't hear what's happenin' when he's in there. I'm here to tell you that gettin' into that place again to bug it will be twice as hard as the first time—when we looked for that spoon thing."

"So we've tapped the phone and all we got for all that work was the name of a woman and the chance she's in Iowa. Is that right?" Jeff made no attempt to hide his frustration and anger from Mackie and emphasized that by slamming the telephone headset down hard enough to make every pen, pencil, writing pad, and desk accessory bounce up and down. The ensuing rattle made him even more angry. "I don't know why I keep that guy around!" he said to himself. Then, as logic took over, he instantly cooled off. "Yeah, I know why: he's a good stalker and recon man and is pretty good at break-ins." He shook his head, his mouth a straight line and his eyes almost closed from frustration. "But he can be so damned stupid sometimes!

"I can't tell Dad we installed a phone tap and the guy doesn't use his phones. Dad woulda shot me if I'd been in his office when I told him we had cameras set up to watch what happened inside that Kaaler guy's place and then he put mirror film over all the windows. Good thing I'm here, and he never leaves Chicago." More thought. "'Course, he could send someone here to get me, but that'd put him squarely in charge of everything we do to find that spoon, and if anything went wrong, he'd have to take the blame all by himself." Now Jeff chuckled. "Dad wouldn't do that to himself for any amount of money. So I'm safe. So far." Visualizing his father's tirade after he hears Jeff's report on the wiretap, he thought, *But I've got to get some better results or I'll be in deep kimchee.*

He thought about how to learn who that Kaaler guy was talking to in Iowa, then slapped his forehead when the solution hit him. *If Gerit Pharmaceuticals can't buy someone to find out who Kaaler's talking to in Iowa, no one can.* His frown of frustration was instantly replaced by a smile as he lifted his telephone and dialed the number of a friend who worked in Communications at Gerit Pharmaceuticals.

Chapter 41

What's Next?

November 30, 2004

"Your guys installed that phone tap over a week ago and you got nothing? NOTHING!" Ben Gerit was yelling so loudly that the papers on his oak desk skidded across the desktop, as if dodging his outburst. His face was red, his eyes glared at the speakerphone, and his jaw muscles bulged with every word. "You had that video bug put up so we could watch that Kaaler guy, and what'd he do? He put mirror film over his windows. The only thing we see is our own cameras! Then you tap his phone to find out who he's talking to, and what'd you get? A partial record of only one frappin' call, a gushy one from a woman somewhere in Iowa. So now we've got two illegal bugs there, Kaaler is actin' like he knows they're there, and we're sitting on our tushes just waiting for him to blow the whistle to the cops. And that'll bring not only the local yokels but the FEDS! So how's he able to counter everything we're doin'?" He stopped talking just long enough to look prayerfully at the solid mahogany beams and panels on his office ceiling. "That's *not* the question," he said, resuming his tirade. "The real question is, how's he *know* what we're doin'? You call that progress? I call it a disaster waiting to happen! Now, *what're you going to do about it?*" He screamed into the telephone, each word accompanied by a fist slamming onto his desk.

Jeff expected his father to rant and rave when he reported what happened to their efforts to watch the Kaaler guy, but the intensity of his dad's rage surprised even him. Jeff said nothing for a few seconds, giving himself time to think of some kind of response and, hopefully, to let his dad's bile cool a bit. When he finally spoke, his voice was low and calm, hoping it would translate into an overall lowering of the anger level in Chicago. "First, I don't know how Kaaler knows what we're doing because I don't think he knows we're doing anything. He never came close enough to the windows to be able to see the video cameras. Remember, Dad, we're using cable optics to run from the corner of the windows to cameras mounted just below the window sill and painted the same color as the wall. The cameras are completely invisible from inside the apartment, and the cables are so small they couldn't be seen unless someone was looking closely for them. Secondly, he didn't run out and buy a cell phone right after we bugged his phone. He had to have it with him on the day of that one call we intercepted, because from that time, we never heard him make a single call from his phone. He only got incoming calls, so we didn't alert him to anything about our tap." Jeff noted his father hadn't interrupted him, considered that to be a sign that his dad was listening instead of boiling, and continued. "Third, I don't know what other kind of surveillance to use except to bug his apartment—which is almost impossible—or to do something to force him out of there. That would give us a chance to install our bugs in his new place during the day, while he is working; and his neighbors, if any, would have no reason to think we were anything but hired hands helping get his place set up. You know the kind: cable TV installers, telephone guys, Internet guys, 'n' like that. But remember, we've seen nothing to indicate he has that power spoon, only that he was trying to contact other Kaalers. Why would we go to the trouble to force him into another place? That's what we've tried. What do *you* think might work?" He stopped talking and waited for a response, his level of concern rising with every passing second of silence from his dad, so much so that he didn't even bother to look around his luxurious apartment or at the Golden Gate Bridge.

Finally his father spoke. But he didn't yell or rant; he whispered, his voice dripping with acid. "Doesn't work that way, Jeff," he said. "I hired you—at a very large salary—to get the power spoon. You make headway only after I threaten you. Well, I'm done threatening. From now on, I promise."

Jeff's palms were now sweaty and his throat tense. When his dad was so angry he didn't yell, someone would get hurt. Jeff had no doubt that his dad's next victim would be him.

"You can keep your job for now. *But* if I don't see real progress soon, I'll not only cut off your money, I'll have someone cut off your balls!" For nearly ten seconds, not a sound came from the Chicago end of the circuit. Then, "Did I make myself clear?"

By now Jeff's forehead was so sweaty that the salty drops were flowing over his eyebrows and into his eyes. He'd seen his father threaten others that way, and those who didn't do as directed were always seriously injured. But he'd never been threatened before. He was in deep trouble, so deep that he believed his life might well be at stake. Making it worse, he knew his thoughts about taking over the company by using the power spoon himself against his dad were doomed to failure because that would take time. And now he didn't have any time to spare. "Yes," he said.

"Good. Just remember: I'll be watching!" With those words the line went dead, and for the first time in his life, Jeff realized how evil his father could be. He immediately called the woman at Gerit Pharmaceuticals who said she'd get the name and number of Kaaler's friend in Iowa. *If she doesn't know it by now, I'm dead!*

Chapter 42

A Metal Grasshopper

December 1, 2004

"Again, something strange Sense I, Lee."

Lee now believed FarCaller's Sensings but didn't believe he had that gift. "Please explain."

FarCaller squinted as if trying to peer at Lee through fog. "A device to me unknown."

With FarCaller's recent Sensings about surveillance of his apartment, Lee's first thought was that it might be a Sensing of a bulldozer crashing through his apartment. "What's it look like?"

"My friend, to describe it I am red faced. A fool you will of me think."

"Never! Our worlds have major differences and many similarities. Describe what you Sensed as carefully as you can."

"Very well, but foolish will I sound."

Lee nodded his head in a gesture FarCaller now recognized as meaning, "Get on with it."

"A very large insect. Short legs has it, and a fat body, but thin wings that in flat circles move." He stopped, closing his eyes. When he opened them, he wore a satisfied smile. "A small circular wing on the end of its body it also has."

By the time FarCaller finished, Lee was smiling. "That is a machine that flies."

FarCaller's eyes widened in disbelief and shock. "Possible that is?"

That question once again made Lee realize how different their worlds were. "Yes, but it takes a lot of special kinds of science and study before they can be made. I don't know either of those subjects well enough to try to explain them, but it doesn't matter. You described a helicopter very accurately."

FarCaller looked relieved. "Glad am I, Lee, because such a thing never before imagine could I." Before Lee could say anything, FarCaller added, "But not so important as something else is that."

"Tell me."

"This machine you enter and to somewhere far away go. But like yourself look you do not."

Lee thought for a few seconds. "Do you remember I told you of the woman who called and Challenged me?"

"Of course. Through the printed paper her, met you. To visit her, plan you."

"True, but I've been trying to decide how I could do that without being recognized. You Sensed what I must do—use a disguise. Thank you."

FarCaller was about to say something when Lee felt as if he were in the air, floating above a scene, watching it unfold before him. *I'm Sensing! I can't believe this!* When he looked closely at the scene and willed himself to "fly" lower, Lee could see FarCaller surrounded by a group of men yelling and carrying large clubs.

"FarCaller! I've just Sensed something—something awful!"

The little man's usually smiling face suddenly turned dark, his eyes widened in apprehension. "What?"

"I think some people are going to attack you, maybe even try to kill you."

It took the better part of an hour for the two men to understand what Lee Sensed, but at the end both knew what FarCaller needed to do.

"This house leave will I, and to a secret place ride will I. There dry and safe is, and food and water have will I until no further danger in my future Sense you. Only then to my home return will I."

"Take your plate or I won't be able to contact you."

"I will. What your plan is?"

"To fly out of here by helicopter, wearing a disguise, just as you Sensed. And I'll take the spoon."

Chapter 43

Thommy K.

November 30, 2004

Lee knew he couldn't develop a useful disguise without assistance. After thinking about how to obtain a good one, he remembered someone who might be able to help: Thomas K. Pajaro, his best friend in college. He was a smart, good-looking Nebraskan whose roots seemed to be an admixture of Finnish, Latino, and something else. Thommy K., as he chose to be called, never talked much about his background even though the two of them spent many hours studying, talking, and occasionally double-dating. Lee recalled that Thommy K. was born and grew up in the South but loved the Midwest, especially Omaha. He had wanted to get a job in a bank there, settle down with some never-described blond and loving woman, and raise little Pajaros.

It took twenty seconds on the Internet to locate a Thomas Pajaro in Plattsmouth, a small town south of Omaha—less to raise someone at the number.

"Hello." A woman's voice.

He's married? "I'm trying to reach a Thommy K. Pajaro, ma'am," Lee said. "Is this his number?"

"Just a minute."

Some muffled conversation Lee couldn't quite make out, then, "This is Thommy K. Pajaro."

After nearly ten minutes of joyous reunion, Thommy K. asked the inevitable question. "Why are you calling out of the blue, Lee? I honestly thought I'd never hear from you after graduation."

The direct approach is the best approach. "I need some help on a matter I'd really rather not explain, if you don't mind."

"Go ahead." Thommy K.'s voice was lowered in both pitch and volume, excitement replaced with caution.

"You worked in Portland during the summers, didn't you?"

"Yes."

"In an area with a fair amount of crime, if I remember correctly."

"Part of a summer lab course. In East Portland. Many families and people there were just one step ahead of the police, as a matter of fact."

"Did you meet anyone who knew how to get fake papers?"

Thommy K.'s voice dropped low and he spoke slowly. "What kind of papers?"

"ID cards, driver's licenses, things like that."

"Lee," his friend said, clearly more confident than a few seconds earlier, "are you in trouble?"

Lee couldn't keep a small snicker from escaping his mouth. "No, but I believe I'm being watched pretty closely concerning something I can't tell you about, and I need to leave Oregon without being followed. Airlines always check IDs when you buy tickets and check your luggage, but I have to be able to go someplace without leaving any trail."

"It's illegal to use a fake ID, Lee."

"I know, but I really don't have much choice." Before Thommy K. could comment, Lee added, "Look, I don't want to get you into any kind of trouble. If you'd like to forget this call, it won't hurt my feelings."

Thommy K. suddenly changed the direction of their conversation. "You've never thought much about my name, have you?"

"Your name?" Lee thought back to their times in college and many of their talks. "Everyone thought you were some mixture of Finn and Latino, with a touch of the Old South thrown in because you used your middle initial. It didn't really matter."

"Actually, it does, Lee. We have more in common than you think."

Lee thought back to their college days. They majored in different subjects. Thommy K. dated blonds; Lee occasionally dated but never did so based on the girl's hair color. Thommy K. liked rock and roll; Lee liked Baroque, Classical, and disco music. Thommy K. dressed in the most modern fashions; Lee wore more traditional clothes. Thommy K.'s parents were divorced; Lee's were happily married. The further he dwelt in memories and comparisons between the two of them, the more differences Lee found.

"OK," he said. "I give up. All I can think of is that, aside from being friends, we had little in common."

"All true, Lee, but you still miss the point. You're thinking about my last name; I'm talking about my middle one."

"For all I know you don't even have one. I never heard it. Remember, we thought you could be from the South."

"But I'm from the Midwest."

This thing's going nowhere. And I don't have a lot of time. Lee let a tinge of exasperation color his words, certain that his friend would notice. "OK, what is it?"

"My middle name is from my mother's family. My grandmother's maiden name was Kaaler."

Lee caught his breath. "How do you spell that?"

Thommy K. didn't respond directly to Lee's question but instead said, "I'm looking for a different career path, and think I may have found a new calling."

Lee's astonishment continued as the two of them completed the Challenge.

When it was correctly accomplished, Thommy K. spoke softly and a little slyly, "Any questions?"

Regaining his composure, Lee asked, "Why didn't you ever tell me?" Then he smiled at the stupidity of the question. He didn't learn about his Kaaler heritage himself until a few months earlier, several years after he and Thommy K. graduated.

"Served no useful purpose," Thommy K. answered. "Besides, I knew about criminals out to get secrets, and for all I knew, you might be one." Before Lee could say any more, his friend asked, "Now, what's going on?"

After Lee told about the surveillance, the break-ins, and Verry, Thommy K. not only admitted he knew people in Portland who dealt in false identity papers, he gave Lee a name and a telephone number. "When you call this guy, tell him you got his name from me and give him my telephone number. Tell him to call me to confirm you're OK. After I talk to him, he'll help you. Guaranteed."

Much to Lee's surprise, Thommy K.'s friend was still at the number Thommy K. provided. As directed, Lee asked the man to call Thommy K.; after about an hour, he called back, telling Lee that Thommy K. vouched for him. When he learned what Lee needed, he said, "Send me eight passport photos and be here in ten days. Four driver's licenses'll hit you for ten grand—cash." Before Lee could end the call, the man added, "And if you're gonna use a disguise, make certain you have the pitchers taken with it, or you'll get caught for sure."

After that call, Lee headed for the nearest drugstore and purchased key items for his departure: washable black hair dye, a false black mustache, and slate eye shadow. He then went to his optometrist for an eye examination and, while there, bought two sets of cosmetic contact lenses: one brown, one blue. Other items he'd need for his trip to Des Moines he'd get just before his departure. The next day, in disguise, he had the photos taken and overnighted them to a general delivery address at the Portland post office. He used the next week and a half planning what he wanted to do with his life. He also spent much time talking with FarCaller. And every evening he and Verry talked, the subjects getting closer and closer to the matter both were as yet unwilling to discuss: their growing affection.

Chapter 44

Quit?

"Lee," Mr. Younhans, Lee's bank manager, said, "you can't keep taking a vacation day every week or so. I need an assistant manager whom I can rely on to be here when I need him. Besides that, you only have a few vacation hours left. What're you going to do if you decide you want more time off?" Mr. Younhans was shorter than average, extremely thin—almost gaunt, with long slender hands and fingers, and a thin mustache moving in a line down to his small carefully trimmed goatee.

Lee wasn't surprised at the man's response to his request for some time off, but he had held out hope he wouldn't be pressed into making a decision that he didn't want to face. Only a few months ago, he was gloriously single, happy in his job, and enjoying his simple life. After being thrust into the role of Guardian, all of that changed. He spent more and more time talking to FarCaller and Verry, thinking about what he should be doing with his new life, and thinking about the need to have a wife and an heir—all things he never expected to face for years to come.

If he lost his job because he took so much time off, he'd have to find another one. That would be especially difficult in Bend, and very hard anywhere in Oregon. If he couldn't find a decent job, he'd have to start living off the profits from his investments, investments FarCaller suggested he make and which had made Lee a millionaire. If he wasn't extremely careful, that change in lifestyle—from working to apparently being part of the "idle rich"—would draw unwanted attention. With the two break-ins and his concern about the false Challenge and the enemies that represented, becoming more visible was one of the last things he wanted.

I can't believe it's come to a drop-dead decision: spend less time being Guardian or quit a good job so I can learn what being a Guardian is all about. He shook his head in frustration and disgust.

Mr. Younhans smiled across his desk at the young man in front of him. "I'll let you have that Friday off, Lee, but that's it. You have some sick time, but if you use it for anything other than being legitimately sick, I'd have to let you go." His serious expression returned. "I wish there were more options, and I'd really hate to lose you, but I have no real alternatives."

As Lee left the bank that afternoon, he knew he had to quit his job, a job he had worked hard to get. When he left college, he had his employment future pretty well planned, starting with a job as an assistant manager at a small branch bank. That was no longer possible. The shock of the discovery of the powers of the spoon, combined with the ever-increasing tasks of learning more about what a Guardian is and should be, and with the certain need to travel out of Oregon, convinced Lee his responsibility to the Kaaler family had to outweigh any other considerations. With that decision came a series of questions that had to be answered. Questions like *If I'm going to be working with FarCaller, I need a place to live that can be made safe from eavesdropping. My apartment will never be that way.* Another: *If I buy a place of my own, how do I hide my sudden wealth?* Almost as the thought entered his mind, he had a solution. He'd tell a few people, including his parents, that his grandmother had provided for a large sum of money to be given him as part of his inheritance when he reached age twenty-three. It was a secret known only to her and her lawyer and was a sealed codicil to her will. Then another question: what would he do if he weren't working at the bank? His response: he would write a history of the Kaaler family and would do a lot of research involving much travel.

He knew he'd have to think more about that cover story, but at least he had a plan. His first action: prepare for his trip to Des Moines. His second: buy a house.

Chapter 45

I Need a Stick House

December 6, 2004

"Pilot Butte Realty. Louise Chenowith speaking. How may I help you?" Lee often called Louise on bank business and always enjoyed it because her little girl voice rang with excitement and pleasure. In all the time he'd worked in the bank, she was the only realtor who ever radiated enthusiasm every time he called her. "Louise, this is Lee Kaaler."

"What can I do for you, Lee? A foreclosure? A title search? Get an appraisal?"

Every time Lee talked to Louise he smiled, and sometimes laughed. This was another of those times. He stifled the laugh but knew his smile could be heard in every word he spoke. "Nothing like that, Louise. I need your help on a confidential personal matter."

This was the first time he'd ever talked to her about anything personal, and the small delay between his last word and her first told him she was surprised. "A personal matter? In real estate?" Her stream of questions stopped, as if her brain had just caught up with what Lee said. "Confidential?"

"Yes. I need your help in buying a home, and I want as few people as possible to know about it."

"A town house? Not something like your apartment: you know we don't handle those kinds of properties."

"No, Louise, I mean a 'stick house.' On a lot. A nice house on a pretty good-sized plot of land outside of Bend. Maybe east of town a few miles."

There was another microsecond when she said nothing. "You're serious, aren't you?"

"Dead serious. I need a home like that, and I need it pretty soon."

Her voice dropped an octave in pitch, another first in their working together. He took it as a sign of confusion or concern on her part. "There are lots of nice places out east, Lee, but they're pretty expensive. Start about three hundred fifty or four hundred thousand. I didn't think you made an awfully lot of money at the bank. Can you qualify for a mortgage that large?"

Lee's initial reaction to her question was anger, followed by a quick realization that she was just trying to qualify his financial situation well enough to make the kind of search he was asking for. "No mortgage, Louise. Cash. And I want you to do all the paperwork for me."

"Cash? You have that much—" She stopped and seemed to take a deep breath. "This is quite a surprise, as you must know. I'm assuming this is not some kind of joke, or anything like that. You really want me to find you a house out in the country?"

"Yes. And I don't want anyone to know I'm the buyer until and unless it is absolutely essential. I want you to handle everything personally, and I'll be glad to pay anything extra this might require. I need the best help I can get on this, someone whom I can trust to keep this quiet. That's only you—my realtor, and Clem Maestre, my lawyer. Just you two. If you need to contact me, tell Clem. He'll pass your message to me, and if I have to, I'll call you back. I know that sounds weird, but it's how I have to operate right now. Will you help me?"

Chapter 46

Flying and Falling

Mid December 2004

Lee took a taxi to the Bend airport and boarded the helicopter he chartered. It flew directly to a downtown Portland heliport. He then taxied to a small hotel in a seedy part of town and picked up his four fake driver's licenses. Returning to downtown Portland, renting a car using one of his aliases, and providing a cash deposit, he drove two hours to SEATAC, the airport between Seattle and Tacoma. Changing his identification again, he flew to Des Moines, arriving that evening. He stayed in a small motel near the middle of the city, under a third false name, although he doubted the clerk cared about anyone's real one. Once in his room, Lee washed off the makeup that had given him an unshaven appearance, rinsed out the dye that had changed his brown and gray hair to dirty black, removed the brown contact lenses, and pulled off the false mustache. Late the next morning he donned his favorite dark blue suit, put on his dark gray London Fog overcoat against the cold Iowa wind, and hailed a cab. Ten minutes later he entered the Tres Senoritas restaurant, nervously checking his wristwatch, making certain he was exactly on time.

Sitting in the foyer on a red velvet chair was a pretty young woman, her large hazel eyes radiating both excitement and apprehension. She looked just like her photo: a small straight nose, full red mouth, and slightly flushed cheeks. She stood when he entered. Lee could hardly take his eyes off her. Her softly coifed auburn hair reached well below her shoulders. Red leather boots with white furry tops exactly matched the red of her blouse and the two ribbons holding her hair back from her face. Her coat was a long dark blue parka with white fur around the hood and at the cuffs, open in front.

"You're Lee, aren't you?" she said, standing as he entered.

"Yes, ma'am. And you're Verry."

A wonderful smile, immediately followed by an obvious sigh of relief. "You look just like your photo. I was afraid it might be ten years old and you'd have a paunch and chubby face." She flashed a second smile. "But you don't."

Lee nodded at the implied compliment. "And you look lovely," he said. "Better than your photo."

"You're sweet." Pointing to her wristwatch, she said, "It's just eleven o'clock. Why don't I show you around Des Moines before we eat?" She looked up at him, her face radiant, eyes wide and moist. When she unabashedly took his arm to lead him to her car, Faerleigh Faar Kaaler fell in love.

Chapter 47

Too Fast?

December 17, 2004

Back in the Mexican restaurant, Lee and Verry sat across from each other in a booth, occasionally letting silly smiles erupt. Their short sightseeing trip was more useful in letting them be together than in teaching Lee about Des Moines. Thanks to the hours they spent on the telephone before he arrived, they started talking about important things right away rather than engaging in the small talk that usually accompanies a first date.

Tres Senoritas was decorated in a theme Lee characterized as "Modern Mexican American." It had square tables with tops of handmade cheap Mexican tiles and serapes and sombreros tacked onto the beige walls. Along the window sills were tourist trinkets—Mexican dolls and hand-carved donkeys pulling crude carts. The lamps hanging over each table and booth had shades made of thin bronze-colored metal perforated with holes in some motif Lee couldn't quite perceive.

In spite of the touristy facade, the aromas from the kitchen were overwhelmingly tantalizing. They, combined with the beautiful woman sitting across from him, made it one of Lee's best dates; and they hadn't even started to eat.

As they munched on corn chips dripping with fresh salsa and warm refried beans, they talked.

"So you were really surprised to see the Challenge ad I placed in the *Oregonian*," Verry said.

"I sure was. I only looked there because I was upset that more Kaalers apparently weren't reading the Challenge ad I'd placed in several newspapers.

I sort of felt guilty about not doing it myself, I guess." When he finished he looked down at the tabletop and nodded, as if to underline the accuracy of his statement. As he resumed eating his chips and dip, Verry spoke.

"You *did* sound a bit tentative," she said, smiling broadly.

He smiled and nodded back. "I was *really* surprised. And after my experience with the answers I got from my ad in the *Oklahoman,* I was concerned about being trapped by the bad guys, whoever they are."

"That's what you said after we started talking on the phone." Her smile became coy. "Now that you've actually seen me, do you still feel threatened?"

He returned the favor, but his smile wasn't coy. "Of course not. In one of Grandmother's letters, she said only true Kaalers would know *exactly* how to Challenge, and you did." Then he softly added, "Plus the other."

A slight frown, head slightly tilted. "What 'other?' You didn't mention any 'other' on the phone."

Lee suddenly felt embarrassed, something he was not accustomed to. "Shouldn't have said anything," he said. Then, looking up into her lovely hazel eyes, he added, "Forget it."

She shook her head quickly. "I can't forget something you've said, Lee. Tell me."

He kept his eyes locked on hers and took a deep breath. *Here goes!* "She also said I would be very attracted to a Kaaler woman. And," he continued, reddening slightly as he became bolder, "she was right."

Verry maintained the eye contact, her cheeks also reddening, her fingers nervously fiddling among themselves. "Did she say anything else about Kaaler women?"

"She said they would make loving wives and wonderful mothers. And that I could trust a Kaaler wife absolutely."

She continued looking directly into his eyes. "Do you believe that?"

He broke the spell by looking down, surprised to find a corn chip in his right hand, suspended above the small bowl of the spicy red salsa. "I do now."

After a few awkward seconds of silence, Verry said, softly, "This is going pretty fast, Lee."

He quickly looked up expecting to find a concerned expression on her face along with a change of heart about their meeting. Instead he saw a wide, caring smile and, when their eyes met again, she reached over and took his left hand in her right.

"I didn't plan it, Verry," he said, grasping her surprisingly warm and strong hand in his. "Believe me."

"But you came here specifically to meet me."

"Yes. To meet the first Kaaler outside my own family group I'd probably ever have the chance to see. And the woman I've been spending hours on the phone with almost every night since I answered your Challenge ad."

"Armed with your grandmother's description of Kaaler women as wives."

A decisive nod. "That too. But when we first talked, I didn't know how old you were or if you were married or anything about you."

They were interrupted by their dinner: a chicken enchilada with sour cream sauce, refried beans, and rice for her; a pork burrito with red sauce, rice, and beans for him. As a touch of class, he ordered piña coladas. At that point, they stopped serious talking and concentrated on serious eating.

After dinner, Verry drove them toward her folks' ranch. On the way, Lee told her of his warning about danger and his use of disguises and false names to hide his trip to meet her. The false names, of course, were illegal—and he told her that also. He told her more than his grandmother would ever have permitted. It felt right, but he didn't mention FarCaller.

"And," he said, clearly about to end his tale, "I have to reluctantly admit that even coming here might have put you at risk. Now that I know you, Verry, I'm sorry to have done that."

She turned away from her driving to look him squarely in the eyes. "Does that mean you're sorry you came?" After asking that question, she returned her attention to the road.

Lee was more disappointed than surprised by her comment then slowly said, "I can't believe you think that."

She again looked at him, this time with a sympathetic smile. "I don't really. And you have to know that I'm glad we met. I'm not afraid of danger for myself, but I'm already worrying about you." She quickly returned her attention to the road and traffic in front of them.

Armed with that admission of affection, Lee decided to take charge. "Is there a place where you can pull off the highway?"

Another glance, trying to see any indication of sickness or disappointment or a change of attitude. "Is something wrong?"

"No, not at all. But can you stop the car?"

"There's a place over this next hill," she said, pointing to the right. "Maybe another mile."

She turned onto a narrow road leading to a small roadside park: two picnic tables, two barbecues, one Port-a-Potty. When she stopped the car in front of one of the tables and turned to talk with Lee, he released his seat belt, slid over next to her, put his left arm around her neck and shoulder, and kissed her: no warning, no request.

She responded immediately and confidently, obviously having reached her own conclusions on that subject. After a few minutes they broke apart, both breathing hard, faces flushed, wearing silly and satisfied smiles.

Then she loosened her seat belt and moved closer to him. This let her hold him with both arms, smell his cologne and touch his face, and kiss him when she wanted, not just when he started it.

Lee broke the silence. "I'd apologize for being so forward, but I guess I don't need to."

She nodded, her head firmly against his left breast from where she could easily look up and kiss him. "I'm glad," she admitted. "I've wanted to kiss you almost since we first met. And I've *never* felt that way before."

"What do we do now, Verry? I live something like eighteen hundred miles from here. There's no way I can commute on weekends, as much as I'd like to. But I want to be with you."

First she kissed him soundly, letting its sweetness last several minutes. Then she broke off the kiss and pulled back a few inches so she could look into his eyes. "You mean you don't have any suggestions?"

Lee leaned back, searching her face for any indication that she wasn't speaking idly. It was clear that she was absolutely serious even though she wore a luminescent smile. "I have several," he admitted, "but we haven't finished our first date yet."

"What's that got to do with anything? We've known each other for months—if you count all those phone calls," she said. Then she pulled his face to hers and again sweetly kissed him, clearly enjoying the way he responded: firmly yet tenderly, with great spirit, and without any semblance of reluctance.

When that embrace finally ended, Lee's mind swarmed with thoughts, sensual, sexual, serious. At the top of the list: *I love her! I really do! But I can't ask her to marry me. Not yet. She might decide I was just too anxious to trust.*

"Well?" she asked.

"Well, what?"

"Are you going to just sit there, or are you going to say something wonderful?"

He couldn't keep the smile from either his voice or his face. "Verry, what I'm thinking, I'm afraid to say. At least so soon after we've met."

She pushed him away, gently yet firmly. "That's silly, Lee. Even your grandmother—bless her lovely heart—told you I could be trusted." Her smile was lovingly sly and quite disarming.

So they talked more about serious things. Like the distance between their homes. And getting serious. Amidst all of this was an inordinate amount of hugging and kissing and caressing.

Within the hour, both knew where they were heading. This time Verry took the lead.

"I want you to meet my parents. Right now. Today. And I want them to know I'm in love with you. Right now. Already."

"Are you sure that's a very good idea? I'm not even certain how sane it is, considering we just met."

She pulled completely away from him, some anger coloring her expression. "Lee Kaaler," she began—and he knew he was in trouble just from her tone of voice—"if you think I'm not certain how I feel, you're stupid. And if there's anything you're not, it's that. I don't care how it sounds: it's real."

Thousands of thoughts suddenly spilled over Lee, wiggling and crying out for attention, demanding all kinds of conflicting responses. The clearest: *Do it, you idiot! Ask her to marry you. You love her, she's a Kaaler, she's willing, she's smart—and she's pretty, too.* And others: *It's too soon, stupid! No one in his right mind asks someone to marry them after knowing them only a few hours—it's setting the stage for disaster, spelled D-I-V-O-R-C-E!*

But he knew what he had to do. Taking her right hand in his but leaving his left arm around her shoulders, he looked directly into her eyes and said, "Verry Willards, I love you and want to spend the rest of my life with you." Lee thought about the magnitude of what he was about to say, then said, "Will you marry me?"

Verry didn't say anything, just lunged at him and planted the deepest, longest, and most sincere kiss he'd ever experienced. When he had to come up for air, he looked down into eyes that were deep pools of intense love.

"Lee, I'd marry you in a minute!" She smiled at him then said, "And that was the most romantic proposal I ever heard."

He was clearly surprised. "You've been proposed to before?"

"Nope," she said, giggling. "But it was still the best!"

At her parents home, after the introductions, Lee insisted he meet with each of Verry's parents separately, and Challenged them. He wasn't surprised that they responded accurately, but they were clearly surprised that he required this of them before they talked about even trivial things. However, once the Challenges were completed and all were in the living room, he answered every one of their questions about himself, his life, and the fear he felt because of the false Challenge. The subject of the Guardian never arose.

He talked to them about coming to Iowa to meet this woman who placed a Challenge ad, why he answered it, and why she had placed it in the first place: because of pressure from her mother to find a good husband. Then, moving from a stuffed chair by the fireplace over to the couch so he could sit by Verry, he put his arm around her and told them he loved her and had already asked her to marry him.

Joyously, she announced she had accepted his proposal and then planted another short but intense kiss on the man who was now her fiancé. Her father was astounded, both at what he heard and what he saw. Her mother was enthralled and overjoyed. Both women ended up in joyous tears, but Lee's happiness was tempered by concerned about the danger his presence probably brought to these wonderful people and, most especially, to the woman he loved.

Chapter 48

He Left

December 19, 2004

"Mr. Gerit, this is Mackie. In Bend."

"Go ahead."

"Been watchin' that Kaaler guy's place like you tol' me."

Like I'd forget. "And?"

"Followed him to the airport yestiddy. He took a taxi. He warn't there long when a chopper flew in and was towed into a hangar. Kaaler went into the same hangar, then the chopper left, flyin' low headin' northeast. Din't see Kaaler come outta there, so I don't know what happened then."

Jeff felt his anger rising and struggled not to explode in the face of such overwhelming stupidity.

"Let me get this straight, Mackie. You've been staking out the apartment of a man we've been chasing for months and only identified a short time ago. Now, when something interesting finally happens, you delay telling me, making it impossible to check where he went. Did I get that correct?"

The silence from the other end of the line said more than anything the man could have managed.

Assuming his hired idiot was still on the line, Jeff continued. "Here's what I want you to do, Mackie. Listen carefully because I don't want it to seem too complicated." Jeff's anger colored his words with so much acid that Mackie couldn't possibly have missed it.

"I want you to watch Kaaler's place. Stay hidden and don't leave unless something really important comes up. Understand?"

"Yes, sir." Mackie's voice was so soft Jeff could barely hear the man.

"Good. Now let's be certain. What are you supposed to do, Mackie?"

"Watch Kaaler's place. Stay there 'til I have sumthin' 'portent to report."

"Very good, Mackie. Any questions?"

"Only one, sir."

"What?" *It'd better be good!*

"Should I take this cell phone with me when I go eat?"

Before responding, Jeff took three deep breaths. All he could think was, *I'm surrounded by my own assassins!* "Did I say you could leave Kaaler's place?"

"No, sir. But I assumed—"

"I'M NOT PAYING YOU TO ASSUME, MACKIE. I'M PAYING YOU TO FOLLOW INSTRUCTIONS!

"Now, listen again. Go to Kaaler's place AND STAY THERE! Have your meals delivered, but stay hidden from Kaaler. Better yet, buy some food on your way there. BUT DON'T LEAVE UNTIL I TELL YOU TO!

"Now do you understand?"

"Yes, sir," was the thoroughly cowed response. "Keep watchin'."

"One more thing, Mackie."

"Yes, sir?"

"If you mess up a simple job like this, you're hamburger." After slamming his phone onto the desk, Jeff thought, *Maybe I'm more like my dad than I imagined.*

Chapter 49

Is This Man Nuts?

December 20, 2004

Lee timed his return to Portland from Seattle for early evening then flew the short hop to Redmond and took a taxi home, arriving at 10:00 p.m. Once in his apartment, he unpacked the electronic equipment he'd purchased in Denver on the flight back from Des Moines.

Looking at the boxes lying on his living room rug, he shook his head at the reasons he bought them. *Most people, if they saw this, would think I'm certifiably insane at worst, paranoid at best. But there's no way I can explain why I'm doing this without revealing the existence of the spoon. That by itself would probably get me institutionalized.*

The next morning, after installing software to secure his Internet connection, he arranged for a friend in Redmond to install the other equipment.

Red Morriss was a former telephone service technician. His appearance belied technical expertise however, because he spent much of his time tending to his Texas longhorns and small bison herd. His clothes were normally dirty or grimy, often peppered with holes and tears, and his long-sleeved flannel shirts were faded, but he knew telecommunications forward and backward.

It took him twenty minutes to install and check Lee's telephone security device. He spent nearly half of that time checking and rechecking something. Finally he looked up from the device sitting on Lee's desk. When he spoke, his deep bass voice was strangely subdued. "You're not going to believe this, Lee."

Lee felt something grab his heart and squeeze. As soon as he realized it was probably nervous tension caused by anticipating the worst, he forced himself to relax somewhat. "Believe what?"

"Your phone's been tapped," he said slowly, almost apologetically. "I've checked and rechecked everything from the connectors to the outside temperature, and I keep finding a tap."

I bought those boxes because I wanted my calls to be private, but I really didn't think my phone would already be tapped. A flash of confirmation of his fears came over him but just as quickly disappeared. *OK. Those people are more serious than I thought. Can't do anything except live with it—for now.* "Can you tell where it's attached?"

Red's expression betrayed quiet astonishment that Lee could take such news so calmly. He'd forgotten Lee bought the tap-tracing equipment for just that purpose. "My guess would be in or near the telephone service box in this apartment complex. That'd be easiest. If they tried it other places, they'd probably be noticed and reported to the Feds by the telephone company."

I have two choices: leave the tap on the line and try to operate knowing it's there or tell the telephone company and have them check it out. If I do that, it'll let whoever's watching me know I'm on to them, but if I don't it'll mean I have no chance of making any private telephone calls unless the line is encrypted. This confirmed his reasons for buying the boxes. *Just using these voice encryption boxes tells someone I want privacy, but it doesn't necessarily tell him I know my telephone's tapped.* "Leave things as they are, Red. I don't know why the line is tapped, but I'll check it. If things don't change soon, I'll call the telephone company." It was a lie, but a necessary one. Necessary to protect Red if anyone should ever ask him about the tap.

Lee paid him and Red departed, more confused than he would ever have believed.

Lee's next act was to list people who might even consider tapping his telephone. His first candidate was the person who gave that incorrect Challenge in Oklahoma City. The second was the thieves who broke into his apartment and stole his spoons. Lee had assumed these two events weren't related but now wasn't so certain. Even so, it was hard to believe the people who Challenged him in Oklahoma City could find him in the state of Oregon, let alone Bend.

The next candidate . . . His list-making stopped. No names or faces came to mind. There had to be someone else. Someone who might dislike him. Another stop. That didn't seem probable because he'd lived in Bend all his life, had a lot of friends but knew of no enemies. Plus he always kept a low profile.

I need to talk to FarCaller about this. Maybe he'll have some insight. A few more seconds of thought and small grin inched its way onto Lee's face.

He stopped his list-making and headed straight for Clem Maestre's office. As he entered, it occurred to him that even Clem might be on the list of possible telephone tappers. Clem knew more than anyone else about Lee's inheritance, as well as about Lee's sudden success in the stock market. Then common sense asserted itself. That wasn't like Clem. *I think.*

Clem was alone. He was also not busy—something he took perverse pleasure in. He strove to be busy all the time so his income would increase, but he liked to sit back and ponder things, let his moderately rotund stomach rest after his usual large lunch. Relaxing after lunch was his special time. Occasionally he even cheated and took a short nap. Today he just looked through the door of his private office into the small mirror placed so he could see whoever entered his reception area. It let him signal Francine when he wanted to be "too busy" to see the visitor. However, at this day's lunch hour he had no such luck. His first visitor of the afternoon was not a new client but a man who had changed drastically in the past few months. Those changes sometimes made Clem uncomfortable. Like holing up in a nice apartment on beautiful days. Like making spur-of-the-moment investments in the stock market—that turned out to be marvelously successful. Like acting paranoid. Now, suddenly Lee was showing up in person instead of conducting his business on the telephone.

"Y'all come on in, Lee." Uncharacteristically, Lee closed Clem's private office door behind him then sat in the client's chair. That told Clem this conversation was going to be serious.

Clem possessed one talent Lee didn't have and probably never would: the ability to make small talk. Where Lee tended to get right to the point, Clem would talk about people's families, the weather, how the new highway bypass was working (or not working), the upcoming election, and how the Lava Bears were doing in football. As soon as Lee sat down with a shoe box-sized carton on his lap, Clem began his small talk, but Lee held up his right hand, much like a traffic cop.

"Clem, we have to speak—confidentially."

"All raht, Lee." Clem ran his hands through his shaggy brown hair and scratched his scalp slightly, arranged his wire-rimmed spectacles carefully on his slightly bulbous nose, then picked up a pencil. Holding it between his hands, he looked straight at Lee. "What's bothering y'all."

Lee responded by placing a box on Clem's desk.

Without looking at it, Clem asked, "What's this? It's not mah birthday." It was a feeble attempt at humor that failed.

"Mine neither, Clem," Lee responded. "Without going into a litany on the subject, I'll just say that my telephone is tapped. Rather than report it, I thought I'd arrange things so I can talk privately to important people in my life." He stopped looking at Clem and let his eyes wander over the wall opposite him, where Clem had his diplomas and certificates of appreciation. Bachelor of arts in political science from LaSalle University, law degree from Stanford. Coach for Odyssey of the Mind at Bend High School. Photos of Clem with the governor. All properly framed, looking very professional against the beige fabric wall covering.

Lee returned his attention to the lawyer in the brown herringbone suit, white shirt, and, to Lee, an absolutely awful necktie sporting nearly every color of the rainbow arranged in a kaleidoscope of small squares. "I bought you a good cyphony box—it scrambles speech. We can use it when we talk to each other and be certain no one can understand us."

Clem picked up the box, hefted it, and looked at the picture of the innocuous device inside. *Lee may be over the edge.*

Answering a series of questions, Lee convinced the lawyer that there really was a tap on his phone. Then Clem learned that Lee made a trip to Iowa using false identities to meet someone about whom Lee refused to provide additional specifics. *He doesn't seem crazy. Eccentric, perhaps. But not crazy.* Then another quick thought: *How would Ah know? Ah'm a lawyer, not a psychiatrist.*

Lee was out of the office before Clem could ask any more questions, leaving the lawyer holding a box which, so far as he was concerned, performed black magic.

Clem next called the only people he knew who really cared about Lee and who would give straight answers: Lee's parents. They were surprised at Lee's actions but more concerned about Clem's suggestion that Lee get some "spirited counseling" for the things Lee thought might be happening to him.

Throughout the conversation, Lee's father kept repeating that his own mother—Lee's grandmother—was "a little eccentric" and that he believed Lee might have inherited that tendency. "You know Lee," was the father's comment. "He wouldn't hurt a flea—almost literally. If he feels your calls need to go through some kind of scrambling box, and if he can afford to buy that box, I say let him. He's not hurting anyone, it's his money, and he's old enough to look after his own affairs."

After Clem completed the call, he was convinced Lee's entire family was, and always had been, a bit "out to lunch."

Chapter 50

Security and Treachery

December 20, 2004

Because Lee didn't expect his parents to understand his concerns about being hunted, he never discussed the subject with them. So that afternoon, when he broached the subject of a device to scramble calls between them, they reacted much as Clem had.

"Lee," his father began, "this makes no sense. Why on earth would anyone want to put in some black box to keep people from overhearing their telephone calls, when tapping telephones is illegal? I mean, I can understand why a lawyer might have one, and I told Clem Maestre that. But us? A couple of retired people? Your parents? Doesn't make sense."

I've got a long row to hoe, was Lee's first thought, followed immediately by *Clem must have called my folks just after I left that scrambler with him. Now I don't know if he's on my side.*

Lee ignored his mother for the time being because she would always say his dad made the decisions (which everyone knew just wasn't so). His dad made no big decisions without discussing them with her and getting her concurrence. "That isn't so, Dad. If it were, I couldn't even purchase devices like this," he said, pointing at the cyphony box sitting on their coffee table. "The only reason they're sold is because there's a market for them. And while companies use them to keep their proprietary stuff from being stolen, there are other reasons for having them, personal ones."

His father interrupted Lee. "Like what?"

"Like finances. Or medical problems. Or details of a will. Or, like in this case, because someone in the family believes they'll need to talk about sensitive things in the future. These two break-ins have made me cautious—things like that."

"But, Lee, dear," his mother said, "you know you can discuss these things with us any time you want—and we just live across town from you. There's no time lost just driving from your house to ours."

They've both decided against it. He decided to gracefully back out, but not surrender. "Fine," he said, his jaw firm, his eyes glaring with anger and frustration but his voice calm. "Nothing sensitive is ever going to happen. We'll never need to talk using one of these boxes. You already know all the things that are going to happen in the future and see no reason to have one of these things. Is that right?"

He sounded reasonable, but he clearly wasn't. Fortunately his mother was more attuned to nuances than his father and realized that Lee wouldn't have subjected himself to this kind of treatment if he didn't believe it was necessary.

"Faar, dear," she said to her husband, "it can't hurt just to keep the box in the house. After all, he's already purchased it."

Lee's dad looked at her, then Lee, then back at his wife: he'd been outvoted. "Fine. Now let's talk about something else."

* * *

"Macknell here, Mr. Jeff."

"Go ahead, Mackie. What's happening to our favorite Kaaler?"

"For one thing, he's gotta think someone's watching him, 'cause he's doin' things."

"'Things' doesn't cut it. Be specific."

"He keeps the blinds down almost all the time he's there. When he leaves, the blinds go up; he goes straight into town, does something, and comes right back. Then he puts the blinds down. Doesn't hang around, hardly ever even goes to restaurants—which he useta do a lot. And now he's usin' a scrambler."

Mackie assumed Jeff's silence was to allow the man to think about the report. But Jeff couldn't talk because he was so mad his jaw muscles almost cramped. Finally, after several deep breaths to regain control of his temper, he very slowly and quietly said, "How did he find the taps, Mackie?"

Mackie was no genius but knew he was in trouble again. He did the only thing he knew: he tried to cover his tracks. "Don't know, boss. Really don't. We were so careful puttin' that thing in that there's no way we could have been seen. Our recorders don't make a sound on the line, and—"

"BUT HE FOUND OUT!" Jeff screamed. "One of the only ways we have of tracking him is through his telephone, and he's on to us!"

Before Mackie could say anything else, Jeff's next question shot out. "What about the Internet? Have you screwed that up too?"

"Boss, we haven't screwed up anything." The man's words were spewing out of his mouth almost without a break for thought. In the past, Jeff's temper had resulted in some of Mackie's friends disappearing for good, and Mackie didn't want to be the next. "This guy uses the Internet a lot, but when he gets to the good parts, he uses some kinda security software we can't break. But we know who he contacts."

No time to think, no time for Mackie to relax even the slightest. "Who, then? Who's he contact?"

"Places that track down families, graveyard registers, people who keep track of stuff that happened about a hundert years ago. Newspapers, 'n' some kind of places where they store old books 'n' stuff, college liberries. Like that."

Jeff's voice was even softer than before, and Mackie's fears increased accordingly. "And when were you going to tell me about this if I hadn't just asked, Mackie? NEXT CHRISTMAS?" Jeff was now yelling so loudly Mackie could hardly understand the words, but the emotions were unmistakable.

Before he could respond, Jeff broke the contact. Mackie broke out in a cold sweat then made a panicky call.

Chapter 51

Betrayal

Right after talking to Jeff, Mackie made a hurried call to Ebenezer Gerit in Chicago. "Mr. Gerit, this is Macknell Foster. In Bend."

Ben Gerit had attained his considerable wealth by listening when others talked. A call directly from one of Jeff's men demanded his undivided attention. "I remember meeting you a few years ago, Mackie. Why are you calling?"

By the time Mackie finished his tale, the older Gerit was furious and his voice betrayed it. Whenever Mackie seemed to back off a bit in response, Ben reassured the cowboy that *he* was not in trouble, but his *story* was upsetting. He also said he appreciated Mackie calling to report his concerns.

"Do you have enough money to live on, Mackie? If you don't, I'll be glad to help."

"Not needed, sir," was the quick response. "I'm gittin' 'nuff. That's not why I called, sir."

After promising to provide whatever support or protection Mackie needed, Ben ended the call, immediately following it with one to his own man in Bend: Mackie was to be protected. And then, at the right time, he would be wrung dry of anything he knew about Jeff and Jeff's actions.

My son's betraying me. Even as he thought this, Ben couldn't keep a small smile from edging its way onto his face. *But now I've got enough information to neutralize anything Jeff tries, starting with buying off more of his men.*

Chapter 52

No Trail at All

December 22, 2004

Early the next morning, Jeff Gerit received another call from Mackie. When Mackie was stressed, his raspy voice would scratch the copper in the telephone wires connecting the two. Like now. "This is Mackie."

"I'm listening." Jeff's temper still churned from Mackie's last call.

"Been makin' some calls. Found the helicopter comp'ny that flew the Kaaler guy to Portland."

Finally! Useful results. "To Portland airport?"

"No. Hotel heliport. Downtown. Di'n't leave Portland under his own name."

"The airlines gave you that?"

"Don't think you wanta know how I got it."

That's a good answer. He may be smarter than I thought. "OK. But I could kill you for not finding Kaaler's trail in Portland. Seems as how that could be pretty simple."

Mackie said nothing for a second, then said, "Know what I'd do if I was tryin' to hide?"

This scumbag's been around other scum pretty long. I might learn something. "Tell me."

"I'd git some fake ID, put on a wig 'n' glasses, or a beard 'n' colored contact lenses, 'n' take the train or bus to Seattle. Rent a car in Seattle 'n' drive to wherever I wanted. Or take a plane usin' a false name. No one'd know me or where I was goin'."

Jeff carefully absorbed Mackie's words. "If that's true," he said, "it means we probably could never find him."

"Right. First, we'd hafta find who made his fake IDs so we could learn the names our guy used. In Portland that'd be purt' near imposs'ble 'less'n we had a whole lotta time."

"OK, Mackie," Jeff said, closing the conversation, "that's useful. Keep watching Kaaler's place. Report *anything* that happens. Right away." A minuscule break for emphasis, then, "Anything. And right away. Understand?"

Chapter 53

This's Not Weird

"Clem, this is Lee."
"Hi theah, mah friend. What can Ah do for you?"
"You remember the box I left in your office?"
"Certainly. It's right next to mah telephone."
"Is it connected?"
"Yes. Why?"
"Is it turned on?"
"Yes."
"When I count to three, press the red button. OK?"
"Fine."
"One. Two. Three." Lee pressed the encryption button on his scrambler and listened. First there was silence, then white noise, then the connection was again silent.
"Can you hear me, Clem?"
The lawyer couldn't keep his smile out of his voice. "Certainly can, Lee. Makes me feel like James Bond."
"Nice box, hunh?"
"Very. Now will y'all tell me why we're doin' this?"
I'm finally making progress. "You remember I said my telephone line was tapped? And you doubted it?"
Clem shook his head up and down several times while he spoke. "Yes, Ah did. And Ah'm still not convinced it's true. But this scrambler thing tells me y'all absolutely believe it."
"I need a couple of favors, Clem. You're the only guy I can trust. That's why this call is scrambled."
"Tell me what y'all want: unless it's illegal."

Lee sensed the "joke" was more serious than humorous. *Why would he think I'd want him to do something illegal?* "I want you to purchase four digital cell phones, activate them here in Bend, in your name, using your address. Then I'll want them mailed to certain people. I'll pay the charges, of course."

"That's it? That's all?" The relief in his voice was nearly tangible.

"Yes. Today, if at all possible. Plus I want you to use this scrambler whenever you call me here in Bend. You already know you can't use the scrambler on cell phones."

"Then why do y'all want the cell phones?"

"I have to be able to contact certain people on short notice, and I'll not always be near a regular phone. With cell phones, I'll almost be guaranteed to be able to talk to them privately, anytime. You and I are the only people who'll have their cell phone numbers."

"Lee," the portly lawyer said, speaking slowly and carefully, letting "serious" color his words, "are y'all evah goin' t' tell me what this is all about?"

"Not everything." Lee thought about Clem's question. "Does this mean you won't help me?"

"Course not. Ah'm just curious 'bout all the secrecy, y'all's incredible luck on the stock market, and all the security measures y'all're taking. Y'all have to admit it looks pretty weird."

"Not from my end."

Chapter 54

Talk Nice

December 23, 2004

"This is Macknell again, Mr. Gerit."

Ben Gerit immediately recognized Mackie's voice. "Everything OK?"

"Yes, sir."

"No problems with Jeff's people?"

"No, sir. None. In fact, coupla of 'em think I done the right thing."

Ben smiled. *Nice to know I have friends, even my son's employees.* "If they need work, you know what to do?"

"Yes, sir. Let you know, then give 'em your phone number."

"Exactly. Now tell me why you're calling."

"Well, sir, I thought you'd wanna know what's happ'nin' here."

"Is there something interesting to report?"

"Nothin' excitin', sir. Thought you'd like reports every few days or so, just to keep on top of things." Mackie stopped talking, expecting one of the diatribes he usually got from Jeff. When he heard nothing, he took a quick puff on his ubiquitous cigarette then continued. "Kaaler installed more security systems 'round his place. Infrared detectors on the doors and windows, things like you see in banks 'n' stuff. Uses the scrambler talkin' to his lawyer, but so far he's not usin' it to call anyone else. All we can do is record the calls he makes 'n' gits on the phone."

"Keep at it. You never know when we might get lucky."

"Yes, sir. Hope so, sir." Another quick puff, then he threw the butt onto the ground. "Told you we thought he flew to Portland by chopper, didn't I, sir?"

"You did, Mackie."

"Well, sir, we never really saw him, and no one identified him in Portland."

"And you said it would be very difficult to do so unless we knew what names and disguises he used."

"Yes, sir. Well, sir, can't prove he ever really left his house, sir."

Gerit's eyes flitted around his office as he thought about what Mackie just said. "I'm not certain what you mean, Mackie."

"Sir, we proved he hired a chopper to fly to Portland but can't prove he was in it. The pilot and people at the charter place must have got some purty big tips, sir, 'cause they won't say nothin'." Another short silence as Mackie mentally cringed from a possible tirade. Again none came, and again he continued. "Wanted you to know, sir. Don't want to surprise you later on."

Mackie's either an idiot or a genius. Either way, I have to trust him. "Just keep at it, Mackie. Let me know anything else that develops. Especially about any trips Kaaler makes. Or looks like he's making."

"Yes, sir. 'N' thank you, sir."

"For what, Mackie?"

"For speakin' nice, sir."

Gerit gently laid down the telephone handset and leaned back in his soft chair. *Mackie's a jailbird of sorts, but he's honest with me, he's afraid of Jeff, and he's doing all he can. I just don't know if he knows all that can be done.*

Chapter 55

FarCaller's Plea

Christmas Eve, 2004

On the way back from last-minute Christmas shopping, all Lee could think about was how to identify people he could trust. *Someone's checking on what I'm doing. That probably means they're from around here—at least some of them.* He again tried to list those he felt could be trusted, calling their names out as they came to mind. After doing this almost continually since he left his parent's home the previous evening, Lee's entire list had five entries: his parents, Clem Maestre, and Red, the telecoms guy. And Verry.

At the thought of her, all other thinking was impossible. He pictured her in his mind, reliving the entire time they were together. He saw her dress, remembered how it looked on her. Her lips and how soft and sweet they were, and the way she kissed him to emphasize how much she cared for and wanted him. And how it almost drove him insane. *Gotta stop this! There's too much going on to let myself stop thinking about how to protect myself and the spoon.*

"Spoon" reminded him of FarCaller.

Maybe he can help by telling me about the future. And Verry. And how to keep her out of danger.

Back in his apartment, he walked across his living room to the dining nook and its window overlooking Mirror Pond. After a few minutes enjoying the pastoral view, he closed the blinds and walked back to his rocker. Once settled, he took the spoon from his shirt pocket, held it tightly in his right hand, and screamed his thoughts. *FarCaller! Can you hear me?*

Lee repeated this for nearly fifteen minutes. About the time he felt something was either wrong with him or with the spoon, he heard FarCaller's voice, looked into the spoon, and saw a familiar face with an unfamiliar appearance. FarCaller, usually neatly groomed and clean shaven, was unshaven, with messy hair and rumpled clothes. His head jerked back and forth, as if he were afraid of something or someone.

"Lee! Your help need I! To kill me someone tries!"

Chapter 56

They're Not Friends!

Lee sat upright, eyes searching the room as if he himself were threatened. "What do you need?"

Breathing hard, still looking around him for something that clearly frightened him, he said, "What you Sense, tell me."

Lee closed his eyes and thought about his friend, at first Sensing nothing. Then, as before, he felt lifted, found himself looking down on a small bush-covered hill. Near the top, he could see the shadow of a small cave entrance.

A thin trail of smoke wended its way upward from the base of the hill. Willing himself closer to the source, he saw people assembling piles of dry grasses and small twigs. *They're going to burn FarCaller out! Or up!*

Continuing his surveillance, he "moved" his vision around the hill, looking for something—anything—that might give more direct insight into FarCaller's future. Near the base on the other side of the mound, he saw another small opening.

"FarCaller, are you in the cave at the top of a hill?"

"Yes."

"Does it go deeper into the hill?"

"Not know I. At the entrance am I, on my friends building fires down looking."

Why does he keep calling them "friends?" "There's another opening on the opposite side of the hill, at the bottom. Maybe you're in a natural tunnel."

Lee kept his view moving around the hill, looking for other possible escape routes for his friend. After circling the hill several times, looking for other possible exits but seeing none, he saw a familiar head slowly emerge from the hole he first saw, at the bottom of the hill. FarCaller stayed low in the grass then slowly raised his head to look around. Apparently seeing no one else, he slithered under some of the bushes protecting him from direct view by anyone standing at the base of the hill. At that point, Lee ended his Sensing.

"That's it! I see you coming out of the hole at the bottom of the hill. It must really be a tunnel. Continue on through the cave to the bottom of the hill, then call me as soon as you're safe."

"Again, thank you do I, Lee. To cause so much trouble sorry am I."

"Stop talking that way. It's no trouble for a friend to help a friend. Just get away, and find someplace safe."

Chapter 57

Discontent

The winter passed slowly for Lee and Verry. In Bend, the weather was cold, nights below freezing, little snow, partly cloudy skies, gusty winds. The few leafy trees were now nude, the desert colors were now muted, the normal fragrances of juniper and sage brush gone, replaced by whiffs from nearby farms. In Des Moines, the temperatures huddled between zero and freezing, the westerly winds were strong and gusty, everything was white or gray, and most people didn't take deep breaths because the cold air hurt the inside of their noses and lungs. The best things about the winter in both places were the Christmas decorations on eaves and peeking through windows, covering shopping malls with flashing and snakelike lights flickering and flying around like lost trains, and the joyous songs filling the air and airwaves.

For the first time in their lives, both Lee and Verry wished they could spend Christmas with each other rather than participate in their families' traditional holiday activities. Their Christmas gifts to each other were expensive and carefully chosen. Lee sent Verry five pink crystal hearts nesting in a transparent sphere-shaped crystal Christmas ornament. The largest heart was the size of a golf ball, the smallest barely a half inch across. His card to her read, "Keep these in your heart 'til we're together again." Verry's gift to Lee was a light blue faux suede shirt with a matching handkerchief and a complementary silk necktie. Her card read, "Wear this when we next see each other so I can see if it looks as wonderful on you in person as it does in my dreams."

Chapter 58

Whom Can I Trust?

December 26, 2004

Lee let his recliner fit against him, imparting a sense of comfort he knew was false but nevertheless important. *Have to know whom I can trust.* He called FarCaller. This time there was no delay: FarCaller apparently expected the call.

"My life you saved when last talked we. In fact, so surprised at my escape were my friends that now special powers possess I, think they. But instead of jealous being, afraid are they."

"Is that good?" Lee asked. "Couldn't that lead to more danger?"

"For some time not, think I," was the response. "About magic seldom we think, because seldom confront it do we. In my case, about magic never talked have I, but that use it my family and friends now believe do I. Powerful in their eyes that makes me, so to leave me alone started have they. Especially my mother. About a job getting and more things to her giving, bothering me stopped, did she."

"Why do you call those people friends, FarCaller? They were selfish, mean, dangerous, and were thinking about *killing* you. Friends don't do that." Lee was now looking directly at FarCaller's image.

FarCaller picked up on the seriousness. "But why I am as am I, know not they. About the spoon and plate or about you, know not they, and how we each other help also know not they. If those things knew they, so confident a danger to them was I, not would think they."

"And you can't tell them the truth."

"Exactly. Just as no one about me tell you, about you no one tell I."

"But," Lee inserted, now sitting more upright in his recliner as the conversation became more serious, "I will tell my wife when I marry. You haven't told yours."

FarCaller looked at Lee, saying nothing for a few seconds. Then he nodded once and spoke. "True that is. From someone help get I, knows she, but about the gift nothing knows she. And about you nothing knows she."

"And the reason?"

FarCaller looked at Lee, then looked away for a few seconds, then back. For almost a half minute he repeated this behavior, then, "In truth, because our marriage arranged was. A wonderful wife and helpmate sometimes is she, but from the parts of our family who about the FarCaller heritage knew, not is she. Nor my mother. So as you do not about the spoon your friends tell, how you and I communicate, not tell my wife do I. My escape magic was, thinks she. Actually, magic it is, not?"

Lee nodded as he spoke. "Yes, it actually *is* magic. And until this happened, I would never have believed it." Lee had more questions, but it was clear FarCaller wasn't prepared to discuss them, because he hadn't really thought out much of what was happening. Like why his wife would try to hurt him in order to get "things." Then it hit Lee: FarCaller's arranged marriage was a bad match, and he didn't want to talk about it! *Time to move on.*

"FarCaller, I need to talk to you about something. Perhaps something you can help me with."

His friend's attitude instantly changed from thoughtful and pensive to fully attentive. "What?"

"I have no way of telling my friends from my enemies. It's especially important, because I have to go back to Iowa soon."

FarCaller started to say something, but Lee held up his hand, stopping the question before it was asked.

"When I was there, I met and fell in love with a Kaaler woman. I want to be with her again and make plans for our wedding. When you last helped me, I used disguises and false names to keep my identity secret. However, I can't do that in a marriage. Verry—the woman I'm talking about—and her family are willing and ready to protect me. But there are few Kaalers where she lives, and I won't be moving in Kaaler circles most of my life. Is there a way you can help me determine if a stranger is a friend or enemy?"

FarCaller's expression went blank, his eyes blinked in confusion and thought. "Sense your future can I, but the possible actions of others, not can I." He thought more then looked directly into Lee's eyes and shook his head. "No way that to do know I. Failed you have I."

Chapter 59

Anything's Fair

December 27, 2004

"What?" Jeff couldn't believe what his man was telling him. "Mackie's gone?"

"Not gone away, sir," was the response. "He's still in Bend, but he's working for your father. Won't talk to us about anything serious."

Jeff leaned back in his chair, trying to relax even though he knew the effort was doomed to failure. Whenever something as bad as this happened, he couldn't relax until he took what he considered appropriate action. That didn't include throwing something.

So Dad bought one of my men to help him. His anger subsided, replaced by cold determination. *I have to show Dad I know what he's done without telling him.* He stopped thinking and let his mind roam.

"Banjo?"

"Yes, sir."

"Arrange a traffic accident for Mackie. A serious one." *Mackie's one of his buddies. This'll not only get rid of Mackie, it'll tell me a lot about Banjo.*

At first there was only silence on the other end of the line. Then, "Understand."

Jeff replaced the handset, ending the long-distance call, and thought some more. This time he didn't remain in his chair but paced around his office, looking out at the bay, thinking about the people enjoying their sailboats as they flitted back and forth across the blue waters. *Some people have their money and time to enjoy it. Others have to keep earning theirs.* After a few minutes, he knew what to do.

A call to his father's bookkeeper increased the amount of money he siphoned off his father's investments. Shares would be sold and the proceeds deposited in an account ostensibly in his father's name but accessible to Jeff through a few secret machinations implemented by the friendly accountant. *For a good percentage of the take.*

This'll make it harder for good old Dad to keep financing his own efforts to get control of the spoon. He smiled wryly. *Nice of him to finance both of our efforts.*

Another call, this one to a reporter friend with a Chicago paper. *It's a terrible thing,* he thought, *when a man of the stature of Ebenezer Gerit suffers so many business losses. It's even worse when the newspapers begin reporting rumors to that effect.* Another smile, this one broad and beaming.

Chapter 60

Talk to the Burglar

Mid January 2005

It was after midnight when the phone's insistent ring roused Lee from deep sleep. He fumbled around, trying to find it then picked it up. "Hello," he said, his voice unsteady from being awakened.

"Lee, this is your dad." Hearing his father's normally steady voice colored with a quaver of fear brought Lee straight out of his sleep-induced stupor.

"Are you OK? Why are you calling me so late?"

"I'm sorry for awakening you, Lee, but we thought you ought to know."

"Darn it, Dad! Know what? Are you OK? Is Mom OK?"

"Well, yes, as a matter of fact. We're OK. But we thought you should know that our home was just burgled—or at least a man broke in and tried to steal something."

By now Lee was fully awake. "Did he get anything? How did you know he was there? What—"

His father cut him off in midsentence, something totally out of character for the normally quiet and almost withdrawn man. "We took your advice and bought a burglar alarm system. Turns out you were right about our needing it, son. The man set it off and the police were here within minutes. In fact, we got a telephone check from the police about the same time a squad car arrived. They were very nice. Quite professional."

"Dad, I want to know if anything was taken, if the police captured the burglar—all of that."

"Yes, son, I know." He heard his father take a deep breath then heard something muffled being spoken. "Your mother says nothing was taken so far as she can tell. At least not yet."

"You don't know?"

"I only know they took him away. The police arrested the man on the sidewalk just down the way a bit, then took him to jail, I think."

His dad's answer startled Lee. *Being on the sidewalk right after a burglary doesn't make sense.* "OK, Dad. I'm coming right over."

"I don't understand, Lee. What is there to learn besides he wanted to steal something? Surely you don't think there was anything else involved, do you? And why would you think such a thing? Your mother says to tell you not to worry, and—"

Lee cut him off by simply pushing the Off button on the handset, then pulled on his favorite sweatshirt, his flannel-lined jeans, his old boots and hustled to the garage.

He was at their place in less than ten minutes, having broken every speed law between his home and theirs without spinning out of control on the icy streets. Once satisfied they were not injured, he drove north of town to the sheriff's office, where the county jail held both city and state law offenders.

Bend, Oregon, was a growing and industrious city, a prosperous one, but small by many people's standards. It had just over fifty-five thousand people but was in the center of one of the most popular growth areas in the country, so it had a constant influx of outsiders. On any given day, you could see license plates from nearly every state in the Union, plus many Canadian provinces. Because of that, there were people who needed but couldn't find jobs; and that led to an upsurge in petty theft, burglaries, and occasional muggings.

Lee knew the desk sergeant, Wilson Beamer, because they attended the same church; but they weren't really friends. Will said the burglar didn't even try to run from the police when they arrived—they'd never had a burglar hang around after breaking into a house. While booking him, the burglar told them he was from Idaho and was a stranger in Bend, but the police didn't believe him because he'd been seen hanging around one of the local minibreweries for several months. He'd never been in trouble in Bend before, but they expected the fingerprint search from the national files to turn up something interesting.

While Lee was there, the sergeant took a call on the intercom. Speaking guardedly and occasionally glancing up at Lee, he replaced the instrument and looked at Lee, a puzzled expression on his face.

"Did your dad recognize this guy, Lee?"

"He didn't say, but I'm sure he'd have told the police if he did. Based on what you said about the guy's hangouts, I'd be surprised if he'd ever even seen my dad, let alone their house."

"And you don't know him?"

At first Lee chuckled, as if the question were asked in jest. But when he realized his friend was serious, Lee quickly changed his demeanor. "Will," he said, "I don't know the man's name, because you never said it. I haven't seen his photos because you haven't shown them to me. There's *no way* I could know if I know him—if you get what I mean."

The sergeant looked at Lee for several seconds, his face not displaying doubt so much as deep thought. Then he nodded once and said, "Right." Reaching behind him, he picked up an official file. Quickly opening it, he held it up and showed Lee a photograph.

The man in the photo was thin, almost gaunt, had a long but thin mustache, dark eyes deep-set into his skull, ears that stuck out from his head, and bushy and unkempt black hair.

"This the burglar?" Lee asked.

A slow nod.

"Never seen him."

Will glanced at the clock on his desk. Lee quickly checked his wristwatch: 2:35 a.m. "He's been here a little over an hour and a half, Lee. Answered our questions like he was used to the drill, offered no information on his own. 'Bout what you'd expect from a petty criminal, part-time laborer—you know the type."

Lee nodded as if he understood, even though he wasn't familiar with small-time crooks at all.

"That call," Will said, nodding toward the intercom handset he'd just set down, "was from the jail duty officer. He said this guy"—tapping on the custody folder—"just asked for *you*."

Chapter 61

We Want It!

After swearing Lee to secrecy about being allowed into the cellblock instead of being led to the visitors' room as was usually done, one of the deputies took Lee directly to the cellblock. Once there, Lee was handed off to a jailer and escorted to the cell holding the man who burgled Lee's parents' home.

When the deputy knocked on the cell door, its occupant moved to the door and peered through the small barred window just below waist height.

"Your name Kaaler?" His voice was high and tinny.

Lee knelt so he could see the man's face and was a bit taken aback at the man's directness. He answered in kind. "One of them."

"This isn't a game, mister," the little man said, his voice both menacing and insistent. "You got an apartment near the river?"

Lee maintained eye contact with the burglar, but his mind was whirling. *How does the guy who broke into Dad's place know this about me?* He nodded.

"Listen, Kaaler," the man began, "I'm in this place fer only one reason, and it ain't burglary. It's ta tell ya sumpth'n."

Lee's eyes betrayed his surprise. Before he could respond, the small dark man continued. "Ya got somethin' my boss wants. He said t' tell ya that we can reach anyone ya know, do anythin' we want to 'em, and ya can't stop him, no matter how hard ya try."

Lee felt a hot sphere begin to build inside his chest, throbbing in synch with his heart, threatening to devour him.

"Why are you telling me this? I don't know you or your boss."

"It's what 'm paid ta do, mister."

"But you haven't said why your boss told you to say this. Or what he wants. Or who he is."

"Won't say who he is. He calls ya a Guardian 'n' wants that spoon yer guardin'."

Chapter 62

Why Have a Guardian?

As Lee walked back to his car, one thought kept gnawing away at him: *These people know I have a spoon, and I have no idea how they know it. They think it's powerful but can't know what it does. None of them has ever seen it or knows how it works or that they need the gift to use it.*

On the drive back to his apartment, he kept turning the night's events over in his mind. *I can't believe the Kaalers have been protecting the spoon and its powers for generations just for the wealth it could bring the Guardian.* His thoughts were interrupted by an eighteen-wheeler blocking the intersection where he usually turned to return home. *There has to be something else, something incredibly special about the spoon's powers. But why didn't Grandma mention it in her letters? Why would she leave me to flail around like this?*

Chapter 63

Scare Him!

Later that morning, Jeff Gerit received a call from his man Briggs, in Bend. Tapping the speakerphone button, he said, "Go ahead, Briggs."

"Two things, Mr. Jeff. Mackie was in a bad car accident, and Tigger delivered your message."

Jeff thought about the report on Mackie. "Tell me about Mackie. I thought he was a pretty good driver."

"He was, Mr. Jeff. Broadsided in front of a bar south of town. Truck's brakes failed; rammed Mackie's pickup. Killed him."

"And the other driver?"

"Can't find him, sir."

"What's that mean? Didn't the police interrogate him? Doesn't he have a name and address?"

"Yes, sir. But after he was interrogated by the police, he disappeared."

"Do you mean he *holed up* somewhere and no one can find him, or do you mean he's left town without a trace?"

"Left town. Someone paid his bail in cash. Name and address were false."

"You mean Mackie was murdered and the murderer got away?" Jeff yelled.

"My opinion, sir?"

"Of course!" he yelled. "Why do you think I asked?"

Briggs was taken aback at the ferocity of Jeff's response, but not so much that he didn't realize he was in a dangerous position with this very rich and powerful man. "I think someone wiped him, sir. He'd never had any trouble until he started working with us, then suddenly this happens. Especially the part about the driver's ID being rigged."

Jeff began pacing the floor, smiling. *So it's done. Just like I wanted. Mackie double-crossed me. Should be no way for anyone to learn that I arranged it.* "Thanks, Briggs. Tell the guys to take care of any family Mackie might have. If they need money, just let me know. But don't tell them Mackie worked for me."

"Will do, sir."

"One more thing, Briggs."

"Yes, sir?"

"You said Tigger delivered my message to Kaaler?"

"Yes, sir. Just like you said."

"And he called Kaaler a 'Guardian?'"

"Yes, sir."

"What did Kaaler say or do then?"

"Nothin'."

"Nothing at all? Didn't ask what Tigger meant, or anything?"

"Nothin', sir. He just left the jail."

"Okay, Briggs, I want you to bail Tigger out of jail. Tell him I'll get a good lawyer for him, and I'll send you $500 to give him for his efforts. Make sure he gets all of it." It was a scarcely veiled threat, and both parties knew it. Jeff's reputation for dealing hard with anyone who cheated him was well known: his people didn't cheat. Not if they wanted to live.

"Yes, sir. Is that all?"

"No. Send another strong message to the Kaaler. Use your own judgment, but don't hurt *him*. Understand?"

"Yes, sir. When?"

"Soon." After he ended the call, Jeff slyly grinned. *Looks like my bluff about Kaaler having the spoon worked. We don't have to work anymore to find the Guardian: the idiot just told us he was it.*

Chapter 64

Strong Message

"FarCaller! Can you hear me?"

The wait always seemed interminable yet seldom lasted more than a few seconds now. "Here am I, Lee."

"How are you, my friend?" Lee peered at the wall behind the image of FarCaller. "Where are you? I don't recognize the room you're in."

FarCaller smiled, almost lighting up Lee's living room. "In my home am I. My new home." His smile broadened more than Lee would have thought possible.

"New? You've moved?"

Many nods of the dark head of hair, the smile seemingly unwilling to relax. "That I was worth something, decided my mother. Then enough money a house to build me found she. On her property my home is, but from her house nearly an hour's walk. Much room we have, lots of privacy and very comfortable are we. But the reason you called that is not, Lee. Why we are talking tell me."

Lee's expression grew more and more serious. FarCaller noticed the change almost immediately.

"What's wrong, Lee? In danger are you?"

"Probably," Lee answered, then told of the attempted burglary of his parents' home and what he learned from the burglar. When he finished, FarCaller was silent.

"Such violence threaten they," FarCaller said. "Why?"

"They want the spoon, FarCaller, and I need your help with some more investments so I can afford to keep myself and my parents safe. And, right now, I'm beginning to fear for Verry as well."

"Verry?"

"The woman I want to marry. If those people discover who she is, they may try to harm her. Or even kidnap her."

"And some investments you want to make because—"

"Because," Lee said, continuing FarCaller's thought, "I may have to support myself and my parents for a while, and I've got to have enough money to do that and keep them and myself and Verry in safe places. Only you can help me with that."

"Yes. And perhaps for me you the same can do." He reached out to touch his silver plate and simultaneously closed his eyes in concentration. Nearly half a minute later, he opened them. "I Sense another company. Soon it will an important change announce. Perhaps this will help you make more money."

Three days later, Lee had completed investing the way FarCaller recommended, again against Jackie's advice—but softer advice than before his first two investments.

In one week, Lee made nearly a quarter-million dollars, and Jackie profited as well. Lee transferred his earnings to several Swiss accounts Clem had arranged for him.

Chapter 65

It's War!

January 20, 2005

Ben Gerit decided to tie up some loose ends and started by calling Etta, his female agent in Bend. She would give him a unbiased view of how things were really going in the hunt for the power spoon and, more specifically, for the Kaaler guy Jeff insisted was the Guardian.

After she answered the phone, Ben wasted no time on small talk. "I'm trying to find out how things are going and especially if Mackie is being taken care of."

"Oh, Ben, honey, didn't you hear?"

He never liked answers that started with "Didn't you hear." "Hear what?" he asked. "What happened?" His temper was already rising just from knowing he was going to be surprised, but he contained himself because Etta was the messenger, not the message.

"Mackie got run into by a hit-and-run driver. Died on the spot. I was going to call you a bit later, but you beat me to it."

"Tell me what happened. Who hit him, where, all of it."

She said nothing for a few seconds. "He was going back to his place from his favorite bar. When he drove away from the curb someone creamed him. Car was totaled; Mackie was all busted up. Lost a lot of blood. EMTs couldn't save him."

Ben's mouth became straight line, jaw muscles so tight they looked like small acorns on each side of his mouth. His eyes were narrow slits. "No witnesses? Police have any leads?"

"No, honey. Nothing. It was after midnight; the street was apparently deserted. The crash made enough noise that a couple of the bar patrons ran out to see what happened." Before Ben could say anything, she added, "I didn't know you knew him very well, Ben."

"Well enough. Mackie have any family?"

"Don't know. I can try to find out for you."

"Do that. Call me by noon tomorrow, no matter what you find."

"Will do, Ben, honey." Her voice changed from serious to inviting. "You still haven't said when you're going to visit me."

"Later." His reply was curt, his voice tense. "Don't have time right now." Before Etta could say anything more, Ben ended the call and leaned back in his leather armchair. He looked at the ceiling, eyes wandering aimlessly as he thought about what he had just learned. After a few seconds, he smiled, not in humor but with malicious intent. *Mackie sells out to me. Jeff's showing me he knows it.* His face slowly blackened, dark eyes glared hatred and anger. As his anger spurred his mind to think about how he would retaliate, he methodically broke every pencil in the miniature Jim Beam barrel on his desk, spraying yellow shards of cedar and black pieces of graphite all over his desk pad. *So he arranges an accident for a simple little guy like Mackie. With his luck, Jeff might have put himself in the evidence loop and ended up in prison. And, worse, me with him. That was stupid.*

Chapter 66

Rest

Because there was only one easily identifiable season on FarCaller's world, life there continued as it had for centuries. FarCaller and Lee talked two or three times a month which, Lee assured him, was only a matter of every few Earth days. Their talks were informative and often fun, but since nothing serious or dangerous seemed to be happening to Lee, the calls were more to ensure each was healthy and safe than to try to solve problems.

For Jeff Gerit, the only good thing about winter was the series of parties thrown by his friends or business partners in the San Francisco area. Twice he flew to Maui for a week of debauchery to get his mind off the incredibly boring reports coming to him from his people in Bend. All that told him was the "Kaaler guy" went to work in the morning, had lunch at a wide range of inexpensive restaurants, sometimes alone, sometimes with someone, and went home about the same time every day. The video cameras Jeff's people installed outside the Kaaler guy's apartment remained useless, just like the bug on his telephone. As convinced as Jeff was that they had identified and located the Guardian his old great-great-uncle Thomas Gerit wrote about, he had not yet seen or heard anything that proved he was right.

Ben Gerit was still angry, but from frustration, not because of any mistakes Jeff or his men made. He finally believed the "Kaaler guy" was the Guardian and had the power spoon but knew he was no closer to getting it for his own use than he had been nearly nine months earlier. He drowned his frustrations in his work: planning acquisitions of competing pharmaceutical companies as part of his aim to control the industry and taking working vacations in southern Mexico.

Nothing important was happening in Bend, and both Jeff's and Ben's teams felt they dared not try to force any action by the "Kaaler guy." At least not without orders. In October, both teams had been making small and subtle attacks at the other, but this grew old and began to feel childish. They had now stopped their little game.

The only benefit to Lee of the competition between the Gerits was that it detracted their attention from him. When the Gerits stopped fighting between themselves and took their vacations, both of their teams in Bend became lax and careless, spending most of their time and money on the Oregon lottery, illegal card games, alcohol, and women.

The winter and early spring were overall the most restful times for Lee since he discovered the spoon, its powers, and his legacy as Guardian.

Then, on the Ides of March, Lee's mother was in a hit-and-run accident, extracted from her car by firemen using the jaws of life, and taken to the hospital for emergency surgery.

Part V

Collisions

Chapter 67

Fire!

April 2, 2005

FarCaller was becoming more and more amazed at the Sensing gift. From his grandfather he had learned that he and his counterpart could help each other. But actually doing it, experiencing it, knowing it was so, no amount of talk could adequately describe. Now he had been rescued from certain death by this man whose face he knew from watching it in a silver dinner plate. In turn, he had helped that man in much the same way—a man who saw FarCaller and his world through a silver teaspoon. It made no logical sense but was nevertheless real.

Lee's Sensings had led FarCaller to several places on his land that were rich in precious metals and gems. With these finds, FarCaller no longer was a beggar in his family, no longer looked upon with such disdain in his village. He now had wealth, could pay his own way for anything, and tried very hard to use his newfound wealth sparingly and wisely. It didn't please some neighbors that he wouldn't support their plans for his wealth, but they knew he didn't dislike them for their self-serving suggestions.

This evening, he decided to walk into the hills on his land to relax and be alone. His "wife" was very attentive and just a little demanding of his time, especially at night, and thus jealous whenever he left her for any length of time. She was unaware of this strange gift he and Lee shared, and FarCaller intended to keep it that way until he knew her much better. Right now, he had no alternative but to be alone so he could be safe from eavesdroppers or spies.

His favorite place on his property was high on the west side of a small hill about a half mile from his house. From there, he could look at the sunset or stars, listen to the birds, the insects' buzzes and clicks, the croaking of frogs, and just wallow in nature's bosom. Once he found a dry spot where he could sit on the soft grasses, he removed the plate from inside his shirt where he had hidden it, held it on his knees, looked into it, and thought about Lee.

These thoughts were different from so many others because he was neither calling nor answering Lee but trying to Sense Lee's future. Relying on experience, he concentrated on Lee's face and what he had seen of Lee's home and the view of those very high rocky hills Lee called mountains.

At first he saw nothing other than his own reflection, then he recognized the misty appearance of the plate's surface: he was about to Sense something.

As the image formed out of the mists, he saw things that, as often happened, he didn't understand. Boxes with windows and wheels that seemed to move about on their own, carrying people within them. Many homes—huge buildings with many rooms and lights coming from their windows. Animals like small wolves moving about the short grasses and bushes surrounding these buildings. And small forest cats with long tails.

His vision moved closer to one building, smaller than many surrounding it, but well kept and neatly groomed. He saw two people in an upstairs bedroom, sitting up in bed, talking. The man looked much like an older Lee might look; the woman had Lee's eyes, except both of hers were blackened. There was a white strip on her forehead, just above her left eye. Her left arm was in a stiff white sleeve that prevented her from bending her elbow, and her head was wrapped with several white pieces of cloth, tied in a manner FarCaller recognized as being the wrapping for a wound. Similarly, her left leg seemed too thick and stiff to be natural: she probably had a stiff sleeve on it also. His brain finally caught up with his eyes—she had been badly injured!

"Stop fussing around me, Faar," the woman said, conveying both frustration and love. "The doctor said I would heal, and I'm feeling better." When her husband heard that, he looked closely at her face, as if examining evidence that belied her statement. She recognized the look, reached out, touched his face gently with her right hand, and softly said, "Really."

The man put his hand on hers, holding it against his cheek, then gently kissed her palm. It was a moment of tenderness FarCaller had never before seen, and he knew he was intruding on a something private. But the Sensing continued: he was to see something important to Lee.

"I know what Lee said, honey," he heard the man say, "but that doesn't mean I feel good about all of this," gesturing up and down her body, slowing when he pointed at her head, left arm, and left leg. "You've got two breaks in your leg, a broken arm, and a sprained wrist; you've had a concussion and cuts and bruises on your head, the guy who drove the car that hit you is still loose, and I'm supposed to relax?" It was said partially in jest, but she recognized the seriousness in his voice.

"OK," she said, conceding some point between them, "I'll stop trying to do much of anything—even telephone calls. But," she added, pointing at her casts, "you don't really believe I can do anything strenuous, do you?" She was smiling. The discussion was over.

Suddenly her husband sat up straight, looked around in alarm, and began sniffing the air.

"What's wrong, Faar?"

He looked around the room, still sniffing, and got off bed, quickly moved to the window and lifted the sash. "Don't you smell it?"

His wife was now clearly concerned but could do little to help him, adding frustration to her feeling of helplessness. "Smell what, Faar? Since they gave me this pain medicine, I really don't smell anything very well."

"Smoke! I smell smoke!"

Upset by this scene, FarCaller willed his view back from inside the room to outside it and was startled to see flames climbing from below a window at the back of the house. *By the gods, their whole house on fire soon will be!*

Then FarCaller understood. He had wanted to Sense Lee's future, and this was in it. These two people were Lee's father and mother, and now they could be burnt alive.

Chapter 68

A Prescient Warning?

Lee woke from a deep sleep full of beautiful dreams about Verry and their future honeymoon, about endless lovemaking, endless energy, endless pleasure, endless sharing. In his dream, they were in their second straight day in their hotel room in Las Vegas when FarCaller's image interrupted their favorite movie. Lee was so shocked that FarCaller would interrupt their honeymoon that he woke up cursing FarCaller's intrusion into such a magnificent experience. Then it hit him: *FarCaller's calling!*

He turned on the bedside table lamp and withdrew the spoon from beneath a pile of handkerchiefs he kept in the drawer of his nightstand. Holding it up in the light, he saw his friend's face. Before he could say anything, FarCaller was shouting.

"Lee! Finally! For almost a day calling you have I!"

That alone impressed Lee about the seriousness of the contact: a day of FarCaller's time was about an hour of Lee's.

"Why? What's happened?"

FarCaller violently shook his head back and forth. "What *has* happened it is not, Lee. Sensed your parents did I, and afire their house was! On the back of their house."

It took Lee a few seconds to translate FarCaller's description into reality. "There's a fire on the back of my folks' house?" As he spoke, he shed his pajamas and began pulling underwear from his drawer.

"Not. A Sensing it was. But if something soon is not done, their house on fire will be. And die they could!"

At 2:00 a.m., Lee called his parents. His father particularly resented Lee waking his mother from her badly needed healing sleep. But Lee was so insistent that they were in danger that his father finally agreed to listen. To let his wife go back to sleep, he went downstairs to their living room. Lee went straight to the purpose of his call. "Dad, I can't tell you why I know what I'm saying is true, but your house will be set afire soon, and both of you will be either killed or seriously injured. You *have* to believe me! And you have to do something to protect yourselves."

His father settled back in his favorite overstuffed rocker, put his feet up on the footrest, and pushed down the lever letting the chair recline. "Lee, this is ridiculous. Until you can tell me why I should believe you know our future, your mom and I aren't moving anywhere."

Lee was fully awake, his frustration level rising rapidly. *How do I convince my dad anything about this warning without telling him about the spoon?* "Dad," he began, searching for the right words, "I don't know how to convince you without"—*he's an honorable man; maybe he'll believe the truth*—"breaking my word to someone."

His father's eyes opened wide, but he said nothing.

"I've been very fortunate to have"—again Lee searched for something he could say without revealing what he had to protect—"a special friend who has a talent for seeing into the near future. He's never been wrong so far. In fact, his suggestions led me to make some very lucrative investments, investments that my broker and lawyer said were very risky."

His father now brought his chair upright, but he remained silent.

"My friend called me just minutes ago and told me he believed your house would soon be set afire. He said the burning would start at the back. He was absolutely certain that it would be set soon and that both you and Mom would be seriously injured if you didn't get out of the house right away. You can't expect me to suddenly ignore advice from someone who's never been wrong about predicting short-range future events—just because it would disturb your sleep."

At first Lee heard nothing, then his father said, "Lee, we both love you very much, as I'm sure you know. But I'm not going to move your mother at two in the morning because you got a call from some mystic. If you want to talk more about this, call me after nine."

Chapter 69

Hogwash!

"What was that all about, Faar?" Lee's mother asked, her words slurred with sleep.

"One of Lee's cockamamy ideas. I told him to call me in the morning if he still wants to talk about it."

"But it was strange for him to call at such an awful hour. Especially since he seldom calls at all. Maybe it really *was* important."

"It was hogwash." He checked her face for any signs of pain or discomfort. Aside from eyes puffy with sleep, she looked as good as he could expect. "Go back to sleep, Mama. Maybe Lee'll come to his senses in the morning."

Two hours later, Lee's father awoke smelling smoke. Sitting up with a start, he turned on his reading lamp and saw a noxious black and gray cloud entering their bedroom from the upstairs hallway. He jumped out of bed and ran to the nearest window and opened it so they could breathe fresh air. His sudden movement awoke his wife. She was terror stricken when she saw the smoke and smelled the fumes. "Faar," she screamed, "help me! I can't move!"

He called 911 then threw aside the blankets and gently picked her up, trying to minimize stress on her broken leg. Her sudden gasps told him she was in pain, but she said nothing. By the time he got out the front door, sirens were coming down the street.

The night air was freezing, made worse by the chill from strong wind gusts. He could see the winds whipping flames up at the back corner of the house but was almost too cold to think about the damage being done to his home. When the firefighters and ambulance arrived, the entire back corner of the house was burning, studs visible through most of the walls, wooden siding now merely charred strips. The EMTs took Lee's parents into the ambulance, covered them with warmed blankets, and gave them hot coffee to drink. At their request, after confirming they had no new injuries and Lee's mother's leg and arm were still safely in its casts, they moved to their car, where they could close the doors to protect themselves from the winds and the heater could warm them. It took less than an hour for the fire department to extinguish the fire and another to learn the cause. Their conclusion was foregone: arson. The fire was started with barbecue lighting fluid splashed over the kitchen's outside wall.

From the ambulance, using a cell phone borrowed from one of the EMTs, Faar told Lee what happened. Lee arrived ten minutes later. Both of his parents were shocked, his father was staring at the damage to their home and the firemen were struggling to clean up their equipment, fighting the cold that kept freezing everything touched by the water from the hoses. Lee's mother was lying in the back seat of their car, struggling to get comfortable, now shivering from the cold air still inside the car.

Lee ran up to his father, put his arm around the older man's shoulder, and said, gently, "Dad, let's leave. I'll put you up at my place until you decide what to do."

The look in his father's eyes revealed appreciation, shock, and a certain amount of fear of this son who told him their house would be set ablaze two hours before it happened.

Chapter 70

Sooner!

Lee's parents were established in his bedroom, finally asleep, and Lee was on the sofa bed in his living room. He couldn't sleep, so he called Verry on his cell phone, knowing she would be awake by then. They talked about the fire for some time, then Lee made the most difficult decision of his life.

"Verry, someone around here is hurting my family, and I think they're doing it to get to me." His eyes filled with tears as he steeled himself for what he had to say next. "I can't intentionally put you in danger by marrying you."

Silence from both ends of circuit, then Verry fairly yelled at him. "How dare you? How dare you tell me you love me, that you want to marry me, that I am the one for you, and then—all by yourself—decide it's too dangerous for us to get married? How dare you do that, Lee? Don't I have any say in this? Besides that, it seems to me that, if what you say is true, I'm *already* in danger!" Where he expected tears, she was attacking.

He was totally unprepared for such an outburst. "But I thought—" he began, his voice revealing his sudden loss of confidence.

"You thought you could make that decision for me? Is that what you thought?" Before he could respond, she continued unabated, scarcely pausing to breathe. "You asked me to be your wife, and I accepted. I don't care about the danger—you warned me about it. I thought wives were supposed to stand by their husbands in time of danger and stress and were supposed to support their husbands, and they were supposed to fight together for what they wanted. Was I wrong?" Before he could formulate any answer, she added, "Why aren't you answering me, Lee?"

What kind of woman is this? "Well," he began, "I, uh, didn't expect you'd want to get married when there is this threat to me and my family. So I—"

"So you decided for me?" Her voice softened. "To protect me?"

"I don't want to put you in danger or increase the chance of your getting hurt or—"

Her voice was now very soft, almost caressing, but her feelings radiated strongly. "Lee, I appreciate that and love you for it. But don't you think I'd rather be with you when you are in danger than in Des Moines worrying about what might happen to you and whether I might never see you again?"

"I never thought about it that way."

"Well, Lee Kaaler, that's how I feel. Now stop all this useless worrying and talk and tell me when you're coming here so we can be married and start our lives together." He started to fumble with an answer when she again interrupted him, "Or do you want me to come there?"

Lee couldn't help but smile at that thought. "Verry," he began, "I love you so much I can't begin to tell you. And I'd marry you right now if you were here. But don't you want to have a wedding with all your friends and relatives around you?"

"Of course I do. I've always wanted that. But I'd rather marry you right now and help you win your battles than go through the months of planning and preparation it takes to put together a wedding like that and leave you facing some kind of danger all by yourself."

Seems she's made our decision for us. "OK, let's get married soon. Give me a couple of weeks to get things organized here, and I'll come to Des Moines. You get things organized on your end, and we can get married as soon as I get there. In the meantime, just know I love you and can hardly wait!"

Chapter 71

Coronary

April 5, 2005

Ben Gerit felt good. He was in his living room, smoking a mild Cuban cigar nearly an inch in diameter and sipping a glass of port from the best winery in New York. As usual, he was relaxing in his leather recliner, wearing a silk brocade smoking jacket given him by a female admirer a few—was it already three?—years ago, and enjoying the night view of Chicago's skyline.

"Life's good, you know it?" he asked no one. "Couldn't get much better than this. Now for some more action."

He picked up his telephone and dialed a number in Central Oregon. It rang twice, then he heard the familiar female voice.

"Hello?"

"This is Ben Gerit, Etta."

"Why, hello, Ben, honey."

"Missed working with you, Etta. Thought you might like a chance to get back in the saddle with me."

"What've you got?"

Just like her to get to business at exactly the right time in a conversation. Always knows just when to do something.

"I need a couple of favors. Very quiet, very professional, and very soon. Find out what Jeff's people are doing and let me know. Wouldn't surprise me if they're getting lazy."

After falsely promising to see her soon, Ben ended the call and sat back in his chair, suddenly feeling quite tired. The longer he sat, the hotter he felt, his face breaking out in a full sweat, his arms and legs feeling very weak. Then he felt two separate and distressing symptoms: a sudden painful and spasmodic tightening of his chest and nerves tingling, starting on the lower left side of his jaw and radiating all the way down his left arm.

Just as he reached for the telephone to call a doctor, he felt something in the middle of his chest expand into a burning ball, trying to eat him alive. He barely had the strength to call 911.

At the same time, two of Etta's men took positions outside Jeff's office in San Francisco with instructions to keep track of his every movement and report back to Etta at least twice a day.

One of Jeff's men saw he was being spied on and reported it to Jeff. He was so enraged that he tossed a chair through his office window, the glass shards and chair falling more than twenty stories onto the street below. Then he overturned his desk, spilling its contents all over the office floor, breaking every bottle in his liquor cabinet, ruining a Persian rug, and screaming so loudly he strained his vocal cords until he couldn't make another sound.

It was at that point the police entered his office and arrested him for reckless endangerment of the cars and pedestrians on the street below. He would have been out on bail in less than two hours if he hadn't tried to hit the officers. He received a sentence of three days in jail, a $2,000 fine, and was directed to perform one hundred forty hours of community service.

Jeff didn't learn of his father's heart attack until the next day, after his lawyer paid his fine and got the judge to suspend the sentence pending completion of the community service work. By that time, Jeff could only consider his old man's ailment as somehow befitting for such a cantankerous old coot.

After two days to calm down, he called his father's doctor, an old friend of both of the men, but one who was on a permanent retainer from Jeff.

"I need a favor, Doc."

Never one to mix friendship with business, the older man responded in his most professional air. "Of course, Jeff. You know I'd do anything for someone I've known so long and so well."

"My father had a heart attack, right?"

"Absolutely. I don't expect he'll be able to work for many months—I told him he should take at least six months off before even attempting to go back to work part time."

"I'm just as concerned about Dad's health as you are, Doctor. So much, in fact, that I think he should get plenty of rest. I'm certain you have something that will allow him to heal, but not feel well enough to work. That way he'll ultimately be better off. In fact, if this works well, we'll all be better off, including you."

There was a short silence on the other end, then the doctor said, "I know just the thing for your father, Jeff. Unfortunately, it's a bit expensive, but—" he left the sentence unfinished.

"You just let me know the costs, and I'll pay them in cash. How about a $10,000 advance. Would that help?"

"Very much, thank you. You can be assured your father will get all the rest he needs."

Chapter 72

Plan It Correctly

April 6, 2005

"Clem, this is Lee. On my count, activate the black box."
Clem wasn't expecting Lee's call and had a client with him but also didn't want to delay talking to Lee when he insisted the security box be used. That meant something serious was happening.

After excusing himself from his client, he did as Lee asked. "OK, my friend, what can I do for you?"

"I've got two things I need to have done for me, and right now you're the only one I can trust to do them. First, please write this down and get on it today. I have to leave here soon, but I can't unless these arrangements are made." He told Clem exactly what he needed done. When Clem indicated he had written that task, Lee continued. "The second favor: I've asked Louise Chenowith, at Pilot Butte Realty, to find me a house to buy. I told her I've asked you to be my point of contact on this and that she should get in touch with me through you. I hope you don't mind. Tell her I'll look at her best choices when I get back, which should be late next week." Before Clem could say anything, Lee added, "Call me as soon as the first favor is done, Clem. I'll be at home, so use the box or your cell phone." Before Clem could say anything more, Lee closed the circuit.

It occurred to Clem that his client heard not a word about who the caller was, where the call came from, or what Clem was supposed to do. *Pretty smart, Lee, my boy. Kinda like double security: Ah say nothin' unless ovah a secured telephone line, and y'all get all y'alls instructions passed without being overheard.* Returning his attention to his client, he said, "Now, Mr. Gerit, wherah were we?"

Chapter 73

I Could Buy This!

April 13, 2005

Lee's parents couldn't believe his obsession with secrecy, but the warning about the attack on their home convinced them something strange was going on and he was acting in their best interests. What they didn't know was that he barely thought about them from the time he and Verry set the wedding date until he left Bend. Had they seen what Lee did that day, they would have been convinced he suffered from delusions of danger.

Immediately after Verry's insistence that they get married as soon as possible, Lee devised a plan to let him leave Bend without being noticed, much as he had done when he flew to Des Moines. On the day before his Sunday departure for Des Moines, he borrowed his dad's old Stetson. Sunday morning he asked his dad to drive him to the ten-thirty church service. His excuse for not taking his own car was that he was going to spend the day with a few of his friends, and they would bring him home. He wore a light-weight tan jacket with many pockets that he had filled with the disguise makeup he used on his first trip to Iowa. Just as his dad stopped his car in front of the church's main entrance to let Lee out, Lee gave him two sealed envelopes. The first was addressed to his mom and dad and was to be opened at five o'clock that evening. It would tell them that he was leaving town for a week or more and that he would call them when he was returning. The second was to be delivered the next day to his boss. It contained his resignation from his job.

Sunday was a beautiful spring day: clear skies, crisp and clean air, light wind, and unobstructed views of the Cascade Range, over twenty-five miles away. It occurred to Lee how glad he was that he and Verry would live there, because he didn't want to lose the lift he felt from seeing Mount Bachelor, the Three Sisters, and Mount Jefferson every day. All were snow-topped year round; all were breathtakingly beautiful when seen against the clear blue sky so common in the High Desert of Central Oregon.

After church, he joined a few of his friends for brunch at a restaurant Lee suggested. It was on the south end of Bend, on the main route out of town. When the fun-filled meal was over, rather than having his friends take him home, he told them he was going to walk to the factory outlet mall just across the street, do some shopping there, and then find a ride home. Once his friends left the restaurant, Lee walked out the restaurant's back door, donned his dad's Stetson, and walked a half block south and the same distance west to the Goodwill store. There he bought some scruffy jeans, used cowboy boots, a slightly faded blue Western shirt, and an old suitcase. In the restroom there, Lee used the eye makeup to give himself a "five o'clock shadow," attached the bushy black false mustache, and inserted the blue contact lenses. His church clothes he put into the suitcase he had just purchased. When he left the store, his appearance had changed so much that he knew even his parents couldn't have recognized him. His next stop was the convenience store in the gas station across the highway from Goodwill, where he purchased a toothbrush and toothpaste, some deodorant, a comb, and some snacks. These he also put into the suitcase. He then walked the few blocks north to one of the Greyhound bus stops. He hated few things as much as riding a bus for long distances, and his friends and family knew it. For that very reason, he chose to take the bus to Boise.

While recognizing that the bus line served a real purpose, especially for people who had little money and for towns that had no airport or train station, Lee detested the experience. After leaving Bend and seeing no sign of anything unusual—like someone watching him—Lee pondered the circumstances that made him assume he was being watched. The conclusion was simple enough: someone in Bend was dangerous enough to torch his parents' home, install a video camera to look into his apartment, and tap his telephone. That forced him to don a disguise just to leave town unseen. If those unknown people were still trying to watch him, in a few days without seeing him they'd know he wasn't in Bend. Looking around for him would be useless because they could trace him only to the restaurant where he shared Sunday lunch with his friends, and after that he disappeared.

On the long trip, he was surrounded by elements typical of all long bus rides: squalling children, numerous stops at incredibly tiny "towns" for dropping off and picking up people and packages, and the occasional cold, stale, and expensive sandwiches and soft drinks.

The drive to Boise from Bend would consume about six hours by car, but on a bus it was closer to fourteen. Sitting in a narrow seat that barely reclined, the false mustache making his upper lip itch, and smelling body odors, stale cigarette smoke, dirty diapers, and diesel fuel, Lee hated his unseen foes more for each minute he endured the ride.

He was a cash millionaire, something he seldom thought about. But while riding in a vehicle he could purchase by simply writing a check, he thought about what money could buy and how much he wanted to live his life in a more leisurely and comfortable manner. He constantly thought about the threats to him and his family from someone who wanted to use the spoon for their own benefits, someone who had no concern for the harm it could cause to others on this world, as well as what it could do to FarCaller and the people on Spoonworld. Ironically, they couldn't know they'd never be able to use the spoon even if they captured it: they didn't have the Gift.

I'm on my way to marry an incredible woman while fleeing from someone I've never seen. I'll put her in the same danger I'm in, yet she insists she'd have it no other way—and I agree with her! How incredibly selfish can I be?

His mind shifted to thoughts about their upcoming honeymoon and Verry's soft, beautiful body, their deep and fulfilling kisses, their electric caresses. Quickly he realized he had to change the subject or he'd embarrass himself. Putting her out of his mind was incredibly difficult.

At four o'clock Monday morning he arrived in Boise without screaming from the claustrophobic experience of riding that bus. He was hungry and anxious to begin his drive to Des Moines. He couldn't sleep in spite of his exhaustion, so he decided to stay in the station until some restaurants opened for breakfast. An hour later, a small cafe less than a block from the bus depot opened. Lee gulped down three pancakes, four limp slices of bacon, and two cups of coffee that tasted like they might contain battery acid. He then taxied to the RV rental agency where Clem had made reservations for him and pawed through his suitcase to find the fake driver's license he had to use for the rental. *I couldn't be acting more like a fugitive if I tried. Only I'm not a fugitive from the law, I'm a fugitive from outlaws.*

It took ten minutes to get to the RV rental office, another thirty to complete the paperwork and the walk-around inspection, a seemingly interminable series of explanations of the workings of the twenty-eight-foot motor home, and three minutes to buy a sheaf of maps to all the states adjacent to Idaho—so the rental agent couldn't tell where he really was headed. Finally, at 8:30 he drove up Cole Avenue to the intersection with Interstate 84 and headed for Salt Lake City and points east.

One thing Lee wanted to invent was some way to let FarCaller see the landscape go by while Lee drove across Idaho, the northeast part of Utah, across Wyoming and Nebraska, and into Iowa. He knew he had to keep in touch with FarCaller and couldn't afford to spend hours without any contact or to stop his RV just to talk to his—now—closest friend.

His mind wandered. *Is FarCaller a giant or more the size of a microbe? Is his world smaller or bigger than Earth?* He shook his head to erase the thoughts.

When he neared Mountain Home, Idaho, the traffic eased; and he looked at the spoon he had attached to the sun visor with clear tape, smiled at what he was about to do, then yelled, "FarCaller! Are you there?" *I am so glad no one can see me do this. They'd think I'm crazy as a loon.*

Chapter 74

Tipster

"Here am I." FarCaller's image and voice appeared only a few seconds after Lee's hailing. Then he frowned in confusion and peered closely at Lee and his surroundings. Because Lee had to keep his eyes on the road, he didn't see FarCaller scan the area behind the driver's seat, moving his head up and down as he tried to get a better view of the area in which Lee sat.

"Where you are, Lee? From this place never before contacted me have you, and always before directly at me looked you. Something wrong is?"

Lee's smile erased any doubts FarCaller had about his mood but did nothing to explain the change of surroundings. "I'm OK," Lee said, still looking down the freeway, checking the traffic, but only occasionally glancing at the spoon directly above his field of view. "I'm driving to meet my future wife, and I have to look closely at the road in order to keep from having an accident. I left Bend on a bus, in disguise, then switched to this motor home in Boise—a larger city—so it would be harder for someone to follow me."

"The disguise I understand; where you are understand I not," FarCaller responded. "In a small room or building sitting are you, yet as if you are moving you look and talk."

I need to put this to rest once and for all. "FarCaller, can you hear me when you can't see my face?"

"Yes."

"OK, then, look at this." Lee flipped the sun visor down so it and the silver spoon faced the road ahead. Interstate 84 passed through lands that were alternatively fields of grasses and grains, the Snake River basin, a raptor sanctuary, and granite outcroppings. Adding to the beauty, the colors varied from blue skies to tan soil to green fields and black granite. Making the view and driving interesting, the road gently curved through the land, letting Lee's perspective of southwestern Idaho change while keeping his attention level high.

An hour later, when he flipped the visor back up, FarCaller's eyes were wide with wonder. "Never could I have these things imagined, Lee," he said. "The land beautiful is, with many colors and shapes that new to me are. Yet in a small room sit you. Moving fast on a very smooth road are you. A table and a bench covered in blue plaid has it, and a sink. Even a place your meals to cook. What wonders are these?"

Lee clearly enjoyed his friend's questions. "I'm in what we call a motor home. It's exactly as you described: a small house on wheels that can be driven from one place to another. At night I pull off the road, close the curtains, then cook and eat my meal, and sleep in the bed in back. It even has a small toilet and a place to bathe."

FarCaller just shook his head, clearly amazed. "This believe not can I! Our vehicles all drawn by animals are, and our roads as smooth as yours are not."

"I'm sure that's true," Lee said. Before he could continue, he steered the motor home to the right edge of the road to let a large semi pass him just as the road narrowed. Stifling several swear words, he shook his head in disgust, checked the other traffic, moved back into the center of his lane, and quickly glanced up at the spoon. FarCaller was again trying to look around the room and behind Lee's head.

"Would you like to see the inside of this place better?"

"If a problem cause it would not, yes."

Lee turned the visor so it pointed to the back of the RV then returned his attention to the road. "Better?"

"Very much." FarCaller looked around, then he stopped his gawking. "But you called me why? Surely to show me this moving home it was not."

"Motor home," Lee corrected. "No, something else."

"Ask me, then."

"Part of my question has been answered: I don't have to see your face to be able to talk with you."

"Using the spoon and plate each other to call also needed is not, if well enough together we work."

"Really? Without using the plate and spoon?"

"What my grandfather FarCaller said that is."

"Maybe we can practice that later."

When Lee completed the story about his parents, the arson attempt FarCaller envisioned, his mother's injury, and his concerns about Verry, FarCaller simply said, "Whatever you need, support I will. However—"

The silence was so sudden and unexpected that Lee was forced to look up, checking that FarCaller was still there. He was, but with a quizzical expression on his face. Then he spoke again. "Lee, remember about good investments you to advise, you asked me?"

"Of course. I made a lot of money with your help. Enough so that I won't have to work anymore for the rest of my life."

FarCaller's astonishment was written all over his face. "Possible that is? That much money gained you?"

"Yes. It is amazing, isn't it? But why do you ask?"

"Because another such thing Sense I. A company that medicines makes and sells, something very special soon announce will it, and the company's value greatly increase will."

"What can you tell me about it?" He slowed the motor home to fifty-five miles per hour in spite of the problems it caused those behind him. When he couldn't give all his attention to driving—and right now he didn't want to—he knew he had to drive more slowly.

"A picture I sense, a drawing perhaps. The roof of a house it shows, with a small house built upon the roof of the porch, and on one of the posts a snake climbing up is." A few seconds more, then, "Strange it sounds, but sense does it make?"

"You described the symbol for one of this country's biggest medical drug companies. It's very famous for its medicines and medical research and is named after its owner: Gerit Pharmaceuticals. Last time you gave me a tip like this, FarCaller, I learned I have to act on it right away. So, if you don't mind, I'll do that now. You can watch if you want."

"Nothing about this did my grandfather understand. Perhaps watching this help me to write will."

"OK." Lee lifted his cell phone from its charger on the RV's dashboard, obtained Jackie's telephone number through the cell phone information service, and listened while her telephone rang. She answered on the third ring.

"Jackie, this is Lee Kaaler."

"Why, hi there, Lee. Got any hot tips for me today?" His previous success had become a not-funny joke with Jackie, because she had always cautioned against his making the investments FarCaller recommended.

"As a matter of fact, I do," he said. "I'd like to buy some shares of Gerit Pharmaceuticals."

"Really?" He could hear her tapping on her computer keyboard. "I'm not showing anything special or new about them."

"You wouldn't believe me if I told you, Jackie."

"Like last time?"

"Like last time."

"OK, then. It's at $95 per share right now, not 50¢ each like Pyramid Textiles was. It's been at that level pretty much for the past several months. How much do you want to buy?"

Lee swallowed hard before making his decision. If the purchase didn't go well, he'd lose a large sum of money. "A thousand shares, I think."

The line was silent as she made her calculation. "That'll cost $95,000 plus commission, Lee. You sure that's what you want to do? I can think of a lot of stocks that should do better than Gerit."

"I've been pretty lucky so far. See no reason to change now."

He could hear her take a deep breath. "You got it, then. I'll send out the order right away." When next she spoke, her voice was softer. "There's not that much money in your account, Lee. What do you want me to do—buy what I can with the $65,000 that's there?"

"Yes. Then contact Clem Maestre and ask him to arrange a transfer of another $50,000 into the account. That'll take care of this buy plus give me something to work with if I decide to buy something else later."

"I know how successful you've been, Lee," she said, her voice steady but lower in pitch than normal, "and Lord knows I made some money off of your tips myself. But Gerit Pharmaceuticals?"

"Just do it, Jackie. Buy that stock right now. Today." He was getting frustrated and feared his voice betrayed his feelings.

She apparently picked up on it. "Done, then. I'll call Clem and take care of the rest for you. Just remember what I said, Lee. I think this buy is wrong."

Lee flipped the cell phone closed and replaced it in its charger. Remembering his contact with FarCaller, he said, "That's how it works, FarCaller. Learn anything?"

His friend's deep voice was unsteady, as if bad news were imminent. "Saw did I, Lee, but learned not did I. So many questions have I."

Lee couldn't contain his smile. *I'll bet that's the understatement of his life. He knows nothing about electricity, let alone batteries and radio and manufacturing techniques and whatever else is involved in using cell phones, or how a stock market might work.*

He accelerated the motor home to highway speeds. "Ask your questions. I'll answer them if I can."

"Where to start I know not," FarCaller began. "Any answers too difficult to understand will be, I fear. Only one now have I: what makes your house on wheels move?"

The next two hours consisted of a series of simple questions from FarCaller and incredibly difficult answers for Lee to provide.

Chapter 75

The Interceptor

Lee kept the spoon facing forward, letting FarCaller watch the changing panorama of southern Idaho farmlands, open range, irrigation canals and sprinkler systems, and the incredible range and numbers of vehicles they met.

They talked for several hours about many things—including the threats both Lee and FarCaller received and the help they provided each other. Then Lee felt the beginning of the sensation he now associated with Sensing.

"Don't talk for a bit, FarCaller," he said, "I Sense something."

FarCaller knew he should remain silent until Lee spoke again. FarCaller believed the fact a Sensing came to Lee without bidding foretold of bad news.

Just as the Sensing began, Lee pulled the RV over to the side of the road, not wanting to lose concentration.

Unlike his other Sensings, this one began as soon as Lee could apply his attention to it. Also different: there was no floating sensation. It began with a view of a large stone house with a newly thatched roof, surrounded by fields filled with a wide variety of vegetable plants. Judging from the dewdrops on the leaves and shrubs, Lee concluded it was early morning. Someone was carefully walking up to the side of the house carrying a burning torch, its yellow flame making no telltale smoke. Lee forced his view as close as possible to the man's image, memorizing it. Then the vision ceased.

The man with the torch was small and lithe, in his early twenties, with hair reaching below his shoulders. It was blond, matted, and stringy, as if it hadn't been washed in weeks. He wore a long-sleeved dark tunic and baggy brown pants, his feet unshod, filthy, and calloused. His eyebrows, lashes, and bushy mustache were all black. His eyes burned with fanatic zeal. At this hour, unless the occupants were early risers, any fire would certainly destroy the building interior and roof and, quite probably, kill anyone inside.

Lee was surprised at FarCaller's reaction to his Sensing: steely rage nearly matching that of the arsonist who, Lee now realized, closely resembled FarCaller.

"I'm sorry to bring you this kind of Sensing, FarCaller," Lee began, "but—"

His friend vigorously shook his head back and forth. "Good it is that you did, Lee. My younger brother you described, who we the Interceptor call because, as his mission in life, every good thing to stop has he. Often here, once our ages about fifteen years have we reached and our behavior and interests to our families and friends known are, as names titles carry we. The FarCaller gift have I, and by tradition FarCaller am called, although no others here the reasons know. Every good thing anyone did, resented did my brother. Usually to stop them before those deeds could be accomplished tried he. Thus, the title Interceptor has he.

"This title as a compliment believes he, when actually a bad term is it." FarCaller looked back at Lee, his face still grim. "Many of us think a sickness in his mind has he, but prove it or treat it not can we. One reason is that away from most people keeps he. Many people hurt, or tried to hurt, has he." FarCaller looked away slightly, blinking in concentration. "That you have seen him near my mother's home surprises me. Never before our family threatened has he." A deep breath, then, "Stop him must I." He turned away and added as he walked away from the silver plate and out of Lee's vision, "But how I know not."

* * *

It was after 11:00 p.m. before Lee relaxed enough to let exhaustion put his body and mind to sleep. As he drifted off, he heard someone yelling his name.

"Lee! Hear me can you, Lee? Please come!"

Lee shook his head a few times to bring himself fully awake then forced his eyes as wide open as possible to clear his vision. While this was happening, he tried to figure out how anyone near him would know him well enough to call out his name.

"Lee! Please answer!"

Good grief, it's FarCaller! He rose and went to the wall by the shower and toilet, seeing by the light from the overhead floodlights in the RV park, then rummaged through his underwear drawer until he found the small black pencil box in which he kept the spoon. Quickly removing it, he returned to his bed, turned off the reading light, then held the spoon up so FarCaller could see him.

"I'm here, FarCaller. What's wrong?"

"Thank the gods, Lee! That something bad to you had happened, afraid was I. For many hours calling you have I been." Concern still colored his face, but as he talked, his expression relaxed and the more familiar smile returned.

"I've been very busy, so I guess I just didn't hear you."

"All right it now is, Lee," FarCaller said, clearly relaxing. "So upset were you with your Sensing about my brother when last we talked that afraid something had happened to you on your travels was I."

"I've driven more than six hundred miles in the past two days, FarCaller. Plus I've had to talk with some friends about this trip, so I've been pretty busy."

"Far that sounds, Lee, but the word 'miles' I understand not."

Now what? Lee asked himself. *How to explain a mile?* His mind scanned through a series of alternative methods of making FarCaller understand then hit on one he liked. "A mile, FarCaller, is about two thousand paces. I can give a better definition, but first I need to know if you understand the word 'hour.'"

"Yes. Also 'hours' use we. In each day twenty-five there are."

That's close enough. "Well, here the average walking speed is four miles an hour."

FarCaller's mind digested what Lee just said, then his eyes widened in surprise and disbelief, his eyebrows rising in tune with them. "Six hundred miles moved you? In two days?"

Lee's confusion showed: eyes blinking, slight frown, mouth slightly askew. "But it's only about three hundred or so miles a day."

First FarCaller peered closely at Lee then moved back slightly and shook his head. "Lee, in this world to go three hundred miles in a month fortunate would be we."

That made Lee recall their earlier conversations about FarCaller's use of animals and carts, and he again realized their two technologies were literally worlds apart. Intentionally changing the subject, Lee asked, "Your mother. Is she safe and healthy?"

"Oh yes!" FarCaller said, his face again lit with a smile. "Of the torches and flames warned you, so my brother to stop able were we, and any harm coming to my mother to prevent."

"What did you do to him?"

Again the man's face radiated confusion. "Do? Not understand I. What to do would there be?"

"Well," Lee began, "we'd have him arrested for attempting to damage that home. He'd have to pay a fine or spend time in jail or perhaps some of both."

"But my brother is he," FarCaller insisted. "Anything like that, to him happening, stop would we!" As he spoke, he shook his head: clearly upset about even thinking of such punishment.

"Then what *did* you do?"

"First, from coming into the yard with his torch, him stopped we, then the torch extinguished, then all of us harshly to him spoke. After that, welcome at our homes he was not, if to damage them or us he again tried, to him told we."

"And then?"

"Away, went he. What else to do could he?"

Lee hadn't convinced FarCaller something more should be done to stop his brother's evil acts, so he decided to change the subject, especially since he was exhausted. But before he could say anything, he once again felt a Sensing begin. He held tightly to the spoon and cleared his mind so whatever image formed would be sharply presented.

It was a scene of the room from where FarCaller communicated with Lee. Two rustic end tables were tipped over, the dark brown handmade braided rug was askew, as if it had been dragged by one corner from its usual place. Broken pieces of red ceramic mugs were spread on the floor, along with two or three small paintings in broken frames.

Suddenly two men rolled into view, arms grasped around each other, faces flushed and clothes torn: fighting. One was FarCaller; the other his brother. In the midst of the grappling, the Interceptor picked up a large piece of one of the mugs and tried to slash FarCaller's throat. FarCaller pushed the jagged edges away from his face just before they could have torn his throat open, smashing them on the floor alongside his left cheek.

One of the worst parts of the Sensing was that it was silent, played out as if observed by deaf people. Before Lee could think more about that, the scene faded away. He was back in his RV, looking at the far wall of his small sleeping area, his eyes still unfocused as his mind absorbed the violence. When he could talk, he looked back into the spoon at his friend's face. "FarCaller, I've—"

"My future Sensed have you, Lee. Bad it is?"

What else would it be? Since when do these things bring good news? He answered his own question: *The investment advice was perfect. But the other stuff . . .* He let the thought drift away and returned his attention to the face in the spoon and described his vision. "Tell me again why you don't do something to stop this guy, FarCaller. He's tried to kill you at least once, he's tried to torch your mother's home, and now it looks like he's going to try to kill you and take the plate away for his own selfish benefit. Are you going to continue to put up with all of this stuff until he kills you or your mother? What would a Guardian do if there were no FarCaller?"

FarCaller peered closely at Lee, listening to every word and checking for every nuance in Lee's expressions, then looked down at the floor. Finally he looked up again. "Greatly him I fear, Lee," FarCaller admitted. "A ferocity he has to match not can I. A drive for whatever he wants to get has he. These talents never possessed have I. But, as you say, evil is he." Again he looked away, this time toward one of the walls. "To confront him time it is, fear I."

Lee's view of FarCaller changed as FarCaller moved his plate out of the room, holding it in front of him. Then he heard FarCaller quietly say, "If gods you have, to them for me please pray."

Chapter 76

Warning

Jeff Gerit returned to his room in the Park Motel in Bend. It was furnished with a Northwest decor: photos of Crater Lake, the Cascades Range, and people fly-fishing and hunting. The room was finished in tans, pastels, and sky blue, with a faux hardwood floor. Jeff reluctantly admitted it was attractive and comfortable. He had just left Clem's office after a second talk on a real estate transaction that he never intended to make, for land he didn't want, in this world of lava rocks, juniper trees, sagebrush, rabbitbrush, and people who seemed to flourish in the dry climate.

"Mr. Kaaler," he said into Lee's answering machine, enjoying the opportunity to personally pressure the Guardian, "you don't seem to realize how easily you can protect yourself and your family from danger. You have nothing to gain and everything to lose if you insist on behaving so childishly. All you have to do is hand over that spoon and you will save your family and friends a great deal of grief."

He was sitting in a recliner, looking out his window at the trees and the lake in Pioneer Park, just south of the motel. Wryly he admitted to himself that Bend really was a pretty place. Except it wasn't in the Bay Area.

He continued with his message. "We know a lot about you, Mr. Kaaler, including members of your family and where they are, and even the fact you have a special friend in Des Moines. We really don't like threatening innocent people, but you're giving us little choice because of your selfish attitude.

"This is your last warning. If we don't get that spoon, your loved ones will soon have accidents. Preventable ones. You wouldn't want them to be hurt, would you? Remember, it'll be *your* fault."

Jeff put the phone down and smiled. "If he doesn't get *that* message, he's too stupid to waste time reasoning with."

After Jeff hung up the telephone, the man Jeff hired to copy Lee's incoming telephone calls stopped the tape recorder, copied the tape containing Jeff's warning, and put the copy in his shirt pocket. By that evening, Jeff's dad knew exactly what Jeff said.

All Jeff had been thinking about was how this "preemptive strike" would effectively eliminate any impact his father might have on Jeff's recovering the spoon and taking control of a great deal of money and people. However, his father was quietly irate, a state anyone who knew him tried hard to avoid. "Calling Kaaler was monumentally stupid. I'll give Jeff something more useful to think about while I get things done properly."

He called his bookkeeper and stopped Jeff's monthly stipend and closed a series of bank accounts through methods Jeff couldn't know, using contacts Jeff was unaware of, to obtain results Jeff wouldn't like.

Chapter 77

Breaks and Bruises

The Ides of April 2005

Verry winced from a deep, dull headache, then from lights so bright they blasted through her eyelids. She squeezed them tightly together, trying to block out the light. After a few seconds, she confirmed that her toes could move, that her knee was numb, that her left arm ached, and that her face felt hot in some places. Then she heard sounds: rhythmic electronic beeps, people talking in hushed tones, and wheeled carts moving about.

"She's waking up, Doctor." A woman.

I'm in a hospital? What happened? Why can't I remember?

"Vital signs?" A man.

"Normal post-op."

"Good." Verry felt a cool hand rest on her forehead.

"Ms. Willards, can you hear me?" he asked.

She slowly forced her eyes open, blinking several times and letting her tears flush them and help dissipate the pain caused by the lights. "Yes," she answered. "What happened?"

Someone gently wiped the moisture from her face. As they did so, her vision cleared, and she could see the handsome young Asian man in a white coat looking at her. Behind and above him, like snakes hanging from tree limbs, were white, yellow, and red tubes and gray electrical cords. "You were in a car accident," he said. "And you were pretty lucky."

She tried to shake her head back and forth to disagree, but it hurt too much, so she slowly said, "Don't feel lucky."

"Probably true. You've suffered a mild concussion. I imagine your head hurts quite a lot. And you might have some temporary amnesia."

She nodded slowly, trying to prevent more pain. "I think I do. Can't remember how I got hurt."

"Your left elbow was badly sprained," he continued as if he didn't hear the question implied in Verry's comment. "It's in a splint and should feel better in a few days. We had to operate to fix your knee. It's in a cast and should be like new in a few weeks. Your headaches will continue for a while, but we'll give you something to help you with all your pain. You need to stay here for a few days to make certain you don't have any serious problems from your concussion."

Verry closed her eyes and lay still, absorbing the information her doctor gave her, thinking about little, conscious of her headache more than anything else. *Terrific!* she thought. *I'm on my way to work with my girlfriend and—*

That jolted her out of her complacency. Her eyes snapped open. "What about Julie?" she asked. "Is she all right?"

The doctor's expression immediately became neutral. He looked across her bed at someone else, gave a minute nod, then said, "She was very badly injured."

He's hiding the truth. "Doctor, I'm not dying, right?"

He shook his head, sensing what was coming, but said nothing more.

"Then I'm strong enough to know if Julie's alive or not, aren't I?"

He looked at Verry for a few seconds, as if calculating whether or not to say anything. Then, very softly, he said, "The driver's side of the car took the brunt of the impact. We did all we could for her, but she was too badly injured."

Verry's eyes again filled with tears, but this time not from her pain but for Julie, her best friend from high school and a college classmate. She looked for tissues and saw a woman's hand holding one up for her. Wiping away her tears then clumsily blowing her nose one-handed, she asked, "Her family know?"

"Oh yes, Verry," the nurse answered. "And your parents and your sister were told about your injuries."

Then it hit her: *Lee! I've got to tell Lee! He warned me about the threats to him and his concerns about my safety, and now I'm injured.* Another thought hit her just as hard: *What if that wasn't an accident? What if Lee's warning came true?* "Nurse," she said, "can I talk to my sister? She works in ICU."

"We know Drella," the doctor said, nodding to the nurse and joining her in a grin. "We almost had to shackle her to keep her away after you were admitted. She's outside waiting to see you." He smiled reassuringly and gave Verry's hand a quick squeeze. "We'll get her right away."

A few seconds later, she heard a familiar voice. "Verry! I've been so worried!" Drella then broke into tears, holding Verry's hand and sobbing away the fears she carried ever since Verry was admitted.

"I'm OK, Drella," Verry said, "but someone has to tell Lee about this. Where's my cell phone?"

Drella was blinking away tears of relief and at the same time blinking in confusion about Verry's statement. "Your cell phone was destroyed in the accident."

Verry looked at her sister then painfully extended her right hand and grabbed Drella's wrist. "Dorella Janine Willards," she began, her voice weak but intense, knowing her sister's full name would grab the other woman's attention more than anything else she could do. "Someone has to tell Lee I've been hurt. If I can't use my cell phone, then either I use yours or you call him. BUT SOMEONE HAS TO CALL HIM!"

Drella's eyes widened in surprise at her sister's intensity and determination, especially after just awakening from general anesthetic. "OK," she said, "I'll do it. What's his number?"

Chapter 78

Need Cash; Must Hide

Lee finally completed most of the long drive up the foothills of the Rockies. He was on Interstate 80 just outside Rawlins, Wyoming, dead tired and tense from his concerns about FarCaller. Cell phone chirps brought him out of the funk that often accompanied worrying and driving for long stretches.

He was surprised and concerned when he saw the caller ID number displayed. The only two people who knew his cell phone number were Clem and Verry, and this call was from neither of them. His first inclination was to ignore the call, but something told him to answer it. Gingerly, almost as if fearing he could be hurt by just touching the Send button, he removed his cell phone from its holder on the dashboard and opened the circuit. His voice was low in pitch and volume and hesitant rather than radiating his usual sense of confidence. "Hello."

A woman's voice—not Verry's—said, "Is this Lee?"

God, don't let this be either a junk phone call or one of those people chasing me! Not about to give any more information than necessary, he said, "Who's calling?"

"This is Drella Willards, Verry Willard's sister," came the now insistent voice. "I have to talk with Lee Kaaler. Is this Lee?"

Still uncertain that this call didn't come from some kind of enemy, Lee responded tentatively. "Yes, this is Lee."

"Before I say anything more," she began, "I have to do something." Taking a deep breath, she said, "I'm looking for a different career path, and think I may have found a new calling."

"Drella," Lee said impatiently, concern for his future wife seeping throughout his body, "this is serious. If you're calling me and not using Verry's cell phone, it must mean something has happened to her."

"If you're Lee Kaaler, say what you're supposed to or I'm hanging up!"

For two seconds, Lee thought about Verry, then this woman who claimed to be his future sister-in-law. He needed to know she was a Kaaler and when he thought about what Drella was doing he realized it was exactly what he would have done before talking to a complete stranger about a family matter. He remained silent a few more seconds, calming himself some, then said, "A new calling can be very hard to find. Did you have any preferences?"

"Something in long distances."

"Worldwide, I presume," Lee responded. Before Drella could say anything, he said, "OK, now tell me why you're calling."

By the time she finished telling about Verry's accident and hospitalization, Lee was in a state of near panic, feeling helpless, in the middle of nowhere in a rented RV traveling under a false name. Then he began thinking logically. "Do two things, Drella. Right away."

"OK."

"Tell Verry I love her and I'll arrange some help for her as soon as I can. In the meantime, *stay with her*! Don't leave her for any reason unless one of 'us'"—stressing the word to indicate he meant a Kaaler—"is guarding her. Understand?"

"Guarding her? She said she was in danger. Who from? What—"

Lee was getting more frustrated, yet he knew Drella's concerns were real. "Drella! Stop talking and answer me. Do you understand?"

"Yes. Stay with her. Or have one of my family here."

"Right. I'll call you back on this number as soon as I can arrange some help. Hopefully it'll be in only a few hours. And don't forget to tell Verry I love her, Drella."

"I won't forget," she said. Then the magnitude of his statement hit her. "Love her? Verry didn't say anything about love! Is that why you're coming? To get married?" Drella was bubbling like an excited child, her mood totally opposite from that at the start of the call.

"Goodbye, Drella," Lee said, closing his cell phone's flip top and ending the call. *That's all I need: a well-intended but excited woman who might talk too much.*

Lee spotted a small RV park with a vacancy on the east side of Rawlins, but the place looked like an old drive-in theater. Instead of poles sprouting speakers, they had electrical and water connections.

"That'll be $20 for the night, sir," the small, portly but friendly desk clerk said as she prepared his receipt. "TV hookups are two dollars extra."

Habit took over. Lee withdrew his billfold and pulled out his favorite credit card. Handing it to the woman, he did what he always did as his credit card was processed: thought about nothing and looked around. Cigarettes for sale behind the clerk, several display racks holding small packages of hand soap, dishwashing liquid, holding tank deodorant, and drinking water hoses. He just started to turn around and look behind him when the clerk said, "I'm sorry, Mr. Kaaler, but your credit card has been rejected." She looked concerned and serious, but not threatening.

What's happened? he asked himself. *I've been using that card for years and never had any problem before. My account's all paid up, and—it's those guys who are looking for me. They've messed up my credit cards somehow. But how'd they get my numbers? And—*

He stopped thinking and stood still, eyes closed. *I'm not at all comfortable being in disguise, and I'm not thinking like I should. I tried to use my real credit card, and if it hadn't been messed up by someone, I'd have compromised my entire attempt to hide.* He blinked a few times then smiled at the clerk. *I've got to get out of here and solve this problem.* "I'm really very sorry, ma'am," he said, taking back his card and looking into his billfold. "Don't know what happened, 'cause I've used this card for years. I'll get some cash and come back." *Darn! I should have gotten a couple hundred dollars in cash before I left. Really stupid!*

Just down the road from the RV park was a huge truck stop with acres of parking spaces scarcely half full of long-haul rigs. That reminded him of how hungry he was after his long, uphill drive, so he parked in front of the truck stop's attached restaurant and ate the ubiquitous buffet dinner special. He paid for his meal with his last $20 bill then had an epiphany. *Why am I trying to stay overnight in RV parks? I could park my RV behind some big semi in the back of one of these truck stops and no one would ever think about it. It'd let me sleep, stay hidden, and save me money at the same time.*

That decision made, he called Clem. After relating how his credit card had been messed with, Clem agreed to wire cash to him using the appropriate false name. Acting on a whim, Lee checked the voice mail at his home phone and heard the threatening message from Jeff Gerit. He then realized his credit card problem was just one of a series of difficulties these people—whomever they were—could cause. *And they might have arranged Verry's "accident."*

From his cell phone directory service, he got the address of the Western Union office in Rawlins, drove there, and retrieved the five hundred dollars Clem wired him. While hunting for the Western Union office, his overriding thought: *Those people know way too much about me.*

Chapter 79

Help's on the Way

April 15, 2005

After parking behind a large moving van in the truck stop parking lot, Lee spent the rest of the evening worrying about how to get Verry out of the hospital before he arrived in Des Moines. Just as he was about asleep, he thought of a way to protect her and called an old friend on his cell phone. *These things are marvelous! In one hand you can hold a device that lets you contact nearly anyone in the world!* He was surprised that his friend answered the telephone himself, as the last time Lee called it was answered by a woman. "This is Lee again, Thommy K. I need some more help. But your wife might object."

A spontaneous laugh, followed by a muffled conversation Lee couldn't make out, then a woman's laugh. "No problem, Lee. My wife won't object because I don't have one." Both Thommy K. and the woman again laughed.

"But I thought—"

"Lee, stop worrying about me and tell me why you're calling. Up until a couple of weeks ago we hadn't talked in years, and suddenly you're on the telephone asking for more help. Something serious must be up."

As Thommy K. talked, Lee nodded. *Still cuts right to the heart of the matter.* "It is," Lee admitted, trying to decide what to say while still keeping much of the background material out of the discussion. "I'm supposed to get married next weekend, but I just learned my fiancée was in a car accident. Without going into detail, let me say that I have reason to believe it might not have been an 'accidental' accident, if you know what I mean."

"Someone arranged it?"

"Possibly."

"But why? What'd she do to anyone?"

Again he goes to the core. His friend's skill in processing data didn't help Lee keep some things secret. "Nothing. But it might be a message to me."

Thommy K. said nothing for a few seconds, obviously considering the meaning of Lee's statement. "You mean someone's willing to hurt an innocent person just to get to you?"

"Maybe. They—or somebody—already torched my folks' home. And someone left a voice mail message saying they're willing to keep it up."

"But why? Are you involved in something illegal—besides using fake IDs?"

"No. But right now I need someone to go to Des Moines as soon as possible and get my fiancée to someplace that's safe from whomever's trying to get something I have. There's no way I can confirm her injury wasn't an accident, but I can't risk her life."

That admission convinced Thommy K. "Just tell me what to do," he said, "and I can leave in thirty minutes. But can I ask another question?"

"Ask away."

"I don't know any clever way to say this, Lee, but—is this a Kaaler matter? And are you supposed to solve it?"

Lee was stopped cold by the question, partly because no one had ever asked it before and partly because it told him Thommy K. thought Lee might be the Guardian. "Let's talk about this when we get together," he said, evading the question. "What about your lady friend?" referring to the woman in Thommy K.'s place.

"She lives here," was the matter-of-fact answer. "She'll do fine while I'm gone."

A sudden panicky spasm: "Did she hear the Challenge when we talked the first time?" Lee asked.

"Nope. In the other room watching television. Now tell me all I need to know."

Chapter 80

Unexpected Help

Clem didn't like people who tried to be mysterious: it was cheap melodrama, something better filmed in black and white than in color. And when these threats affected his friends, it angered him, something he had trained himself to avoid.

As a lawyer, he was constantly confronted with angry people—he believed that was why the legal profession existed: to resolve arguments. To keep from being part of the problem instead of part of the solution, Clem didn't let himself get angry while working because it prevented him from properly representing his clients. Now, however, a really nice guy had been threatened. A guy who hurt no one and, so far as Clem knew, didn't have an angry muscle in his body. Threatening such a man was, in his lawyer's mind, tantamount to assault. *That* he could deal with.

After he received Lee's call for help, Clem decided to help in ways Lee couldn't know about, even with his background in banking. The next Monday, Clem retrieved bank account numbers from Lee's personal file and, with the help of a banking friend in Portland, began manipulating Lee's finances. His friend's regular job was to transfer money around the world via the bank's computer, so Clem had him electronically transfer more than one hundred thousand dollars from Lee's account in Bend to an account Clem kept for his own purposes in a Belgian bank. Then they established a new bank account in a Portland bank in Lee's grandmother's maiden name, with Lee as the co-depositor. That made it look like a joint account for a married couple and, they hoped, would put Lee's money in an account that was essentially untraceable. It was, strictly speaking, illegal to open a bank account in a dead person's name, but both Clem amd his friend were willing to take the chance. They could always change it later, and they were certain no one would check to ensure both parties were alive. That done, they transferred Lee's money into the new account.

Lee was on the road, thinking about Verry and her safety, still worrying about protecting her, but comforted by Drella's assurance that Verry would heal completely and by Thommy K.'s agreement to help. The last thing he expected was a call from his lawyer, but when he checked the caller ID and saw Clem's number, his first thought was that it was an emergency report. "Are my parents OK?" His voice betrayed his concern.

"They'ah fine," Clem said in his smoothest and most reassuring voice, "Everahthin's OK here. But after Ah transferred that money to y'all, Ah got to thinking 'bout y'all's situation and did somethin' moah. Can y'all write some stuff down right now? Y'all need to use it at the first bank y'all find."

Lee pulled the RV off the road so he could give his full attention to what his lawyer wanted. "OK, Clem, go."

When Clem completed passing the new bank account information to Lee, there was only silence on the line. "Lee, are y'all OK?"

Lee nodded, forgetting no one could see him. "Yes," he responded, trying hard to keep the catch out of his voice. "I didn't expect to receive help right now, and I really needed it. You don't know how much it means."

"Just do as Ah instructed when y'all get to a bank. Whatever y'all do, however, don't sign anathin' using a false name. That'd be a criminal act, and everythin' would stop. Y'all might tell the bankers to call me 'bout the secrecy y'all want to maintain. Ah think Ah can convince them to keep this whole thing quiet. In fact, Ah know some legal threats that might make them lose sleep just *thinkin'* 'bout saying anathin' 'bout the transactions."

"Thanks much, Clem."

"Just be careful. And when y'all get back here, y'all can tell me what this is about."

Chapter 81

Take Her!

"Billy, this is Jeff Gerit." The response was instantaneous. "Yes, sir. What do you need?"

"I need someone there in Des Moines you can trust to do a very important job."

"My guys are pretty good, but if you're worried about secrecy, maybe I'm your man."

He broke the code! "I was hoping you'd feel that way, Billy."

"What do you need?"

"There's a woman right where you are, in Des Moines. Her name is Vera Willards. She may be the key to getting what we need from Kaaler. She's very close to this Kaaler guy we've been hunting, I think. Right now she's in a downtown hospital. Had an unfortunate "accident" we arranged for her. I want her moved to a place *we* control. We'll use her for *our* purposes."

"For leverage."

"Strong leverage. I think Kaaler will be much more cooperative when he knows she'll be hurt if he doesn't give me what I want."

"I can do that."

"It has to be done pretty soon, Billy. Kaaler is probably headed to Des Moines already."

"Give me her name and I'll have her in twenty-four hours."

"Her name is Vera Willards. She's the key to getting what we need from Kaaler."

Chapter 82

Final Thrust

One of the best things in FarCaller's life was the joy he experienced when he walked through the forests on his land. So often was he there that he knew the homes of every small animal, knew which family of birds would be nesting in which trees, and knew the best places to simply sit against a tree to watch this small world go about finding food, mating, and raising the young. On this day, however, after Lee's Sensing about the Interceptor's clear desire to kill him, FarCaller left the forest he loved for the privacy of his barn. First he sat on a large bundle of dry grass to think about the danger he was fated to confront. Perhaps worse, he wondered what he must do to save his own life from someone with whom he should share a bond of love instead of being separated by fear and hatred. The animal odors of the barn, usually comforting and familiar, now seemed to reek with the scent of danger and death. The joy he got from cleaning the stalls for his beloved working horses was erased by the fear he would never again enjoy this special place and its memories.

In this place once radiating pleasure, FarCaller prepared for a confrontation with the Interceptor in a manner he had never before attempted: he armed himself. He first hid a dagger under his right pant leg, just below his knee. Next he took a digging pick from its pegs on the back wall of the barn and practiced swinging it, getting a feel for its heft and movement, imagining the pain and injuries it could inflict if he had to hit his brother with it.

Throughout all of this, he was as depressed and sad as he had ever been. Instead of feeling joy at a family homecoming, he was preparing to fight his brother to the death if need be. The silver plate used by FarCaller and his ancestors to contact the Guardians had always been passed to the eldest child in that family line, but the Interceptor didn't care. Even though he knew almost nothing about the plate and what FarCaller did with it, he wanted the power that he believed came with that plate. He wanted his own way regardless of whom he hurt, how old or young, how rich or poor, friend or family.

"To him," FarCaller said to himself, "only his own desires important are. Unimportant all else is." He resumed swinging the pick at a sheaf of hay he'd placed upright as a target, then his thoughts returned to his brother. "An evil man he is, evil things doing. About the harm he does to others nothing cares he." FarCaller took two hard swings at the sheaves of grass, the second cutting one sheaf in half, dust and pieces of dry grass flying all over the barn, coating FarCaller's clothes and getting into his eyes. As he blinked them to wash the dust out and return clear vision, he continued thinking aloud. "Control of the silver plate he cannot gain. Centuries of tradition would he destroy his own selfish ends just to serve. And much Lee would suffer."

He let the pick rest on the barn's dirt floor and allowed himself a brief respite from his exertions, wiping perspiration and dust from his brow onto the sleeve of his blue work shirt. *If I practice too hard, so tired will I be that myself defend I cannot. That would any good no one do, except the Interceptor. The Evil Interceptor.*

Taking several more deep breaths, coughing as he inhaled the dusty air inside the barn, he walked toward the door to meet a man he should love but couldn't: a man with whom he should share his home but whom he could trust with nothing.

As he pushed open the barn door, he sensed something wrong and instinctively crouched to lower his silhouette and give him time see whatever set off his perception of approaching danger. As he did so, he felt and heard a swoosh followed by the smash of something on the barn door directly above his head. Quickly looking up after wincing from the sound of the blow, he saw his brother raising an ax above his head, readying for a second blow, a blow clearly designed to separate FarCaller's head from his body. The eyes of the Interceptor were black pools of evil radiating hatred to the total exclusion of everything else. He was FarCaller's height, but more muscular, his large biceps and strong hands exuding power, his knuckles white with his effort to crush his brother with the next blow of his ax. His dirty blue overalls were covered with streaks of mud and bloodstains, as if he had butchered a large animal several days earlier and never washed either his clothes or his body since. And he was on a mission of murder!

FarCaller had never fought anyone for anything, never before even contemplated anything like it. But he was smart, his body was pumping adrenaline and giving him strength he didn't know he possessed, and his mind was working more quickly than he could ever have imagined. In a split second, he saw the Interceptor's weakness. His brother was so intent in attacking and so confident in his power that he didn't think about defending himself. FarCaller leaped out of his crouch straight for the Interceptor, just as his brother's ax was headed for the space where FarCaller's head had been. Shoving the pick handle straight toward his brother, FarCaller jammed it into his brother's groin with all the strength he could muster, trying to slow the other man enough to allow FarCaller to regain his strength and think more about how to defend himself as well as incapacitate his brother.

His brother's reaction was that of any normal man, so much so that it surprised FarCaller. His brother grabbed at his testicles and fell to the ground screaming an unearthly, high-pitched wail that almost hurt FarCaller because so much pain lay behind it. The ax skittered aimlessly across the barn floor. As that happened, FarCaller struck the man across the forehead with the pick, willing all his strength into the blow, trying to slow the attack enough that he could gain his breath and prepare for the next onslaught. The Interceptor now lay on the ground, blood streaming onto the dusty earth from the open crease on his skull. There would be no "next" onslaught. Seeing that evil man lying in the dust and straw, still clutching his groin, FarCaller felt as if he himself had suffered this quick death.

He was the victor in the Intercepter's terms, but in his own eyes he lost. He was unharmed physically. He had done his world a favor while losing his own sense of humanity. Kneeling down in the dirt, he hugged the Interceptor's lifeless body to his chest, crying and moaning aloud at the loss of a brother and his own innocence.

His mother found him several hours later, still in that position. She had come to bury FarCaller. He, in her eyes, had no chance against his brother, a brother so certain of his strength and cause that he even bragged about his intent to kill FarCaller. Seeing FarCaller's grief, she realized how much and for how long she misunderstood him, and wept at her own shortcomings. Much later, they put the Intercepter's body on a cart hitched to their gentlest mare and took it into the farthest reaches of their land. Together they dug a grave deep into the soft, beloved, and familiar land they had known all their lives and quietly and quickly deposited the body of the son and brother they once knew. Only a small line of rocks outlined the grave. They then silently rode the cart back to FarCaller's home. After unhitching the mare and letting her loose in the pasture, they embraced each other and again cried together. Then his mother left FarCaller alone, now unquestionably the patriarch of his family. But at such a price.

Chapter 83

Get Out!

No matter how hard hospitals try to make patient accommodations pleasant, they fail. At least that was what Verry felt. With nothing to do and only time on her hands, she studied her room's decor. Pastel blue walls matching some of the spots in the vinyl floor tiles, intentionally or otherwise. Window curtains with a spring garden motif on a mottled pastel background designed to match anything and everything in the room. Light green sheets and pillowcase. And on and on. Even the brilliant spring sun's rays didn't help.

Interspersed in this tedium were thoughts of Lee, of the life they would have together, of their handsome sons and beautiful daughters, of a cozy home in a beautiful place with only spring blossoms and snowcapped peaks year round. And no threats.

Verry was not only bored and depressed, she felt she wasn't healing. Deep down she knew she was, but her whole world—except for the accident and Lee—was *boring*. But then every time she thought about her accident, she thought about Julie, her best friend for the last ten years. Then she cried.

Before she could mire herself much deeper into an emotional morass, the door to her private room slowly opened, and a familiar head pushed its way in. Drella was wearing green surgical scrubs, her long and lustrous brown hair covered by a thin white medical hairnet, her hospital ID badge hanging from a silver necklace about her neck. Her face was beautiful and bright with excitement.

"What's wrong, Drella? I've never seen you excited and quiet at the same time. What's happened?"

"Lee asked one of his friends to come to Des Moines and sneak you out of here. And that guy—Thommy K. somebody—asked me to help!" The excited smile on Drella's face was so contagious the whole room seemed to light up and smile with her. But she still spoke very softly—quickly, but softly.

Verry's happiness at seeing her sister and sharing the "good news" was suddenly tempered by inherent good sense. "But why would Lee want someone to sneak me out of here?"

"I can't explain it, Verry," Drella continued, "but Thommy K. Challenged me and everything—just like I did to Lee. When I responded correctly, he said to quickly get you and your things ready to leave, and he'd be here early this evening. I'm supposed to find a small house or apartment where we can stay until Lee gets here tomorrow or the next day."

Verry would have jumped up in bed if her arm and leg casts didn't prevent it, but she was so excited she pounded the bed with her good right arm and smiled just as broadly as Drella. "Tomorrow? Oh, thank God!"

Drella's face turned slyly secretive. "And Thommy K. said Lee said he loves you. And Lee told me the same thing a couple of days ago. But when I asked him if you were going to get married, he hung up!" She hurried over to Verry's bed and grabbed her right hand, wringing it tightly. "When, Verry? When's the wedding?" Drella was literally jumping up and down in excitement, albeit only a few inches.

"Drella, will you stop hopping around and tell me how a twenty-four-year-old woman can change so quickly from a competent intensive care nurse to someone sounding like a giggling teenager?" Before Drella could say anything more, Verry asked, "Who's Thommy K.?"

"Lee's friend. From Omaha." Her eyes widened in sudden realization of something she forgot. "Oh darn! I've still got to find a safe place for you to stay."

Before Verry could say anything, Drella quickly left, slowing only enough to close the door quietly behind her. Verry first commented to herself about how young her sister sometimes acted but then remembered the salient feature in everything Drella said: *Lee's friends are going to try to sneak me out of here tonight because I'm in danger!* With that realization, her heartbeat accelerated, her breath came in gasps, the pain in her knee increased, and her stomach quivered.

Chapter 84

SOS

The intensive care unit in a large general hospital had been the most stressful environment in Drella's life—until now. This afternoon she realized she had been lucky. She was now on her own in a situation in which a mistake might cost her sister's life: she no longer had others to rely on, as she did at work.

She didn't dare ask her parents for help because they'd react emotionally and try to take Verry home with them. From her short talks with Lee and Thommy K., she believed that would endanger her whole family.

She had to do it alone, yet there *were* people who could help. Newspaper ads listed houses for rent, even small furnished houses like she needed, but that usually took days to sort out: calling the person or company who placed the ad, finding out where the house was, arranging for a visit—and on and on. Each step important, each taking time. She had no time, but there was a housing source closer at hand.

A key component of a college or university situated in the middle of any town was the Student Housing Office. Student housing had to be cheap, available, and close to school. Verry worked in the alumni office and knew people in University Housing. Since the campus was barely a mile from the hospital, she started there.

She confided to the student assistant in the housing office that the need was immediate and that Verry would vouch for the renter. She didn't tell the girl that Verry herself would be the tenant. They found three potential rentals.

The first was cheap. It was a mess and smelled like it hadn't been cleaned in a year.

The second was better. It was a Cape Cod-style house, and it had two bedrooms, but they were upstairs, and the bathroom was downstairs. *Can't use it: getting Verry up and down stairs is way too hard.* Drella believed Thommy K.

and possibly Lee would be staying there with Verry and herself, so whatever she rented had to have at least two, and preferably three, bedrooms. But the prospects weren't looking good.

The third was just behind the string of strip malls surrounding the hospital: the office complexes for the medical professionals who worked at or supported the hospital. Two blocks behind that complex of expensive offices was a working-class neighborhood. The people who kept Des Moines alive lived there: bus drivers, sanitation workers, street cleaners, janitors, store clerks, shoe salesmen. They had low or modest incomes, couldn't afford really nice homes—even small ones—but were the people often called the salt of the earth. That neighborhood had vacancies in houses formerly occupied by college students.

Drella walked through the house tentatively. It was already early evening, and Thommy K. was due to call in less than an hour. Crunch time.

This one had only one bedroom. It also had a rickety but serviceable tan velour sofa bed in the front room along with a brown plaid futon, a small living/dining room, a working toilet, and an old, stained, cast-iron bathtub with eagle claw feet. The kitchen/dining area had green floral wallpaper with a white lattice fence pattern up to wainscot height: very "in" forty or more years earlier. The floor in both rooms was in a faux hardwood pattern. It wasn't what she'd wanted, but she didn't have a lot of time to continue her hunt, and this place would work for a few days.

Drella turned to the rental agent. "I'll take it." She sat in one of the metal dining chairs with blue plastic upholstery and gestured for him to sit opposite her. "I need to move in here tonight. That's not a problem, is it?"

The young man's eyebrows shot up in surprise at how quickly Drella made her decision. "Not if you provide the cash deposit first."

Cash? I don't have any cash. She took a deep breath and let her shoulders slump, hoping to give the impression of deep exhaustion. "I just don't want to look anymore, and this is the right place!"

He acted like he'd heard it before but shook his head, his expression unchanged.

Then Drella played a hunch, something as a nurse she had been trained never to do. "What about this? What if I move in right now? I'll lock the door behind me. Then I'll go to the bank and get the $400, go to your office, sign the papers, and pay the deposit. It'll save me an extra trip clear across town to get my stuff. And it'll give the owners rent starting today, and everyone'll be pleased." She accompanied her suggestion with what she hoped was a delighted smile, one with just a tinge of sexuality and availability.

The agent just shook his head. "Ma'am," he began, "can't give anyone the keys until they've paid the deposit. Regardless."

This isn't working the way it's supposed to!

She tried a different strategy. She thought about the saddest thing she'd ever seen: the slow death of a small girl in the cancer ward. A lovely eight-year-old with a pretty face, quick mind, and delightful sense of humor, but with a body feeding a cancer so virulent that there was no hope except to keep her in as little pain as possible until the inevitable end. She let herself tear up and, instead of letting the thought go away, purposely recalled the little girl's funeral, the other little children, and the children's songs, like "Jesus Loves Me." Inside of a minute, tears were running down her cheeks, her breath coming in small gasps, and she looked absolutely distraught. The agent didn't have a chance.

Within ten minutes, Drella had the keys and was driving with Verry's bank card to the closest ATM. After getting the rental deposit, she drove to the housing office, signed the lease, gave the young man a smile guaranteed to make his day, and rushed back to the house.

Drella didn't have the experience to know what she had really done, but she was now the tenant of what most law enforcement and intelligence agencies would call a "safe house." It was a place where people could relax in the midst of danger, in a neighborhood where outsiders rarely visited, situated among working people and students who constantly moved in and out.

Once inside, she called Thommy K. on her cell phone and told him what she had done. Then she gave him the safe house's address, directions to it and the hospital, and Verry's room number. "Drella," he said, "I don't know anyone else who could have put all of this together so quickly. I know I'd not have been able to even if I'd started this morning. I owe you a gesture of thanks, probably starting with a big hug and kiss."

Before she could respond, he closed the circuit.

Both sound marvelous! I wonder if he's single. Or good looking. Then she rushed out to buy enough groceries for four people for four days.

Chapter 85

This Is Serious, Counselor

April 16, 2005

It was midafternoon, and Clem had just counseled a young couple on the legal problems caused by declaring bankruptcy. After they left, he'd wondered how two young people could get themselves so deeply in debt, when his thoughts were interrupted by a telephone call. After Francine forwarded it to him, he picked up the receiver and was about to answer it when the caller said, "Mr. Maestre?" Clem quickly checked the caller ID box: it displayed Unknown Caller. "Yes. To whom am Ah speaking, please?"

"That doesn't matter, Mr. Maestre," the voice said.

Clem quickly and expertly analyzed both his situation and the tone of voice on the other end of the line, skills honed in the many court trials he'd watched and participated in. "It does to me," Clem countered. "Ah don't talk to people who won't identify themselves." As he spoke, he pulled a yellow legal pad close enough that he could make notes. The first thing he wrote: used to being in charge; likes to act big.

"This call isn't for you: it's for your client, Faerleigh Kaaler," the voice said. "It is very much to his advantage that you listen to what I say." The man continued before Clem could say anything more. "Mr. Kaaler is having problems with his credit cards. A lawyer with your credentials can take care of the matter easily, since it's mostly a nuisance. The point of it was to inform Mr. Kaaler, and you, that we are aware of every detail of his life and can continue these little games as long as we choose."

Clem's curiosity was now aroused. "But what's he done to y'all to deserve this?"

"That's not important, Mr. Maestre. What's important is that both he and you understand we are serious. But to answer your question, he has something we want badly and intend to obtain. This can be done in several ways, some painful for Mr. Kaaler, some easily accomplished."

"What is it y'all want?" Again Clem's curiosity was piqued. He knew a fair amount about his friend and client, and to his knowledge Lee had nothing of particular value. Certainly nothing that should cause this almost comic-strip act by an unknown foe.

"If he wants you to know, Mr. Maestre, he can tell you. What is important is that he be given this message as soon as possible. And that he understand further delays in acceding to our wishes will cause additional pain to his family and loved ones."

Before Clem could respond, the line went dead.

Chapter 86

Verry's Flight

"Drella, this is Thommy K. I'm about an hour out of Des Moines. Now listen carefully, OK?" His baritone voice had a slight edge to it, as if he were worrying or concentrating very hard on something.

Drella was so excited at hearing his voice again that she almost forgot that talking with her wasn't his reason for calling. Quickly putting things back into proper perspective, she said, "Right." She pulled a small notebook out of her purse and put it on the bed next to Verry. "I'm ready to copy."

"All we need to do is get her from the hospital to the house. Can you work some kind of transportation?"

As he was talking, Drella was thinking about just how to accomplish that task. "Yes," she said as she wrote the task on her notepad. An illegal or unauthorized use of an ambulance was a possibility. She smiled as she remembered one of the women ambulance drivers she had helped pass the medical part of the written exam to get her job. "I know someone who'll help me and keep her mouth shut."

"OK. When I get to the hospital, I'll come straight to Verry's room, and we can sneak her out." He paused. "Can't we?"

Drella was again thinking about the difficulties of the task they had undertaken, now trying to visualize a path through the hospital where a woman on a gurney would least likely be noticed. She wrote the task in the notepad while she was thinking how to accomplish it. She had about half the route planned when Thommy K. said, "Drella? You there?"

What a time to get lost in thought. "Right. I'm thinking about the route we can take in the hospital, and I've just about got it. I'll have it and an ambulance arranged by the time you get here."

"OK, then. What's her room number?"

After Drella gave Thommy K. the number and directions on how to find the room, he said only, "Good. See you at 8:00."

One of these days I hope we'll be able to have a decent conversation. He might be a nice guy, but right now he's all business. She shook her thoughts away from what would have been carnal images and back to the matter at hand. Verry was looking at her, a slightly lewd smile on her face.

"I know what you're thinking," Verry said, her smile broadening, "and you ought to be ashamed of yourself!"

"Speak for yourself," Drella retorted. "Now let me alone while I make a couple of important calls, then maybe we'll be able to talk about who should be ashamed of what."

Drella obtained her ambulance driver friend's reluctant agreement to move Verry out of the hospital. After tracing and retracing the route they would take to minimize the chance of anyone seeing them on their way out, she left Verry's room and returned less than thirty minutes later with some clothes from her apartment. The sisters were the same size, so that part of the escape was easy. Getting them on Verry while fighting the interference caused by Verry's leg cast and arm sling wasn't. Just as she was trying to get Verry's right sock on, there was a light knock, and the door slowly opened. A man in a hospital orderly's uniform entered, carrying a plastic tray full of syringes and test tubes used for collecting blood samples. He appeared a bit unsure of himself, as if he were new to his job.

Drella was in her nurse's scrubs and instantly went on the offensive. Stepping between the orderly and Verry, hoping the man didn't notice Verry was wearing regular clothes instead of a hospital gown, she said, "This patient isn't scheduled for any blood work at this time of night. You've got the wrong room."

The handsome orderly didn't look surprised or check his hospital orders: he smiled. "No," he said, "I don't think so. Are you Drella?" His voice was low, his smile wide, his eyes dark brown, and his body trim.

Drella stopped in mid-thought, not expecting to hear this unknown orderly say her name, then realized he couldn't be an orderly. No matter how realistic he looked, he didn't have his hospital ID badge hooked onto his white pullover shirt. "Depends on who you are."

"I'm Thommy K. Pajaro. And I owe you something."

Quickly putting the blood work tray on the foot of Verry's bed, Thommy K. embraced Drella and planted a kiss full on her lips. Before she could react other than blush—to her sister's delight—Thommy K. quickly returned to business.

"OK, both of you," he said, moving quickly to grasp Verry's free hand, "we need to get that gurney here so we can move out."

Drella had recovered her "professional" persona and was now all business. "The gurney will be here in"—she checked her wristwatch and the clock just above the room's door—"about three minutes."

As she spoke, the door opened and a woman in an ambulance service uniform entered, pushing a gurney. Seeing Drella, she moved the gurney next to Verry's bed. "Drella, help me."

It took two minutes to move Verry onto the gurney and cover her with a sheet so her street clothes couldn't be seen, being careful to cover her IV drip of a half liter of saline solution. Then all three of them followed Drella out of the room. Drella's friend pushed the gurney with practiced ease, and Thommy K. held Verry's right hand as if to reassure her things would be OK. They followed Drella down the hall, into a staff elevator, then up other halls and down other elevators until they reached the hospital service entrance, now closed for the night. Turning toward her friend, she asked, "Is everything all set up here?"

Two nods. "Yes. Give me thirty seconds and I'll have the door open and ready for Verry."

Soon they were in a white ambulance with red stripes and letters, moving out the service driveway; no emergency lights flashing, no siren, nothing to indicate there was anyone but the driver in an off-duty ambulance.

Ten slow minutes later, they were at the safe house. In another fifteen Verry was in bed and the gurney, the driver, and Thommy K. were out the door. While Drella helped Verry tend to her personal needs and then get arranged in the noisy and oversoft bed, Thommy K. rode back to the hospital wearing his orderly uniform, then changed into his own clothes, transferred to his own car, and returned to the safe house.

As Thommy K. drove away from the hospital, a tall, slender man with skin tanned dark from long exposure to the winds of the plains approached the visitor information desk at the main entrance. He wore faded denim pants and a short denim jacket. When he reached the information desk, he smiled an engaging smile to the young woman sitting there and said, "I'd like to visit Vera Willards, ma'am. Could you please tell me her room number?"

She typed something on her computer keyboard and looked at the ensuing display. To the ruggedly handsome man standing before her, she said, "I'm sorry, sir, but Ms. Willards can't have visitors tonight. You could see her tomorrow morning after nine."

"Thank you, ma'am," he said. "I'll return then."

His next stop was a telephone booth in the hospital lobby. He made a quick call, waited until he heard a familiar voice answer it, then said only, "Found her."

Chapter 87

Warm and Loving

April 17, 2005

The closer Lee got to Des Moines, the more he thought about Verry, their marriage, and honeymooning. The traffic increased so much as he neared Des Moines that he had to force thoughts of Verry out of his mind and pay attention to what was happening around him. His first goal was to see her, but he didn't know where she was. He stopped at a small county park just west of the city and dialed Drella's cell phone number.

It rang six times before anyone answered, causing Lee to worry even more about Verry's safety. When Drella finally answered, he recognized her voice and felt a load of worry escape his body: he was more nervous than he thought.

"This is Lee. Is Verry OK?"

"Want to talk to her?"

"Put her on, please. It's been a long drive."

He heard a muffled conversation, then, "Lee? Is that you?"

He didn't remember much about that conversation in spite of the fact it lasted over thirty minutes. The salient features, however, were etched into his brain: Verry was feeling better; they were safe; Thommy K. was a great help; and Verry wanted to see him *now*. At ten o'clock at night.

"OK," he said, "but first I have to know how to find you." He said it with a touch of humor in his voice, but the message was clear.

"Oh my gosh, Lee," she said, her voice changing from the loving and caring woman to that of a confused one, "I don't know where we are for certain. Drella can tell you." Before she handed the phone to her sister, Verry added, "Be careful!"

Drella's instructions took him through several middle-class and lower-class neighborhoods, full of small houses, streets almost clogged with old and battered cars and pickups, and everything needing repair. The houses needed repainting, the streets had more potholes than smooth sections, and the vehicles were either sun-scorched or rusted and dented. The predominant color was gray; the predominant odor was garbage. It took Lee fifteen minutes to find the house, his heart pounding in his ears the entire trip, trying to pay attention to traffic while negotiating his way though a place he'd only visited once, to a section of town he'd never even heard of, let alone seen. As he parked the RV on the gently sloping street, the front door of the house opened, and the familiar shape of Thommy K. bounced down the cracked cement sidewalk, reaching the RV door about the same time Lee opened it.

A quick handshake followed by a hefty hug, some quick words of thanks as they walked back to the house, and a hug for Drella—ignoring her knowing smile, and shutting the door behind him he rushed into the bedroom to be with the woman he loved.

Amid all the hugs and kisses and caresses and loving looks, all Lee could think was, *God, I love this woman.* From her responses, he knew she felt the same.

After about ten minutes, someone knocked on the bedroom door. They were ignored for several minutes.

"Come on," Drella called through the door, "you'll have time for this stuff later. We have to talk."

Lee and Verry finished a very deep kiss, shared quick and loving smiles, and, finally, Verry said, "OK."

Instantly the door opened, and Drella and Thommy K. entered. Neither Thommy K. nor Drella said anything right away, nor made any attempt to conceal their curiosity at how flushed the couple looked nor how fast they might be breathing. Finally Thommy K. broke the silence. "Well, you obviously recognize each other. Now, Lee, tell us what's happening." Before Lee could say anything, Thommy K. added, "And then maybe you'll answer that question I asked."

Both men knew exactly what he meant, but neither sister did.

Lee spoke first, looking Thommy K. directly in the eyes. "The answer is yes, it's a Kaaler family matter." Thommy K.'s eyes widened. It was clear from that answer that Lee didn't want to discuss the matter further, at least then. Thommy K. gave a quick nod then continued as if nothing had been said, "And how was the trip?"

Drella couldn't stand the seemingly innocent repartee between the men. "Stop it!" she said, stomping one foot lightly on the floor to emphasize her impatience. "The only thing that matters is getting you guys married!"

"Not so," Lee said, withdrawing his arm from around Verry's shoulders. "The only thing that matters is getting Verry and me out of this town safely and secretly." He looked Drella straight in the eyes then turned and nodded at Thommy K. "No one knows about your role in this, so you two should be safe. But we're not."

Chapter 88

FarKiller

Instead of feeling elation from eliminating the threat posed by his brother, FarCaller felt remorse, grief, and sorrow. "What else would you someone call whom his own brother slays? FarCaller me they call," he said to no one in particular, "but Far*Killer* say they should." His mind told him he'd had no choice: the Interceptor needed to be killed or he would keep killing anyone who got in the way of getting whatever he wanted—whenever he wanted it. But FarCaller's heart told him he had done something wrong, and no amount of rationalization seemed to change that. He was in his house, pacing back and forth between the great room and his bedroom, not knowing where he was going or why he was walking, only knowing he could not erase from his mind the burden of having killed his own brother. When he returned to his home after burying his brother, he tore off the clothes he wore during the fight and incinerated them in his fireplace. Then he walked the thousand paces to the small stream at the edge of his property and washed himself with strong soap and a stiff brush. When he finished, his skin was raw from being rubbed so hard and his flesh burned from the lye in the soap. He knew he was clean on the outside, but inside he still felt dirty. That night he couldn't sleep—he thought—until he heard cows lowing. When he looked around, he realized it was already midmorning. He had indeed slept, and slept hard. He pulled on a pair of clean dark blue work pants and a light blue shirt and rushed to the barn.

After tending to his cows and horses, he returned to his house to rest but found his mind refused to do so, still flashing the views of his brother lying in the dirt outside the barn, blood oozing from his scalp and ears. To get his mind away from self-incrimination, FarCaller busied himself around the house, beginning with dusting his books using a well-worn and moth-eaten old sock.

Pulling each volume from the bookcase to dust off every surface, he came across a brown leather volume with his grandfather's name engraved in gold on it. It was cracked with age, its thin oak veneer starting to peel off its pine backing. Something made FarCaller stop dusting and open the book only to suffer another surprise—it was a journal. He never knew his grandfather kept a journal and he'd never seen it before. Perhaps his mother had kept it away from FarCaller until his brother was forever out of the way and then decided to put it in a bookshelf in his new house.

He put the slightly damp dust rag on top of the waist-high pine bookcase and took the journal to his favorite chair, placed so he could look directly at the fireplace. Above the mantel, in a position of honor, was the silver plate, his window into Lee's world, a world no one else in *his* world knew existed. He stopped thinking in words, letting vague concepts roll over him. Then he recognized something he'd missed in all his thoughts about the Interceptor: *Bad the death of my brother is, but if I died the line of FarCallers forever ended would be. Worse than the death of my brother that would be.*

Two shocks of recognition struck him: the journal was written in a system of symbols he'd never seen before, and he could read them! *More FarCaller magic this is. But why Grandfather FarCaller about this never revealed?* The answer struck him almost as hard as the shock of being able to read the text: *This a special part of the FarCaller gift is, that to discover for ourselves we must.*

He then felt much better. Almost immediately he saw the words "Guardian Ima"—Lee's grandmother. Leafing through the thick pages, he noted the words, "golden set." *What? Only of a silver set did Grandfather tell me.* He continued turning and scanning the pages. In the next twenty he found three references to a golden plate and golden spoon. FarCaller stopped then, sat down in his favorite chair, and thought about this discovery. He came to only one conclusion. *About this must Lee be told.*

Chapter 89

Disturbing Discovery

FarCaller pored over his grandfather's journal, searching for anything about a second spoon and plate set. Unfortunately, related entries were scattered throughout the volume, making it impossible to efficiently find all the information in one or even two spots. However, after searching until late in the evening, he had many pages of notes extracted from the journal entries and finally had time to read them seriously. It was later than he usually stayed up, but he was too involved to sleep.

His grandfather wrote of rumors about a second spoon and plate set, passed from his predecessors. Most importantly, the reports from the other FarCallers always said the second spoon and plate set was in Lee's world. Instead of silver, it appeared to be of gold.

From there the information was less definite, but it still carried the feeling of evil or, if not evil, of powers best left alone. According to FarCaller's grandfather, those powers were more powerful than those of the silver, the set used by the Guardian and his FarCaller. *That possible is? Who the golden set made: Ewan the Smith, the first Guardian? If the entire set in Lee's world is, how was it there taken? And what the second set does?*

After long hours of worry and thinking, he fell asleep in his favorite chair. His grandfather's journal lay on the table next to him, his research notes on his lap, his mind full of more questions than he believed possible, and the death of his brother forgotten.

Chapter 90

Second Opinion

Ben Gerit was sick and tired of being sick and tired. He knew he'd had a mild heart attack: both his physician and his cardiologist confirmed that. They even told him that stress caused the attack and that he had to change his diet, start exercising, and remove stress from his life. These would help speed his recovery and decrease the probability of any subsequent "cardiac event." *Why can't these idiots speak English?*

He'd been in the hospital several days and was feeling worse, not better. The more he thought about it, the less sense it made, yet his doctor insisted it was to be expected. One evening, he called a business friend who had experienced a similar attack. "Tell me about your recovery, Byron," he said. "I'm only hearing stuff from my doctor and don't know whether I should believe him or not. Doctors speak in so many generalities I don't really know what to expect."

He listened intently as his friend told about his attack—how it felt, what he did, what treatment he had.

"When did you start feeling better?" he asked. "I'm really tired all the time and didn't expect that."

"I was at first, but not after the first week or so," was the response. "My doctor gave me exercises to do and made me start walking around the hospital. After a few days, I started to get my breath back. I was weak, of course, but I was feeling better. And sleeping better." Then Ben could hear a smile in his friend's voice. "My doctor even said sex would be good for my heart, so of course I obeyed his orders!"

That report angered Ben so much he felt his heartbeat accelerate and chest pains begin anew.

OK, he told himself, *I've really had a heart attack, and I really need to take care of myself. That means I have to stop getting as angry as I used to.* He took several slow, deep breaths, trying to relax, letting his heart resume its normal rate, hoping his blood pressure would drop. From the way he had wires all over his chest leading to an EKG screen above his bed and at the ward nurse's station, he had no doubt he'd be checked on almost immediately. No sooner had he completed that thought than a tiny plump nurse in scrubs sewn from a pink cotton print with yellow and black daisies entered his room and checked the EKG cables, all the time looking at the monitor.

"Mr. Gerit," she said, "you must have had a bad dream or something, because your heartbeat and blood pressure took a real jump. If you need anything to keep you calm, just let me know. Your doctor has already given us orders for medications." She smiled as she began to leave. "We don't like to give medicine unless it's really needed, but you need to keep ahead of your pain."

Ben Gerit gave her a few minutes to get back to her station and recheck his EKG there, believing it would show things were more nearly normal. He again reached for the telephone, dialed the hospital switchboard, and asked to speak to a cardiologist he knew well.

"Jim, this is Ben Gerit."

"Heard you had a heart attack. That true? I wasn't called about it, but the administrators had to know you're my patient."

"It's OK, and I'm doing OK, I think. However, I'd like you to come here this evening or tomorrow night so we can talk without anyone interrupting us, if you know what I mean. I want you to check the medicine I'm receiving. A second opinion."

"I'm here in the hospital right now, checking on my patients. See you in about a half hour."

After he arrived, they talked at some length. His friend was short, dark, and bald, with a black handlebar mustache and hairy hands and arms. He was also one of the best cardiologists in Chicago. After their talk, the doctor checked Ben's medical records, listened intently to his heartbeat, and studied the display on the EKG right next to Ben's bed. When he finished, he said, "You wanted a second opinion, right?"

"Exactly. I want to know if I'm being treated the same way you'd treat me."

The doctor sat in one of the guest chairs. "It's always hard to step into a case on short notice, especially if you don't have the chance to talk to the attending physician."

Ben waved his hand, cutting the man off in midspeech. "Don't give me a bunch of professional disclaimers, Jim. All I want to know is if I'm being treated the way you'd treat a patient in my situation."

A quick smile in response. "That's easy to say, Ben, but—"

"But nothing, Jim. That's a yes-or-no question."

Two nods, then he looked at the door to the room, making certain it was closed. "If that's my only choice, then the answer is no."

"Why?"

"The medicine you're taking sedates more than I'd prescribe. You're weak, certainly, but this wasn't a really serious attack. The medicine you're getting probably keeps you feeling tired, although it doesn't hurt anything except keep you from the exercises you need."

"What if I stopped taking it? Would I have withdrawal pains or something like that?"

Two quick head shakes accompanied by a frown. "Normally not."

"OK, that's what I wanted to know." He looked at his friend, even now rising from the chair. "I needed an honest answer, and you gave me one." Gerit extended his hand, and the doctor responded with a firm handshake. "And if this happens again, Jim, I want you to treat me."

His friend responded with a modest smile, nodded once, then left as quietly as he entered.

Gerit placed two more calls. The first was to Etta, in Bend; the second to one of his most trusted men in Chicago.

Etta immediately packed up her records of the actions of Jeff's men in Bend and put them in an Express Mail envelope to go out the next morning. The man who answered Ben's second call left his apartment as soon as he received Ben's call.

* * *

Heart Surgeon Attacked

Last night, police and emergency personnel, responding to a 911 call, found Dr. Phillip Stevens, a prominent cardiologist, in his home, attacked and beaten by unknown assailants. Both his arms had been broken, and he suffered multiple injuries to his face and ribs.

The police also reported that the 911 call did not come from Dr. Stevens's home but from a pay phone some distance from his apartment complex.

Police have no leads as to the identity of the assailants nor the motive for the attack, as nothing appeared to have been stolen from the doctor's apartment.

Anyone with any information about this attack should contact the Chicago Police Department.

Chapter 91

Injured but Strong

Drella proved herself an expert organizer in a way that became apparent right away. She had stocked the kitchen with food and the bathroom with soap, towels, and washcloths and put sheets and blankets on Verry's bed, on the sofa bed for Lee, and on Thommy K.'s futon.

Everyone in the small house spent a restless night. Verry slept poorly because her sprained arm throbbed and her knee hurt. She also couldn't sleep because Lee was there and she kept dreaming about her future as his wife. Even though Drella was back in her own apartment and in her own bed, she slept poorly because of the excitement of sneaking around and moving Verry from the hospital, and from meeting a really neat guy—Thommy K. Thommy K. slept poorly because the futon was uncomfortable, because the house smelled strongly of pine-scented disinfectant, because of the excitement of helping Lee avert real danger, and because he kept dreaming about Drella, her body, her smile, the clever way she spirited Verry out of the hospital, her body . . .

Lee lay awake on the sofa bed, thinking about Verry, about her injuries and how any movement might slow down her healing, about how much he loved her, and that this major part of his journey was really over. He was overtired and unable to sleep in the little house, but he had an alternative: his RV was parked on the street in front of the house. He was accustomed to sleeping in it, although not when it wasn't level. At 1:00 a.m., he pulled his jeans and pullover sweater on over his pajamas and quietly left the house, shivered at the chill in the spring air, locked the door behind him, and entered the RV. There he lay down and, in spite of the slight downward slant at which he had to park, fell soundly asleep. He woke about 6:30, when local traffic noises began in earnest. He rose, showered and shaved, and returned to the house without waking Thommy K. or Verry. The only person up was Drella, who must have seen Lee's empty bed, guessed he was in the RV, and went about her business.

Lee joined her in the kitchen where she had already begun frying bacon for their breakfast. She wore a bright red apron over a light blue short-sleeved T-shirt and pink jeans, her long hair held in place by a Kansas City Chiefs baseball-style cap. He walked up behind her, put his hands on her shoulders, and began rubbing her tense muscles. She stopped cooking, let her shoulders slump, and put her head back, letting the massage ease the tension. Just before stopping his massage, Lee leaned forward and whispered, "Thanks, Drella. This was really thoughtful. Especially for a future sister-in-law." Then he quickly kissed the top of her head and started to move away to go to greet Verry. Drella, however, wasn't ready for that. She turned, grabbed him around the waist and, when he turned to see why, gave him a big hug.

"Thanks yourself, Lee," she said. Then looked into his eyes, smiled broadly, and gave him a quick peck on the cheek. "I needed that." Before he could say anything more, she pushed him away. "Now go wake up my sister!"

When he entered the bedroom, he was surprised to see that Verry had somehow already managed to wash and put on her makeup. *With Drella's help?* he asked himself. She looked great, and he told her so, whereupon she pulled him down to her with her right arm and, when he sat on the edge of the bed and leaned over to kiss her, put her left arm—splint and all—around his back and pulled him hard against her.

"Now," Verry said between deep breaths, "tell me what's next."

"I think someone should tell your folks where you are," Lee said. "If they find out from the hospital that you're missing, there's no telling what they'll do."

Her eyes widened in recognition of a major oversight. "Oh no! I forgot all about telling them!" Then, smiling, she pulled him down to her again and kissed him soundly. "See how you affect me?"

Lee pulled his cell phone off his belt and handed it to her. "If you don't call them right now, I'm likely to do something we'll both like, and this is neither the time nor the place."

Verry then surprised him. Large tears flowed down both sides of her face, smearing some of her mascara.

"What's wrong, Verry? Did I hurt you?"

First she pulled him hard against her again, her strength surprising him especially since she could only use her right arm properly. After some more sobbing and a few quiet and carefully placed kisses, she put her mouth close to his ear and said, "No, you didn't hurt me. I'm just so sorry!"

Lee broke her embrace and sat up, resting both arms on the bed beside her shoulders, and looked down into her face. "Sorry about what?" Inwardly he feared she was backing away from their marriage.

"Not you," she said. "Me." She pointed to her thick bandaged elbow and to her leg cast. "What kind of honeymoon are we going to have with me wrapped up like King Tut?" She smiled through her tears, but her emotions were clear.

"Lady," Lee said, leaning forward and putting his weight on his elbows so his face would be next to hers, "if you think a little thing like a leg cast and arm sling can stop us from having a honeymoon, you have too little faith in the power of love. Remember, it's just your arm and knee that's involved, not anything else." Before she could say anything, he kissed her soundly.

This time Lee broke their embrace and sat back up. "We've either got to get married soon, or I've got to go back to Bend. I can't take much more of this 'almost' stuff." He was smiling but serious.

She grabbed his cell phone from the edge of the bed where he dropped it. "Maybe the best way to cool off is for me to talk to my mother."

The hospital had already notified her parents she was missing, and they were nearly out of their minds with worry. Fortunately they hadn't yet called the police.

"Momma," Verry said, her voice carrying an edge of both love and impatience, "calm down. I'm absolutely OK. Lee's here with me and—"

Lee heard her mother's voice saying something so loudly that Verry couldn't hold the receiver to her ear, but not so loud that he could understand what was said. After a few seconds, Verry put the telephone back to her ear and shouted, "Mother! Stop! Lee came here and took me from the hospital because something happened to make him think I might be in danger." When her mother said something else, Verry gave Lee a look that indicated she was patiently bearing all the interruptions. "I don't know the specifics, and I don't want to, Mother," she said. "I want you to call the hospital, tell them you've talked to me, that I'm fine, and apologize for having such a thoughtless daughter, and they should send you my bill. You've made this kind of call before, and you can do it again. Do you understand me, Mother?"

This time the delay was only a few seconds.

"No. I'm not going to tell you where I am because it won't help anything. I'm in good hands, Drella's with me along with Lee, and I'll call you again tomorrow. Now do as I asked and don't say anything to anyone else until I tell you. Do you understand, Mother?"

Another short wait, then Verry said, her voice now loving and soft, "Thank you, Mother. Tell Daddy I'm OK, that I love you both very much, and not to worry. I know that's hard, but you have to."

Verry folded the telephone and handed it back to Lee. "She doesn't like it at all, but she'll do exactly what I asked. My mom's a very strong person when she has to be, but she does her darnest not to have to be."

Lee looked at Verry, gave her a quick kiss on her lips, and rose from the bed before she could even start to respond. "So are you, lady. I'm just glad you're on my side."

Part VI

Picking Up Pieces

Chapter 92

It Isn't Cheap, Lee

Clem *believed* in the law. It colored everything he did. He considered the lawyer/client privilege one of the most important elements of the law and tenaciously observed it. But working with Lee had strained Clem's ideas about many things, and being the middleman in purchasing a house was one thing he never could have imagined doing. Fortunately for Clem, Louise Chenowith, Lee's realtor, was not only immensely competent, she kept Clem informed of every major development in her search for a home for Lee. Like Clem, her work was hampered by her inability to talk to Lee directly and made more difficult because Clem was reluctant to call Lee unless something truly unusual or threatening developed. So when she finally found a house both thought Lee would like, neither could be certain he would buy it unseen. It was time for a call to Lee, only this time Louise would be part of the conversation.

She was tall, attractive but not particularly pretty. Her dark blond hair was short and neatly combed, and she was always dressed to impress. Best, she knew the local real estate market better than any five other realtors.

It was her first visit to Clem's office, and she was impressed by the tasteful masculine furnishings and the rogue's gallery of photos of Clem with noted political, professional, and well-known sports personalities. Plus, of course, his prominently displayed diplomas and certificates of membership in a plethora of professional, honorary, and service organizations and associations. It was early afternoon in Bend when he placed the call, turning on his speakerphone so Louise could particpate. Lee answered after only two rings.

"Yes, Clem," he began, obviously having checked his caller ID before saying anything. "Is something wrong?" His voice was calm, but Clem suspected his friend was feeling the stress of his long drive and was still worried about his parents, especially how well his mother's broken leg was healing.

"No, suh," Clem said. "In fact, things around heah are goin' pretty well. If Ah may, Ah'd like to inquire about your bride-to-be. Is she well?" He expected a pro forma answer to the effect that things were fine.

"You remember, Clem," Lee began, "that I told you of a number of things about my life that made you feel I might not be quite normal?"

Clem nodded as he said, "Yes, suh, Ah do. Ah was quite concerned, as Ah remember."

"Well, they haven't stopped. When I was about halfway here, Verry was in a car accident. Her knee was badly injured and had to be operated on, and her elbow was pretty badly sprained, so she's still in pain and bedridden. But the worse part of the 'accident' was that it killed her best friend."

Louise was sitting next to Clem so she could clearly hear Lee. When she heard his description of what had happened to Verry, she gasped in shock. That resulted in an awkward silence on both ends of the call.

Lee noticed the unexpected sound. "Is someone with you, Clem?"

"Yes," Clem began. Before he could complete his sentence, Louise said, "It's me, Lee—Louise Chenowith. We're making this call together because we have to talk about this house you asked me to find for you. But I'm so sorry to hear about your future wife's injury and her best friend's death." Her voice resonated with her concern.

There was another short silence: Lee was apparently thinking about something to say. Finally he spoke. "She'll heal, Louise, but it'll take about six weeks. And, Clem," he added, "without going into details, I'll tell you that I think this has something to do with the things we talked about before I left."

"Ah understand, Lee," Clem said. "Also without going into details, Ah must tell you that Ah've had some unexpected things happen to me as well. The result is that Ah no longer doubt anathing you've told me, even though Ah still don't know the reason these things are happenin' to y'all."

"I'm sorry about your doubts, Clem," Lee responded, "but I'm glad what you've learned just now helps you understand some of the things I've told you." Before Clem could say anything, Lee said, "I'm in a small house right now, and I'm going to walk out to my RV so we can talk more privately. Give me a few seconds before we get into anything very serious."

Louise couldn't handle the ambiguity of the men's conversation and spoke up, her voice and words reflecting her frustration. "What are you two talking about? What's happened?"

Before Clem could respond, Lee said, "I'm in the RV now, Louise. To answer your questions, there are people who think I have something that could be of value to them. They are trying a number of malicious things to pressure me into giving it to them. Their efforts have become very bothersome and, in several cases, criminal: arson, breaking and entering, malicious damage. I supposed you heard that my parents' home was set afire a few weeks ago."

"Yes, I did. But are you saying that was part of some kind of plot against you?" she asked.

"Louise, why do you think I hired you and Clem to secretly help me buy a house outside of town, especially when I'm a couple of thousand miles away and don't know for certain when I'll return?"

"But what—" she began.

Lee cut her off in midsentence. "I can't talk about it now, Louise. And besides, this is your call."

Her expression reflected disappointment at being kept ignorant of the meat of their conversation, but she was smart enough to let that pass and respond to Lee's request. "I've found a wonderful place about eight miles east of town, Lee. A few miles northeast of the airport. It was custom built and professionally decorated for a local dentist who died just before the final papers were signed. Four bedrooms, three baths, large kitchen, living room and family room, manicured lawn front and back. It's on a country road and a bit too far out of town and too big for most people. Plus the ten-acre lot is relatively small for being out in the country and has so many lava rocks and so much mesquite that no farmer would buy it. All that aside, I think the whole thing is absolutely stunning, and it's never been occupied. Other than being a bit dusty inside, it's in perfect condition and ready to move into. But," she said, slowly, "it isn't cheap. I need instructions before doing anything more on it or continuing my search for something else." Before Lee could respond, she added, "If you want, I can fax you some photos of it."

"That's a good idea, Louise, but it'd force me out in the open. That's neither clever nor wise right now." Lee weighed the magnitude of the decision he had to make. "Clem, have you seen it?"

"Yes, Ah have, Lee. It's everythin' Louise said. Quite beautiful. It's even high enough that y'all can see the Cascade mountains all the way from Mount Bachelor here in Bend north almost to Mount Hood."

"And the price?"

Louise gave him the asking price and suggested a lower price to offer if he was interested. His answer surprised both his friends.

"How soon could the sale be completed?"

Louise and Clem exchanged surprised glances, then she said, "Within a few weeks, believe it or not. All the title research and things were ready for the sale when the dentist died. I think all that will be needed is to check your credit, change the papers to make you the new owner, and prepare the mortgage and insurance documents. The credit check takes the most time, of course."

"It'll be a cash sale, so no mortgage or credit check will be needed. Shouldn't that speed things up a bit?"

"Why, yes," she said, her voice scarcely concealing her astonished look. When she looked at Clem for some kind of support, he only grinned broadly and nodded. "I could probably get the papers ready in just a few days if I smile prettily and coax the title company a bit." She turned to Clem and flashed a tentative smile accompanied by a shrug of her shoulders. She wasn't certain where things were going, but it looked like the biggest sale of the year for her.

"OK, then, I'll trust you both. Clem, you know a lot about my finances, if I remember correctly."

Clem chuckled and nodded to no one in particular. "Yes, Ah do."

"Don't I have enough to cover this?"

"Yes, but it'll take about half of y'all's savings that Ah know about. Do y'all want to spend that much?"

"I think so. It sounds like a good place, with privacy and a good view, and plenty big enough for Verry and me as well as my folks."

"Y'all's folks?" Clem asked. "They're going to live with you two?"

"Only as long as it takes to get their place repaired. I expect that'll be several weeks more, at least. Don't you agree?" Before his friends could respond, Lee blurted, "Brackafrass! I don't have enough furniture to support just Verry and me, let alone Mom and Dad." He thought some more. "Louise, do you know any good interior decorator or shopper or someone like that who would furnish it for me? Soon?"

Louise nodded as she answered him. "Yes. A couple of them, as a matter of fact."

"How would this be handled?" Lee asked. "I mean, do I just tell you I like contemporary designed furniture and accessories then give you a budget and say go?"

Now Louise smiled. "Yes, that's about all it takes. We'd have to make arrangements to pay for everything she buys for you and get it moved to the house, but that's about it."

"What's a reasonable budget for all that?" Lee asked.

She looked down at the top of Clem's dark walnut desk, took a couple of deep breaths for thought, then began mentally calculating the size of the job. "New contemporary furniture, pictures and other accessories, kitchen utensils, dishes, and towels and bed linens. Delivered in a week or so? Is that what you need?"

"That sounds about right. I'm still not certain when we'll return, but the sooner the house is ready for my parents, the better."

She nodded, then her lips tightened into a straight line. "For the whole house, ready to go, I think you'll need to budget somewhere between twenty and twenty-five thousand dollars, Lee."

The connection was silent for a few seconds, then they heard a loud, "Whew!" followed by, "It seems really high, but I don't know furniture from sour cumquats, so I'll take your word. Go with that, but bid that lower price you suggested for the house." Before either Clem or Louise could respond, Lee added, his voice intense, "Just don't tell anyone who's buying the place. OK?"

"OK," she said. "All but the title company. It has to know, but I doubt they really care about who buys what. And anyway, the sale will be public record as soon as they get it recorded." She looked directly into Clem's eyes then shook her head in wonder.

Lee interrupted their thoughts. "Can't help that, I guess. Is that it? Have we settled everything?"

Clem looked at Louise and raised his eyebrows in a silent question. She nodded. "Yes, Lee," Clem said. "Ah'll need a special powers of attorney foah signin' the papers for y'all. Y'all could get a foahm at a local bank, Ahm sure. Or Ah can contact a lawyer and have him prepare it foah y'all. Y'all'd have to overnight it to me, of course, so everythin' will be ready at closin'."

"OK, it's a deal, then. You and Louise get the paperwork started. Contact a lawyer here in Des Moines, like you said, and have him call you when he's got the form ready. Then you let me know and I'll go to his office and sign it. He can overnight the stuff to you.

"Anything more?" he asked them.

They exchanged head shakes and Clem said, "No, Lee. That's it."

"Fine, then. I appreciate both your help on this. I'll call my folks right away and warn them they'll be moving out of my apartment soon."

Lee closed the circuit, and Clem pressed the button that turned off his speakerphone. Louise shook her head in disbelief. "That young man is going to spend three-quarters of a million dollars on a place he's never seen!"

Clem nodded slowly. "That puts a lot of responsibility on us, Louise. We've got to be 'specially careful that we do everythin' correct foah ouah good friend."

* * *

Lee's parents were astonished and thrilled. Lee was relieved that this part of his plan to be a full-time Guardian was complete but a bit awed that he could spend so much money on a home. Six months earlier, he'd not have been able to buy a $100,000 home in Bend if there was one available that cheaply.

Chapter 93

More Differences

That evening, after a long goodbye kiss with Verry, Lee decided to sleep in the RV instead of the sofa bed. Not only did he need a good night's sleep, he needed to contact FarCaller. There was no way he could do that if he stayed with the others.

He was in a mental and emotional quandary: he knew he should call FarCaller and he wanted Verry to be part of that experience—but they weren't yet married, and somehow it didn't seem right. That made him feel guilty. *Can't I trust my wife-to-be? If not, is she the wrong woman for me?*

The answer came to him almost immediately, and it startled him. *I'm the Guardian, not Verry. She has no right to participate in such contacts, wife or not.*

The release he felt from that realization was palpable as well as psychological. His shoulders felt as if a heavy weight had been taken from them, his breathing became deeper and more relaxed. Fumbling around in his shirt pocket for the spoon, he held it up and thought about FarCaller. His friend appeared instantly, saying nothing. "FarCaller?" Lee said, obviously surprised. "I didn't expect to see you so soon. Were you about to call me?"

"No. But a feeling you would call had I, so readied myself did I. A few minutes only waiting am I."

Lee just shook his head in wonder. In the months since he'd learned how to use the spoon, this was the first time they'd "met" without one or the other having to expend physical or psychological energy calling and waiting, sometimes for days, until the other responded.

"Last time we talked I was concerned because you feared you'd not be back. You were about to face the Interceptor and were afraid you'd be killed."

FarCaller looked down, his mouth tightened into a distressed line, then he looked back at Lee. "No longer the Interceptor anyone will bother." When he finished that statement, he kept his eyes locked on Lee, as if saying, "Into details go will I not."

For his part, Lee maintained the eye contact while he thought about what FarCaller said. Then he understood, and he hurt for his friend. "Are you OK?"

"Injured was I not, but hurt am I."

"You would be, I think." Lee broke eye contact, not only to relieve the pressure but to indicate he was going to change the subject. "It has been several days since we last talked," he said, "and much has happened here."

"Several weeks to me and fairly quiet has it been, thank the gods, so time without interruptions to read and learn had I. Even my mother pestering me has stopped." With that statement, FarCaller smiled, the first of this contact.

"That had to be a godsend," Lee responded, returning the smile. "Here, we've moved Verry out of the hospital and away from the danger I felt for her. We will be getting married soon."

FarCaller frowned in confusion. "Hospital? That word I know not."

I keep making assumptions about how similar our worlds are, then FarCaller shows me how really different they are. "A hospital is a place where we take sick or injured people to be treated."

"Ah! Now understand do I. Here a healer's house it is." A quick nod. "Every talk, more learn I. Continue please."

Lee related the story of recruiting Thommy K. only to find he was a relative, how they sneaked Verry to their little house, and how much he loved her.

FarCaller listened intently but after a few minutes began showing signs of impatience. By now Lee was attuned to the nuances of communicating with him and ended his tale. "Now tell me about what you have done while I was so involved with my fiancée and friends."

The small man with the intensely dark eyes held up a sheaf of papers for Lee to see. "Much reading did I. A reference to another spoon and plate set found."

Lee stared in astonishment. "What?"

"My grandfather's journal found I, and unexpected information discovered." He looked down at his notes, then related what he'd learned.

For Lee, FarCaller's report was both fascinating and disturbing: another spoon and plate, attuned to each other, on Earth, and carrying the reputation of evil or danger.

"No hint of where they might be? Or their purpose?"

"None. Except a vague sentence about *them*—the second set—the Guardian to find trying. Of that no further explanation."

"And nothing about how to locate them?"

"Correct. Only that gold are they."

Both men were silent for several seconds, letting their minds mull over this information. FarCaller was mentally reviewing what he had read; Lee was trying to apply this new information to Earth. It only generated more questions.

"Anything about their size or shape?"

"Not."

"So they could be large or small, they could look old or new—or anything in between."

With each option, FarCaller nodded his head in agreement. "That help I cannot provide, regret do I," he said. "Every page of my grandfather's journal have I read and nothing more found."

Lee let that bounce around his brain and discovered another question. "This may be obvious, but are there other journals written by previous FarCallers?"

FarCaller's expression went absolutely blank, only blinking eyes revealing he was thinking. Then he tilted his head and squinted, obviously thinking very hard. Finally he looked back at Lee, a querulous expression on his face.

"That know I not." He held up the well-worn binder with its three inches of pages. "This book found I. But once found, stopped searching did I."

"OK, tell you what. Keep looking for more about that set, and I'll think about ways I might be able to locate the set here. I've already thought about it a bit and don't like the choices."

"Choices? What choices?"

"Oh, I could check with antique shops and places like that, but there are probably tens of thousands of them in this country alone, so that isn't an efficient way to search."

FarCaller blinked in confusion. "The word 'antique' also understand not I."

Lee smiled sheepishly. "We've done pretty well in our conversations so far, haven't we? Sometimes I forget we don't live in the same place and use the same words."

FarCaller only nodded.

"An antique is something over a hundred years old. But antique stores sell all kinds of used things, some very old and some relatively new. A logical place to try to find this golden set would be an antique shop, because the golden set would be old and handmade. And if it's real gold, it'll be expensive. But there are too many shops to complete such a search in less than a decade. And that's just in this country."

"No such shops have we, because everything until it breaks use we. Such stores in some of the larger cities might be."

It was Lee's turn to become fascinated with the insight into another world. "How big is a 'big' city? And how big is the nearest one to you?"

"Capital City the biggest one is. About ten days ride from here is it. Over ten thousand people has it. *Very* big is that, say you not?"

Lee became thoughtful. If he answered this question, it might embarrass his friend or sound like bragging. Or it might make FarCaller think Lee was lying. *Probably not, though.* "Our biggest city has over fifteen million people, FarCaller. And there are many with populations of over a million. The nearest to where I am is probably Chicago, and it has several million people. The biggest city closest to my home is a place called Portland. It has nearly seven hundred fifty thousand people."

FarCaller didn't seem to doubt Lee, merely shook his head in wonder. "So many! Much food and wood for cooking and heating to need would they. And fresh water to them every day brought. How any place that big could survive understand not I."

Lee knew that he couldn't respond to that impression in the time they had available. "FarCaller, let's leave this discussion for another time. I need to get some sleep or I'll drop off right now, and it takes a very long time to tell you about big cities. I'll try to contact you in a day or so."

Lee had just fallen asleep when someone knocked loudly on his bedroom window. Before he could get out of bed, he heard Thommy K. saying loudly, "Come back to the house, Lee. Verry's sick."

Chapter 94

Justice or Retribution?

Jeff Gerit was concerned about his father, but only about his whereabouts, not his health. Almost daily since the heart attack and his talk with his father's doctor, Jeff called the hospital and received the same report: he was doing well.

That's what I call good work! he thought, visualizing how his father's doctor was keeping the old man in bed so he couldn't interfere with Jeff's activities and plans.

It was 5:00 p.m. on the West Coast: 7:00 p.m. in Chicago. *Dinner is over, the doctor's rounds are completed, and visiting hours are about to begin. A great time to call.*

"Doctor's Hospital," said the ever-pleasant voice of the hospital operator. "How may I help you?"

"This is Jefferson Gerit. I'm calling to check on the status of my father, Ebenezer Gerit, in room 1222."

"Just a moment, please." Jeff visualized what was happening during this hold: a few seconds for the operator to call his father's room number up on her computer and read what the doctor said in his last examination. Then she came back on the line. "Mr. Gerit checked out of the hospital this morning, sir."

For the second time in his life, terror gripped Jeff. He knew the kind of revenge an angry Ebenezer Gerit could exact. Trying hard to control his shaking voice, Jeff asked, "Could I talk to his physician, please? I expected my father to be in the hospital several more days and had no idea he was doing so well." *He wasn't supposed to be well enough to get out of the hospital until I've put my plans in place. This not only screws that up, it puts me in danger!*

"You didn't hear, sir?"

"Hear what?" *Not more bad news. Please, no more bad news.*

"Dr. Stevens was mugged a two nights ago, sir. He's a patient here himself. Your father's new cardiologist, Dr. Benjamin, signed your father's release orders."

Jeff ended the call without saying anything, his hands and face breaking out in a cold sweat. His arms were shaking, eyes blinking away perspiration flowing into them, its saltiness seeping into his mouth. He sat still in his new recliner, looking out onto the lights of the bay, thinking about what he'd just heard. *If Dad's out, it's because he found out about the medicine he was getting. If Dr. Stevens was mugged, it's because Dad found out that doctor was my buddy and was keeping him sedated—for me. And if Dad's out because of those things, I'm about to be attacked!*

He tossed his bourbon and water down, scarcely feeling it and missing its normally calming effect. Now he sat motionless, in shock, trying to figure out what he could do to protect himself, and having no idea where to start.

Then it hit him: *Tracking the Guardian takes money. Bribing doctors takes money. Everything I've been doing takes money, and Dad's been providing it. He'll shut off my money and try to get to my personal accounts.*

Flailing around in the drawer in the telephone table, Jeff finally found an old bank statement, and frantically looked for his bank's telephone number. He dialed it and said to the woman answering his call, "This is Jefferson Gerit. I'd like to check the status of my checking account."

After giving his account number to her, he heard a series of clicks. There was a short silence, then he heard more clicks. Finally the woman spoke. "Our records show you closed your account yesterday, sir. We certainly hope any problems with our service didn't affect your decision on this matter."

Jeff hung up without saying anything. He rose from his chair and nearly ran across the room to the closet that held his personal safe. Checking all of his secret bank accounts, he confirmed each was still untouched.

A sense of relief began to settle over him, his breathing slowed, the sweating stopped. *Thank god Dad couldn't get to these! He doesn't even know they exist.* He rushed out of his suite, the private elevator dropping him off at the lobby, then walked directly to the ATM there, inserted one of his bank cards, and entered his PIN number. His hands were still shaking from the stress of the attack he knew he was under.

When he could check his balances, he was greatly relieved. He withdrew five hundred dollars from each of the other accounts, hoping it would tide him over for a few days. Jeff's father had always been wealthy, always provided the best for his son, even staked him in the business of hunting for the Guardian. Jeff had been siphoning money from those accounts, adding it to the healthy allowance his father provided every month, until he was a millionaire in his own right. Now, however, he began to fear that his money would be taken, hidden, or tied up in so many legal ropes that he wouldn't be able to get to it.

"Clever," he said to himself. "Dad knows I like expensive things, and he'll try to take them." Then he realized his brain was working at the wrong end of the problem: he should have thought about consequences *before* he began cheating his dad. Now it was too late.

Chapter 95

The Doctor

Verry lay in her bed, face flushed, body slumping as if under a massive weight. Her eyelids flickered slightly, her breath came in shallow gasps, her nightgown and sheets were dark with sweat. Lee sat at the edge of her bed holding her right hand, his concerns barely eased by her feeble attempts to hold on to him.

"What now?" he asked Drella. "What's wrong with her?"

For the second time in her professional life, Drella had difficulty separating the nurse from the sister. The first occasion was a few days earlier, when Verry was in the accident. She didn't like the feeling because it prevented her from being the excellent nurse she knew she was. Forcing thoughts of her sister out of her mind, Drella tried to see Verry as a patient. That helped but couldn't hide the fact the woman in need was not just another someone in the hospital.

"I don't know exactly what's wrong!" she said, her frustration coming out defensively. "She's not been drinking much water, so she's probably dehydrated, and I think she has an infection of some type. And even if this is correct, I can't get the right medicines and supplies without a doctor's orders."

"Can't we call a doctor?" Thommy K. asked, interjecting himself into the conversation.

Drella nodded; Lee shook his head. "Sure we can," he said. "All it'll do is reveal her location, probably get us in a mess for taking her out of the hospital before paying her bill, and a few hundred other things." He looked at them, frustration and anger coloring his grim countenance. "Come on, think!"

A red flush of anger colored Thommy K.'s face then faded when he realized Lee was right. Perhaps Lee's choice of words could have been better, but his conclusion was dead on. "OK, then what?"

The three exchanged glances, ignoring Verry. Then Lee looked at Drella and said, "Are there any Kaalers who are doctors?"

The simplicity and power of his question startled the others. Drella's eyes began flitting around as she thought about all the Kaalers she knew, trying to associate any of them with the medical profession. Thommy K. did the same, but the only Kaalers he knew, besides these three, were in the Omaha and Council Bluffs area: he couldn't help.

Drella shook her head, but not in surrender. "I don't know any," she said, speaking slowly, "but Mom and Dad will."

In ten minutes, Drella had the names of three Kaaler physicians in the Des Moines area, one of whom was attached to a hospital less than five miles away. Lee immediately called that doctor's office and quietly demanded to talk to the doctor. When the receptionist insisted that was not possible, Lee quietly said, "Tell him the Guardian is calling in regard to an emergency. I'll hold."

It was the first time he had ever introduced himself as the Guardian, but all he could think about was this wonderful woman at his side, a woman they had stolen from the professional care she needed, a woman suffering from something they couldn't treat. He wasn't about to let her suffer any longer because of fear of discovery. Or even the possibility that the receptionist or someone in the doctor's office was on the "other side."

In a short time, another woman came on the line. "This is Dr. Zoren. Unless you have an extraordinarily good explanation for the message you gave my receptionist, I'm going to hang up this telephone so fast it'll make your head swim! My patients are used to the attention they deserve and don't appreciate my being called away from them to answer telephone calls that could be delayed until I'm done with their examinations. You're obviously not a doctor, and just as obviously like playing jokes."

"Dr. Zoren," Lee said, trying to remain calm in spite of his concerns about Verry, "I appreciate and understand your anger. But before I say much more, I'd like to say this: I'm looking for a different career path."

When he completed the first sentence of the Challenge, he was met by an intense silence. Finally the woman on the other end of the line said, "Would you mind repeating that?"

Finally! She's listening! Lee did as she asked and was immensely relieved to hear her respond correctly. When they had completed the Challenge, Lee said, "The message your receptionist gave you is accurate, Doctor. But I'm not the one in medical trouble: it's my fiancée, whom we had to 'liberate' from a hospital where I feared that she would be in great danger. I'd like to send someone to pick you up and bring you here to treat her."

"That could take too much time," Dr. Zoren responded. "If you'll just give me the address, I'll leave in a few minutes and come right there."

"No, Doctor," Lee said, finally starting to relax, "I don't want to give out the address on the telephone. Thommy K. Pajaro, my best friend, will be at your office in about ten minutes. If you prefer, he can lead you here. But I won't give the address over the telephone." *Unless she leaves me no choice!*

Dr. Zoren said nothing, but Lee could hear her breathing deeply. He couldn't tell if she was angry, frustrated, or what. "If that's what has to be done, OK," she said. "I don't like it, but I'll do it. I'll cancel my appointments for the next hour or so." Before Lee could close the circuit, she added, "But there is one condition."

"Name it."

"If you're really the Guardian, and if this is really an emergency, then when I get there you must show me what you're guarding."

It was Lee's turn to be silent. He had never before shown the spoon to anyone and hadn't intended to do so until he and Verry were married. But this woman was a true Kaaler, recommended by Verry's parents, and he didn't want to delay Verry's treatment any longer than absolutely necessary.

Finally he made his decision. "Very well, Doctor," he said. "If that's the price, I'll pay it. But you'll have to swear secrecy—I know of no living person besides myself who has ever seen it."

"Mr. Kaaler," Dr. Zoren said, "you don't have to worry about that. I just subjected you to a test—possibly a very unfair one. But if you hadn't answered as you did, I wouldn't help your fiancee. As it is, I'll be there, and you don't have to show me anything—even money."

Chapter 96

Diagnosis and Treatment

Dr. Zoren sized Lee up quickly then went directly to Verry's room and shut the door. After what seemed like an hour, she returned and walked over to Lee, who was nervously sitting on the sofa bed wishing he had something useful to do, knowing he didn't.

She was a short, slightly stocky woman in her late thirties, her shoulder-length hair dyed black with a bleached streak starting above her right eyebrow and tapering across the top of her head. As with many slightly overweight women, she wore a dark dress. Her dark eyes were large, with an almost liquid quality, and a kind and caring look. When Lee stood at her approach, she said, "You're Mr. Kaaler?"

He nodded.

"That woman is your fiancée, is that correct?"

Another nod.

"And you Challenged me." It was a statement.

"It was necessary," Lee said. "I'd been told you were a Kaaler, but I had to be certain."

She looked intently at him for a few seconds then sat beside him. Very quietly she whispered into his ear, "I'm not certain what I'd do in your case, but for what it's worth, you did the correct thing. I'd never have thought of it."

Lee started to ask about Verry, but the doctor raised her hand, stopping him before he started.

"Your fiancée suffers from a combination of lack of trace elements, dehydration, and a slight throat and ear infection." She reached into her black bag and withdrew a handful of pill packets, putting them on the small coffee table, then knelt and separated the small packets into piles. "She should take these," she said, pointing at one pile, "for her infection. It's an antibiotic that should nip it within a few days." She looked up to ensure Lee was paying attention and quickly saw he was concentrating on every word. "She's to take them all." Then she pointed at the second pile. "These will ease the pain from her injuries." She looked him directly in the eyes again, ignoring Thommy K. and Drella. "I changed the bandage over the incision on her knee with the material I brought with me. You understand that she really should be in a hospital, don't you?"

"Yes, ma'am," Lee answered, "but it's not possible."

"You haven't broken any law or something stupid like that, have you?"

Lee could only smile at the question, regardless of how seriously it was intended. "No, ma'am, at least I don't think so. Her hospital bill will be paid today, so we're not stealing anything. I didn't think taking her out of the hospital was a crime—" He stopped, looked at both Drella and Thommy K. for any response. Both shrugged their shoulders.

He returned his attention to Dr. Zoren. "It's not, is it?"

She also shrugged but didn't smile. "I don't know either, as a matter of fact. But, aside from that, you're not in legal trouble?"

"Not to my knowledge."

"But you had to take her out of the hospital."

"Yes. For her own safety."

That stopped her again. For a second time, she looked deep into his eyes, as if doing so could provide proof he was telling the truth. She blinked and leaned over to whisper. "And you are the Guardian."

Lee was silent a few seconds then whispered back, "Thommy K. thinks I am. No one else in this world, besides you, knows for certain." Before the doctor could respond, Lee whispered back, "When Verry needs to know, I'll tell her. Sometimes too much information is a curse rather than a blessing."

"A curse—yes," she said, exhaling quickly through her nose as if mimicking a snort. "That's exactly what I'd consider it." Her eyes widened, as if she suddenly remembered something.

"I forgot to tell you what to do about her dehydration," she said, her voice returning to normal volume. Turning to Drella, she said, "Can your sister keep fluids down?"

"Yes, Doctor," Drella answered, assuming her nurse persona.

"Give her as much as she can drink. It'll help her fever drop, clear out a bunch of wastes in her blood, and do her a lot of good." She smiled then added, "But you already know that, don't you." Before Drella could say anything, Dr. Zoren glanced around the living and dining rooms. "Do you have a bedpan? She's going to need one if she drinks nearly a gallon of water a day. Getting up a lot at this stage of her recovery isn't a good idea."

"We don't have one yet," Drella admitted, "but we'll get one right away."

Dr. Zoren rose, straightened her dress, then reached out and shook Lee's hand. "This may sound strange to you, Mr. Kaaler, but I'll always remember meeting you." She turned to Thommy K. "Ready to take me back?"

Before Thommy K. could answer, Lee interrupted. "Dr. Zoren, thank you for coming here under what had to be unusual circumstances, and at a personal and professional inconvenience. I'll always be in your debt for helping Verry."

"Not at all," she said, smiling. "The pleasure of the occasion is mine. I'll probably never have this opportunity again, and I can assure you it means more than you'll ever know." With that she nodded to Lee and Drella and headed for the front door. Without another word, she was gone.

Lee started to go into Verry's room when Drella stepped in front of him, stopping his progress. "Why was she so happy to meet you?" She peered intently at him. "Is there something about you that you haven't told us?"

Lee looked her directly in the eyes—intensely. "Drella, if you needed to know that, I'd have already told you. Knowing some things could place you in a great deal of danger, and I don't want to do that. It's bad enough that my family and I are already in danger. I even tried to talk your sister out of getting married right away because it would imperil her. But she insisted, and frankly, I'm glad, because I don't want to wait to marry her. With all the trouble that's going on around me and those I care about, adding you to the list is just plain unfair." Throughout his answer, he kept his eyes locked on hers. When he finished, he reached out, pulled her close to him in a loving but nonthreatening hug, then released it slightly and kissed her forehead. "Now can I see your sister?" Before she could say anything, Lee walked into Verry's bedroom and closed the door.

This was their first crisis; it was also their first cry together. Verry still felt ill, and Lee just wanted to comfort her. He held her and kissed away her tears only to realize he was also crying. She looked weak, and it worried him.

"Lee," she said, holding him close and whispering in his ear, her eyes closed and tearing, "I should be better soon, according to the doctor, but I want to marry you so much I'd do it right now if I didn't look so awful." After wiping away her tears, Lee stopped her apologies by kissing her. When he started to pull back, she held on tightly and said, "Tell me why someone I don't know would try to hurt me." Then she loosened her hug and let him up so she could look at him while he answered her.

She became a target in spite of my efforts, and now we're in this dumpy little house trying to evade the people hunting me and hurting others to get to me. For the spoon. "Your Kaaler family secrets didn't include anything about the Guardian, did they?"

She looked at him, a puzzled expression on her pale and puffy face. "I know there is one, and we're to support him or her in every way we can. My folks never told me anything more specific, and I don't think they know anything more. So what's a Guardian?"

His expression and eyes were as serious as he could make them. "Me, Verry. I'm the Kaaler Guardian. I have something some people want to use for their own purposes, and they're willing to kill, injure, burn—almost anything to get it. They burned my parents' home and arranged a car accident that injured my mother—to force me to give them what they want. They even called my home and told me that. Now they've come after you—to get to me."

Lee leaned closer to emphasize his words. "That's why I didn't want to let anyone know about you, because I didn't want the people chasing me to hurt you. But they already have. And they'll probably try again once you get back into circulation." Finally he smiled. "So there's no reason to delay getting married. Then I'll take you home with me—to a new place I just bought and haven't even seen. We'll be safe there after I get some more security things installed, but more importantly, we'll be together." He nodded, his speech finished.

She smiled weakly but sincerely. "The last time you were here, I asked you when you were going to propose to me, and you did right then. Now I want to know *when* we're going to get married."

He smiled and gave her a peck on her lips. "How long does it take to get a marriage license and find a minister?"

She smiled back, a small twinkle in her hazel eyes. "Three days, and they're good for two weeks." Before he could say anything about the three-day waiting period, she added, "I got it last week."

Chapter 97

A Threat of Murder

Lee went to the RV again that night. As soon as he was settled, he intentionally left the spoon in his pocket when he thought about FarCaller. After that he retrieved the spoon. In a very few seconds, FarCaller spoke. "Lee," he said, "your call very clearly this time I heard. Why?"

Lee did the only thing he could. He laughed.

FarCaller completely missed the humor and was about to speak when Lee cut him off. "I just thought your name, FarCaller." "Just like you said our grandparents did. And it worked."

"Next time that try will I. Now, why talking are we, please tell me."

"I've been thinking about the second set of instruments and your feeling they may be evil or bad or something like that. Maybe one way to learn if that is so is to look into my future a bit. Would you?"

Many nods, accompanied by a big smile. "This not always fun is, but always interesting is."

Lee closed his eyes while FarCaller sought to find something in the future that might provide insight into those two instruments. Apparently Lee fell asleep, because the next thing he knew, he heard FarCaller yelling at him.

"Yes, FarCaller. I'm here." He looked into his friend's face, trying to determine what he might have learned, but the dim lights and the small image in the spoon prevented getting any preview of the results.

"Lee, no danger in your life did I see, but a person in a light coat saw I, with long hair, a box big enough for two large boots carrying. Walking slowly was he, toward the front door of a house where the paths of a long piece of smooth stone were made. Night it was, so little light there was, and afraid acted he."

I wonder what that means. It could be anyone, anyplace. His eyes widened in surprise. *Or it could be here!*

FarCaller interrupted Lee's thoughts. "Lee, the same for me would you do? Something planning have I been, and what you can see to know I want."

"Of course." Lee closed his eyes and sought the out-of-body feeling that accompanied his voyages into FarCaller's future. Very quickly he found himself looking back into FarCaller's house. He was in the living room looking into the kitchen. He saw a slender, very attractive young brunette, sharpening a short knife and talking to someone.

"What to do know I. The next time to bed go we, with this knife fix him will I. Suspect me he will not, but this place inherit and in luxury live will we." The most chilling part of the Sensing: she was very calm about planning to murder FarCaller.

The scene suddenly disappeared. The look on his face told FarCaller much.

"What is it, Lee? What saw you?"

There's no easy way to pass on bad news. He described his vision, trying to remain distant from the picture he painted. When he finished, FarCaller had a stricken look on his face.

"The woman I'm living with described did you. The good news about a new wife to tell you was I, but taught me, did you, after my money and my life is she."

Chapter 98

Fortune-Telling

"Once again, Lee, from death you saved me. From my brother first, and from the woman I would have married now. Forever in your debt am I."

"No, you aren't," Lee said, all the time shaking his head. "You've certainly saved my life several times, so let's not talk about debt."

FarCaller flashed his big smile again. "Some good news have I."

"I could use some." Lee looked around the little sleeping area in the RV. "This thing has probably saved my life, but I'm getting tired of living in a cabin on wheels when I have a really nice home quite a ways away."

"Lee, something most unusual Sensed have I."

At that statement, Lee's degree of attention doubled.

"Listen. A woman shorter than you. Strong, but with a nice shape." He made an hourglass motion with his hands. "Her eyes a peculiar color are: sometimes green, sometimes brown, sometimes blue—never eyes like that seen have I."

Lee was about to interrupt, but FarCaller shook his head: Lee was to do or say nothing right then. "Her hair red is; dark brown eyelashes, and eyebrows she has. In this place as being 'child-built' describe her would we: her hips wide are, her waist narrow. A beautiful smile and a loving heart has she. Such a woman know you?"

The more FarCaller spoke, the wider Lee's smile became, until it almost hurt his face. "I certainly do! You've just described the woman I'm going to marry."

FarCaller's expression changed from concern to relief. "So glad am I," he said. "If knowing her you did not, prepared was I to tell you that the woman you intended to marry for you not the right one was."

"Why?"

"Because the only person I've Sensed she is, besides you, who the *gift* possesses. For you no other wife could there be."

Lee was struck silent. He looked at his friend's image in the small spoon, again wondering at its power as well as the amazing friendship that had developed between him and this man whom he would never meet in person. But could this Sensing be correct? Only the Guardians' firstborns were supposed to have the gift. *This whole gift thing is supposed to be more magical than genetic. And I don't think Grandma knew that. Wait a minute! Maybe FarCaller's Sensing meant Verry could only communicate through the spoon, not Sense the future like the Guardian and FarCaller do. It's still weird, but it makes more sense, if anything in this whole Guardian thing makes any sense at all.* Lee did the only thing he could right then: close the conversation. "I thank you for that, FarCaller. It's the finest wedding gift I could ever receive."

"Glad am I, Lee. Someday to see you two together, hope I."

"We'll make it happen, FarCaller. Now, however, I have to get back to the house. I came here so we could talk without being overheard."

"Understand do I, Lee. Careful must you be."

Lee nodded at FarCaller's statement and put the spoon in his shirt pocket. He then moved to the small sofa where he could relax as well as look out the window and see the house.

For several minutes, he just sat and stared, thinking about FarCaller's Sensing about Verry. Just as he felt sleep begin to sneak up on him, he noted movement reflected from the streetlight onto a person wearing a white coat, gingerly walking toward the house. Fear grabbed his chest as he thought of FarCaller's earlier warning. As silently as he could, he opened the RV door and quietly moved toward the unexpected and unknown visitor.

The person in the white coat walked slowly and carried a package with both hands, as if the package were heavy or its contents were dangerous. Once he reached the front stoop, he seemed reluctant to step onto the small porch, apparently so intent on private thoughts that Lee's approach was completely missed. Lee walked quietly up the walk and when he was within an arm's length of the unknown visitor said, "May I help you?"

The visitor jumped straight up and spun around, nearly losing the package. To keep from dropping it, she put it under her left arm and held it tight against her chest, her right hand over her mouth to stifle a scream. When she faced Lee, her eyes were wide in terror, her pupils completely invisible in the dim light.

"Good grief! You frightened me!" she said, breathing deeply. Then she leaned over, as if trying to avert a fainting spell. After two or three deep breaths, she slowly straightened up.

Before she could say anything more, Lee asked, "What are you doing here at"—he checked his watch—"one o'clock in the morning, Dr. Zoren?"

"Mr. Kaaler," she said, her breath still coming in small gasps, "is there some place we can talk privately?"

Lee let a smile sneak onto his face, not certain whether his unexpected visitor could see it. "If you'll just accompany me into my private office, Doctor." He pointed toward the RV with an arm outstretched in an overdone chivalrous gesture. "But please call me Lee."

Inside the RV, he could see much more about the woman before him. She had taken great care with her appearance before coming but was clearly nervous. Even her lovely dark eyes found it hard to meet Lee's. "Tell me why you're here at this ungodly hour."

She sat at the small dinette table and placed the large box before her then slowly and gingerly pushed it toward Lee. "This belongs to you, Guardian."

Before she could pull her hands back, Lee reached around the package, cradling it between his arms, and took both of her hands in his. They were cold, slightly damp and quivering. *Is she really that nervous?* "No one has ever called me that before, Doctor."

She looked directly at him, and her expression remained serious. "My grandfather gave this to me when I was a young woman. He said it came to him from an old man, also a Kaaler, he met once on a visit to the East Coast. Since the man's name was Kaaler, and after some small talk, my grandfather decided to Challenge the man. The other responded correctly and looked greatly relieved, saying he'd been holding a package for the Guardian, whom he didn't know and knew no one who had ever met a Guardian. However, he said he had a compulsion to pass it to another Kaaler, one who lived further West, in hopes it could be given to the Guardian.

"My grandfather was quite upset at the man's statement, because Grandpa was comfortable being a person who had an unusual family secret with no other obligations except to keep that secret and pass the story on to his eldest child. Now he was about to assume an obligation: it destroyed his previous comfort at only holding a secret, because now he had to do something. He told me that all he knew about being a Kaaler was that there were good ones and bad ones, and you couldn't tell one from the other except by the Challenge. The 'good' Kaalers he knew he could trust. It was an act of faith: he knew it was important to be a Kaaler, but he didn't know why.

"He said something special when he gave me this. He made me memorize it and promise to pass it on to either the Guardian or a person who would try to find and give this to the Guardian. This is the message:

"To the present Guardian from Fwan, the first Guardian: Greetings.

"This package was brought to our world many years ago as the only weapon the Kaalers would ever have that could protect their identities and their lives. You are to use it wisely, as it has great power, and you are to share its use only with a Kaaler in whom you have absolute trust. Use of it against you could cost you that which you guard.

"The person who delivers this package to you is unaware of its contents or their use, as well as being unaware of that which you guard. It is to remain so. The act of passing this to you is proof of his or her honesty and dedication. No reward for this act is expected, but it is permitted providing it is something only you can provide.

"This is your calling."

Dr. Zoren took two deep breaths before continuing, as if relieved of some awful weight. "I've had this for nearly ten years," she said. "It has been a terrible burden. Always on the alert for another Kaaler—who almost had to be a stranger. Wondering why something so important would just randomly circulate among our family members, with no direction, no way of identifying anyone who might be a Guardian." She took another deep breath. "I hope this is useful, because God only knows how many people have dedicated their lives to protecting it."

All the time she spoke, Lee held her hands, feeling them quiver, knowing she was frightened as she recited the words that made sense only to him. Giving her hands a quick squeeze, he released them then put the package on the seat beside him so nothing would be between them. She didn't move her hands, and he again took them in both of his.

"Dr. Zoren, I—"

"Amelia," she said, interrupting him. "My name's Amelia."

"OK, then, Amelia, I want to thank you for bringing this. If it's what I think it is, it's something I have only recently learned about. It will hopefully help me get out of living in an RV, wearing a disguise, and using false names. And fearing for the welfare of those I love." Now he smiled, again squeezing her hands. "And that includes you, Amelia." Before she could say anything, Lee added, "I want to give you something."

"No," she said, vigorously shaking her head. "I don't want anything for this."

Lee again squeezed her hands. "It will not be money or anything like that, and I'm not certain I can even give it. But I'm going to try, and I want you to stay here until I come back from the bedroom. What I have to do you cannot witness."

Before she could say anything, he rose and walked the few steps back to the bedroom area, quietly sliding the small door closed behind him. Sitting on the bed, he pulled the spoon out of his pocket and thought intensely about FarCaller.

Almost instantly his far-off friend's image appeared.

"Yes, Lee. Again I heard you call loudly. Most surprising it is, but pleasant."

"FarCaller, I need a favor."

"Anything for you that I can do, will I. Know that you do."

"I think I have just received the second set of"—Lee searched for a word the doctor could not overhear or understand, not trusting the door to protect what he said from being overheard—"equipment. The one you read about in your grandfather's journal."

FarCaller's face lit up. "Truth?"

Lee shook his head, trying to silence FarCaller. "It was brought to me by the doctor who treated Verry, along with a memorized message from the first Guardian—whose name was Ewan, by the way. I want to give this woman a gift and wondered if you could help me by Sensing her future."

"Not, think I, but perhaps able are you."

Lee was dumbstruck. "I didn't think that was possible. I thought I could only Sense *your* future."

"Our own futures we cannot sense true is. But—" He let the words drop off. Then he added, "Try will I."

This time he did something Lee never had before seen. Before FarCaller closed his eyes to try to Sense Dr. Zoren's future, he reached forward and touched the plate that connected him with Lee. It was almost as if this gave him extra power.

After a few minutes, he opened his eyes, blinked a few times, then shook his head.

"Nothing Sense I, Lee. Perhaps to try should you."

"Very well. Thanks, FarCaller."

Lee wasted no time. Closing his eyes and gripping the spoon tightly in both hands, he concentrated on Amelia, her appearance, her loyalty, and the fears she overcame in just coming to deliver the package. After several seconds of absolutely nothing, he felt the beginning of the Sensing. He saw a scene in which Dr. Zoren was in a hospital bed, her hair plastered over her head from perspiration, tired but elated, looking down at what appeared to be a baby held closely to her left breast. Then the scene disappeared. *Well, I'll be . . .*

Returning to the "dining room," he found Dr. Zoren sitting just as he left her, but a slightly curious expression on her face.

"I heard talking," she admitted. "Did you make a telephone call?"

"Something like that,"

"I won't accept anything for bringing this," she said, a clear note of insistence coloring her words.

Lee ignored her protest. "I have to ask some questions."

One nod. "Fine, ask away. But don't try to give me anything."

Lady, you have no idea what you're saying. "You're married, right?"

"Yes. Nearly fifteen years." She frowned in confusion. "What does that have to do with anything?"

"Just bear with me, Amelia. Any children?"

Her mouth became a straight line, her expression more grim. "No."

"Amelia, I know these questions are personal, but please listen and answer."

"Go ahead, Guardian." She smiled now, intentionally using Lee's title to make a point: she would do as he asked because he wanted her to, both as a friend and as the Guardian whose role in life she neither knew nor understood.

"Did you want a family?"

"Persistent, aren't you?" Two more deep breaths. "We tried, but I couldn't get pregnant. So we went on with our lives."

For the first time in his life, Lee felt suddenly and inexplicably humbled.

"I'm a doctor, Lee. Just say what you're thinking."

"One of the special things Guardians can do is learn a few things in advance of their happening."

Her eyes widened, her mouth opened in surprise and amazement. "You don't mean you can tell the future." She looked askance at Lee and frowned in doubt. "Surely you don't mean that."

"A little bit. Sometimes. I want to tell you something about yours." He grasped her hands even harder, leaning forward until their faces were less than a foot apart. "You must swear to me that you will tell no one about this gift Guardians have. It's a Kaaler family secret, probably second in importance only to the Guardian's name."

Normally she would have simply let such words flow off her like rain from a duck's back, but his seriousness prevented her from assuming that flippant posture. "I swear," she said, quite serious now.

"You will have a baby." He felt her jump up and try to take her hands from his grasp, but he kept his grip firm. "I don't know when, or if it's going to be a girl or a boy, but you will have a child."

The next thing Amelia did surprised both of them: her head slowly fell to the table, and she began sobbing. Lee immediately released her hands and began stroking her head. In just a few minutes, she regained enough composure to reach into her smock pocket and withdraw several tissues. She blew her nose and wiped tears from her face.

She said nothing for a short time then asked, "Are you certain? I don't want to be disappointed again."

"I hesitate to say this, but yes, I'm sure." He smiled, certain she was both happy and accepting of his words. "Now you understand why I couldn't describe this gift. I am so happy for you."

She rose from the dinette and moved around, standing close to him. Then, almost as an afterthought, she grasped his head between her hands, tilted it up so she could look directly into his eyes, and planted a gentle kiss directly on his lips. "I'll never forget this, Lee. Never in my whole life. And that child will bear your name."

She turned away, stepped carefully down from the entry onto the curb, and quickly walked down the street.

Chapter 99

The Stupidest Thing

"This is Jeff."

"This is unexpected," Ben said. *If he can't see through that lie, he's in really bad shape! He declared a war and I'm winning.*

"Probably true. We haven't had much direct contact lately."

The first admission, the elder Gerit thought. *Sounds like he's about to make a deal. Or try to.*

Jeff continued. "Seems as if our people get on opposite sides of things every once in a while." Even as Jeff spoke, Ben Gerit wore a smile. He rose from his desk, holding his cordless phone to his ear, and walked over to the window looking out onto the beautiful panorama of downtown Chicago and Lake Michigan. It was a sight he enjoyed every time he saw it. Only a call from his son could lessen its impact.

"I've decided it's silly for us to work against each other instead of toward the original goal," Jeff said.

You're right! Most stupid thing you ever did. "If you mean things could be more efficient, I completely agree. What do you have in mind?"

"First, I've already told my people to pull back from the Guardian's house—assuming we've been right about that."

He's worrying about the loss of his assets: money talks. "Smart move. I've heard they were a little too obvious in their surveillance. People could sometimes see some of them around Kaaler's apartment."

"You heard that?" Surprise colored Jeff's words, bringing pleasure to his father. "Who from?"

Nice try. "I have a few friends in Bend. They call me when they see something that might interest me."

"Well, my guys're not there now. I felt we could learn more about Kaaler if we focused our energies in other directions."

"Like what, for example?" Ben asked.

"Like checking more closely on his lawyer. Maybe he knows something we could use."

"And how do you expect to get him to cooperate with you? If the two of them are good friends, he's not likely to offer much help. And if the lawyer's ethical, you'll get even less."

Jeff was silent several seconds, thinking of way to force the lawyer to talk about his client. "It'll be tough, especially since they talk over scrambled lines. Or use cell phones. But there are ways to obtain information from one side of the conversation. That should be better than nothing at all."

He's back to bugging offices. Sometimes it's smart, sometimes not. "Think you can manage it?"

"Have to try. No one's seen the Kaaler guy for over a week. That's not proof he's gone, but my guys reported hearing a helicopter arrive at the airport and leave right away, about a week ago. He could have left in it, but we don't know where he is."

"Jeff," the elder Gerit said, finally deciding to break the conversation, "your people already tried to get information from the chopper crew and didn't get the time of day." *Might as well tell him some things to make him realize how stupid he's been.* "My people traced a bunch of Kaalers and found a group in Des Moines that probably met this guy. We even arranged an accident for Kaaler's girlfriend using the info you bribed Francine in Communications to get for you. Seems as how she disappeared from the hospital the night before my man was going to call on her. That's a pretty strong indication he's there. At this point, we have the same problem you have: finding someone no one admits to knowing or seeing.

"You've torched his folks' place, arranged an accident for his mother, and got nothing. In fact, if my information is correct, that Kaller guy's parents are safe and well in his apartment right now. Plus you've lost a couple of your people to stupid mistakes." He let the magnitude of his information sink in then gave Jeff a few more minutes to realize how much he'd been outfoxed.

"I don't want you to think I don't appreciate your call, because I do. But if *we're* going to work this thing together, then *we're* going to have to coordinate our efforts. That means *you'll* listen to what I say and do what I say. If you don't, you'll be penniless and you'll get not a single dime from all the money we'll have once we get that spoon. Further, until you agree to do what I say, I'll not send you one measly buck more. "Now, do we understand each other?"

Before Jeff could respond, his father hung up on him. Immediately after that Ben called Etta.

"Isolate every one of Jeff's men. Have your people show themselves and tell Jeff's guys that they're to go back to their rooms and stay there until they get specific instructions from *me*. Make them understand they'll be closely watched, and anyone who decides to be a hero will be badly hurt.

"Also try to find some cops or sheriff's deputies in Bend who need some extra spending money. When you have them on the string, tell them to be very slow in answering any calls for help coming from Kaaler's place. Got it?"

"You bet, Ben, honey. Now when're you going to come to my place so we can have some private times? I miss you a whole lot."

You miss my money, honey. But you're worth it.

Chapter 100

The Package

The package Amelia gave Lee was heavier than he expected, tightly wrapped with strong cord and heavy yellow paper. It smelled old—that curiously acid, somehow comforting scent of times past.

The knots in the cord rejected any attempts at untying, so he used his paring knife to cut them. He carefully cut close to the knots, feeling that somehow the box and its wrappings deserved special treatment.

Noisily unfolding the stiff paper protecting its contents, he was surprised to find a box of lightweight but strong dark brown wood, held closed with a golden clasp. Hands and fingers quivering with excitement, he pulled up the clasp and slowly opened the lid.

Red velvet lined the chest. Lifting the piece of rich cloth protecting the contents, he was surprised at how much care had been taken to protect them. In the center of the box, cradled in a depression obviously designed for a single purpose, was a thick golden plate with octagonal sides. At the top of the beautiful plate was the same strange symbol embossed on his silver spoon. To the right of the plate was a spoon, also gold, also bearing the same symbol.

For the first few minutes after opening the chest, Lee sat transfixed, somehow knowing he was in the presence of power. Remembering what FarCaller said about the plate, Lee's "antennas" were fully out, trying to sense anything evil, anything unusual, anything emanating from either the plate or spoon in front of him, but he felt nothing like that. For all purposes, the objects were simply golden antiques packaged in their original container. He knew that was incorrect: whatever the golden plate and spoon were, they were not simple.

With both hands, Lee carefully and slowly lifted the golden spoon from its cradle. As with the plate, there was nothing unusual in its feel. Turning it over, he looked for anything special, trying to determine how it differed from the silver spoon he'd been using these past several months. *Only several months? Feels like I've been battling the "whomevers" for years.*

After a minute or so, he became aware of a warmth emanating from the spoon. It didn't feel alive but more like something inside it was awake, generating enough heat to warm itself and his hand. He felt no danger, but it clearly wasn't just some old antique.

Out of habit, he looked into the spoon, trying to see if there was an image like he'd found in the silver counterpart. He saw nothing. *That's wrong! I don't see "nothing," I see darkness, or something dark.* His smile returned, pushing away the serious expression he'd had when he first entered his RV. *This definitely is a special spoon. It's got to be the one FarCaller told me about.*

Carefully replacing it, he just as gently picked up the golden plate, performing the same inspection as he'd done with the spoon.

Resting the plate in its cradle, he looked into it, pretending it was his silver spoon but on a larger scale. At first he saw only his own reflection: a disappointment. He remembered how it and the spoon had been given to him by Amelia Zoren, so very early that morning, and how he had frightened her by his approach.

After the bottom of the plate seemed to cloud over, the scene he just remembered came back to him in amazing detail: the old oak tree, its leaves just unfolded after a winter's sleep, the dirty old concrete sidewalk leading from the curb to the house. The single step up to the house, the concrete porch with square wooden columns once painted white, now supporting a dilapidated gabled porch. The screen door with the many small holes formed when the metal rotted away from lack of care. The front door with the small square windows about eye height, glass dirty and speckled with dried, muddy drops of water, probably blown there by the strong windstorms that arose during the tornado season.

Suddenly Lee realized something so obvious it frightened him: he wasn't recalling these things, he was *seeing* them! In the plate.

Holy Shamockaway! I thought it might show me more of Spoonworld, but it doesn't. It's connected to what I'm thinking!

He returned the plate to its cradle then sat back and wondered why this thing gave FarCaller's grandfather the impression of evil. More thought, reviewing as best he could his memories of the conversations he'd had about this plate and spoon. *He didn't say it was evil; he said he got the impression it was evil. Or dangerous.* Lee dropped the idea of evil from his thoughts and concentrated on the "dangerous." *I wonder if it's dangerous to the user. If it is, why would the first Guardian have it?* He envisioned one of his ancestors using the plate for whatever purpose it had and became more convinced of one thing. *It isn't dangerous to the user: it's dangerous to someone else. Enemies?*

He sat transfixed in his chair, seeing or hearing nothing, letting that conclusion sink over him. *Is this our weapon?* Again he was struck with the enormous ramifications of his conclusion, only to reach another: *I don't know what I'm talking about. For all I know this plate was designed to serve golden fish to King Midas.*

Almost reverently, Lee repacked the plate and spoon in their wooden case and put it in the small hall closet in the RV.

Chapter 101

I Present to You . . .

Two days later

The wedding wasn't taken from *Brides Magazine* or *Vogue* or anything Verry planned or ever imagined as she grew up. Instead of being a major event in the sanctuary of their family's large, old, friendly, and comfortable church, it was held in the living room of a small run-down old house. Instead of flowers, there was the scent of floral room deodorant; instead of five bridesmaids, there were none. Drella, the maid of honor, wore a pastel blue silk dress Lee bought for her. Worst of all, Verry didn't walk down the aisle on her father's arm to the strains of Mendelsohn's wedding march: she sat in a wheelchair in the middle of the living room. No music, no audience of friends and acquaintances to share this special time. There would be no reception and opening of gifts, because there were no gifts and no guests.

She thought about someone not there, someone she always intended to share her wedding with, someone now forever gone—Julie. Her best friend. Verry corrected her thought—her *late* best friend. Blinking away her tears, she forced herself to think about this day, this place, and these friends.

Lee wasn't in the tuxedo she'd envisioned but instead wore a dark blue suit, the blue shirt and the tie Verry gave him for Christmas, and new, wing-tipped black oxfords. He didn't have a white carnation boutonniere to match those normally worn by his best man and groomsmen: there *were* no groomsmen or ushers, only Thommy K., as best man, wearing the same outfit as Lee but with a white shirt. Lee bought both of their outfits.

But it was *her* wedding, to a man she loved more than she could have imagined, a man who loved her and treated her so well that she felt like a beloved queen in his presence. Best of all, Verry's sister and Lee's old friend were the witnesses as well as being the only other members of the wedding party. They knew more about the stresses and strains the bride and groom faced than anyone else in the world.

Her minister, who had reluctantly agreed to perform the ceremony, especially on his day off, was more than slightly distressed at the location. However, both Verry and Lee were insistent on that point, finally telling him that if he wouldn't perform it where they wanted, they'd get a justice of the peace to do it their way without any fuss. Faced with such a determined and inflexible onslaught on this point, especially from such a lovely young woman he'd known since she was in grade school, he agreed. Once he got into the swing of it, he gave it every ounce of his energy and love; and it showed in his voice, his manner, and his smile.

Verry couldn't go to the jewelry store to pick out their rings, so she chose a set in a catalog Drella obtained from one of the largest jewelry stores. Lee purchased exactly what Verry chose, except he changed the stone size on the engagement ring from one to three carats. When Verry saw it—just before he placed it and the wedding ring on her finger—her eyes bulged, she gasped in surprise, and almost pulled her hand away to protest the extravagance. Then she realized it was too late—she'd have to accept that ring or no other, and joyously did so.

When the minister finally told Lee he could kiss his bride, Lee silently and carefully knelt beside Verry, leaned forward, and gave her a long, solid kiss which she enthusiastically returned. It wasn't until they heard Thommy K. cough that they realized they'd forgotten where they were. They then reluctantly broke off what had been one of their very best kisses. So far.

The minister introduced Lee and Verry to Drella and Thommy K. as "Mr. and Mrs. Faerleigh Faar Kaaler." Thommy K. then paid the minister and again swore him to secrecy until Lee and Verry had told both sets of parents. The minister once again congratulated Verry and Lee, smiled at all four members of the wedding party, and left. Thommy K. and Drella also headed out.

Neither Lee nor Verry expected to be left alone so soon, but before they could say anything and before Thommy K. closed the front door, he turned around and held up Drella's cell phone and the keys to the RV. With a huge and knowing smile on his face, he said, "If you need us, call." Drella looked back at the newlyweds and winked knowingly.

Lee had been correct: Verry's cast didn't prevent any honeymooning.

Chapter 102

Envy

Thommy K. and Drella left the house and immediately went into Lee's RV. They turned on the television mounted in the console on the wall next to the shower/toilet, then sat on the sofa, intending to spend some time together before dinner. And they talked. About how Lee and Verry met, about the marriage ceremony, about how Thommy K. and Drella got swept into this whirlpool of danger and excitement because of their relationships with the newlyweds. And about themselves. One thing was immediately obvious: both had strong loyalties to Lee and Verry, loyalties that superseded personal friendships.

"But I still don't understand why these *things* happen to Lee or his family," Drella said. "He's a great guy, he doesn't seem to look for trouble or anything like that, yet bad things keep happening. Why?" She looked intently at Thommy K., seemingly certain he knew the answer. His response wasn't what she expected.

"He said he has something the bad guys want," he said, sliding down in the sofa and looking up at the RV's beige ceiling. "I don't know what it is."

Drella was listening so hard she frowned. About the same time, one reason for her frown occurred to both of them: the TV was on, but neither was watching it, and the audio interfered with their attempts to communicate. Thommy K. went up front and turned it off. When he turned around, Drella had moved from the end of the sofa to the middle. No matter where he sat, he'd have to sit close to her.

First he shed his coat and loosened his tie. Not only was their talk intense, the spring weather in Des Moines was beginning to get hot. Drella noticed his discomfort and innocently asked, "Doesn't this high-tech house on wheels have air-conditioning?"

Thommy K.'s reaction was typical of him: he shrugged. He'd been so intent on Drella and their conversation that he'd stopped thinking about anything else. He immediately turned on the AC and decided what to do about Drella's move. *If I can't recognize that as an invitation, I've got no business here.*

He sat on her right, put his left arm around her, then slowly pulled her closer, leaning forward and gently kissing her. She responded with fervor, and the kiss lasted for several minutes. Finally Thommy K. broke it off and regained enough control over his breathing to talk. "We'd better take it easy for a while." Drella slowly nodded, her head against his chest, still holding him tightly.

"But," he said, pulling back slightly and looking down at the top of her head, "that doesn't mean we can't continue it."

Drella let a small smile sneak onto her face then looked up into Thommy K.'s handsome countenance. "When?"

He responded with a grin and said, "How 'bout after dinner?"

It was one of the best either had eaten in a long time: chateaubriand with all the trimmings in the finest steak house in Des Moines, a pleasant cabernet, baked Alaska for dessert, and three hours of dancing to disco, big band, and Latin music. At one in the morning, it was clearly time to leave, something neither wanted because it also meant the end of a very special day. Their parting kiss at the door of Drella's apartment contained more promise than content, but still was memorable.

Neither slept well, especially when they thought about Lee and Verry and the envy that arose with those images.

Chapter 103

The Tale

Being married had several immediate impacts on Lee, some expected, others not. He thought he knew what to expect from sex, but not the deep psychological impact it had when shared with someone he loved. He fell more and deeper in love with this wonderful, caring, responsive woman whose openness regarding sex surprised them both.

Another big surprise: he found himself not wanting to leave her for anything, even though that was impossible. With Drella's departure, he became Verry's caregiver, a role that involved helping Verry with her toilet, bringing drinking water, helping her wash and with some exercises Dr. Zoren prescribed. Verry seemed not to mind this sudden intrusion of a man into what was an intimacy that was never discussed during their short courtship. Her cast was on her leg and her arm was wrapped carefully and securely. It didn't change the fact that she could neither walk on that leg nor use crutches. Her only option was a wheelchair.

For this first twenty-four hours of marriage, she didn't need to walk on anything. Her husband was with her, sharing his body with her, joining in learning about both their bodies, and blessed with a sexual appetite that fully complemented her own. Even in their most intense moments of intimacy, however, in the back of his mind, Lee worried about their safety and decided they had to leave Des Moines as soon as possible. He didn't think it was a smart idea to take Verry, with her injured knee and recovering from surgery, some eighteen-hundred-plus miles across the United States in a small RV.

A quick call to his Swiss bank the next morning confirmed his money was safe and untouched. After that, he arranged for a small business jet to carry them to Reno the following day. Then another realization hit him: *I've got to get the RV* back to Boise. He shook his head in frustration. *Maybe Thommy K. can help—even more. I have no idea how I'll repay him for what he's already done.*

They soon discovered another wedding gift from Drella: a refrigerator full of precooked meals. *Someday I'll return the favor* was all Lee could think.

After dinner that evening, Verry asked Lee the question he both dreaded and expected. They were in bed, Verry's head pillowed by his left arm. She spoke softly and lovingly, but her need for an answer was clear. "When are you going to tell me why we're in so much danger?" Before he could answer, she pulled his head down and kissed him firmly but not sensually. This was talking time, not lovemaking time.

There's no way like the direct way. "It's a long story."

An hour later, she knew about the spoon and how Lee learned about it and its powers, about his grandmother's role as Guardian, about her letters, how the spoon let the Guardian and his counterpart see a short way into the future, and how Lee had been targeted by someone who would injure his loved ones and damage his property if he didn't give them the spoon.

"So your grandmother was the last Guardian, and her name was Ima Faar Kaaler?"

Lee nodded, no longer looking at his wife but staring straight ahead, thinking of all he'd learned since receiving that little artifact from his grandmother. "Her married name was Mainor, but I guess she wanted me to carry the Kaaler name, so she paid my parents to change their family name to Kaaler." He took a deep breath before continuing. "She was really generous. I sort of blindly accepted it until she died and I found her letters to me." He thought some more about her then added, "I feel guilty now about taking so much for granted."

Apparently Verry wasn't listening to his last comment, because she said, "But her name sounds just like 'I'm a far caller'—that's almost silly."

"So's mine, then. Mine sounds like 'Fairly far caller.'"

"And the man you communicate with is called the FarCaller?"

"His *name* is FarCaller. It's not a title. But he calls me Lee, not Guardian. Guardian is my title. He only used it when we first made contact."

"And each of you can see into the other's future."

"For short periods. It's like we're seeing what will happen if we do nothing to change it. If it's bad, we do something; if it's not, we don't. Like, he described you to me and I described his wife to him. Except my fortune was good and his was bad: she'd have killed him if I hadn't had that look ahead. FarCaller says that gift is called 'Sensing,' so that's what I call it."

"Good heavens, Lee," was her response, then she lapsed into silence for several minutes. Occasionally she'd hug him, and once he felt her tears drip onto his chest, but he knew he shouldn't move. It seemed to be a special moment for Verry. Finally she took a deep breath then rolled away from him to get a tissue and blow her nose, returning to embrace him—all without a word being spoken.

After kissing his chest again, obviously enjoying the feeling of his chest hair against her face, she said, "You didn't want to marry me because you were protecting me. Then I was injured, and you were even more certain you didn't want to bring me into what you thought was more danger."

He looked down at her and gave her a quick kiss. "But you wouldn't have any part of it."

She hugged him again, firmly, with what seemed to Lee to be a newly found strength and determination. "I didn't have any real understanding about why you felt that way—couldn't have." She seemed to be talking to herself as much as to Lee. "No one in their wildest dreams would have thought such a thing could exist, let alone be so valuable that people would stoop to the levels they have just to force you to give it up."

Verry rolled onto her back then struggled to a sitting position. "So I didn't just marry you, I married *the* Guardian."

"Right. And the only people who know this are you and Amelia Zoren. Thommy K. suspects it, however."

Verry's eyebrows rose in surprise at the mention of the doctor, but Lee waved it off. Meaning: We'll talk about that later. "Well?" she asked, an expectant smile radiating toward her husband.

Lee was puzzled by her question, frowning slightly and peering at her face. "Well—what?"

"When can I see this heirloom that put you—and now me—in so much danger?"

Chapter 104

That Can't Be True!

Verry's initiation into Lee's world as Guardian came right after breakfast. Lee had brought the spoon with him from the RV when he showered and shaved before the wedding, wanting the luxury of a larger bathroom to prepare for the occasion. The package Amelia Zoren gave him remained in one of the van's closets.

Sitting on the bed beside Verry, Lee handed her the spoon. She looked at it carefully, turning it over, searching for something special, finding nothing. Wordlessly, she handed it back to him, leaned back against the headboard, and watched as he held it up so he could look into it.

As he thought about FarCaller, his awareness of Verry faded. This time he had to wait a few minutes, during which he again became aware of Verry because she was squirming impatiently beside him.

Suddenly FarCaller appeared, smiling broadly. "Lee, my friend," he said, "beginning to think, was I, that something to you bad had happened." His smile remained as he added, "Something other than a wedding, meant I."

When she heard another man's voice, Verry's first reaction was fear. She covered herself more tightly with the sheet and looked around for the source. Noting Lee didn't move or react, reality grasped her: everything he had told her about that spoon and his world as Guardian suddenly became real.

"I'm fine, FarCaller," Lee responded. "But before I tell you why I called, I'd like to show you someone." He turned around to face his startled wife, holding the spoon so FarCaller could see her. "This is my wife, Verry. I've told her about this spoon and how we communicate, how we've helped each other, and she wanted to know more." Holding it close enough so Verry could more clearly see the small image of Lee's Spoonworld friend, he said simply, "Verry, this is FarCaller, a man who has saved both our lives."

Before she could say anything at all, FarCaller flashed her a large, joyous smile and said, "Congratulations, Verry. To see you at last, happy am I. Much about how he felt about you told me has Lee, and now understand I. Beautiful you *are*."

Verry reddened, not only as a "blushing bride" but because the compliment sounded so sincere that she absolutely believed "that man in the spoon" meant what he said. If Lee had said the same thing, she'd have taken it as a reflection of how he perceived her as his wife in all its facets. But coming from "that man in the spoon," she accepted it differently and wished she'd been properly dressed and had her makeup on.

Lee turned the spoon back toward his own face, leaving his wife still blushing and aghast. "FarCaller," he said, "I again need you to Sense my—our," he corrected, momentarily forgetting he was now married, "future. I want to fly at least part of the way back home and need to know if you Sense anything dangerous."

FarCaller looked up, again reaching out and touching the plate. Closing his eyes, he stood motionless for a minute or more, his expressions wavering between smiles and frowns. Finally he opened his eyes and let his hand drop away from the plate.

"Nothing dangerous see I, Lee," he began. "How machines can fly still don't understand I, but it appears you and your wife home safely arrive will." He closed his eyes as if thinking or reviewing what he had Sensed then opened them and shook his head. "That's correct: no danger see I." Then he smiled and added, "My wedding gift to you and your beautiful bride please this consider."

"Thank you, FarCaller. We'll be home in a month or so in your time, I think. I'll call you from there unless something happens. OK?"

"Of course. But the favor return would you, please? Another potential wife have I found, Lee, after many weeks searching since the last one . . ." he hesitated, as if seeking the best word, then said, "left." None of the customary smiles this time. That had been a dangerously close call.

Lee nodded. "Absolutely. Just a minute." He let the spoon rest on his thigh, closed his eyes, and sought the sensation of flying that now preceded any glimpse into FarCaller's future. A pastoral scene appeared: green fields high and thick with alfalfa, cattle calmly eating and occasionally lowing, bluebirds and swallows flitting around a large oak tree. Sitting side by side, leaning against its trunk, were FarCaller and a beautiful young woman. She had light blond hair worn in two long braids trailing down across her chest, deep blue eyes set off by suntanned skin, a sensuous mouth, lovely complexion, and overall beautiful face. They were talking, laughing, touching, and occasionally kissing, seemingly unaware of anything but themselves.

Without warning the nature of the vision changed. Both FarCaller and the young woman looked up at some unexpected sound, then Lee saw a giant bull began to charge at them, clearly angry. FarCaller and the woman both jumped to their feet and looked around for a safe place, but there appeared to be none. The woman then grabbed his arm and pulled him behind the tree so the bull could no longer see him, but she stood slightly away from the tree, making herself its target. She screamed at the bull and waved her arms, clearly trying to keep its attention riveted on her.

Just before the bull could gore her, FarCaller stepped out from behind the trunk and pulled her into the safety afforded by the tree. The bull rushed past them, slowing quickly and turning around, his hooves cutting loose large hunks of turf and soil, raising a cloud of dust around him.

FarCaller and the woman stood beside the tree, looking at the enraged animal as if trying to determine what, if anything, they could do to protect themselves. The woman said something, and pointed to a large branch just out of his reach: obviously telling him to climb the tree. When he shook his head and reached out for her, she pulled away, again shouted something and pointed at the limb, then pushed him against the trunk. As he jumped up and grabbed the tree limb, pulling himself up to safety, she rushed at the bull, screaming and waving her arms.

The bull appeared fully taken aback and, instead of charging her, he backed up a few paces then turned and trotted away, not returning to his attack.

She then ran back to the tree and said something to FarCaller, after which he dropped to the ground and walked toward her. Unexpectedly, she ran into his arms, holding him tightly and saying something, then pulling slightly away, looking up into his eyes, and kissing him hard, passionately.

Returning his attention to FarCaller's image in the spoon, Lee described the vision exactly as he Sensed it. When he finished, he said, "It looked like she was willing to risk her life for yours, FarCaller. I'd take that as a good sign."

At first FarCaller was silent, then he smiled weakly. "Agree, Lee. But what a scene! About that bull us charging and in danger herself placing. Frightening!" Then he said, "Very much you thank I. It seems finally found someone have I, someone to both love and trust can I."

"I really hope so, FarCaller," Lee said. "You deserve a good woman more than anyone I've ever known."

At those words, FarCaller looked directly into Lee's eyes, his own now filled with tears. "Something wonderful have said you, Lee. Again you thank I. Please my regards your lovely wife give. Both a happy life together will you have, trust I." Now he smiled broadly. "As it so far has been."

Before either Lee or Verry could say anything else, FarCaller disappeared from the spoon. When Lee turned to say something to Verry, he found her staring at him, then the spoon, then back at his face, speechless.

* * *

A sudden loud electronic beeping pierced their sleep. Both Lee and Verry jumped at the interruption, first looking around in shock. When they recovered enough to realize the source of the sound, they exchanged sheepish glances. Lee rose and retrieved his cell phone from atop the dresser where he'd left it the previous evening. A quick glance at the caller ID told him much.

"Hello, Clem," he said. "What can I do for you?" He glanced at the small bedside alarm clock; he and Verry had slept until after 10:00 a.m.

"Not much right now," his friend responded. "Ah thought y'all needed to know what's happenin' on yoah house purchase is all. Have Ah interrupted somethin'?"

Lee couldn't keep from smiling, and his voice revealed it. "Not much, Clem. Verry and I were just honeymooning is all."

Clem chuckled, then spoke. "Ah am truly sorry if Ah've inconvenienced y'all, Lee. Ah could call back later if y'all would prefer."

"Not necessary. How's the house?"

"Well, Ah'd consider it fine. Things've gone quite well heah. Louise certainly knows her way around title companies and insurance companies, Ah can assuah y'all. All the papers are signed, the monies are transferred, and y'all own a lovely place as of just an owah ago."

"How about the furniture and all that?"

"Also fine. Louise fudged a bit and had it delivered yesterday, as a matter of fact, and the interior decorator is puttin' the finishin' touches on it as we speak. Ah'd guess it'll be done by noon tomorrah."

"Do my folks know?"

"Oh yeahs. Yoah mother is thrilled. Yoah dad is also excited, but he doesn't show it as much, certainly. They'll be movin' in tonight, Ah'd guess."

"That's wonderful, Clem. Can't thank you enough."

"That's not exactly correct, of coahse, Lee. Ah mean, Ah've taken the liberty of adding my fees to the administrative costs of the purchase, so that kind of thanks is already received. But Ah was thinkin' moah in the way of learnin' about why all of this happened in the first place."

Lee nodded to himself. "I can't tell you everything, Clem, but I'll tell you as much as I can when I get home." As he spoke, another important thought occurred to him. "Which reminds me. I've already told you Verry and I are married. I think we'll be leaving here in a day or so. If you don't mind, I might call you or Louise before we get back. That way someone can lead us to our new home."

"It'd be mah pleasure, Ah can assuah you, my friend. Call me just befoah you depart Boise after returnin' the RV, and Ah'll meet y'all and greet y'all as only a Southern lawyer can."

Lee had come to take Clem's assistance for granted, but it had been critical to Lee and his future with Verry. That thought made him realize the many things that were important in life and what he really had that was valuable: Verry, the Guardianship, good friends, family. He thought some more, playing back his trip from Bend, the long stretches of highway, the types of people he met on that drive—people from a totally different life than he had even imagined. To the things he already had on his "Thanks, God" list, he added: *enough money to be comfortable and the freedom to travel as we want, when we want, where we want.* Another thought about Verry and the things he was thankful for: *Verry's healing, safety from harm, the incredible technology that allowed me to keep in touch with people even while on the road. And, always, a God who continues to love and look out for us.*

Chapter 105

Stopped!

The logistics of the departure from Des Moines were more complicated than anyone had anticipated, not because they were complex but because no one planned anything. Lee and Verry were more caught up in themselves and their honeymooning than anything else. Similarly, Thommy K. and Drella were enjoying each other's company too much to think about getting Verry into either a car or the RV for the drive to the airport. But when it came time to pack suitcases and depart, the magnitude of their problems struck.

Drella started it. "How're you going to get Verry into the RV? Or are you going to drive it to the airport? And why are you going to Reno? I thought you lived in Bend."

Lee looked around, and all of the others seemed to have the same question on their minds. "I thought it was obvious," he began, "but I guess I was wrong." The others nodded. "We're going to Reno *because* we'll live in Bend. I don't think anyone knows of our marriage except the four of us and the minister. By departing for Reno, I think it'll look to everyone like we're going there to get married, so that's where they'll look for us. But just because we're starting out for Reno doesn't mean we will arrive there." There was a small chorus of, "Oh," and "I see," then everyone returned to the more immediate problems.

Thommy K. asked, "Do you want me to turn in the RV for you, Lee? Or can you do that in Des Moines?"

Lee's answer: "I'd really like you to do it for me. Just send me the credit card receipt."

Verry asked Lee, "Can I get into the airplane in a wheelchair?"

"Yes," he said. "They'll use a small one to carry you into the plane. Drella can return this one to the hospital, or wherever she got it."

How'd I let this all happen? Lee asked himself. Then he realized how it came about. *My mind has been running in a single track this week, that's what!* But it still didn't prepare him for the magnitude of the effort to prepare to fly the two of them out of Des Moines.

By the time all of these things were discussed and decided upon, it was already ten thirty in the morning, and they were to depart Des Moines at four. Unbelievable to Lee, they left the little house, fully packed, three hours prior to their intended departure, allowing themselves plenty of time to get to the airport.

Things went as planned until they entered the small private aviation terminal. At the security gate, two serious-looking men stood between them and the baggage check-in counter. Neither wore the uniforms most airport security agencies used. Both were in blue jeans and plaid flannel shirts, one red, one dark blue, with dirty and scruffy cowboy boots, wide tooled leather belts, and large silver buckles with rodeo scenes embossed on them. They would fit well in the general populace around Des Moines and its surrounds, yet they looked out of place to Lee. Unfortunately, there were no obvious airport security people in sight.

Might as well pretend they're not there, Lee thought, not at all certain the ploy would work. In the meantime, the three others noticed something was wrong but waited to follow Lee's lead.

"You really think it's them, Mal?" whispered the first man, not wanting his uncertainty to show.

"Right size, right color hair, looks like his picture, except for the mustache. But Mr. Gerit said our guy is single." Now both men were whispering.

"Yeah, and there's four of 'em, not just one. And they look 'real,' if you get my meanin'."

"Have to stop 'em anyway. Like Mr. Gerit directed."

"What if they call security? What'll we do then?"

The first glared at the other. "Things're bad enough already, Mal. Don't try to make 'em worse."

They turned back to face Lee's group, trying to look official but too awkward to appear anything but strange.

Lee smiled at them as if he were being nice to strangers and continued pushing Verry's wheelchair toward the check-in counter, trying to move around the two men as if they were merely an impolite obstacle rather than a roadblock. Verry was terrified, the only evidence being how tightly she held Dr. Zoren's "present" against her chest.

The closest man reached out with a strong and rough hand and slowly but firmly brought Verry's wheelchair to a stop. Before Lee could say anything, the man said, "Mr. Kaaler?"

It's them! They've finally found me! Then Lee remembered FarCaller's Sensing of the future. *Somehow we're going to get through this.* Looking at the two men, though, he began to doubt his own confidence.

"No, sir," Lee responded. "Jimmie Williamson. Me and my fiancée here're flying to Reno to get married." He smiled his most beguiling smile. "Now, if you'll please excuse us."

His accuser gave what was supposed to be a smile, something he clearly hadn't had much practice doing. "We think you're Mr. Kaaler," he repeated. "Our boss would like to talk to you."

Verry and Drella were terrified, and their eyes showed it. For his part, Thommy K. looked around for security guards to help them but saw none.

"My name is Williamson," Lee insisted, reluctantly retrieving his wallet and showing an Idaho driver's license with his photo, mustache, and all. "If you don't get out of our way, we'll miss our flight." He looked down at Verry, frozen in her wheelchair, afraid to say or do anything. "Her folks don't really like me too much yet," he continued, as if oblivious to any threat these men might pose, "so we decided to elope. That'll let us get on with our lives right now, and we'll worry about her parents later."

The confident expression in both the men's faces began to wane. This wasn't how they expected their prey to act. Or look.

Lee leaned forward again, as if to share a confidence. "Her folks also don't like me because I don't have a job, but I inherited plenty. Otherwise, I couldn't hire one of these private jets to fly us to Reno." A quick smile. "I think they'd rather I worked for everything. Know what I mean?"

The men looked at each other for guidance, received nothing in return but puzzled expressions.

Lee decided to keep talking and take advantage of the confusion the two men were already showing. "We're getting married early this evening, and if we don't get there on time, we'll lose our reservations for the pastor and the chapel." He smiled broadly. "We're going to the Chapel of Love. Ever hear of it?"

Again the two hunters exchanged puzzled glances. After a few seconds, some kind of message passed between them; and the first said, "Thank you for your time, Mr. Williamson. Sorry we bothered you. It's just that our boss was really anxious to talk to this other man, and you look a lot like him."

Thank you, Lord! Lee thought, trying not to show his relief. "No offense taken." He looked for a way to steer Verry's wheelchair around the two men, who had not yet moved out of the way. "Now, if you'll excuse us, we've got a wedding to go to."

The two men again exchanged concerned glances then stepped aside and let Lee's party continue to the check-in counter.

Until takeoff, Verry's entire vocabulary, from getting out of the RV in front of the Des Moines airport until they got into their jet, consisted solely of grunts indicating she hurt somewhere. Not until they were airborne did she calm down enough to talk. Her first words: "Those men were going to kidnap us!"

They sat side by side on the bench seat in the rear of the business jet, facing the open cockpit door. Her words were nearly drowned out by the high-pitched whine of the two small jets mounted just forward of the tail section. Lee put his arm around his bride and pulled her close to him, awkwardly trying to offer comfort to a terrified young woman.

"I'm really sorry this happened, Verry," he began. "I expected some kind of confrontation, but because FarCaller said we wouldn't be in danger I didn't worry too much about it. That's what saved us in the end, because those two goons probably expected 'Mr. Kaaler' to try to run away or go stiff with fear or something like that." He kissed her cheek then tentatively added, "If you want, we'll take you back to Des Moines and give you time to rethink this."

Verry instantly turned to face him, her fear replaced by anger. "Lee, don't you even suggest that! I didn't say I wanted out, I'm just scared." Her flashing hazel eyes became soft and loving. "I told you a long time ago that I wanted to marry you in spite of whatever dangers you were in because I thought we should be together. Now that we've had some time together"—a loving, tender smile accompanied by a quick kiss, reminding him of their intimacy—"I'm even more certain I was right. Now what do we do?"

He unfastened his seat belt and began the slow crouching walk toward the cockpit. "First, we change our destination."

Chapter 106

Two Idiots

Jeff Gerit couldn't believe his ears. "You did *what*?" The response was mumbled, but he clearly understood what the man said. "You let them go because he had ID and there was a party of four, not just one or two." *How was I blessed with two such numbskulls?*

After a few seconds to regain his control, he very quietly asked, "And where were they going?" More mumbling, then "Reno! What a wonderful place for a wedding! Isn't it nice that they gave you all that information?" Before the man could answer, Jeff added, "Get out of that city and my life. Call back in two weeks to see if you still have a job. If you call before that, Mal, you'll regret it!" Before the man could respond, Jeff slammed the telephone handset onto its charging platform.

Jeff dialed another number. After three rings, he heard the click of an answering machine beginning its litany. When the time came to give his message, he said, "Get your people in Nevada to check every airport for the arrival of a business jet carrying a woman in a wheelchair accompanied by a man. Both young, both good looking. Report where they go, what they do, and when they leave. Every hour if you have to. And whatever you do, don't lose 'em!" Just before he ended the call, Jeff added, "And check the wedding chapels!"

What an idiot! Two idiots! They had their hands on the man we've been hunting for years and very calmly let him go. Really wonderful. Dad's gonna love it.

Chapter 107

Even Richer!

Ben Gerit's reaction was the worst Jeff could have hoped for. Fuming rage would have been best. His dad would throw things around and vent the anger and frustration out of his system right in Chicago, leaving Jeff untouched. Next best would have been a seething rage that involved a vicious verbal tirade and threats against Jeff and everyone connected with him. But instead he got nothing but stony silence for several minutes.

The elder Gerit wasn't screaming and yelling because he knew it would kill him, yet he was so angry he had to do something or the stress of holding back would do the same. Gently putting the telephone handset down on his desk, he walked to the window overlooking the city, now sheeted with rain and hail from a spring thunderstorm. Putting his hand hard against the cold glass, he tried to let the sound of rainfall comfort him, ease his anger, help him regain control, and thereby save his life.

A few minutes of this, several deep breaths, and he returned to his desk and picked up the handset again.

"Get rid of both of them. I'll get back to you in a while." He softly placed the handset in its cradle then returned to his recliner and slowly sat down, letting himself absorb the soft and relaxing vibrations coming from inside it. *Jeff doesn't know how lucky he is that I'm still recovering from that heart attack and the maltreatment my former doctor gave me on his behalf. If I was half the man I'd been before that thing, he'd suffer the same fate as his doctor friend.*

He forced himself to relax, pushing his anger away just as his new doctor said. First he took two of the small white pills the doctor prescribed to calm him. As he checked off the remaining steps in the process, carefully following the procedure his doctor gave him, he felt his heartbeat slow, his breathing become deeper and more relaxed, his perspiration stop. *This is one of those times when blood shouldn't run thicker than water. If it'd been anyone else who screwed up so badly, he'd suffer for three or four weeks before we finally let him die. As it is . . .* He let the thought fade then grabbed it back and reviewed what they really had going for them. *At least we know who the Guardian is and where he lives. That means we also know he probably keeps that power spoon with him.* A few seconds more, then a smile softened his grim features. *And we know who his new bride is. So we know her family.*

Another good thing, he thought. He let the vibrating massage emanating from the recliner do its magic, feeling calmness and normality return. *Jeff had the guts to call me instead of trying to hide this screwup. Shows he's trying to work with me. For a change. We'll get rid of that Guardian for good and get that power spoon, then we'll run pharmaceuticals on this whole continent.*

His smile broadened just before he fell asleep.

Chapter 108

Don't Shoot!

"What did you say to the pilots, Lee?" Lee answered as he rebuckled himself into the bench seat he shared with Verry in the chartered business jet. "I changed our destination from Reno to Walla Walla."

"Is that a place? I thought it was just a brand of apples." She was telling the truth and Lee was astounded.

"You've never heard of Walla Walla, the town people like so much they named it twice?"

Verry chuckled. She just shook her head but held on to his left hand. "Not before now," she admitted. "Where is it besides in Washington State? And why don't we just fly to Bend—or wherever the nearest airport is?"

"Walla Walla's northeast of Bend and should be a place where those people hunting me wouldn't look. From there I'll rent a van and drive to Bend. That should throw them even further off our trail, because they'll expect just what you said—that we'll fly directly to Bend." He looked her directly in the eyes, signaling something serious was near. "It's a long drive, Verry, and it'll be hard on you, but I think it's safest."

She squeezed his hand then gave him a quick peck on the lips. "I'll be OK as long as we can find a toilet I can use. These casts make everything twice as hard as it should be."

"Well," he began, bolding somewhat, "it's a darned good thing you're wearing a baggy dress, then. Even shorts would make your life a lot harder."

She smiled back, enjoying another aspect of marital intimacy—understanding. "What're we going to do after we get home?" The thought of "home" being where she and Lee would live together strangely warmed her. A place of their own, where they could start their lives together, a new place where there were no preconceived notions about her that they had to overcome. And in an area Lee loved. It made their marriage seem somehow more real.

"First you'll meet my folks. I haven't told them about our wedding, so they're really going to be surprised." Answering her unasked question, he added, "They'll love you. You're the kind of woman my mother really likes. Just remember neither of them know anything about"—he looked around from force of habit, checking to see if they were being overheard; they weren't, of course, but he still felt caution was the best course—"about the spoon and the Guardianship," he continued. "So don't talk about anything involving it."

Her frown telegraphed her mental state: confusion. "But I thought your dad was the oldest son, and he got the—thing—from his mother."

Lee shook his head. "He didn't want anything to do with whatever grandmother had, so she told him nothing and then willed it to me. That's why she wrote me those—" He stopped in mid sentence, mouth agape.

"What's wrong, Lee?" Fear tinged Verry's voice. "Is something wrong?"

He shook his head, turning to look at her and calm her. "No. It's just that there's one more letter from her that I should have opened a long time ago. Her others were very helpful; don't know how I forgot."

He smiled again, clearly not nervous. "Why don't we just try to sleep in this noise box? We can talk all we want after we get into the van." Then another thought made him feel like an idiot. *Cripes! I still don't know my new address. About all I can hope for is to rent a van with a GPS thing and trust it to get me home. So the next thing I do is call Clem, ask for the address of my house, and thank him for his offer—I'm not going to get him up at dawn just so he can to lead me home.*

* * *

The GPS worked perfectly. They arrived in Bend early the next morning, after driving and talking most of the night. Lee was too excited and on edge to sleep, but Verry's need to heal overcame her desire to stay awake with her husband. By dawn, she had already slept more than five hours and was sleeping hard. Lee's thought: *We must really be married. She snores.*

Following instructions from the GPS, Lee carefully drove down the paved country road near his new home, hoping to minimize any bumping or loud road noises so Verry could get as much sleep as possible before they arrived. Turning onto the road to his home, the rising sun shown directly into his eyes, making it impossible to see well and impossible to lower the sun visors enough to shield himself from the bright glare. He had to get out of the van, push his home's fence gate open, then drive through and close it behind him.

After maneuvering Verry into her wheelchair and pushing it up the walk to the front door, he pressed the doorbell button and heard a pleasant chiming. In just a few seconds, it was opened by his father—pointing a deer rifle at Lee's chest.

Both men were shocked. Lee never expected to see his father frightened enough to use a gun for protection, and his dad didn't expect to see Lee at five thirty in the morning, especially without any warning. One of the things that helped defuse the matter was the woman in the wheelchair behind Lee. His dad instantly understood the significance. A big smile replaced his apprehensive expression; he leaned the gun against the wall then turned around and called back, "Honey, come here! It's Lee! With a surprise." Lee turned Verry's wheel chair around and slowly and carefully pulled it up the two stairs onto the small porch. When that was done, he pushed the wheelchair into the house, nodding for his father to close the door behind them. Just then, Lee's mother wheeled herself into the room, wearing a pink lace trimmed dressing gown, still not recovered from the injuries she suffered in the hit-and-run accident, but clearly curious and excited. From behind the wheelchair, Lee leaned down so his face was next to Verry's head, put his hands on her shoulders and smiled at his folks. "Mom and Dad, I'd like you to meet Vera Willards Kaaler—my wife. Verry, these are my parents."

His dad immediately leaned down and gave Verry a gentle but lingering hug. Lee's mom reacted totally differently. "Oh, Lee, how wonderful!" She wheeled herself beside Verry and tried to enclose her new daughter-in-law in her arms, but two people hugging each other while sitting in wheelchairs was impossible. "I'm so glad Lee found a beautiful wife. Oh, my dear! What happened? Are you in pain? Can I do anything to help? Do you need—" Then she started to cry, clearly tears of joy, but nonetheless tears. Lee and his father were a bit uncomfortable with it, but Verry instantly knew it was a good sign.

Lee put his hand on his mother's shoulder and turned her so she faced him. "Mother, Verry's dead tired and her arm and leg both hurt. Right now we both need some good solid sleep—that'll do us more good than anything else. So if you don't mind, we'll go straight to my—our," he corrected himself, smiling a bit sheepishly at his wife, "room and crash. We'll probably be up after noon, and then we can tell you what's happened." He looked at both his parents, checking their expressions. "OK?" he said. It was not a question, regardless of how it sounded.

Both his parents nodded and smiled. "Good to have you back, son," his dad said. His mother beamed at Verry then gave both of them a quick peck on their cheeks. "We'll see you when you get up. Don't worry about a thing." She then had another thought. "But you don't know where your room is, do you?" She smiled and pointed toward a long hall just past the kitchen. "It's at the end, on the right. You can't miss it."

Mom, Lee thought, *you're acting like this is your house and you're the hostess!* A few seconds more, then, *Which is exactly what she's been ever since they got here a few days ago. I'll bet she's even rearranged the kitchen cupboards and linen closets.* Letting those thoughts die, he wheeled his bride into their bedroom and closed the door behind them.

Chapter 109

Just Stay Here

The newlyweds awoke in midafternoon, still tired, but not sleepy. Both recognized the problem: they'd been under more stress than they'd realized, and their bodies were now commandeering the resources to permit healing to occur. After brushing his teeth and washing his face and hands, Lee returned to his bride, took her in his arms, and kissed her soundly. Very shortly afterward, they initiated their bedroom.

After that, when Verry began moving toward the bathroom, Lee heard a soft moan.

"What's wrong?" He was still in bed, still enjoying watching his wife hobble around, especially when she was wearing only perfume.

She turned, her face slightly contorted. "The truth is," she began, "both my arm and leg still hurt, mostly when I get up in the morning. The medicine Dr. Zoren gave me barely controls the pain. Once I get moving about, especially after a hot sponge bath, the pain subsides."

When he heard that, Lee realized for the first time that she'd been in pain their entire marriage, and their honeymooning unquestionably contributed to her suffering. "I'm so sorry. If I hadn't been so selfish, I'd have let you sleep more, and—"

Before he could complete his sentence, Verry hopped on her good leg over to him and put her hand over his mouth. "If I'd been in so much pain that I couldn't stand it, I'd have told you." She kissed him, then added, "Besides, what we did made me forget the pain, so I figure I gained a full day of relief from pain in the two days we've been married!"

It gave them the first real laugh of their marriage and also taught Lee more about his wife: she was not only strong willed, she was strong. And she loved him a great deal.

They joined their parents sometime later, after her sponge bath—administered by Lee, complicated by Verry's cast. He insisted Verry use the wheelchair until her knee didn't hurt most of the time, and she agreed.

His parents were obviously anxious to meet their new daughter-in-law and delighted when the newlyweds appeared. After the expected questions about how Verry felt (fine, considering) and whether the two of them were hungry (they were), the real talk began. Uncharacteristically, Lee started the discussion by describing what happened to them in Des Moines, beginning with Verry's accident and why Lee believed it was aimed at him.

It didn't take long for his parents to understand more fully Lee's concerns about them: the arson attempt at their own home, Verry's accident, his mom's accident, and the confrontation with the unknown men at the Des Moines airport. Lee's mother went straight to the heart of the matter.

"But *why* is all of this happening to you, Lee? What did you do?" She was as sincere and concerned as Lee had ever seen.

When Lee's mother asked that question, Verry flinched slightly—enough that Lee could feel it but not enough his parents would have noticed.

Now what do I do? How do I answer that question without revealing stuff neither of them can be told? "Dad," he began, "do you remember ever talking with grandmother about some family secrets she wanted to share with you?"

His dad blinked slowly, thinking back several decades. "Yes, son, once, when I was a teenager, I think." He frowned as he talked, obviously trying hard to remember whatever Lee was talking about. "Don't remember the details, I'm afraid." He again blinked, but this time with curiosity instead of concentration. "Why do you ask? How could that have anything to do with burning our house? Or hurting Verry?"

All eyes were turned to Lee, two pair out of curiosity and concern, the third from another perspective: wondering how he was going to answer such a difficult question.

"Well, Dad, because of a decision you made then, Grandmother kept those secrets from you and told them to me. Then, in her will, she bequeathed me something valuable. I've had it ever since, and a few months ago, someone who knew about that thing found out I had it—or thought I had it. It can be very powerful if used for selfish purposes, and that's what they want to do. So they started hurting people dear to me in order to force me to give it to them. In fact," he said, pointing at his telephone answering machine, "while I was gone, they even left a message telling me just that."

One deep breath. "That's all I can tell you." He looked straight at his mother, sitting on the sofa, holding his dad's arm, looking absolutely shocked. "But to answer you directly, Mom, I've done nothing wrong to cause all of this trouble." He looked at Verry, gave her hand a hard squeeze which she just as firmly returned.

"But now that we're here, I intend to try to do something to protect myself and my loved ones from these people."

He returned his attention to his parents. "Until then, I want you to stay here and let the work on your house continue as long as it takes. I'll increase the overall security of this place now that I'm back. And," he continued, again looking at Verry and squeezing her hand, "Verry will help me in what I have to do."

"And *we* can't." It was a statement from his mother. She looked Lee straight in his eyes but nodded slightly: his desire to be left alone for whatever reason was OK with her and she was not offended.

"Exactly," he said. "The best way to help me right now is to stay here, where I know you're safe." Gesturing around the room, he added, "This place is more than big enough for Verry and me, so we can live our life and you can live yours, and we won't have to impose on each other or interfere with anything. I'll do most of my stuff in my office," looking at the end of the room to the walnut-paneled door. "When I'm in there, I'd appreciate your leaving me alone. That's about all I ask. The rest of the time we can spend getting to know each other as married couples instead of parents and children."

That brought smiles all around. Lee's dad took the hint and retrieved a bottle of his favorite wine, that he bought and stored in Lee's small wine cellar. "Let's start with a toast to the bride and groom."

After two days of getting reacquainted with his parents, of Verry learning about them and her new home, and of short personal telephone calls to Verry's parents, Thommy K., and Drella, Lee felt he could no longer put aside learning his responsibilities as the Guardian. First priority, since he'd received no calls from FarCaller and therefore wasn't worried about his friend, was to thoroughly examine the contents of the package Amelia Zoren had left him.

Chapter 110

Squeeze 'Em

"This idiocy must stop!" Ben yelled at his son. "I've been more than patient, but all your people do is screw things up! From now on we'll do exactly what we agreed: you and your goons will work with me and mine and do exactly what *I* say."

Jeff listened quietly, more frightened than usual because he knew, from past experience, that his father had never before kept such close self-control when he was really angry. It meant his old man was either playing a game or afraid of another heart attack. Both were serious. "Tell me what you want."

Jeff's quiet response helped calm his father a bit; an argument would have probably cost Jeff everything but his life.

"Starting right now, we squeeze Kaaler. You don't know where he is; you only know he didn't get to Reno. But I'll bet he's in touch with his friends and relatives. So I want your people in Bend to start harassing everyone Kaaler knows. Spray paint, car accidents, rocks through windows of his friends' homes or businesses—anything to make our point. You warned him to cooperate or we'd start hurting his friends and family, so we do just that. I want him to realize we're still around and still serious."

At first Ben heard nothing on the line, then Jeff quietly said, "I'll contact my people right after we hang up."

"And you can be sure I'll contact mine as well!"

Ben's first call was to Etta, his female friend in Bend who'd never failed him in anything. After the customary greetings and innuendoes about visits and time together, he told her exactly what he wanted, closing with, "Start with the lawyer! Those shysters will do anything they can to stop me, and this guy's going to pay for it."

"Can I ask what he did, Ben?"

"Helped Kaaler."

* * *

"Mal, this is Jeff Gerit."

The big man was still in his small apartment, still waiting for this call, still fearing what Jeff might do to him. "Yes, sir."

"Got a job for you. One you better get right."

"Yes, sir. What?"

"You remember the Kaaler guy, right?" It was rhetorical. Mal would never forget "Mr. Williamson" and how much trouble he got into because that man bluffed his way out of the airport.

"Right."

"I thought so. Find out who this guy married and start doing things to her family—you know the bit."

Mal nodded as he responded. "Yes, sir."

"Good. Then get with it." Just before Mal hung up, he heard Jeff's voice again.

"Sorry, sir, I didn't hear what you said."

"I said, 'And don't screw this up.'"

Part VII

Retribution

Chapter 111

Another Discovery

The Guardian had some work to do. Lee carried the golden set from his bedroom into his new office and set it on the desk. One of the first things he noticed was how comfortable the room felt. It was a good-sized room, with walnut paneling and thick light brown carpeting. Three walls were covered with bookshelves already half full. On the fourth wall, just to the right of the door, were his desk with a cordless telephone connected to his cyphony box, and his Macintosh. On that same wall, directly above the desk, the decorator had hung his college and high school diplomas, a few pictures of himself and some college friends, and a large poster of Forsyth Park in Savannah—one of the places he intended to take Verry when this mess was over. He pulled out the new brown leather office chair and sat, savoring the smell of the new leather and enjoying how it supported his body.

Sometimes you don't realize how lucky you are.

Wasting no more time, he opened the wooden case and laid the golden plate and spoon flat on his desk. *I already know the plate shows me what I'm thinking. What more can it do?* He let that thought percolate for a while then picked it up.

First he visualized the Des Moines air terminal, where he and Verry were stopped and questioned by two men he was certain worked for whomever was trying to get the spoon. Just as before, the image of the terminal appeared in the plate. Only this time, the two men weren't visible.

The picture in the plate clouded, gold and black and brown streaks and clouds moving through the interior of the plate as if it were being swirled about by a forty-niner trying to pan gold. Then the image re-formed into a totally unfamiliar scene.

A small living room somewhere. Dark beige wall-to-wall carpet. The square furniture usually found in cheap motels or furniture stores advertising "The Sale of the Century!" or something just as idiotic. Cheap tan wallpaper covered with colored specks or buds. Scenes of waterfalls and forests in frames above the sofa, a small TV opposite the sofa, cheap end tables on both ends of it. Sitting on the sofa, a can of Coors in his hand, was the man who did most of the talking in the terminal.

This thing not only shows what I think about, it finds *whoever I think about!* The next thing Lee was conscious of was how much he resented that man and what he represented. He made no effort to hide these feelings as he had to do when that man tried to kidnap him and Verry and take them to his boss.

Lee's jaws clenched with anger and resentment; he found himself wishing that man could realize just how much Lee disliked him and everything he represented. Before that thought left his mind, the man suddenly jumped up, dropping his can of beer, and began wildly checking the apartment, as if looking for something or someone. His breath came in deep gasps, and his normally ruddy complexion was white: he was terrified!

Lee quickly stopped that thought and, just as quickly but gently, replaced the plate into its bed in the carton in front of him.

This is *a weapon! That man felt exactly how much I detested him and what he stands for.*

He sat back, both hands on the arms of his chair, intentionally not touching the items on his desk. *If a person wanted to, he could probably scare someone to death with that thing.*

His shocked expression was slowly replaced by a mischievous grin.

Chapter 112

Threats

Most of Lee's day was spent studying the "golden set," as he called it. Once he had Verry take the golden spoon into their bedroom then called to her through the golden plate. When he saw her image in the plate, a series of goose bumps ran up and down his spine, thrilled that he had discovered another way to use it.

Immediately after, she wheeled herself to his office, pounded on the door, and, as soon as he opened it, began speaking so fast he could hardly follow her.

"Lee, that was awful! Frightening! I saw you in the spoon and heard you call my name. I don't think I ever want to do that again." She held the spoon away from her body, her arm outstretched toward her husband. The clear message: *Take this thing away from me—now!*

He did as she wanted then sat down and took both her hands in his. Speaking softly but with excitement, he said, "Verry, calm down and listen to me."

She nodded but struggled to regain her composure.

"I needed to confirm two things." He stopped speaking and looked directly into her hazel eyes, assuring he had her full attention. "Do you realize what we just did?"

Still saying nothing, she let her eyes go blank as she tried to reconstruct what had just happened. Then she realized where he was leading her. "The spoon worked with me!" Her fear dissolved into muted joy. Before she could say anything more, Lee continued.

"Absolutely. It proves a lot of things I wanted to know. For one thing, you *do* have the gift—just as FarCaller said. So our kids probably will."

It was the first time they'd talked about family and having children. At first Verry was a bit embarrassed then realized it was totally unwarranted. She was a happily married woman who wanted to bear her husband's children. Someday. Not yet.

Lee continued unabated. "It also means you could possibly contact FarCaller if something ever happened to me."

"No, Lee," she said, shaking her head, "I don't want to be Guardian. That's something I could never do."

"I'm not talking about *being* Guardian," he said, squeezing her hands again. "You can't be a Guardian unless something happens to me before our oldest is ready for that responsibility. I'm not planning on letting that happen. "What I'm so pleased about is that it's something *we* can do, not just something I do." He leaned forward and gave her a light peck on her lips. "That means a lot."

She nodded. He couldn't tell if it was in agreement or surrender. "OK, then," she asked, "what's next?"

Before he could answer, his telephone rang, its sharp chirp so intrusive that both of them jumped. When they realized what happened, they both laughed, breaking up the seriousness of their conversation.

"Hello."

"Lee, this is Clem Maestre."

He covered the mouthpiece with his hand and whispered to Verry, "It's my lawyer."

She nodded, said nothing.

"Let's go secure, Clem. Are you ready?"

"Go, Lee."

"On three." Lee heard the white noise for a fraction of a second, then the line was silent. "Good to hear from you, Clem."

"When do Ah get to meet the blushing bride?"

Lee smiled at Verry then said, "First of all, she's not blushing." Before Clem could respond, Lee continued, "But you can come anytime. She's still a bit gimpy from the injuries she got in the a car accident in Des Moines."

"That's kind of what I wanted to talk to y'all about, Lee."

Lee's confused expression concerned Verry, so she motioned that he should turn the handset so she could hear both sides of the conversation. He did so before speaking. "Don't understand, Clem."

"Well, my friend, things that also seem to revolve around y'all are happenin' around here as well."

Fifteen minutes later, Lee and Verry understood the magnitude of the efforts against them: Clem's office windows had been smashed, his furniture spray painted, office machines ruined. Lee's bank called Clem, believing Lee was still out of town, and two San Francisco banks reported that Lee had written bad checks. Lee's parents' house, whose repairs were nearly complete, had been struck by a supposedly drunken driver, knocking the entire front corner out, damaging the house enough to require more weeks of work before they could move back in.

As Clem spoke, Lee and Verry just looked at each other, barely able to believe what they were hearing. When he finished, Lee said, "And you think I'm the only common thread in all of this."

"Ah think y'all may be," the lawyer responded. "Ah've been tryin' to figure out anathin' else that might tie all those things together, but the calls to the bank are definitely about y'all. Y'all's parents wouldn't hurt a flea, so the damage to their house is almost certainly pointed at y'all." He was silent just a second or two, then, "Lee, do y'all remember when we talked, coupla weeks ago, and Ah asked y'all what was going on and if y'all'd evah tell me?"

"Of course."

"Well, my friend, maybe the time has come. Seems to me that this is gettin' out of hand. Maybe the two of us can find a way to stop all of this. But Ah'm totally in the dark, and that's not a good way for a lawyer to be. Not if he's tryin' to help his client."

"How soon can you get here, Clem?"

Chapter 113

Destruction

"Verry? This is Drella." Her voice quavered as if she'd been crying or was under great stress.

Verry was in the bedroom, resting her leg. "What is it? You sound upset." Then a terrible thought hit her. "Mom and Dad! Are they all right?" Verry's heart was beating fast and hard, and her breathing sped up.

"They're OK." Drella's voice seemed to be somewhat more in control. "But bad things are happening, and you and Lee need to know about them."

"Just a minute—I'll get Lee on the line."

Before Drella could tell Verry not to bother, she heard Verry talking to someone then heard a click on the line.

"He's on now, Drella."

"Hi, Drella," Lee said. "What's happened?"

"All kinds of things. Some of the folks' cattle were killed and mutilated, some of their farm equipment was vandalized, my car was spray painted and the windows broken out, the hospital has received complaints about my work with demands that I be fired—all kinds of things."

"Oh no, Drella," Verry said. "You didn't lose your job!"

"No. At first the administrator's office was all upset, then they started checking the calls and found none of the people who called were ever in the ICU when I was. Now they're upset that such calls were made but convinced that they're from some nuts." Her breathing had slowed, and the tremor in her voice had nearly disappeared, making everyone feel better. "But it's not funny."

Lee responded first. "I'm so sorry, Drella. I hoped this wouldn't happen. It's all my fault."

Both sisters responded with exactly the same words: "That's stupid!" It made all three of them laugh and considerably lowered the stress level. But the matter remained serious.

"For what it's worth, Drella," Lee began, "those kinds of things have happened here too."

Drella was silent, something in itself abnormal. "You mean—"

"Just that," he said, continuing. "Someone's putting pressure on me, just like they said they would."

"But what're you going to do, Lee? This stuff can't continue—it'll ruin people." Her concern had again arisen, her voice almost a wail.

"I think there *is* something I can do," Lee began. Before he could continue, Drella interrupted.

"You're not going to surrender."

"No. Just tell your parents how sorry we are and that I'm going to try to stop this stuff. They'll have to trust me—which may be a bit difficult, considering I stole their daughter away from them without so much as a 'How do you do.'"

Drella chuckled. She was definitely feeling better. "I told them about how we got Verry out of the hospital and the wedding and where you spent your honeymoon. Even told them about the thing at the airport. Mom even thought it was very romantic."

Before Lee could respond, Verry said, "It was!" Her smile was also obvious in her voice.

"You girls talk away," Lee said. "I'm going back to work."

"What kind of work?" Drella asked Verry after Lee left the line.

"You wouldn't believe it if I told you."

Chapter 114

And to FarCaller As Well

After Clem's and Drella's calls, Lee thought about what he could do to stop the attacks on his friends and recognized the solution immediately: he had to stop the leaders. The problem: he didn't know who they were.

Before this train of thought could continue, he felt/heard FarCaller calling. He retrieved the silver spoon from his shirt pocket, where he now carried it all the time, and looked into it. Looking back was the very worried countenance of his friend.

"What's wrong, FarCaller?"

"Sorry to bother you I am, Lee, but again your help I need."

No hesitation. "What kind?"

"Some of my friends my wife and me attacking are, threats making, even one of my cows killed."

"Why?"

"Helping them enough I am not, they say. Animals to them I've given, and carts, even one of them build a new house I helped."

"And this is how they thank you?" Lee made no attempt to hide how badly he thought of those people.

"Good people basically are they, Lee," FarCaller began, "but—"

"Excuse me for interrupting, FarCaller," Lee said, "but you say that about nearly every person who tries to harm you. If they're so good, why are they so darned selfish? If they're so good, why don't they express their thanks for what you've done for them instead of making more demands and threatening you if they don't get whatever they want?"

Never before had Lee spoken this way to FarCaller, and it shocked him. So shocked was he that he looked away, clearly thinking about what Lee said.

Finally he looked back, slightly embarrassed. "Sorry am I," he began. "The way you think not do I, and that really being used was I, saw not I. To work this out myself, try will I."

"Don't be silly. I'll be glad to help, I just wanted you to see that you're being abused by ungrateful people." Now Lee smiled. "Let me tell you some of the things that have happened to me in the past few weeks."

After reviewing the wedding and its aftermath, especially the confrontation in the air terminal, Lee told FarCaller about the golden plate and spoon. "And," he said, ending his exposition, "I've learned much about it. So much, in fact, that I think I can help you by using it."

FarCaller looked at Lee, puzzlement growing on his face. "Understand I not," he said. "Evil can help me how?"

"It's not evil," Lee corrected, "it's powerful. The plate's a weapon. Now, if you'll give me an idea of what these people look like, I think I can help put a stop to this stuff."

"Their appearance?" FarCaller was obviously confused. "Never before have you this asked."

"Never before did I need it."

The lack of explanation told FarCaller he would receive no more information at that time. In itself, that was unusual. "Perhaps if into my future you looked—" He let the matter drop, knowing Lee would understand.

"Excellent. I should have known enough to do that. Please wait a few minutes."

FarCaller just nodded as Lee closed his eyes and again sought the soaring sensation that told him he was looking into his friend's future. It quickly came. Lee felt himself lifted so he could look down on FarCaller's house and yard. Outside it, pounding on the rail fence, were four men and two women, screaming something. One of them opened a sack and emptied it on the ground. From its deep insides rolled out dozens of fist-sized rocks. Next he withdrew from one of his pockets a device that looked like a slingshot without the Y-shaped frame. *It's a sling, like David used against Goliath!*

Willing himself closer to the people, Lee scrutinized their faces, committing them to memory. That completed, he opened his eyes.

"Something useful seen you have?"

"Indeed I have, FarCaller. For one thing, if we don't stop those people soon, they'll start stoning your house with large rocks. That could not only damage your home but might even injure you. Keep this contact open. I'm going to disappear for a bit."

Lee turned away and picked up the golden plate. First he looked into it and recalled the face of the man who seemed to be the leader of the attack against FarCaller. When he appeared, Lee immediately thought about hurting the man, about breaking his arms, beating his face raw, all the time saying things like, "You miserable creature! Why are you attacking the only person in your village who cared enough about you and your worthless family to even try to help you? Go away and never bother him again, or you'll suffer everything you just imagined!"

He then did the same things to the other men and women, intentionally trying to terrorize them and put the blame for this attack directly back on their own selfish actions. In less than ten minutes, he finished, and all of the would-be attackers had fallen to the ground, writhing in pain.

Putting the plate down, he picked up the spoon, found FarCaller waiting. "I'm done now, FarCaller. I doubt they'll ever bother you again, and they'll probably tell their friends not to do so either. In fact, it wouldn't surprise me if people started treating you with a little more gratitude." Now Lee was smiling, a knowing smile devoid of information.

FarCaller was too smart to let the matter alone. "Lee, what you did, tell me you must. Those my friends are, even if thoughtful they are not. Changing that I want not."

For a few seconds, Lee thought about whether he should tell FarCaller about the golden plate. *Hiding this from FarCaller is stupid. He's the one who told me about it in the first place.*

After explaining his use of the golden plate as a weapon, Lee turned the silver spoon so FarCaller could see that plate. Holding it there for a few seconds, he then moved the spoon so he could see his friend. "That's it, FarCaller. If you hadn't told me about it, I'd probably never even tried to use it and wouldn't have been able to help you just now."

FarCaller's usual smile was gone; the man looked shocked. After a few seconds of looking around his living room blankly, he said, "Lee, like the plate I have on my wall exactly it looks, except of gold it is. Anything more about what it can do, know you?"

"Not yet. But I'm about to use it against my own enemies. If that works out, I'll have time to try other things with it. If I find something useful, I'll pass it on."

"Please do so, Lee. Of something else I read in my grandfather's journals it reminds me. While you are your enemies fighting, to find those entries try will I."

"Right now the important thing is that you should be safe. When I've completed my own battles here, I'll contact you again." He broke the contact by putting the spoon back into his pocket.

Picking up the telephone, he dialed Clem Maestre's office. *If Clem can get me some photos of my enemies, I'll give them a taste of their own medicine.*

Chapter 115

Inflicting Great Pain

"Mr. Flogenson, this is Faerleigh Farr Kaaler. My lawyer received a complaint from you about a bad check I supposedly wrote and cashed in a San Francisco bank. Do you remember this?"

He did. After expressing his deepest apologies for ever having to contact Lee on such a matter, Lee said, "Do you know how much money is in my account with your bank?"

"Well, sir," the banker began, "I had my people check it when we first received the call. It seems there should have been adequate money to cover a $2,500 check."

"Yes, sir, it does," Lee said. "If my memory serves, I should have in excess of $150,000 in that account. Is that correct?"

"Ah, well, ah, yes, Mr. Kaaler. Our records showed a balance of $165,331.76 on the day the check was supposedly cashed."

"So what did you tell them?" Lee felt anger rising. His dislike in dealing with accountants was exceeded only by his hatred of government bureaucrats—any level of government.

"Well, Mr. Kaaler, we told them we didn't understand the complaint, as there was adequate money in the account to cover such a check."

"And they said?"

"Curiously, sir," he began, "they seemed not at all surprised."

Lee let that sink into his brain for a few seconds. "Did the caller leave his name?"

"Her name," the banker corrected. "She left her name and telephone number after insisting this was very serious. One of their best customers, a Mr. Jefferson Gerit, had called them, she said, violently complaining about how they handled your supposedly bad check."

"And you returned the call to that number, not the bank."

The silence on the other end of the line told Lee he'd hit the weak spot in the entire matter.

"Mr. Kaaler, are you suggesting that this call didn't come from the South Bay Bank?"

"Mr. Flogenson, will you please check the bank directory and tell me if the number that woman gave you is one of the numbers used by that bank?"

"If you'll give me just a few minutes."

Two minutes later, the man came back on the line. "I don't know how to say this, Mr. Kaaler, but it appears that number is not used by the bank."

"You confirmed this?"

"Yes, sir. Just now."

"May I ask a question, Mr. Flogenson?"

"Of course, sir."

"Why didn't your people do that before contacting my lawyer about a bad check that couldn't possibly have been a bad check?" Before the man could answer, Lee hung up the telephone. *Useless idiot!*

He sat back in his chair, thinking about all the things that had happened in the past few months. *My telephone lines were tapped, my home was watched day and night, my folks' home was torched, my lawyer's office was broken into and smashed, Verry was hurt in an automobile accident that killed her best friend, her folks' farm was vandalized . . .* He stopped recalling and reviewing, as he was getting more angry with each item. Then he made a decision. Picking up the telephone, he dialed Clem's number. When the lawyer answered, Lee said, "On my count, Clem?"

"I've got a client, Lee."

"I'll call back later."

Then Lee thought about what the banker had said. *The complaint supposedly came from a Jefferson Gerit.* His brain went into a controlled loop, trying to put that family name into a place Lee could remember. In just a few seconds, he had the answer. *Gerit Pharmaceuticals! I made a lot of money from their stock a short time ago. You don't suppose . . .* He thought some more then decided what to do.

Fifteen long minutes later, during which he forced himself out of the office to join Verry and his parents in a conversation about interesting and fun places to visit, Clem called back.

Lee activated the scrambler and asked Clem to have someone research Jefferson Gerit. The portly lawyer, now a good friend, thought it was a terrific idea.

Booting up his Mac, Lee went to Google and searched on the name Jefferson Gerit. Two things about Google continually amazed Lee: the speed of its responses to nearly every query he'd ever made and the number of responses he received. Today he had only five responses. The first referred to a newspaper clipping about

Jeff's high school graduation and his father's gift: a fishing trip to the Bahamas, along with a photo of Jeff and a two-hundred-pound marlin. The second item was similar to the first except the occasion was his college graduation. This time the photo showed Jeff standing by a magnificent sable antelope he'd shot in Africa. That trip, like the other, was also a gift from his father, Ebenezer Gerit, "founder and CEO of Gerit Pharmaceuticals."

That ties Jeff to Gerit Pharmaceuticals, and the banker tied Jeff, by way of a second party, to the false complaint about an NSF check on my account. But it doesn't tie Jeff to the destruction and mutilations being aimed at both Verry's and my families. He shook his head in frustration. *Before I do anything serious, I have to* know *this guy—or these guys—are behind all the harassment.*

Lee immediately checked the three remaining references to Jeff Gerit still on his screen and saw a Gerit family tree compiled by someone in San Francisco who studied millionaires from that area. It showed Jefferson Gerit was directly related to Philemon Gerit, who built the Gerit Pharmaceutical industry from the meager beginning of selling snake oil to gold prospectors in the mid-1800s. The last two references were to the Gerit family more than Jefferson Gerit and provided Lee no useful information.

He closed the Web site and sat, thinking, for several minutes. *So what do I really know? Jefferson Gerit is the son of the CEO of Gerit Pharmaceuticals.* More thought. *Terrific! That doesn't help me tie him to all the stuff that's happened to me or Verry, and—*

Thinking about Verry reminded Lee of the men who stopped them in the airline terminal in Des Moines, one of whom Lee found by using the golden plate and then accidentally nearly scared the man to death. Then Lee got more insight into the matter.

That guy has to know who hired him. Maybe he might tell me what I want to know. Smiling to himself, Lee reached under his desk to retrieve the golden plate. Leaning it up against the computer screen, he again thought about the tall man who seemed to be in charge of the effort to intercept and possibly kidnap him and Verry.

Lee applied two minutes of intense pressure on the man. When he stopped, his target was writhing in pain on his living room floor, his face contorted, crying and sobbing, begging for the pain to stop, and yelling out answers to every question Lee asked. Lee didn't enjoy inflicting so much pain, but he felt he had no choice: he got his answer. Both of the men in the airport were hired by Jeff Gerit. They were not to hurt Lee but had clear instructions to hold him and everything he had with him in a motel in Des Moines until Jeff Gerit arrived to talk to him. The man's last words to his unknown and unseen assailant were, "Please, don't kill me!"

After assuring Jeff's henchman that Jeff would never know anything about his revelation, Lee broke the contact. *OK, I know who is behind all of this harassment, but I don't know what he looks like now.* He thought some more. *But Clem has a lot of contacts.* He picked up his telephone and punched in Clem Maestre's telephone number. As soon as the call was secure, Lee said, "Clem, I'm now pretty certain this guy, Jeff Gerit, is responsible for much, if not all, of the bad things happening to my family and to my friends—like you. Do your people have anything on him?"

Normally long on small talk, Clem went straight to the point. "He's the man who complained to the bank about yoah supposedly bad checks. He's some kind of big time hotshot who has no apparent source of income but lives high on the hog. But his dad owns Gerit Pharmaceuticals, so—"

"So he and his dad *have* been behind all of this."

"That's what Ah was about to tell y'all. He and his dad usually work together on whatever his dad wants, and sometimes he gets in trouble. Had his office and apartment trashed a few weeks ago: no evidence, no suspects. Unsolved mystery and all of that."

"Sounds like you had someone working pretty hard on this."

"As it turns out," his lawyer responded, "the guy Ah called worked foah Jeff Gerit in the past and didn't like the man at all. Seems as if none of the PIs in San Francisco like young Gerit, but his money's good. Anyway, mah guy had a file on Jeff Gerit and even faxed me his photo. Ah seem to remember y'all wanting that."

Lee shook his head in amazement and joy. "You're incredible, Clem. Fax it to me ASAP. I'll be surprised if we have any more problems from that guy after I get through with him."

"'Through with him?'" Clem asked. "What's that mean? Are y'all goin' to San Francisco?"

I almost blew it. After all the times I've told people to keep their mouths shut about our secrets, I darned near blow the whole thing myself. "No, I didn't mean that. But I think I can make this guy back off without resorting to any kind of violence."

"Lee," Clem said, his voice now cautious, "if y'all're planning anything illegal, Ah can't be a part of it."

"Sounds that way maybe, Clem, but it isn't illegal."

"One other thing, Lee."

"Yes?"

"Jefferson Gerit was in mah office a couple of times several weeks ago. On some possible real estate deal. We talked, then he left. Until now, Ah saw no reason to suspect anything at all."

Lee closed his eyes as the enormity of Clem's report hit him. *Gerit was here, probably talking to his buddies, maybe even made that threatening message on my answering machine.* "I appreciate your help—again, Clem. Trust me not to do something illegal."

Lee had the photo two minutes later.

As he did with the man in Des Moines and with FarCaller's friends, Lee let the plate locate Jeff Gerit then poured out his anger and frustration. *You attacked the Kaalers, and they did nothing to you! You hurt them, you burned their homes, you attacked their women, you tried to ruin them financially. You're greedy, and if you're greedy again, your greed will kill you!* Lee kept that thought in his mind, watching the man wince and shrink from the invisible onslaught. Then he grabbed his chest, obviously in pain; he looked around, eyes bulging, trying to find his attacker.

And, Lee thought toward Jeff Gerit, *all of this happened because you wanted something you can't have. Now you will feel great pain whenever you think of the Kaalers.*

Lee cut off his attack on Jeff Gerit and closed his eyes, thinking about how much Jeff hurt, hoping Jeff would keep himself and his people away from Lee and his family from that point on. When Lee last looked at the man's image, Jeff was writhing in agony on the floor of his apartment, sweating profusely, screaming for mercy and help.

Now for Papa Gerit. Lee remembered receiving a prospectus kit from Gerit Pharmaceuticals just after he returned home with Verry and began searching his investment files for it. Very shortly he found it. A thank-you letter, an annual report, and a prospectus from Gerit Pharmaceuticals. *Owner: Ebenezer Gerit. And it even has his photograph. That, my good man,* he said to the picture of the smiling man on the front cover of the annual report, *may have been one of the biggest mistakes of your life.* Then an ironic thought made him smile. *I wonder if you know how much money I made from your company.*

He picked up the prospectus, held it right next to the plate, and again looked into the golden plate. Concentrating on Ben Gerit's image, he shifted his attention to the plate.

After the multicolored swirl stopped, a view of a very expensive office appeared. Sitting at an obviously valuable dark oak desk was Ebenezer Gerit, looking very much like the photo Lee was using to find him. *Why is he wearing pajamas?* A split second later, he had an answer: *He's not in his office at work, he's at home. I wonder why.* Not letting any sympathetic thoughts hinder his mission, Lee resumed his main course of action.

"Well, sir," Lee said aloud, letting his anger and frustrations boil up, gain strength, and empower the plate, "let's see how you like a dose of *my* harassment!"

When Lee finished with him, Ebenezer Gerit was slumped on the floor and seemed to be calling out to someone. It was a frightening thing to watch and made Lee reconsider whether he wanted to exact further punishment. He shook his head, took a deep breath, then withdrew from the image in the plate, letting it disappear in the same kind of swirl which announced its appearance.

If he ever tries it again, I'll hit him harder.

He sat back, surprised to find himself perspiring freely. Taking several deep breaths to relax himself from what was really a distasteful job, he calmed down, letting his anger with the Gerits diminish, finding it partially replaced with regret at having to strike back. *No choice. If it's them or me and my family, they lose.*

Chapter 116

It Hurts!

It took both Gerits no time to realize something drastic had happened to them in addition to their sudden panic attacks. Every time they thought about "the Kaaler guy" or his family, or the powerful spoon they were certain he owned, they suffered more pain and panic. Each attack was more acute and terrifying than the previous.

Neither told the other about their experiences for nearly a week. Then Jeff, in a call to his dad, confessed about being overcome with terror one day with no warning and his feeling that it was directly related to their pursuit of the Kaalers

To Jeff's great surprise, his father responded with, "So it hit you too. I thought maybe I was going crazy."

"I wasn't going to tell you because you might think I was losing it or something."

Jeff couldn't see his father shaking his head. "Too real. Just hope it doesn't happen again." He shifted his thoughts to their main goal. "OK, then, what should we do next?"

At the thought of resuming their attacks, both men were stricken with a repeat of their previous experiences, and again they heard the unknown voice threatening them with even worse punishment if they ever tried to resume the attacks.

It was several minutes before either could speak or think straight, each having dropped their telephones in reaction to the pain they suffered.

Finally, Jeff picked up his handset and spoke. "Sorry, Dad. I just had another one of those awful attacks." His entire body shook as he recalled the pain. Before he could continue, his father said, "Me too. Call me tomorrow. Maybe we can do something then."

After three days of the same panic attacks and warnings, both Gerits decided to go on vacation.

In the meantime, their agents in Bend, Oregon, with no instructions and no one to report to, stopped harassing anyone associated with the Kaalers. None of them understood why they were receiving a thousand dollars a week for doing nothing; neither were they about to ask.

Part VIII

Housewarming

Chapter 117

Gifts

It was the first party Lee had ever hosted, and he was a nervous wreck. Always before his mother or grandmother had taken care of the major details and he'd been given little tasks. Here, now, in his own home for only six weeks, he was supposed to be the host. Never in his life had he felt so ill prepared. But his mother and wife were marvelous. While the idea for the party was his mother's, Verry joyously agreed. "Oh, Lee, it'll be wonderful! I'll meet your friends, you can show them our house, my folks and Drella will be here to see us and our home, and it has such a beautiful view of the mountains that they'll be just overwhelmed, and—"

He was outvoted before it ever came up. He nearly had a nervous breakdown trying to sweat all the details of his fiesta until Verry sat him down one afternoon, kissed him warmly, and explained how everything worked. Bottom line: all he had to do was help with the decorations and get the yard fixed up. Verry and his mother would take care of the guest list, the food, the drinks, and the cleanup. It sounded so easy.

But what they forgot (?) to tell him was that the food would be catered, they would both get completely new outfits, and he and his dad would have to stay out of the way and put out whatever "fires" arose, like not enough ice or where to park all the cars.

Every night for a week, he took long soaking baths in their spa to ease the pains in seldom-used muscles caused by hauling lava rocks around the yard to improve the border fencing, outline the driveway, and upgrade the terracing for their new flowers. And load and push and unload wheelbarrow loads of dirt and gravel and bark mulch to make everything look "just right." Once again he learned something about married life: it was "their" party, and "their" house, but the wife was the final arbiter of all conflicts. He also realized he was in poor physical condition and needed to do the landscaping himself instead of hiring someone.

His wife was also pretty, excited, warm, and loving; and her knee was healing so well that the doctor let her replace the heavy leg cast with an elastic bandage. Her arm splint was also gone. Her leg was still weak, but she could walk on both legs.

One thing Lee insisted be done that Verry thought was unnecessary and his parents knew nothing about: he wanted the silver spoon put someplace so that FarCaller could attend, if only remotely. Verry decided to include the spoon in a bouquet of dried flowers to be placed on the fireplace mantel, and from then on Lee was an enthusiastic participant.

When "the day" finally arrived, Lee almost felt good about the entire affair and was particularly pleased when he had FarCaller "call" to the silver spoon so he could see their party. Lee and Verry carefully placed the reception line so FarCaller could see everyone who came and hear their names called out. He was very much a part of Lee and Verry's family, albeit invisible.

One of the first guests to arrive was, to Lee's surprise, Clem Maestre. Clem, of course, knew Verry by now, but didn't know her parents and truly impressed them with his Southern charm. A bigger surprise: he was accompanied by Louise Chenowith, Lee's realtor. He'd never known Clem to have a date of any kind before this.

After everyone had arrived, Lee took Clem to the fireplace "where they could talk privately." As soon as that happened, Clem unfolded his tale.

"It seems the Gerits were behind all of your troubles. Ah just got word from ouah sheriff's office that a large group of Gerits' former employees heah in Deschutes County got into a big fight in a bar the othah night. They'd been drinking a lot, tempers flared, and the whole group of them—ten or fifteen or so—got into a melee. Once the cops and deputies made theah arrests, those people, including several women, began relating theah life stories.

"They'd all been hired by one of the Gerits—father or son—to watch y'all, tap y'all's telephone lines—just like y'all said, by the way," he bowed to Lee, acknowledging the doubts he once had about Lee's sanity on the matter, "cause some accidents—all kinds of things. They gave the police the names and times and dates and all kinds of details. Sheriff told me it'll go a long way to indictin' many of those people and possibly both Gerits." He shook his head slightly and looked Lee directly in the eyes. "If the Gerits are as smart as Ah think, it'll be verra difficult to tie them to anathin' illegal, hearsay evidence notwithstandin'."

He stopped then looked at Lee very suspiciously. "The one thing they couldn't explain was how and why the two Gerits suddenly stopped all the pesterin' of y'all, yoah folks, and yoah friends." He now smiled. "Like me, for instance. But, whatevah the reason, those two are goin' to be in big trouble foah some time, if only financial."

He stopped talking, looked around the room at all the guests, talking, laughing, and having a seriously good time. "I'm really glad," Clem said, continuing, "because both of y'all deserve some good breaks. Y'all've got a lot of friends hereabouts, and they're all glad y'all found such a wonderful woman, although, Lee," and his smile widened, "they don't understand whatever made her marry you in the first place."

They both laughed at the joke, both knew it was partly true, and both knew Lee and Verry were so much in love that it was impossible to miss.

After the barbecued pork disappeared, along with the coleslaw and potato salad and seven bean salad and hot fresh bread and peach cobbler and ice cream, and when people felt they'd had enough of the talking and drinking and hugging, they began to leave. By ten o'clock, six hours after the party began, Lee and Verry were finally alone. Her parents were staying with Lee's folks in their newly refurbished home, and Thommy K. and Drella were somewhere else, paying attention to each other and not wanting to be interrupted.

Before going to bed, Lee and Verry went to the fireplace and stood in front of the mantle so they could see the silver spoon.

"FarCaller? Are you still there?"

"Yes, Lee," came the answer. It was difficult to see his face because they were so far from the spoon, but he was still sitting in his favorite chair, across the room from the silver plate. "Here am I, and amazed. That party you shared appreciate I also: something from another world was it."

He was absolutely serious, and so was Lee. "FarCaller, that is *exactly* what it was. I don't know where your world is, but it is different from ours in many ways." As he spoke, he put his arm around Verry and pulled her close. "It wouldn't have been right to have such a celebration without you here, because all three of us know that it wouldn't have been possible without your help. You saved my life; you helped me make enough money so I could protect myself, go to Iowa and marry the love of my life, and get back here safely. I'm sure part of this evening was boring, but you had to be here for it to be right for us."

When he mentioned Verry, she gave him a strong hug.

FarCaller stood up and walked toward them. "Many of your friends gifts brought. Usual is that?"

"Yes, FarCaller," Verry said. "They're called housewarming gifts. We give them to help people celebrate moving into a new home. However, some of them were also wedding gifts—they were the ones wrapped in white paper."

"As I thought," he answered. "For you also a gift have I."

Both Lee and Verry shook their heads. "You don't need to give us anything, FarCaller," Lee said. "Besides, how could you ever give us something? We don't know how to send anything to you other than pictures and sound."

FarCaller motioned to someone out of sight, immediately after which a beautiful young woman entered, carrying a very small baby.

"This my wife, Lovely, is—the woman who from the angry bull saved me." Both men smiled at the reference; FarCaller's wife blushed.

"Our gift she carries—our son. Lee FarCaller named him have we. A symbol of our friendship that is."

Lee was speechless, looking first at the beautiful woman holding the baby, then at the handsome baby, and then at FarCaller, who was beaming.

"I don't know what to say. I had no idea your wife was pregnant. And the time rates between us are so hard to compute I didn't realize you'd been together long enough to already have a family." Beside him, he heard Verry sniffing back tears then felt her embrace him, letting her tears soak through the white silk shirt she'd bought him to wear at their party.

"But young Lee our only gift is not." FarCaller nodded at Lovely, who gave him their baby and left the room, appearing seconds later holding another small child. Now FarCaller's smile fairly lit Lee's living room. "Not simply a son have we, but two babies." He nodded for Lovely to approach the silver plate and pull down the white blanket covering the baby's face.

"This our daughter is, whom Verry named have we." He stopped talking and looked at Lee & Verry. "You this gift will accept, we hope. Very sincere it is, because very special you are. If here you were, a ceremony would we have. Formally your names to our children give you would, and to help them grow up to be strong in body and soul, agree you would. Such a ceremony have you?"

Both Lee and Verry nodded, their eyes now filled with tears. "Yes, FarCaller," Lee said. "That ceremony would make us your children's godparents. It is a great honor, my friend, one I cannot repay and one I will never forget."

"Good that is, Lee and Verry." One of the babies began to cry, followed almost immediately by the other. "Time to go it is."

Lee and Verry nodded their understanding, still embracing each other, tears now running down their cheeks.

"When we will next meet know I not, my friends," FarCaller said, "but to again sharing with you forward look I. Now goodbye say must I, and the happiest of lives together to both of you wish."

Part IX

The Mystery

Chapter 118

Travel?

The house was still a mess and Verry was getting ready for bed, but Lee couldn't relax. He went to his office and from his safe retrieved his grandmother's last letter. As he held it, he thought about the amazing past few months and the changes they had wrought in his life. But, in spite of the glow of a wonderful party and the thrill of seeing FarCaller's twins, one thing nagged at Lee.

Why? Why does my family have the gift and the silver spoon? Why was the golden plate made, and by whom? None of this can be just to keep the Guardian and his family in financial comfort. There has to be a bigger and better reason, something Grandma Mainor couldn't tell me, assuming she knew what it was. He stopped thinking about the unknowns and focused his attention on the envelope. *Maybe this will help.*

Gently opening it, he withdrew the single sheet inside and was immediately disappointed in the very few words he saw.

> My dearest grandson,
> If you live to read this letter, you have undergone a most terrifying battle, done some awful things in order to win, and are doubting yourself and whether you should ever have been entrusted with knowledge of Spoonworld. The answer must be yes, my dearest, for you and you alone are its protector.
> For now, at least, Spoonworld and our secrets are safe. You must pass these Guardian duties on to your firstborn. And he or she must be told *everything* that happened to you on this journey.
> One final item. In my last talk with my FarCaller, he told me something sinister was in my future, that I would face a series of attacks

and dangers threatening not only me but perhaps my country. That hasn't happened yet, but since the gift is never wrong, I'm afraid these things may be in store for you. Just be careful and alert. We Guardians often feel we *attract* troubles.

A last request: When next you feel the urge to travel to someplace interesting, grab the spoon, hold on to your wife, and think about the stars. On this, trust me.

I love you dearly, Lee, and regret I'll never see you again.

With my love forever,
Grandma

The End . . . of the Beginning

Printed in the United States
100316LV00003B/29/A